DESTINY MADE OF RANIDETRO- FROM NADIR TO ZENITH

RAFFLESIA PAUL

Copyright © Rafflesia Paul
All Rights Reserved.

This book has been self-published with all reasonable efforts taken to make the material error-free by the author. No part of this book shall be used, reproduced in any manner whatsoever without written permission from the author, except in the case of brief quotations embodied in critical articles and reviews.

The Author of this book is solely responsible and liable for its content including but not limited to the views, representations, descriptions, statements, information, opinions and references ["Content"]. The Content of this book shall not constitute or be construed or deemed to reflect the opinion or expression of the Publisher or Editor. Neither the Publisher nor Editor endorse or approve the Content of this book or guarantee the reliability, accuracy or completeness of the Content published herein and do not make any representations or warranties of any kind, express or implied, including but not limited to the implied warranties of merchantability, fitness for a particular purpose. The Publisher and Editor shall not be liable whatsoever for any errors, omissions, whether such errors or omissions result from negligence, accident, or any other cause or claims for loss or damages of any kind, including without limitation, indirect or consequential loss or damage arising out of use, inability to use, or about the reliability, accuracy or sufficiency of the information contained in this book.

Made with ♥ on the Notion Press Platform
www.notionpress.com

In the dedication of memories of my dearest grandfather who worked in Military.

Contents

The Toughest Committee Selections — vii

1. The First Day Of College — 1
2. Explorations! — 7
3. The Secret — 12
4. The Tattoo Removal! — 27
5. The Toughest Selections Ever! — 51
6. More Secrets Revealed — 73
7. Worst Training Ever! — 117
8. Not Riding But Jumping Over The Horse! — 143
9. Preparation To Hunt Him Down — 162
10. Do Or Die! — 175

The Toughest Committee Selections

It is 23 September, the day of committee selections.Laila wished them luck before they left the hostel and she stayed back as she couldn't apply for the Committee which had strict rules on no tattoos for candidates who are applying. There are six hundred twenty four students in total who are reporting in the University grounds occupying their chairs classwise. Mumkin, Pamela and John are sitting there too. They had to come well groomed with only one pen in their hand. All students had to ensure that they didn't carry any watch, handkerchief or any other accessory. Principal Blacksmith enters the ground and facilitates everyone to keep quiet and soon the selection starts. The students are asked to check under their tables ,they find chits consisting of different numbers written on both sides with pink and green color each. Principal tells them to choose the number written on the pink color side ,follow group leaders and keep the dual colored chits safe. As pre directed the sixty leaders including Benny Sabastian's group the students based on their numbers. Each group has twenty students. These groups are taken to thirty one different halls of the University, where testing will take place. Mumkin and John are now in two different groups. Pamela is in a group with Benny and Ren. In each hall, there are well groomed people who don't belong to the University as they haven't seen here before. In the hall where Mumkin is sitting, a Classy man enters, goes to the podium and gives instructions. In all halls consisting of twenty to twenty one students, instructions given are the same. When a classy person goes to the podium, tell them to sit according to the roll number allotted on the green side of the chit. Mumkin's number is 207, John is 330 and Pamela is 128. The students are instructed to unseal answer sheets when instructed. They are given a sealed question paper that has hunderend questions to be done in sixty minutes. The instructor instructs to write roll numbers and unseal both question paper and answer sheets and start writing answers. Mumkin observes on the top right side written as "Unique Association for Success(UAS)", he quickly realizes that the writing material is from the Amrisk's shop. He goes into deep thinking. He recalls the day when Amrisk was busy, probably it was because he was trying to provide the University with writing material for an upcoming exam. But he doubted why Amrisk didn't give this info to the trio when they reached his shop that day. He suddenly gets out of his thoughts and he remembered that the time was running out ,he quickly opened the booklet that contained twenty aptitude questions based on analogies, classifications, reasoning and mirror images , twenty each questions based on general knowledge, basic science ,mathematical skills and puzzles.

 Students were rigorously solving questions, most of them struggling in mathematics and science as they have humanities background and Science students struggled with general knowledge . Few struggled with aptitude. Few finished the exam and they were asked to shut their mouths and wait by the examiner upon asking to leave early. As it seemed that there's very few minutes left or time was already up, then the Examiner rang the bell and asked them to lift their both hands up, stand up, move in que and leave the room .Mumkin, Pamela and John met each other . Pamela tells them that like criminals they've been asked to lift up their hands and walk. This college is not just a zoo but a prison too. John replies that 'Yeah, zoo where violent animals like you Pamela take admission to learn humaness through psychology'. Pamela lightly punches John on his shoulder indicating him to shut up.

 Along with other students they move out, where they are served coffee and hot dogs. As the trio are standing in que, the discussion happens.

 Mumkin:How was the test? For a moment I thought I wouldn't be able to complete it!

 Pamela said that she did all hundred questions and John did some ninety of them. Still skeptical about his performance, Mumkin tells Pamela and John that he thinks he won't be able to make it in the next round. Ren, Benny ,Fred and Daniel join the trio too. Fred and Daniel are self assured with their selections. Benny doesn't share any thought , instead he snatches Pamela's hotdog, takes a bite and returns it back with the purpose of teasing her. As Pamela sees Ren, he makes eye contact with her, turns back after taking his snacks and returns back to Janny who isn't taking the committee selection test but she has come to support him. Suddenly John comes in front of Pamela, he asks her to move away from a big wolf spider . Pamela shouts out loudly and takes three steps backward, loses balance and is about to hit the ground when John holds her hand and lifts her up. Mumkin steps on the spider and kills it finally. They hear an announcement.

Prof Olivia: All, return back to your seats now. Quick or else it will be taken as rustication from the committee selections.

All students return to their seats. There comes a gentleman with spectacles from the committee selection team who introduces himself as Philip Hielmaster .

Hielmaster: Good morning, ladies and gentlemen(crowd wish him back). So feeble, who all missed eating the snacks?Was prof Olivia the reason for speaking so feebly as you are scared of her?

The crowd laughs and Prof Olivia standing on the left side down the podium gives a quasi smile for half a second and becomes unresponsive again with a stern face.

Hielmaster : I'm going to announce names to students who made it to the next round of the committee based on an intelligence test. Those who don't need to leave university quickly as per directions of the committee. The selected ones will be guided by respective leaders. The people who are selected for next round are- Jim Gua, Manasa, Lilly John, Benny Sabastian, Diha Azan, Alax Pitruda, Pamela Brown, Kiki Won, Bessy Thomson, John Breze, Palkunia Johnson, Ren, Alacia, Bravoz Woodsmith.......

Many students didn't hear their name and got a message from Hielmaster that they weren't selected.This included Mumkin and Fred . As Mumkin was moving back to the University he got various thoughts that it might be a mistake , a miserable mistake where Hielmaester might have announced the names of unselected students as selected, thus reversing the order. He feels as if he has missed an opportunity. He goes to the canteen of his hostel and buys two lemon balm tea. He heads towards the Prism tower which is the longest tower of his University. This is the first time when he isn't having his friends John and Pamela with him.They both made it to the next round. After reading the top he finds Janny there. She recognizes him and tells her that she isn't in love with Ren. She considers Ren as an immature guy who is emotionally and physically dependent on her. She doesn't find her future with him . In Fact she is with him due to his affluent family background. She wants to be into journalism. Ren's endearment has enslaved her. She further tells Mumkin that she doesn't want Ren anymore. She goes near Mumkin and her eyes get filled with tears and she gets closer further where Mumkin can feel warm air blowing through her exhale. She is about to kiss him, but Mumkin takes a step back, says sorry and leaves. He hears an inner voice that Ren is his friend who loves Janny, letting Janny kiss him is actually perfidy on Ren. Mumkin leaves the place.He finds Laila in front of the hostel .She tries to communicate with him, she goes near him and holds his hand.

Laila: Mumkin, I want to talk with you.

Mumkin: (Leaving her hand) Sorry Laila, now.

He takes the sideway of Laila and starts moving in the direction opposite to her. She stops him

Laila:I know it's Mumkin, that you couldn't make it in committee . That is why you're sad and seeking alone time. Fred told me about you and him.

Mumkin stops, moves back to Laila.

Mumkin: Yes, I wanted to be there in the committee. I'm disappointed that I did not make it.

Laila: Don't worry , you can try for selection next year if they conduct selections. Who knows what the committee is all about? It can be a futile committee too.

Mumkin: No idea if such selections will be conducted again and a committee will be made for it! Indeed I believe that it's not futile but a paramount. That's why selections are so tough! Majority of the students couldn't make it.

Laila takes Mumkin to a shady place in the park where the red, pink and yellow roses are blooming and colorful butterflies are flying. They both sit there under a banyan tree.

Laila: You know Mumkin, these colorful butterflies are actually transparent . They are not two legged but four legged. This is the reflection through the multi miniature scales, due to which we see colors. Do you know how many days they can live?

Mumkin: Probably a few weeks.

Laila: Yes ,four weeks . But that doesn't make it debilitated, through pollination butterflies become predominant in the ecosystem. Its colorless wings aren't weak but strongest as change of its behavior can flip and change the ecosystem's egalitarianism. That's the power of a butterfly! What can be the potential of this six point two feet tall and seventy three kg boy with his brain power of around one thousand three hundred seventy grams.(pointing towards Mumkin).

On hearing Laila Mumkin starts chortling of this new transformation. How an introverted tattooed girl in class who once was addicted to alcohol parties is now a motivator in his life . She is interpreting human existence, their strength and probably making Mumkin fall in love with her. On asking this, Laila reiterates about the book that Pamela reads for her written by Devkali Neelghanti Paul . Mumkin too recalls that he hasn't seen the book due to his over ornate routine from the past three days. She tells him the meaning of Brahmana and various quotes for salvation of human beings. They both discuss the human brain, the speciality of human organs, the bewilderness of the Universe and Mumkin shares his dream of selling weapons through the Armed Forces for the first time with Laila. She provides moral support to him by saying that she trusts his abilities. Then they go back to their respective hostel rooms after a kiss between them. Mumkin assures himself that he will read the books given by Miss Isabela to him .He also plans that he will exchange the books with Pamela once he's done with reading.

On the other hand the selected students are just one twenty in number selected for the next round of committee selections. Pamela, John, Ren and Benny are feeling bad for Mumkin and Fred. Hielmaster tells them to go back to their respective hostels and arrive tomorrow morning at 8 AM for the second stage. As John enters the room, he sees Mumkin sleeping with his hand placed on the book which is kept on the table.John wakes him up. They chit chat and then John leaves the room to get a fever medicine as he is feeling febrile. Mumkin opens one of the two books written by Devkali Neelghanti Paul which is the same as that of Pamela``The sages said this". He reads eleven pages of it and could make connections with Laila's contentment. Mumkin understands that the part that Pamela called boring is actually healing Laila. He appreciates Bhagwat Geeta's quotes and closes the book on twenty third pages. He then keeps this book on table and picks up the second book just to take a glance of it, as he decides that he makes a plan that he will go out with John after reading a little from the second book. As he opens the book, he finds that it's actually not a book. In Fact it's like the written notes of someone. As he turns the pages and moves to the first one, he realizes that it's a diary entry named "ALORA DIARIES". Mumkin assumes that the book has mistakenly come to him. He glances through it.

ALORA DIARIES

10 June,

"There faces were worth watching ,when they saw me sitting and gaping upon them wearing the dog's leash. From the fire of my eyes itself they got to know that the leader of the student council is revolting against the notice of the University to make Uniform necessary. Almost three fourth of the University students are rebellious , after all we're not school students. And finally kudos to this knockout girl, yeah I'm referring to my brilliant idea that the whole shitting plan of University to control students and make their lives excruciating is in vain. From now onwards till forever, no student in Himbertown University would ever have to wear the Uniform! This all drama I created wearing my bra and panti only with that 'Fuck off uniform written ,we're not dogs' written on our flag of protest. Every professor and principal were just gazing at me. But this time there was a handsome man who was just looking at me as if I'm acting immature.

14 July 1934, 11 AM, As I walked through the corridor I realized a group of students working on some sort of plan. I peeped in . They invited me to be a part of a chemistry project. A project that is envisioned to make our military stronger. I straight away said yes! and joined the team. I don't know much about the military although my dad was in it whom we lost when I was a kid. I joined this programme because I know that my intellect will be stimulated,along with that I'll get new resources for Chemistry experimentation. I don't know where I'll be heading with this project. Today working wasn't easy as I wore a crop top and pants . With a little more cleavage, others found it difficult to focus too. Swear I need to be less fashionable to work here"

Few pages of the book were torn. There was inconsistency in writing.

25 Aug,

"It's going well! Project's plan is riveting.I have in fact very similar people. We are a team of ten students working. They made me the vice president of the project. Probably they find me highly intelligent! Haha. Not just that Alora, it's just that I'm gifted with passion to work deliberately in this field. Blueprints are made, soon we'll start with a project. I am going to U.M.B.A.S. book store. It's Unique MIlitary Base Association with Students. The shop is specifically designed to collaborate students with the Military to prepare them for war. Probably I might find something which can help our project to grow at a fast pace as the Government is hinting that in future we might face a war due to fast progress of our country.I don't care about war, but I do care about becoming the best scientist. Yeah but I will not shy away from standing with the country during war, the way my father did!It's like a single arrow hitting two targets. Both country's need and my ambition "

16 Sept ,

"Wook man. I searched a lot and finally discovered four books that have specific mention of what the military requires. I wrote a letter for the same to the Military. Soon there will be personnels from the Military and other students from separate courses who will be joining us in the project for guidance and assistance. And Alora the most lively part of today is Amrisk, he's the bookseller. I've spoken to him. He mentioned that he recently joined his ancestral business and they provide all books, especially to the books related to the military. He will further assist me in searching for good books in the Military. Indeed a very helpful person, I appreciate his helpfulness.The best thing about his shop is the black coffee and doughnuts that he offers exclusively to me whenever I visit him. My tummy is filled with that. I am lying on my bed with a cozy blanket. Very sleepy, good night Alora . "

20 Nov,

Soon Mumkin smells that this book is mentioning Amrisk,Military and some project of college students with collaboration of Military personals. He recalls that the story is kind of similar to the batch of 1935 students that the trio found in Amrisk's shop.They were also selected in the Military due to a similar project. He is excited now to know more or written more in the book, whether the dots he's trying to connect are making the right sense or not. He straight away reads the other pages.

30 Dec,

" The day was full of events . Two more people from different backgrounds joined us .Jonathan Williams and Tiger Watson. Tiger is a student from the engineering branch.He is brother of professor William, the one in psychology . He's a funny guy, who became friends with us as soon as we met him. The other guy, Tiger Watson, he's in Business Management. He seems high at intellectual level as he answers most of my doubts. He has a good knowledge of the Military . He says that there's a business with the Military that his family is in. He is an extremely rich person ,but he doesn't interact much with people. Reason is his arrogance! He was quite rude when Leisley asked him out for coffee after work. Weird guy, I mean who refuses by saying "I like coffee of bottle gourd flavor which no shop can provide. Coffee with you in your fuckin dreams!". We'll hope he helps us in making the project complete as not only Leisley ,he's rude with the majority of the other people. He sits in one place and doesn't want to contribute much until I approach him for doubts ."

19 Feb,

"We're making some amendments in the project as we think that the capacity of rifles can be enhanced to eight bullets as compared to the present capacity of five bullets. This is one of the innovative projects as it will actually enhance the capacity of our soldiers too. We're doing the modifications. Amrisk is proving concerned books with knowledge of the same and finally he gave us special writing materials, especially the leathered pen that can work for at least ten years without refilling them . Very useful in making continuous notes. He gave me a pocket diary that is portable. When I tried to pay him money for the stuff, he refused by saying that he considers me as his friend and he won't charge any. "

29 March

"Jonathan Willaims , Tiger Watson and I have been selected to prepare a chemical at a certain price. We three went out today for a coffee so that we can discuss our plan after work. Jonathan is really good at catching ideas but Tiger doesn't seem to be interested.I don't understand why he has been put up in this project? He's highly egoistic, I mean although he has great knowledge and ideas of projects but the heart of a person should matter too. He has a very antisocial personality. He takes everything so seriously and gives an exasperated look at us whenever we laugh at any joke. But at the coffee shop the time was spent intellectually between me and Jonathan. Tiger ignored him completely and answered my two questions. I want to sleep with a light heart now. Let me appreciate that the drizzling in the evening before arriving at the hostel made my mood happy . Work and student life are in balance."

14 May

"Tiger, as he came today in the room where I was experimenting with Jonathan, he threw away the beaker. He tore an empty page of my notes and after snatching my pen from me, writing on the notebook wrote "Come to my place right now!". He tore away the page, gave it to me in my hand and snapped his fingers on my face. The first thing that comes to my mind after seeing his behavior is what an obsessive wild man he is. Am I a slut that he's calling me to his place? Apart from clearing my doubts, he spoke just once till now in all discussions I had with him and Jonathan. He just spoke about his successful business, money and flounting on his ancestral property. Not only me, everyone sees him as a shallow person. I had to say no to and feel sorry for that. He got really angry, bangged the door and walked away. He looked frustrated. I felt that his proposal can never be love, in fact it looked like he's demanding something else...... Poor Tiger, I wish he gets someone better than me as I don't feel anything for him and can't take his tantrums. Now with this behavior, I would never date him my entire life even though he's the last man on earth."

26 July

"None of us can believe what really happened today. General Alexander of Himbertown came today. He really liked the idea explained by me. Of Course my best friend Jonathan also has a huge contribution here. As we displayed our final rifles with increased capacity of bullets, lightweight and advanced chemical formula, he appreciated our work. He kept an option for the three of us to join the Military. I mean seriously man? Who would refuse that but Tiger did! It's a blessing in disguise. Who would like to work with that creep? At the start of the project I was concerned about fulfilling my intellect but now working in a team with the Military personnels has taught me that Military projects are far bigger than my intellect. In Fact both are related. Jonathan and I are excited to join the Military. Woohoo"

17 Aug

"The first day of the Military is unfamiliar. As I recall, my mother always missed my father who sacrificed his life for the country during war. I was just three years old. I'm sure Alora, dad must be proud of me. Just the day before yesterday I realized that history is repeating. Who knows, I might become an important part during the country's emergency! My blood is just driving up the wall for it. I'm excited to meet trainers, and will do everything to keep my mom and family happy. Will never put down my dad. Just going to sleep to wake up tomorrow, timing is antithetical from hostel timings. Hostel's life was full of freedom, no one to do surveillance, we didn't have warden there. But here there are always two or more seniors who check on us. I thought joining military would be like turn up for the books"

17 Sept

"Alora! I can't write....I just can't because the schedules are packed, morning four am till night eleven pm is all continuous work, I and Williams entered the military training. It's the toughest training in an extreme way. There is one senior who wants to harass me. He forcefully bent my head in dirty rain water on the ground, I still don't know the reason for doing so. But I think he believes that I'm not fit to join the Military as I'm a woman. I'm worried till what extent he'll go! I am the only girl present there. Yesterday he made me do forty push ups in heavy rain. I feel lonely but I'm hopeful to become a good soldier. There are many good things here if we ignore him".

27 Oct

"I was going for a break in between training, that same senior stopped me, he asked me to bend down. He was carrying a cane through which he hit trainees. He hit Williams, Joshua and Brian about ten times in each leg. They were crying loudly in pain. As he was about to hit me, I found myself already crying, drops of sweat irritated my eyes and I could read his name on his name plate as AJ Handon. He hit me in the knees after that he said 'For what hell a woman has entered the Military? Fuck'. He kept hitting my knees until they bled profusely. I couldn't speak much as it was really traumatizing. Things turned blur for me, still he didn't stop. Williams told me that he stopped until I was on ground and the sand on earth turned red. Nurse Samantha came to put ointment on wounds and she brought me back to consciousness. Still there wasn't any action taken on beating me like that as none of us can raise our voice against the seniors in the military due to

the hierarchy."

1 Nov

"Jesus, on the third day of training we had rifle practice. I am able to do almost everything but drill parade, oooops, it's one of the most difficult things to do. Probably the most strenuous one, I'm not coordinating that well with six to seven feet tall fellow male trainees. They all blame me for their bad contingent formation. But I want to stay here and prove to others that women are not liabilities but the biggest assets. So far I have understood that here respect is not not given for free, it has to be earned. I will not give up, no matter how much I have to suffer in this training.``

4 Nov

" I had to climb a rock today , but my two feet long hair opened, I lost my balance and was about to meet a mishap. There was a new officer who called the rescue team at the right time through a whistle. The team held my rope and brought me down.Other men trainees with me got exasperated too. He's that officer only who saw me rebelling against the college uniform code. I though he hated me because I was rebelling as a feminist wearing my innerware only, but he actually saved my life. Commander Handon angrily took out his rifle and pointed towards me. He said he would shoot me right away. As I was about to get shot by him something good happened.As I shivered in consternation ,this officer who's supposed to be AJ's friend came in between. He's endearing, the way he wished me"Hello lady, you probably are the only girl from Himbertown University to do the training of the Military to support the armed forces. Proud of you. How's it going? " . I was still tepid. As I was about to say something, Commander Handon pulled his rifle back, he introduced this person to my male batchmates as his fellow commander cum batchmate Charles Chamburt, who has come back to train us after ten days of holidays. AJ Handon , in front of everybody, warned me that if I make such a mistake again, then his rifle will drink my blood away! What a crook he is."

After seeing this name Mumkin is dazed. Charles Chamburt is the name of Mumkin's father. He wants to know now, who's the author of this diary. For a moment he speculates it to be Isabella, as she mentioned it before to Mumkin , Pamela and John in their first meeting. Now he's convinced that the diary belongs to Isabella who is only Lidiya Cheriyan. So now, Prof Olivia's related person Isabella, who probably is her sister, is only Lidiya Cheriyan for which the trio and Ren have been inquiring for a long time in this entire world.He thinks that this is the biggest enlightenment of the world. But there were many more yet to come in reality.

He wants to read more but he doesn't realize that it's ten thirty pm, he looks to his left side and finds John already sleeping there. He keeps the diary back and turns off his light and goes to sleep.

The next morning is the selection process again. Mumkin and Laila wish luck to Pamela, John, Ren and Benny with the selections , after which the two go out of University. Laila sees the various flamboyant wine shops due to which she gets out of her impulse and starts running towards the shop on the other side of the road before she collides with a wheelbarrow carrying garbage. Mumkin runs to reach out to her to help .He holds her hand and lids her up. The person with the wheelbarrow also fell down with his wheelbarrow. He calls Laila an idiot and says 'Are you drunk?Can't you see and walk'. Upon which she replies 'Not yet, but was about to get drunk'. Mumkin chuckles on hearing Laila's answer. Seeing garbage scattered the guy further admonishes Laila,Mumkin firstly defends her by asking the guy to use wise words while interacting with ladies ,but he also asks for an apology on behalf of her as she was the one who collided with the wheelbarrow inorder to get drunk. He helps the guy in keeping his garbage bags back and gives compensation in form of a little money from his pocket money due to which the guy gets happy and leaves from there .He leaves the place by holding Laila's shoulder as her knee is injured to provide her with support. He takes her on his lap where they leave for the University clinic .

Warden Atrika Bloom sees both of them . He comes in front of Mumkin who's breathing heavily as Laila is on his lap.

Bloom: Where are you both going? Why are you going like this? Why is it in your lap? Are the newly formed couple of college? Don't you know the rules of college? Do you have any idea if I should tell Prof Olivia? Do you know what punishment is given to couples in college?

Mumkin whispers in Laila's ear: Have you seen monkeys with cymbals? Once you plug in the key, they keep playing the cymbals. Warden Bloom is like that monkey toy.

Laila chuckles.

Bloom: You didn't answer my question. You think I am a fool to stand here. What do you think of yourself? Don't you know that you're in your first year only? Are you trying to compare yourself with other students of other colleges? Don't you know how undisciplined they are ?

Mumkin : Sir, you can ask these questions later, she's my aunt's daughter and was injured as she fell down on the road as she was running after the candy van to buy candies. We aren't couples as she's technically my cousin. I'm just trying to be kind with her.

Bloom: Put down your cousin right now! Don't hold her like that after all she's your cousin, I'll get a wheelchair arranged . You both wait.

Bloom leaves from there.

Laila gets angry at Mumkin saying 'Oh, so I am your aunt's daughter, your cousin's sister and you're trying to be kind with me! Really(enraged). You're a liar Mumkin, I hate you(blows her cheeks in anger)'.

Mumkin lifts her again and says 'darling ,I had to lie to save ourselves. Also everything is fair in love and war, be it a lie'. He holds her cheeks with his hands and pampers her with love,seeking for forgiveness.

The nurse applies the antiseptic dressing. He drops Laila till her room in a wheelchair and tells her to take care of herself. Then he goes back towards the shop of Amrisk. During the way, he is connecting the dots . Questions that are coming in his mind are- Does Amrisk know about Mumkin's father? Who is Lidiya Cheriyan? The confirmation whether if Prof Olivia's sister Isabella and Lidiya the same person, why Amrisk shop's name is changed from UMBAS (Unique Military Base Association With Students) to UAS(Unique Association with Students), why didn't Amrisk mention about providing material to the University for Committee selection?

As Mumkin was near the University gate he heard John's voice. As he turns back ,he sees John running towards him. He tells him that Principal Blacksmith wants to meet him as he is being pushed for the second stage of committee selections. Mumkin gets astonished with news, on inquiring further John tells him that he doesn't know much about Principal's decision but heard someone near office saying that one staff member of college eyewitnessed that Mumkin ran behind the thief and got him caught by Police on the day while they were returning from Amrisk's shop. This might be the reason for his recommendation into the second stage. Both Mumkin and John head towards the principal's office.They were asked to wait outside. Warden Bloom takes them inside the Office room, which is a fully furnished room with trophies and medals of achievement . Mumkin and John wish morning to Principal Blacksmith.

Principal Blacksmith: Good morning young man, do you know why you've been called here?

Mumkin: No sir.

Principal Blacksmith:Apparently today the game of probability favored you Mumkin, it was your roll number that came out from six hundred twenty three students for one vacancy. You can leave now. Join others for next round selections . All the best!

Mumkin couldn't believe what he heard just now, as till now this was his luckiest day. He has never been that lucky in anything even including ticking the right answer in multiple choice questions of exams. Since morning the day has been great for him,in the beginning he got to spend time with his girlfriend Laila. He also made it to committee.

As Mumkin was listening to Principal Blacksmith, he was stuck to find the photograph of his father with Principal blacksmith and Professor William. He couldn't ask Principal Blacksmith as Warden Bloom comes to take both of them outside the office. After leaving from there, Mumkin feels that he doesn't want to be part of committee selections just based on luck. He believes in his abilities but John tells him not to think in those terms and calls him "estimable ". The duo reunites with rest members selected for the second round of committee selections. Pamela congratulated Mumkin upon his arrival . Then Philip Hielmaster arrived with Prof Olivia,where she asked all students to assemble in Gandhi hall. It's a huge hall painted with green and light green colors with symbols of The rainbow. A rainbow peace flag, the broken rifle, the white poppy, the 'V' hand sign and a big painting of Mahatma Gandhi displaying peace. The students were assigned random numbers on a chit of papers and they were made to sit in an arrangement according to the numbers allotted. Mr. Hielmaster steps up on stage and addresses students about the second stage.

Hielmaster: Dear students, as you have come to the second stage where the number is twenty two now from six forty five. That shows how deserving you all are! Congratulations to all of you for making this far in selections.

Now let's start with the next test, which is based on psychological testing . There is a battery of tests based on human behavior. Mr. Bloom ,please circulate the answer sheets to students.

As Warden Bloom circulated the answer sheets, it was again of Amrisk's shop. Mumkin recalls visiting Amrisk's shop after the second round of selections. Mr. Hielmaster further addresses.

Hielmaster: You will not write anything on the answer sheet until instructed or else it'll lead to your disqualification. A question paper will contain three parts starting with writing a paragraph about yourself for around five hundred words. The second part has completion of sentences, the third part is see, think and wonder based on patterns observed. You can comprehend these patterns into anything you see and imagination is all up to you. Frame your understanding and give a conclusion based on that. Time given is half hours for each. After the bell rings every half hour, move on to the next part. Ensure handwriting is clean. Our psychologists will check the test but assume Prof Olivia is correcting,or without correction ma'am will disqualify you. So write neatly(sarcastically), show trepidation!

Everyone laughs.

Mumkin is a little skeptical with the question paper pattern. Pamela sees the test more as an English test as it has sentence making and paragraph writing etc in the first page.

Hielmaster rings up the first bell to give indication that the test has started.

Mumkin, in the first part, writes about his family members. He writes that he belongs to Ranidetro village where it's rural area based on farming and dairy products. He mentioned about his father whom he loves the most and misses him in his life. He writes about his desires that he had if his father was alive i.e. of going fishing early in the morning in his village's river, polishing his shoe and his father making him sit on his shoulder while returning back. He describes his mother as a serene breath after suffocating tiredness of work. The family of three eat together under a tree while having woodfire cooked fish with rice afternoons, followed by muskmelons.The sugar granules on them are enhancing the taste buds of his mother but his father is disgusted. Still eating quietly. He mentions his dreams of building highly sufficient weaponry to armed forces as his father always spoke about weapons. In the next two fifty words he mentions about the details of his education, his favorite cuisines and his reading habits. He further mentions Isabella's books and how consistent reflection from those is transforming lives of people. He writes about John and Pamela, where both always accompany him. Pamela is a curious cat who brings various life puzzles to solve like the mystery of Lidiya Cheriyan. He also writes about Laila as a new friend in his life who is a supportive and caring person. He writes about his future plans of discontinuing the subject of Psychology and doing a management course next year.

After that the second bell rings giving indication to start with the second part of the exam. Mumkin opens the booklet of sentences like I am in love with a girl who loves someone else I will……., I see an accident , I will….., senior's girlfriend for me is …… biggest promise I have made to someone is ………, I am guilty of……The thing that I hate the most is ……all these fill in the blank sentences are making upto fifty questions. Mumkin starts completing all the sentences as I am in love with a girl who loves someone else I will move on to explore other venues in life and wish her luck, I see an accident call ambulance ,hospitalize and ensure least loss takes place, senior's girlfriend for me is Madam senior, biggest promise I have made to someone is helpful to all and good human, this is promise that I made to my father, I am guilty of nothing , The thing that I hate the most is traitor trying to harm country's peace……

Mumkin keeps on writing the similar sort of responses upto thirty nine when the bell rings for next round. Still there were thirteen sentences left incomplete by him. Mumkin opens the third booklet that contains patterns. It was just dots. He connects them as the dancing dots- belle dancers, people going for picnics in mountains, girl making gift wrap for her lover ,giving a farewell party to seniors and making super technological rifles. He writes the above things in almost twenty pictures before the bell rings .

John writes about himself as the guy who loves to workout. He tries to be a cool dude but dull in studies. He likes modern girls but from inside he wants a girl who loves him deeply. His world revolves around love. The second love of his life is his starting own business and he hates when other people discourage him in doing so. He wants to live life happily with his wife in future and wants to give her a protected life.

After his introduction in the first part, in the second part of sentence completion his answers are metamorphosed into different directions from his introduction. John writes- I am in love with a girl who loves someone else I will buy that girl gifts and win her to steal her away from her boyfriend, I see an accident help in controlling situation , senior's girlfriend for me is attractive or unattractive based on her looks, biggest promise I have made to someone is to not to lie to her, I am guilty of probably making mistakes as I never took help from anyone in knowing how to impress girls so faced various rejections .The thing that I hate the most is reading any book apart from comic …. In the third part he connects the dots with various comic characters doing different things, food testing, stories of movies, children singing songs etc.

Pamela in her introduction writes that she calls herself the lover of this world as she loves every single thing that she might find fun. Like being with children, or on the beach or blowing bubbles from the soap solution. She loves her parents a lot . She believes in the power of healing of every broken thing. She wants to help as many people as she can through her counseling. She hates violence and condemns people who do it especially when there is rape, murder and sexual assault on women and children. But becoming the victim of one of those is her nightmare as she's scared to confront her perpetrator. For her, the perpetrator is evil who not only harms physically but steals the soul away forever leaving a life spiritless.

Whereas Pamela completes the sentences in following way- I am in love with a guy who loves someone else I will give him freedom to make choice, I see an accident will help in giving the first aid by calling for help , senior's boyfriend for me is senior, biggest promise I have made to someone is to nurture people around me ,always, I am guilty of not being able to help a friend through counseling completely ,unfortunately he committed suicide, The thing that I hate the most is sitting idely and doing nothing…. In the third part of the test i.e. connecting dots, she connects the dots while imaging dots as characters that have different ailments with their mental health and she is the center dot which is helping them out for their mental well being .She imagines that the dots are giving her movement therapy, counseling and being a nurse.

Other students too wrote their answers - I am in love with a girl who loves someone else I will give up upon her, fight with the guy,love her more, kill her….., I see an accident i will ignore, I can't see blood, help in call police, give painkiller…..senior's girlfriend for me is senior's girlfriend, beautiful, ugly in comparison to my girlfriend, not matching that great with senior, crazy girl…. biggest promise I have made to someone is to be loyal, make up love everyday, bring money to my family, help in orphanage, drink milk everyday…I am guilty of betraying religion, cheating on my girlfriend, drinking too much late at night, wasting time,stealing hearts of girls, being too good….. The thing that I hate the most is exercise, submitting assignments, someone gaslighting me ,ugly people…..

There were a number of responses written by all people. After the second stage exams the students headed to have their breakfast. Mumkin was just thinking about meeting Amrisk and continuing reading the book given by Lucas that suggests Isabella and Lidiya are the same person. He isn't concerned about his selection in committee for the next stage as if it's death after death then there is no more death. Because he already has seen the rejection in the first stage. So a second rejection will not matter much. All the answers he wrote were his candid responses. In the dining hall Mumkin, Pamela and John are sitting together. Pamela was just getting worried about the result of selections for the next stage . While having breakfast she drops off her spoon in a hurry. As she tries to pick it up, Mumkin picks it for her and she shows her palm to take it from him. But he keeps it away.

Pamela(feeble voice): Mumkin, can you hand over my spoon back to me please.

Mumkin: Pamela, why do you want to use the spoon that has fallen down on the ground? Don't you think it's dirty with germs?

Pamela: Oh yes, it just completely went off my mind. Let me get a new spoon for myself.

Mumkin: Here(giving his spoon to her), you take this. I will drink soup directly from the bowl.Wait, where is your soup?

Pamela: Thanks Mumkin, but I don't think I need a spoon as I forgot to carry my soup from the cafeteria. I just bought sandwitches.I think I need to go back there to get my soup bowl.

THE TOUGHEST COMMITTEE SELECTIONS

Mumkin: What happened to you , you look not that confident as usual!

Pamela: I'm just nervous with my selection.

John: Oh gosh Pamela, for heaven's sake don't be like this. Look at me, whether I make or not in the committee, I'm enjoying my breakfast. You too enjoy it . Don't be a cry baby as it's making me uncomfortable to have food.

Pamela:Why are you feeling uncomfortable?

John: Because you're getting too emotional with selections that's making me also nervous now. So stop it right away.

Pamela feels more disappointed.

Pamela: John I'm not doing it intentionally. I don't feel like eating now.

Mumkin: Okay, Pamela, I understand what you're going through ,but chill. Be like the colorful bird that we see in you everyday. Enjoy your breakfast. John you too, calm down. It's the way she's feeling and she can't deny it.At Least that much I have learnt from our psychology course.

Pamela and John chucke over his last sentence.

The trio eat their breakfast fast and Mumkin assures both of them that the result will be in the favor of the trio only.

As directed at the previous stage everyone is asked to assemble in Gandhi hall again. Hielmaster enters the Hall. He addresses all.

Hielmaser: Hello ladies and gentlemen. So congratulations to all that your writing was readable by our psychologists ,that has been successfully assessed. However there are six of you who made it to the next stage.Let's start with reverse order. These eunoia are -Zeena, Rose, Ren, Pamela, Bessy and last but not the least Mumkin Chamburt. Pamela takes a sign of relief, Mumkin and Ren were unaffected .

Mumkin was deeply thinking about notes in diary after Hielmaster left the stage. He felt a sudden excitement thrilled with anxiety where he got curious about the next stage of committee selections as the diary of Lidiya might give some clues. His thinking is diverted now ,more focused towards the selections. Benny and John are disappointed as they don't hear their names. John says good luck for the next stage to Mumkin and Pamela before he leaves from there kiddingly saying 'You scared me ,but you yourself made it through selections. What a masked girl you are Pamela!'.

Hielmaster: Those selected will have to come after two days on Saturday for the next stage of selection. Good luck to those who couldn't make it. Don't get disappointed as this is not the end but just the beginning. We have our own requirements for the committee.Unfortunately the selected ones will only come to know what the committee is all about,so don't have any regrets in your heart. Should you have? Naah...

Prof Olivia orders everyone to disperse and takes a look at the form handed by Hielmaster. She discusses something with him. While everyone is dispersing ,Mumkin swiftly walks and runs towards the gate to reach the Amrisk's shop. After reaching there, he finds him keeping the books with K.Jalty. He looks at Mumkin,adjusts his spectacles that are on his nose and then welcomes him to get inside. He finds that Mumkin looks tired.

Amrisk: Oh hello Mumkin. Long time, I haven't seen you three for a long time. Where are Pamela and John?

Mumkin: Hi Amrisk(breathing heavily). Was occupied due to committee selections. Pamela and John did not come today.,as in I haven't informed them of me coming here.

Amrisk: So you came alone, leaving your best friends behind!

Mumkin:Yes, I have important work with you .

As Amrisk looks at Mumkin's eyes he finds that his eye lashes are heavy .

Amrisk: Ofcourse. I am always there for you dear. Sit here. (he slightly slides today's newspaper towards Mumkin and starts pouring coffee in a cup).

Mumkin: You're amazing, Amrisk.

Amrisk: Why you're saying it....for the service I give when you visit me...is it?

Mumkin: Yes.

Amrisk: I do it for almost all my customers as they're special to me.

Mumkin: That's not the only thing that makes you amazing.

Amrisk: Then what is it?

Mumkin keeps quiet,his eyes are still heavy and tired.

Amrisk: Mumkin ,I understand that you're rigorously involved with committee selections that's why you look tired. Here you go, drink this black coffee.

Mumkin: Thank you.

Mumkin takes the cup of black coffee from Amrisk. When he takes the first sip, he finds it extremely bitter. So he leaves the cup there itself.

Mumkin: The coffee, it's kind of bitter today.

Amrisk: I've got it made strong....I knew you needed it.....but didn't know that it'll be that strong that you'll leave the cup just after the first sip.

Mumkin: Sorry about that, I can't drink it completely as I prefer a mild taste.

Amrisk: No problem. Is committee selection still going on?

Mumkin: Yes, committee selection is just going on.

Amrisk: So how is it till now?

Mumkin: Me and Pamela made it to the next stage!

Amrisk: Oh congratulations to both of you(giving a shoulder hug to Mumkin).

Mumkin: Thank you sir.

Amrisk: What about John...Didn't he make it?

Mumkin: Unfortunately not!

Amrisk: Where he might have gone wrong?

Mumkin: No idea.

Amrisk: A guy who reads comics can't make into sophisticated committees like these.

Mumkin nods his head in a mixed way, to show his both agreement and disagreement with Amrisk.

Mumkin: I want to ask you something very crucial. I hope you'll not hide anything as it's regarding my dad.

Amrisk: Of Course Mumkin! I ain't sure of your dad's connection with me, but I'm always there to help you. Go ahead(picks up the cup of coffee and starts sipping).(He moved his eyes away from Mumkin staring at the newspaper).

Mumkin: Is Lidiya Cheriyan and Devkali Neelghanti Paul same?

Amrisk: I don't know Devkali Neelghanti Paul in person .

Mumkin: Still, at least you know Lidiya right!

Amrisk: Yes. What you want to say.

Mumkin: Is Lidiya ,Isabella and Devkali Neelghanti Paul, all three the same person?

Amrisk: Wait, what? So many names you took at once, it's very confusing ,don't you think?

Mumkin: Yes ,but can you resolve this mystery?

Amrisk: I know Lidiya, the girl from your College who joined Military. Devkali Neelghanti Paul is a writer. But now who the hell is this Isabella?

Mumkin: Isabella is Professor Olivia's sister.

Amrisk: You're making things too complicated. Listen to me, you focus on plans to make your business in weaponry. You seem unfocused.

Mumkin: No, I don't think that I'm unfocused.

Amrisk: I used to think John is only into women. I didn't know you too are!

Mumkin: Not at all, sorry to say I respect all women, but the ones I am referring to are middle aged women, probably of your age. By no chance I can be interested in them.

Amrisk: So what women are you interested in?

Mumkin: I have a girlfriend ,my classmate.

Amrisk: Let's discuss her then....why are you asking about these middle aged ones?

Mumkin: I want to know more about Lidiya.

Amrisk: I already mentioned about Lidiya that no one including me knows anything about her. She's past for everyone. Better not talk about her,Prof Hastik might have told you the same.

Mumkin: How do you know that Prof Hastik told us this? How do you know the information about the meeting among teachers and students of our college? Don't you think it's all happening inside the college, how that information reached your shop?

Amrisk stops sipping coffee, he keeps the cup back on the table. K. Jalty tells him that a new edition of Educational Sociology is kept on the second floor's third book shelf but Amrisk stops him by telling"we'll discuss this later Jalty". Now Amrisk is looking at Mumkin freezed.

Amrisk: You're asking questions like your warden Bloom.

Mumkin: So you know about all of them, right?

Amrisk: Yes, Professor Hastik came to this shop and he mentioned this incident -that you , Pamela and John reached University late after visiting our shop when you three came here for the first time!

Mumkin: Is this the only truth? How about providing the writing material for committee selection? Why didn't you tell the three of us about it regarding the same?

Amrisk: Oh Mumkin, that was because Committee selections were to be done in a secretive way by the University, so they requested me not to mention anyone regarding the same.

Mumkin: Is it? What about Changing your shop's name from UMBAS (Unique Military Base Association With Students) to UAS(Unique Association with Students)?

Amrisk: Yes Mumkin, that's true that till 1943, we had collaboration with the Military in our shop for war purposes but ours is not the only shop! There was another shop which closed in 1942 ,which was also helping the military in their research and providing writing material to the students. Why are you asking about it? How is this all connected with your father?

Mumkin starts believing what Amrisk is saying as it's matching with events in the diary but he doesn't wish to mention about the diary of Lidiya Cheriyan. Mumkin looks at Amrisk and starts sipping the black coffee.

Amrisk: How are you sipping the coffee that you find strong?

Mumkin: It's alright. I'll finish this cup at least

Amrisk:You're a determined guy. Now what's there in your mind ,tell me frankly.

Mumkin: It's just anything about the military that intrigues me about my father. It refreshes my imaginations with my father.

Amrisk: I understand Mumkin for how much you loved your father. There's something that you're not telling as the conversion of UMBAS to UAS was done in a confidential manner. You were a child at that time. I don't know who gave you this piece of information. Be vigilant to not to share this with anyone as still there are traitors who want to pull the flag of Himbertown down.

Mumkin: Traitors? Who are they?

Amrisk: Like every country has patriots and traitors. We too have people who want to hamper the country 's growth and destroy peace. Now don't ask me more than that, as I'm not entitled to share this information to a teenager for security reasons. Indeed we worked with the Military and I am proud of it too Mumkin. Anything pertaining to the Military I can't share.

Mumkin is fascinated by the words of Amrisk. Upon inquiry by Amrisk , Mumkin shares his experience of how luck which never favored him actually made him luckiest today as out of some six thirty students, his name turned up to sit in second stage becoming twenty second member and ultimately he made it to third round.

Amrisk congratulated him again. He shows him the new collection of books regarding weapons that he ordered specifically for Mumkin as requested by him in their first meeting. He gives him three books regarding weapon technologies, business management and techniques of winning wars with technologies. Mumkin leaves back to his University as it's five thirty in the evening. K. Jalty comes near Amrisk and they have a crucial chat.

K.Jalty: I tried to divert his attention by interrupting you, he knows so much.Principal Blacksmith needs to be informed about the same.

Amrik: Thanks Jalty. I have no idea about the source of this information . Yes, I will inform Principal Blacksmith again about him. Especially about his knowledge of Lidiya and Devkali Neelghanti Paul.

K.Jalty: During the committee selection process, thankfully we informed Principal Blacksmith about the way he , John and Pamela helped Isabella in saving her life. He deserved a second chance at least in psychology testing.

Amrisk: Yes, he was right that luck favors him the least. It was his own kindness that made Principal Blacksmith recommend him for the second stage after we informed him. I am going to meet him again today to inform about today's conversation with Mumkin. He will have a better plan.

K. Jalty: It will as you know the mastermind of all this can never fail in her plans.

Amrisk: Yes, she's moving the waves in her direction. Things will always be the way she wants them to be!

Amrisk wears black hat, coat and sunglasses . He heads towards the University to meet Principal Blacksmith.

Mumkin further goes to the hospital to purchase bandages for Laila's injuries. When he reaches the University, he meets Laila and Pamela. Pamela was changing Laila's knee dressing and Mumkin put bandages on it.

Pamela: Mumkin, are you hiding something? It's been a long time that you haven't interacted openly. You're always in a hurry!

Mumkin : Haha. That's not true(amicably). I am just occupied these days. Did you finish reading Devkali Neelghanti Paul's book?

Pamela: No not yet. Just finished half of it. I too got a little occupied with selections.

Mumkin: Did you find those books as a book or you found something else?

Pamela: What do you mean?

Mumkin: Is her book like other normal books?

Pamela:(befuddled) of course it's a book! What else do you expect from it?

Mumkin: I mean, something peculiar about the books!

Pamela: Not peculiar. The book is slightly boring for me. But Laila likes that ,that's what is peculiar.

Laila: I got it! Yeah Mumkin, these aRen't just books but guides for life. That's what you're asking!

Mumkin: Yeah, I got it. I need to leave for important work given by professor Rehman. Will see you two later. Please excuse.(Mumkin realizes that the books given to Pamela by Lucas are just the published books of Isabella, which doesn't have any information similar to the diary possessed by Mumkin related to Lidiya Cheriyan.)

Mumkin walks towards his hostel room.

Pamela: I don't understand. These days he's behaving bizarre.

Laila: I don't think so. I've been seeing him like this since the time I have known him personally.

Pamela: He used to spend a lot of time with me and John before. But nowadays mostly in his room at the hostel. I 'm concerned about this sudden behavior.

Laila: Probably, you know him since the beginning of class. And you're better at reading people.

Pamela: There's one more reason for his change in behavior(chuckling).

Laila: What's that?

Pamela: Why did he put a bandage on your injury madam?You're a sweetheart for him!(teasing)

Laila: No...ways.

Pamela: Don't lie. You've hypnotized him in your love.

Laila: As you said hypnosis, let's go to a hypnosis therapy workshop.

Pamela: Good idea. Where is it happening and when?

Laila: It's going to happen next week, four days- Monday,Tuesday, Thursday and Friday evening 5 to 6PM.Also, It's by Prof Rehman.

Pamela: Good initiative by Prof Rehman. I'll ask John and Mumkin if they want to join us. Most probably they wouldn't.

Laila: Why won't they join?

Pamela: Because both took psychology forcefully!

They hear a voice"I'm interested to join. Psychology can sometimes be fun". Pamela recognises this voice. It's Ren's voice. As she turns back. She finds Ren smiling at Laila and then he looks at Pamela. The eye contact he makes with her is as deep as she could see layers of brown black colors with sparkles in his eyes. She's speechless to say anything to him as she recalls back that he's been ignorant to him for a long time. She recalls that before a few days he was ignoring her.

He comes near her and starts talking to Laila.

Ren:(laughing) Not in this birth.Just sarcastic. I mean seriously Laila, you're going for that stupid therapy?Not coming for today's party? I'll make some arrangements with the help of my uncle so that you can sneak in.

Laila: No Ren, I just don't feel like being part of anything like a party. I want to live life in a more fulfilling way!

Ren: Party girl what's wrong with you, did you take drugs? What about those tattoos?

Laila: I want to get rid of all past memories that hamper my growth.

Ren: Wait wait...fulfilling, growth and tattoo removal. What's up with you ! Seriously, you don't wanna come?

Pamela: Ren she doesn't want to come. Don't put her into peer pressure. You need not influence her by doing something that's blocking her growth. Stop it!

Ren: I'm not talking to you . Mind your own business. (irked)

Laila: Ren,Pamela is just trying to help me out.

Laila walks away towards her hostel. Now Ren and Pamela are the only ones left near the quadrangle. The sky is blue like blue nightingale's feathers are covering it slowly. Ren turns his back towards Pamela and starts moving away towards the University's exit gate.

Pamela: Ren , why has your behavior towards me has become like this?

Ren: Like what?

Pamela: Before you always teased me and now you are ignoring me.

Ren: What ?

Pamela: It's only after Prof Rehman's therapy class that you are getting more irritated by me. Please answer.

He starts moving quicker but hears her whimpering . As he turns back he sees her face turning red and tears rolling down from her eyes and nose as she is sobbing.

Ren: Stop crying Pamela. You're an overthinker ,there's nothing like that.

She continues crying more. He goes near her. He tells her something due to which her sobbing stops.

Ren: You see, I love my girlfriend Janny very much. During the counseling session of Prof Rehman, the way I could connect with you, I could never do that with any girl including Janny.

Pamela: What do you mean?

Ren: Your serenity and innocence was unavoidable for me. Coming close to you was like losing Janny which I can't imagine even in my dreams as I love her the most. That's why I was impertinent with you and I ain't one responsible for it.

After saying this he starts walking towards the University exit gate. As his image was getting smaller and smaller, she was given a shoulder hug by someone very familiar. It's John who consoles her .

John: Buddy , why are you crying?

Pamela: Nothing John, just like that!

John: Come on, you tease me just like that, I'm seeing you crying after a long time. So please stop!

John again gives a quick friendly hug to her. He covers her with his jacket,and she feels very comfortable .

Pamela: how come you're so caring suddenly?

John: You made it to committee.

Pamela: So I should treat you with an ice cream ,right?

John: Not ice cream!

Pamela: What do you want John?

John: Convince your uncle to recommend me for the committee, like the way Mumkin is recommended by Principal Blacksmith!

Pamela: Shut up Ren. My uncle rarely gets a chance to interact with him.

John: Do something .Please.

Pamela: Okay ,I'll put a word to him. Let's go to the hostel before we reach late.

They both move towards their hostels.

Mumkin enters his hostel room and starts reading Lidiya Cheriyan's diary again.

"Just don't want to give up Alora. Training looks like an impossible mission. If I give up and return back ,probably forgiving myself will be most difficult. My mother,despite being a widow of a military officer, told me to boldly complete the training and prove my worth. I'm the paramount person here as all eyes are on me. If I complete the Military training successfully, it'll open the door for other women to join the Military. But here everyday is a do and die situation for me. I remember my selections.The first day was intelligence testing which was based on verbal and non verbal questions, I'm ain't good at abstract. I practiced many books borrowed from Amrisk and made it to the first round.The second round of psychology which I never studied being a science student seemed like climbing a battlefield but somehow I connected the pattern, had positive affirmations in subject and through this the second stage was like a cake walk for me...............................But initially all the psychology rounds seems to be very ambiguous. I mean what do I write when I have to connect the dots. Whatever I wrote was naturally coming in my mind like a research student creating an antidote for a disease, a college student teaching dance to her batchmates due to which they win the competition and a housewife beautifully decorating her house to accommodate her guests etc. I don't know how they passed me after I wrote all this shit"

As Mumkin reads this he realizes the same pattern of examination is followed in committee selection- Intelligence test and psychology test. Same questions regarding writing a paragraph about oneself, completion of sentences based on vague incomplete sentences . For psychology it's making connections on the dots presented on paper and writing interpretation. He realizes that the pattern of selection of Lidiya in the Military and the committee selection is just the same . Now to read the next line things might become crystal clear, he anticipates that the committee can be somewhere related to Lidiya Cheriyan. To train candidates for the military at the position of commander. This thought revolved again in his head and now there's a strong adrenaline rush in his body. He's getting warmed up with these thoughts running in his head. He tries to read further but is feeling jittery to focus.. He lies on his bed, takes a deep breath and again picks up the same diary to read further steps .If his anticipation is true then he'll have the upper hand over others to be a part of the committee as he will know what will happen in the next stage. He decided to share these secrets with everyone to provide everyone the level playing field.

As he reads through the books Lidiya mentions that the next stage before her selection into the Military is the interview process that lasts for four hours.

"Alora, I wasn to recall an incident before I was asked to join the Military. It was a mauldin experience. I was asked to arrive at the placement room early at 6:30AM.I wore white silhouette . As I entered the room, I was asked to sit down. There was a senior from the Military who was there to interview me. He looked at me for a second and then asked me to take down my seat.He was rude in his tone. I was asked at least twenty questions pertaining to my name, occupation, place of birth ,time of birth, what I like about my name, who kept it, what is famous about my place and what problems I see at my hometown, how can I improve those problems...So many questions that it was difficult for me to keep questions in order and recall them all, but I got the idea that the sole purpose of these questions is to scare me away,of course which I won't be as my name is Lidiya. Lidiya Cheriyan. As I answered around nine out of twelve questions, he asked me to recall back the questions that I've left. I recalled two and answered them on the spot. Then he asked me counter questions from my answers provided to him with respect to the solution of problems in my hometown. I told him women aren't taking up the leadership roles there, he enquired why , I answered patriarchy .He requisitioned me, why is it so? I remained confident and gave him the evidence with respect to unequal pay, job segregation, upbringing of women, gender roles, examples of operation by Military where not even a single woman was involved etc.After my answer Alora, he asked me how do I unroot the patriarchy if I see that as the main problem? I answered him by joining the military, my life will be a chronicle to uproot patriarchy. I don't want women to be either treated as slaves or masters, but give equal treatment where women aren't superior or inferior but indistinguishable, as we all are human beings. Then he asked me further questions regarding my father, what was his role and rank in the military, how I lost him, what was age at that time,how my mother coped up with it, number of siblings I have, what did I do to bring my family to stability etc? All these questions were certainly hysterical for me, but I answered them with firm belief in myself that bad experiences in my life build my strength mentally as I am Lydia. He asked me if I compromised anywhere in my life to meet the daily needs of my family.I answered that I can compromise with daily consumption but never compromise with my values .And needs....needs get fulfilled when one is passionate in life. Another question ,why do I want to join the Military? Is it because I want to give a lesson of feminism to the Military?I answered by saying that keeping up a country's pride is larger than any personal goal. He further asked me to explain my answer. I explained by giving various records where our country had to face many challenges and war-like situations, where both men and women contributed directly or indirectly. Especially when the economy of a country went down, it was both genders who enhanced it. I made a mistake there. Not only both genders but third gender too which contributed. He asked me further about my education project, why did I choose it and how can I contribute to the military through that? After my answers all questions ended.Then he asked me to leave by wishing me the best. I can't forget the propitious day when the Military called me to get trained before joining, giving clear indication that I cleared all stages as I was an honest and learned person. My joining letter made my mother proud. It was all two days after my interview was over."

Mumkin anticipates that for him and the other five candidates selected for the interview is the next round which is going to happen after two days. The next two days, classes are to be attended by all students of college including the ones selected for the next round of the committee. He tells Zeen, Rose, Ren, Pamela and Bessy to meet him after the class near the exit gate ground, under the banyan tree at four thirty pm. After they assemble, Mumkin wants to address them. John arrived there too just to accompany Mumkin.

Mumkin: I have called you all so that you can prepare better for the committee selections. As yesterday, I was walking through the corridor to meet Prof Rehman, I heard someone saying that the next stage will be extensive interview where questions asked will be based on your choices of getting into committee, information about my parents, my name, occupation, place of birth ,time of birth, who kept it, liking and disliking that you may have, what is famous about my place and what problems I see in my place, how can you improve those problems and did you compromise anywhere in your life to meet the daily needs of your family? ....So you have to confidently answer those questions. There will be many counter questions too regarding the same.

Pamela: Haha. The way you are speaking Mumkin, you sound like Warden Atrika Bloom. Is he alive or has his ghost entered your body?

Zeen: Really? Why do you think we shall trust what your ears say? I better inquire about this to Prof Olivia.

Pamela: Trust Mumkin . He's a good guy and there isn't any harm in being prepared for something.

Rose:I agree with Mumkin and Pamela, if he has heard about it then it might be true.

Bessy: Zeen there isn't any point in inquiring from Prof Olivia. Ultimately it might lead to our resignation from the next stage of committee selection.

Ren isn't bothered with what Mumkin says ,but then he stands there to get more ints about the committee selections. They all leave their places . The ones who believe Mumkin start preparing for their interviews which might be the next stage of committee selection. The next few days they attend the classes and meet up for three hours from two thirty to five fifty in the evening. They all discuss their small details and give feedback upon their areas to ameliorate.

Pamela:I'm Pamela, I want to get into committee because I want to be a support system for all in whatever I do. My parents are very supportive towards my goals in life. Being an only child ,I am pampered the most but still I have a soft corner for everybody in this world because I can feel the pain of people. I did my schooling from Christ School.I was born in Himbertown's western part. And I don't remember the exact time but it was Saturday morning around four twenty.I like my name as it means sweet, it resembles me as I've always been sweet with people hitherto except for a few people in my life. One of them is John who's a good friend of mine. We tease each other. Although what I don't like is when people take my winsome nature for granted and try taking advantage. My dad kept my name. My place ,I think it's famous for its river, well planned city, greenery, cuisines like raspberry pudding and wheat champagne etc. Problem in Himbertown can be the crime that is increasing due to unemployment . I think providing quality education, frequent policing, strict laws and of course more jobs can really change the situation. Also these days mental illness is getting common. I want to help people regarding the same. When it comes to compromising with my values ,I ....I (a sudden sobbing),I did it once. I slept with my ex boyfriend, where my parents do not know about it. They trust me a lot. Hiding this from them is like agony of mind. I ...(weeping continues)

Everyone is astonished after hearing this . Not because she isn't a virgin but the way she's taking it on herself like a taboo.

Mumkin goes near her and gives her a shoulder hug.

Mumkin: Don't get worked up!

Ren looks at Pamela and Mumkin and then he looks at her bracelet Pamela is wearing. The stars shaped design is moving, it's shining more and making a pleasant noise.

Rose: Yeah, Pam. This is very normal. I too have parents who don't want me to date multiple people at one time. I still do it, it's my life and after all this time I have four exes. That's not cool according to my parents.

John: Exactly, not a big deal. Just a hiccup. Also you took my name in your interview. What a child you are!

Zeen starts scoffing at Pamela.

Zeen: Really, why Pamela? You will never grow. i think even after sleeping with your ex boyfriend you didn't mature? Trust me ,I can do it better (wicked laugh).

Zeen goes near Pamela and holds her back tightly and she's feeling intimidated with being timorous.

Pamela: Stop it!

Mumkin moves Zeen's hand away from Pamela and John goes near Zeen and punches him on his face due to which his nose starts bleeding.

Mumkin: Shut your damn thing, rascal. Get out of this place.

Angrily Zeen leaves the place.

Situation is quite pensive. Bessy and Rose comfort Pamela. They give her a water bottle . She drinks water from that. After six to seven minutes they rejoin the group. Mumkin tells everyone to reflect on what Pamela answered.

Mumkin: What you don't like can be anything else, saying things like you don't like when people take advantage of winsome nature, that's an undeveloped answer. You can also say the name of a movie or food that you don't like. Like, I don't like bitter gourds!

Bessy: Well, it's a natural answer from my point.

Mumkin: But it's going to cast questions like when people take advantage of yours, why you let them do that and why do they do that etc? You see, it's gonna be chaotic for her to answer such questions.

Bessy: Agree as ultimately one needs to appear confident in one's abilities.

Mumkin: Also you can still hide your dating history as it isn't required! It can also show intense emotions. Remember the selections are for Mi.....secret committee. Who knows what's their demand. So let's be prudent to be confident and avoid hassleness. It's just like a selection that happens to be someone's body guard. One has to always show a strong side of oneself. This is what I heard near the end of Prof Rehman's corridor. I think we shall move to Bessy. Shall we?

All agree and Bessy starts talking about herself. Bessy is a brown skinned girl with beautiful curly hair, her eyes are big with thick eyelashes.

Bessy: I am Bessy Jonas. I apply to this committee as I don't know anything but I look for opportunities. Basically to explore and grow myself. My father is a weaver and mother is a housewife. I have a family of five members with three younger siblings. But in my life I not only want to support my family, but I want to do something great. I was born on the Island of Brijko. I like my name as it means god is bountiful. I'm a very religious person. I like everything in this world. Something that I dislike is wasting food. I wish the world was with zero poverty so that no one had to sleep empty stomach. My grandmother kept my name. My Island is famous for its beach, sea food ,culture especially folk dance and cuisines. The major problem at my place is poverty but we are still highly effective people who use the available resources from the environment to sustain our livelihood. It can be reduced through education, skills development, infrastructure development and big countries can also invest in my country. When it comes to compromising with anything in life , I believe one needs to be ardent in protecting one's traditions and beliefs .But be open minded too. One need not compromise on the above but one can always be diplomatic in making the right choice.

People clapped after she spoke. They mentioned that she is to the point, genuine, practical and her answers show a practical approach towards life. They all discussed their answers and Mumkin was just listening to them to give them feedback to improve their quality of response. It was six pm when Mumkin's turn came. He could only explain the meaning of his name and his passion for his hobbies that includes reading war books. Chamburt is the surname adopted by his great grandfather as they climbed mountains to provide food to village people in Ranidetro village in ancient times. Warden Atrika Bloom came in between his speech to order everyone to get back to their hostels.

They all leave back to their hostel at six three pm and Mumkin decides not to read the diary further as he feels tired and wants to go fresh for tomorrow's selection process. At one point he feels he might miss something very important regarding the selection ,but by not reading further he doesn't have energy to check or overcome that intuitive feeling.

The next morning all of them wake up early as they believe that it is their interview today. That included Zeen too. They all are wearing formal uniforms. The three boys are dressed up in their formal pants,shirt,coats and ties whereas the three girls are wearing formal skirts with full sleeved shirts.It is the third stage of the selection process . All six of them assembled on the ground.Six of them are feeling jittery and anticipating except Zeen who is invigoratingly confident.They are also hiding this important information that the third stage of the process can be an interview. Prof Rehman tells the students to relax as he finds tightness in them. Hielmaster enters with Prof Olivia.

Hielmaster: Good morning everyone! Welcome to the third stage of selections. This is gonna be tough though!

Zeen: I know what this is all about. Just an obtuse interview. Mumkin leaked the information that he heard in the corridor. What a traitor!

Hielmaster: Ooo, that's why you six are dressed so fancy!If what Zeen said is true then your dreams are just magnetic Mumkin. Zeen you too are filled with lovely fantasy as you just now said something about the obtuse interview and traitorhood etc. Did you ever try writing fiction? You'll do great. Believe me.(smirks).

Zeen is atwitter now! Mumkin with Pamela, Ren and other two candidates are too bowled over as they realize that it's not the interviews that'll happen.

Zeen: What do you mean as I am zero percent interested in writing fiction?

Prof Olivia(loud voice): Quiet everyone. Wait for further instructions.

Hielmaster:Thank you Miss Olivia. Interview is never a part of committee selection! Gosh,you guys are just dumb asses.

Pamela raises her left eyebrow and looks at Mumkin as Hielmaster calls them dumbasses.

Hielmaster :Now, without wasting time, run towards the field. Further directions were given there.Five of them assembled near ground running , they were breathing heavily and Hielmaster arrived there after two minutes. Pamela reached ground after him.

Hielmaster: It's a test of intelligence quotient and mental stamina. You're already trained by your teacher regarding the same. What do you see in front?

Mumkin: There's a huge rock with a trophy at top around forty feet from ground.

Zeen: All I see is the shining trophy.

Hielmaster: Okay. Anyone else?

Bessy : A mountain.

Hielmaster: Alright. Your task is to get that top trophy. Can anyone tell its height?

Mumkin: It's forty three feet tall.

Hielmaster: Why that answer ?

Mumkin: The protrusions in the form of small rocks attached are at a distance of two to four feet on the rock. So that'll make up to forty three feets in total.

Hielmaster: What's your name gentleman?

Mumkin: Mumkin Chamburt.

Hielmaster: Yes, what Mr Chamburt said is logical. Remember your mission by using the available resources from that store room(pointing towards the store room attached to the College's sports department building). After completion of the task ,come back to this position, reflection will be done to know the purpose of the task . Results will be announced after that.

As all six of them run towards the store room they find items like rope, fragile wooden stairs of two feet, two feet long log, harness and net. As they check further all these items are just in pairs. Mumkin thinks that just in case one item breaks, another one can be used for backup.

Mumkin: Let's all of us be circumspect while using these items as the number is limited only to two.

Zeen: What do you mean by "us"? It's a competition.I will win. Always. You losers!

Mumkin: Nevertheless, reaching alone to take the trophy is a hardship! We need each other to complete the task. I believe it's teamwork that wins.

Zeen: Shut up you unfastened ! A winner always walks alone with pride(holding the stairs and rope)

Zeen runs with stairs and ropes. He set up the stair near the rock, climbs on stairs and helds first protrusion. Mumkin and other four people- Pamela, Ren, Bessy and Rose take the left material near the ground. Mumkin sets up a stair near a rock at a distance of around five feet from Zeen. Ren climbs on the stairs. He holds the protrusion. Pamela makes a knot with rope and ties it with a log, Mumkin handles the log with a knot attached to it to Ren. Ren climbs the next protrusion around four feet away from the first one easily. However the third protrusion is further away. Mumkin gives Ren the idea that to go to the third protrusion, he needs to keep the log between the second and third protrusion. Ren does it which forms the bridge . He climbs over that temporary bridge and reaches the third protrusion from the second. Now as soon as Rose tries to climb the first protrusion to provide harness to him, the stairs break. She's falling backwards where her head would hit the ground. Fortunately Mumkin and Bessy swiftly provide her support ,holding her through their hands due to which her body turns forward hitting her knee. Meanwhile Pamela also turns her body towards Rose to provide her with the support.

Pamela :Are you okay Rose?

Rose : Yes I am.

Pamela: I think your knee is bleeding.

Rose: Yes it is. The injury is minimal as Mumkin and Bessy gave support at the right time but still I don't know if I can climb again.

Mumkin: Don't worry Rose, you take care of yourself. Pamela, you go ahead.

Pamela: Sure.

Mumkin: You sit on my shoulder as the protrusion is broken now.

Pamela starts giggling.

Pamela: Isn't that awkward that I climb on your shoulder Mumkin?

Mumkin: When you have the right intentions then it's not awkward! Let's do it quickly as we're losing time.

Bessy: Yes, do it Pamela, or else I will climb his shoulder in your place.

Pamela: No, I was just kidding. I will go, Mumkin, just bend yourself.

Pamela sits on Mumkin's shoulder ,Ren passes the log back to Pamela. She ties the harness to the log and lifts the log up . He quickly wears the harness and makes a knot of rope which he ties to one side of the log. The length of the log is smaller to reach the next protrusion. Ren lifts the log till the next protrusion and he gives it a push due to which the knot of one side of rope at log gets fixed to the protrusion.The other side of the rope he ties to his harness and takes a tarzan swing to reach that protrusion .Mumkin starts clapping for Ren's successful efforts to reach the forth protrusion. Other hand Zeen is climbing a second protrusion copying the method of Ren. He keeps the log in order to make a bridge after joining the second and third protrusion and starts to climb it to reach the third protrusion, but suddenly his leg slips and he is losing his grip.His left knee is fixed in log and right leg is in the air. He cries out loud for help. Mumkin goes near him and asks Pamela and Bessy to hold the net as a preventive measure to avoid injury in case Zeen falls down. Pamela is hesitant but Mumkin convinces her to ignore what Zeen did as he looks in trouble which is life threatening.

Mumkin: Zeen , just take a deep breath. Try standing up, then balance yourself and take three steps back. You'll make it to the first protrusion. That's safe.

Zeen: I can't . I just can't. My heart is pumping very fast as I look down.

Bessy: It's not that high. Some nine feet only! Why isn't he able to come down?

Mumkin: Hold on Zeen. Keep your grip on the rope strong.

Zeen loses his grip and falls on the net held by Mumkin,Pamela and Bessy. Due to his overweight the net gets torn and Zeen straight away falls to kiss the ground. Along with him, his log ties with rope also falls down. He cries out loud in affliction. The two nurses wearing white frocks arrive out of nowhere and take Zeen with them on a stretcher.

Pamela: Where did these nurses come from suddenly? It seemed like a scene from a movie!

Mumkin: They might have kept the staff in case of a medical emergency .

Meanwhile Ren looks stuck on protrusion forth as his shoelace is stuck to a nail on rock. He isn't able to move further and is feeling dizzy. Mumkin takes the stairs ,log and rope of Zeen. He makes the arrangement of stairs to climb up, move to first protrusion, uses a log, rope and knot for climbing first,second and third protrusion with techniques of Ren, ultimately he reaches to the forth protrusion where Ren is standing. He unties his shoe lace. Mumkin shows him the way to climb up. But Ren looked a little exhausted so Mumkin took the lead. He starts climbing up one protrusion after the next where Ren follows him. With the support of Ren's hands, Mumkin reaches the top and takes the trophy. The duo climbs down smoothly in a back fashioned way from top to lowest protrusion with the trophy. Pamela and Bessy happily clap for both of them.

The five gather on the ground. Hielmaster comes there.

Hielmaster: So let's reflect! Why did you get the trophy?

Bessy: It's presence of mind because when Ren was stuck, Mumkin went to help him.

Hielmaster: What else do you see?

Pamela: What Zeen did was wrong! Even after knowing the fact that each item is only two,still he took half of the materials with him.

Hielmaster: So what happened after that?

Pamela: He fell down as he wanted to do things alone seeking for self victory.

Hielmaster: Good answer! He believed more in competition than cooperation. Rome wasn't built by a single man, it required a full team. Is there anyone who thinks they could've done the task alone?

Everyone remains silent for a second and then Bessy says no, followed by Pamela and Ren saying "no sir".

Hielmaster: Alright ,hope he learnt a lesson and you follow like this to have a balanced combination of presence of mind and heart! Keep it up .Your team did a good job!

Prof Olivia: Have your snack break, arrive back to know the results.

Hielmaster: Wait miss Olivia, before that I have a question to ask them!......(silence) What do you think the committee is all about?

Bessy:Is it about making us better professionals?

Hielmaster: Think deeply .

Bessy: Yes, making us better counselors, business professionals and theater artists etc. Is it?

Hielmaster: No not at all! Carry on for your snacks break.

All five reach the snack counter, they are handed cheese tomato pasta, muffins,jelly and chocolate milk. This time they also have arrangements to sit and eat. They eat heartily and strike upon interesting conversation.

Bessy:So stupid of Zeen. He didn't think before becoming a joker in selection!

Rose: Yeah, I saw him as a hoaxer who got tricked down by his own actions!

Mumkin and Pamela are eating muffins and listening to them. Mumkin asks Pamella to pass the sugar vessel. As Pamela does so, he adds a spoon of it in his chocolate milk and mixes with the well. Few drops are stuck on his right hand, he wipes it with a tissue with his left hand.

Bessy: By the way, I have heard a lot about Zeen.

Rose: He has a really bad attitude. The way he treated all of us was like a peice of shit .

Pamela: He was behaving like a self conceited person!

Rose:Yes yes, as if he knows everything.

Bessy: Still whatever wrong he does, he's always able to get out of it!

Rose: I don't know much of his wrong doings but I've heard that he was caught carrying weed in his lunch box.

Pamela puts her hand on her face and says 'shoot, how wasn't he rusticated then?'

THE TOUGHEST COMMITTEE SELECTIONS

Rose: Who can rusticate him,no one has that level?
Pamela: No but, even if we come late to the hostel we're given an imposition of five days. Right Mumkin?
Mumkin and Ren are quietly having their food and getting bored in the conversations of ladies.
Mumkin replies in one word 'Yes'.
Pamela: Ya...Then why isn't he rusticated permanently for carrying weed , that too in a tiffin box?
Bessy: He has powerful people backing him!
Pamela: That's why his behavior of entitlement, is it?
Bessy: Do you know he is nephew of whom?
Pamela: No...I'm in first year, I don't know much about the seniors.
Bessy: Do you know Rose?
Rose: No,I don't.
Bessy takes a muffin, puts peanut butter over it and takes a bite. She chews and speaks simultaneously.
Bessy: T...Th(coughing).
The muffin enters her windpipe and she feels choked...Pamela, quickly asks Ren to pass the water jar. As she is waiting for him to fill the glass, he directly goes near Bessy and passes the glass to her saying 'Tiger Watson'.
Rose: What?
Bessy drinks the glass prompt and feels better .
Bessy: Yes, that's what I was trying to say. He is the nephew of Tiger Watson.
Pamela: Tiger toh, he's your uncle's business partner. Isn't Ren.
Ren: Nah, I'm not concerned
Pamela: Okay....(whispering to Bessy and Rose)...He's not less self conceited than Zeen.
They both quietly chuckle after listening to this.
Bessy: Tiger Watson! He's a good friend of our trustee,Silver Bison.
Ren: Mr. Watson is our family friend . He's a nice man.
Bessy:Oh yes, you Ren, you're the nephew of our trustee. Alas, pompous like Zeen is the nephew of a good man like Tiger Watson.
Pamela:I understand now, this is what feeds his delinquency
Bessy:Rightly said Pamela, that's why he is so imperious!
Mumkin: Let's leave this matter here.Hope Zeen recovers quickly. Let's hurry up, Prof Olivia asked to come on time!

All of them reassembled back at the same place . But this time there are seats for them as well as eighty other seats for guests. This wasn't there before. It was all arranged during the time of their break in a bullet train manner. Slowly all guests including faculty members ,student union members and staff members including Pamela's uncle Bidar Nelon arrived there and occupied the seats. SIlver Bison and Tiger Watson also arrived.

Prof Rehman enters, goes on the stage and addresses all sitting guests.
Prof Rehman: Good afternoon. Firstly we would like to thank Mr. Hielmaster for trusting our students for committee selections and giving precious time .It was a strenuous process to screen twenty two out of six hundred and then selecting four members after it finally. The lucky four will be announced by the Principal blacksmith.
Prof Olivia is not present there.
Prof Hashtik in place of Prof Olivia handed a file to Principal Blacksmith while he was climbing up to the podium.
Principal Blacksmith:Good afternoon everyone. Our students have always made us proud. They have been part of various committees. Those involve sports, cultural ,educational reforms, well being etc. When our students have been selected for exclusive projects, that has been a proud moment. This is another such selection which is unique in its own way. This is a salient but secretive committee. The intelligence testing, brain testing via psychology and group compatibility helped in selecting four of you. Also the effort of the team is appreciated in the last stage, helping the fellow student in saving his life and preventing mishappening. Now you all might be wondering what this committee is all about? Again as its name is......It's a secret committee. The selected ones will get full information about the committee's work. The ones not making it here need to assume that their forte lies somewhere else but we appreciate

their efforts. The committee is kept internal as the work or problems related are internal. So the lucky ones are-Ren ....People clap. Tiger Watson shouts"Congratulations Ren. Now next will be the turn of Zeen I know".

Principal Blacksmith: Second is Bessy, third is Rose and forth is Mumkin.

As people clap, Tiger stands up and looks infuriated!

Tiger Watson: Principal Blacksmith, why Zeen's name isn't there?

Principal Blacksmith: He couldn't perform well in the last stage.

TIger Watson: I paid five thousand pound to get him a seat in committee.

Principal Blacksmith: Selections are strict. Your money will be refunded to the person to whom you paid a bribe.

Tiger Watson: Nonsense you took a student through a lucky drawer in a second round! Isn't that dereliction?

Principal Blacksmith: Absolutely not. He (referring to Mumkin)is not selected on the basis of grace or being a super intelligence chap but due to his bravery in saving the life of a woman . Giving him another chance was worth it! He nailed it .

Tiger Watson: Bravery, is it? He made it through a lucky drawer.

Principal Blacksmith: We lied to him and everybody here(adjusting his spectacles). The lie is his selection through the lucky drawer, but he and his two lovely friends- Pamela and John rendered their help in saving the life of a young lady . All three were recommended by committee members to appear in the second stage! Unfortunately John couldn't make it to the next stage, still the committee's decision is reserved in choosing the right candidate at the right time.

Tiger Watson: I'm not here to listen to some benevolence lecture or you being pastoral care to Mumkin. If the committee can change its decision to choose John in future, why don't you take my nephew into consideration?

Principal Blacksmith: Because he's ill mannered.

Tiger Watson: What ?repeat!

Principal Blacksmith:He's ill mannered .I'll mannered like you(smirk).

Tiger Watson: Bloody heck! You'll pay the price of it, you old codger. I wanted my nephew to be the chief of this Secret committee.His name as Zeen Watson was supposed to be published in newspapers, thus enhancing my reputation in public. He's not even made to this stupid secret committee. "They spilled water on my plans".

He wears his black sunglasses back and looks at Bison, holds his collar for a second saying "you! Slothful,so-called best friend". Bison tells him that he can't help as it isn't in his hands. Tiger Watson leaves from there disappointedly.

Principal Blacksmith: Congratulations four of you. Fill up the forms and instructions will be given by Hielmaster. Mr. Bloom escorted the winners to Rama Krishna Hall.

CHAPTER ONE

The first day of college

Hey Honey, wait! Wait! Take your lunch, says Mrs. Chamburt while Mumkin is heading towards his University. He refuses saying "it won't stay fresh mom as the lunch break is at one pm. Anyways i will take it with me, as you have made it with your love and effort.

Mumkin gives her a warm embrace and leaves a kiss on hisr adorable cheeks. He checks his plan from now on, he has three huge bags, one filled with just his passed down books of psychology, the new course that he will pursue in Himbertown University,the second one with clothes from his tenth standard to torn sweaters and the third one, comparatively a smaller one with goodies like home made long lasting candies ,pickle and few juice bottles with chips packets. Mumkin is a nineteen year old son of a widow whose husband went on to the war. Which war? He doesn't know much about it, as neither his mother said anything to him nor he asked. The idea of starting a business in weaponry he got from his father who once served in the Military.

Although he does have zero memory with his father. Mumkin's childhood wasn't up to scratch to remember . He saw his mother in despair and talked about the memories of his father, a brave soldier who lost life while accompanying the forces of his country in a paramount mission . Mumkin always consoled her,hugged her and felt her pain, did whatever he could in order to keep his mother happy including- getting good grades, not dating anyone, keeping a friend's circle of studious people which was zero in his town and giving full attention to his mother. Even trying to figure out if any of his father's brother or friends could remarry his mother so as to alleviate her pain of loneliness. He once got slapped by her at the age of fourteen when his uncle Bruno, who is 10 years younger to Mumkin's father revealed that Mumkin expressed a wish- "he wants me to be his step father".Mumkin remembers the event well. It was sunday morning, when his uncle visited him with rice crackers and chocolate. Mumkin for a second thought that Mr. Bruno can't well fit in the shadow and shape of his father that he created in his mind. His mother got disappointed as she regarded Bruno as his younger brother. His search for mother's groom stopped there itself. Although his mother hasn't improved at all, she still says ""Mumkin, your father was just an amazing man that any woman could dream of, he loved me limitlessly and I miss him a lot. I get worried about you sometimes. I would never want ,whatever happen with him, should happen with you. He could've lived peacefully in Ranidetro,but he was a loyal man. You never follow his footsteps, always stay close to me. Ranidetro has various opportunities to return back home itself after three years of college!. She still treats him like a small kid who can't take care of himself well. Now all he wanted was more stability in life. There's a concord between his mother and an understanding that she has this resistance to change her circumstances and wants to live the way she's living. She gets money support from the government as his father was a soldier. That money was very little though . All Mumkin can do is nothing when it comes to reliving his mother's pain as she misses his father a lot. He can just accept things the way they are! Probably this is what the world calls maturity ,when you helplessly accept the circumstances despite how much serpent hood life carries. However, business is his dream. Whereas she also sees him as a ray of hope, that one day he will become a PhD scholar especially in the new emerging field of psychology .She fears sending him in the Military. He respects her decision .But her protective love towards him can't stop him in being ambitious .He wants to lead bygones to bygones to look at all the possibilities that he has in life. He secretly dreams to run his own business selling weaponry in his village Ranidetro. But his vague idea and bad finances on family struck a pause on his dream. With ideas alive in his mind, he passed the exam where now he is going to attend Himbertown College of Arts choosing a course in psychology his last choice as he has zero interest in this subject. He is granted a scholarship by College till he completes his course due to his outstanding performance in school. Brown haired and gray eyed Mumkin Chamburt continuous reminiscing about the past in a crowded bus to the state of Himbertown which is some hundreds of kilometers away from his house .After getting down from the bus he takes a tonga till his college .Upon reaching he had to leave his two bags as directed by the University's guard. He leaves them near the luggage counter. He looks at himself now in dismay . With all dusty clothes and a huge bag, olive green in color that belonged to his father once, he starts riding a bicycle given by the guard with a chit on which the name of his building, floor number and room number is written. His bag is four times the size of the back seat of the bicycle that falls off nearly ten times before reaching the building. He parks his bicycle, takes his bag and starts running towards the sixth floor, room number 607, a tentative room for psychology students. As he reaches his classroom, there's a huge jitter, everyone is looking at him. All dressed up neatly, with an ambiance of class like that of a hospital. White tiles, white walls,white lights,white benches and white tables. Few students also wore white, while a teacher with a twin look of Albert Einstein encountered him...

"Mr. Chamburt, you're late on the first day. Only difference is that it's college, not school. Spoonfeeding is not possible for your class of 50 students who aim to call themselves psychotherapists and psychologists ....fancy casseroles!know that learning punctuality is demanded here", said Prof Caleb Williams. All Mumkin wants to do is to open his arms and declare that he himself doesn't want to be called a psychologist or a therapist or whatever. All he wants is to live his own dreams. But he kept his mouth shut. He has always been doing that since his childhood, be his teachers picking up on him of stealing the lunchbox of his classmate sitting next to him, but in reality it was the opposite ,or be it wrongly being accused of passing nasty comments on the girl with big zig zag teeth of class in school buy the teacher, which in reality was done by few notorious boys. Mumkin was the first one to be accused as he was outsmarted by the other goons of his class.

They took his name from all acts, but he always kept his calm and remained quiet , took the punishment and moved on from there. An absolute priest of nonviolence. Later on, during his intermediate too his strategy remained the same. To be that innocent lamb, but his good grades protected him from any punishment and the goons got divine retribution of multiple restigations!

Coming back to the present day, his teacher Mr. Willams has been teaching developmental psychology for the past 20 years. , he is strict and wants perfection from his students. At times he gets too harsh but wants students to keep the name of the institution high. Although he looks like Albert Einstein, he's very unlike him. Mumkin stands near the entrance of class and Mr. Williams asks him to take the front seat. Mumkin moves his eyes from blackboard to professor and then to the left and right side with exploring eyes, searching if any old face from life might get discovered. Yes, but none. For the next 45 minutes, learns the professor's lecture through his ears, taking it from one side and throwing it on the other . He kept analyzing his surroundings to see if there's someone similar to him sitting physically in class but absent mentally, he's quite restless from inside. .Mr. Williams was making eye contact with him almost five times every minute. With that demanding situation , he started firmly taking notes, nodding his head as he felt a new challenge, to show diligence as he was late on the first day. Diligence that his full scholarship shouldn't be scrapped if he looks disobedient or a disoriented asshole in class. He was smart enough to understand this fact. He soon realized that eye contact and expectations are too much for him, given from his teacher . Now the last bench will be his lasting place as Mr. William's thick glasses might want to avoid them! Then why is he still sitting in class giving himself this torture? Again reiterating, psychology subject was his last option that he ever wished to take up in studies in the past but the Business management course, his first choice, was costly and it had no scholarship offer from the University. His path to achieve his dream was ambiguous. Psychology to Business in weaponry is a nonsense idea and Mumkin thinks that he should do no nonsense with his life or else he'll lose whatever he has till now! He planned to seek a grant for the next year to join a Business management course.

As the bell rang and Mr. Williams left, Mumkin kept his head down, and saw a sudden hand coming near him. "Hi...I am Pamela Brown, I love psychology. That's why I am here. You see, my parents gave me various choices, even to marry a rich restaurateur of Himbertown who earns millions. But I wanted to complete at least 2 years of education. Class is nice, furniture smells a bit. I like your button on the cream color coat . It's glittering candylike.

Yummm, sweets I hate.You don't look to be from the city. Who are you and which place? I heard prof calling you Chamburt!" says Pamela.

"Hi I am Mumkin and you are Miss Pamela '

"Nooooo, just Pamela, no courtesy please. And how do you know my name?" says Pamela

" well, I recall you introduced yourself by starting with your name." says Mumkin.

"Oppppsy, my bad! Well I am sure you can be my best study partner! You look studious" says Pamela.

Mumkin remains quiet and Pamela looks behind while standing next to him and keeping her hand on his shoulder!

Pamela, an ultra empathic person who catches emotions quickly. She sees life through her feelings. She feels bad for beggars, street dogs, children of orphanages and what not! She makes unnecessary comparisons of a pet dog with a dog sleeping outside,in a cold with an empty stomach and getting bashes of people! She believes that the life of a street dog is hell worse! But almost most of her life she has spent being confused about making decisions. Not getting married wasn't her solid decision. She had to actually spend six months deciding whether to study or marry i.e. go for comfort, sex , companionship etc or choose her passion and interest,ofcourse that too lies in seeking love. Getting direct love after marriage is effortless love according to her. Love had to be hard earned. Similarly she constantly looked at Mumkin while he was taking notes while in Mr. William's class, it took her thirty minutes to decide whether to approach him as a friend or ignore him completely as if he doesn't exist for today. Everyday she compromises with her breakfast time in deciding what to wear, how lucky that dress would be based on her intuition which is very turbulent ! She always says "I hope no one goes through the confusion with which I go through!" . Due to this she chose the course of psychology so as to guide others and being ultra empathetic, she wants to help everyone even if they do not ask for it. Example,one day she wanted to help a blind person while crossing the road. But he shakes her off away from himself as he's just wearing black google and crossing away to get into his Mercedes parked on the other side of the road. Pamela, who commutes mostly by walking or in her paRent's car realizes that a visually impared person also keeps a stick in her mind's language(which is actually a mobility cane) ,how can she be forgetful of such a crucial detail. She isn't detail oriented though .She started feeling bad about herself , not because she mistakenly thought that the person is blind. Instead the guy was affluent enough to be in mercedez but he shook her off away from him that made her feel that she wasn't pretty enough to get his attention. Her feelings are deep. They sometimes make her feel insecure too. But at the end of the day she wants to learn to accept herself the way she is! ,

Pamela again looks back at Mumkin.

Pamela: Mumkin. Sounds weird, but it's a nice name... Mumkin .(gently slapping his shoulder).

Mumkin: Yes it's weird as it's in our native language but the meaning of it is 'possibilities',it's derived from our ancestors.

Pamela: Nice(blinking both eyes together). What's your full name?

"It is Mumkin Chamburt",replied Mumkin.

Pamela: Oh yes, I heard the professor saying this surname! Cahbi....Cambu.....Chanbirth....haha....apolgies I don't get your surname, so will call you by your first name. Mumkin, I always wanted to know the psychology of people. By looking at you I predict you're a diffeRent guy. Something you do diffeRently than any regular guy would. I don't think you're from Himbertown.

Mumkin: diffeRent from others!What(edgy), well do you mean by coming late to class? I don't do that often. It's my first time in Himbertown, I had to travel a long distance to reach here from my village.

Pamela: Yeah, that's what .I see that you're a diligent guy who is focused on learning. The way you entered class and took notes, I could see it.

Mumkin: Well, I had no other option as I was sitting in front of a professor who was constantly making eye contact with me!

Pamela: I see(chuckles and starts playing with her hair). Here he comes. Mumkin, this is John Greze.(pointing towards a guy). My school boyfriend but now a close friend. We did our schooling from Christ School.

John : Shut up Pamela. I was never your boyfriend, nor do I want to be your close friend either!(Pamela lifts her book and hits John on his shoulder).

John: Dude, Mumkin she's trying to be cool. By the way I heard the conversation between both of you, your name ,yeah it's unique and sounds good. I'm John Greze from Himbertown. You're from?

Mumkin: I'm from a Ranidetro village

Pamela: Never heard about it.

Mumkin:You know many brave soldiers hail from my village! They have fought in major wars and gave support to the Military of Himbertown. (mumbling) Hope they supplied weapons, good weapons too so that we never had such casualties of war!

Pamela: Wow, that's cool. Soldiers do a lot for us. My dad also wanted to be a soldier but he left the training soon after enrollment as my grandma was against it completely!

John: I can see your Military connection through your heavy bag! Oh man, four men like you can fit inside it.(lifting Mumkin's bag up) And what's inside it? Stones? It's so damn heavy!

John is a physically fit guy. He is a big time foodie too. He appears to be as passive aggressive sometimes. He has likeability towards the friendly nature of Pamela but he gets vexed when she shows the signs of turbulence and insecurity. He always dreamt of a girl who has high self confidence, is family oriented and someone with more of feminine traits with an hourglass figure. Whereas Pamela was on the chubbier side and of average height. But sometimes John gets completely dedicated towards Pamela. Especially when she smiles a lot, hits him with her book ,teases him and wears something sensual like she wore a red dress during their school graduation at Christ school. With her bulging figure John couldn't take his eyes off her calling her a diva in his mind. But still he always looks for her best as she sometimes acts very innocuous too.

As the bell rings, during the next class the professor is just interactive with white board. No one is listening. People are either playing with paper planes or daydreaming. Mumkin fantasizes holding weapons with high accuracy that can actually destroy targets within two splashes of eye blinks . Highly durable, powerful and maneuverable . His weapons are getting sold at a good price to the armed forces. He's supporting his father, providing him with his newly built gun, Everyone is shoting loudly saying 'fire' and there is extreme bright light. His father proudly put his hand on his shoulder with a serenity on his face, it's all orange bright light around. For a second Mumkin feels that his father was just there with him.

As the bell rings for next hour, Mumkin is alerted to step out of his dream world to reality with Pamela snapping her fingers at him on his face.The professor leaves as it is, without even acknowledging the total number of students present in the class, Only once he moved towards the students, that was when someone threw a paper ball at him from the students that hit his head which was quite painless.

Students were doing rock and roll steps standing just behind him.

The next session was that of Professor Rasko's behavioural psychology. He explained the concept in half an hour and woke up the half sleepy souls... "Mr, Mumkin, join the team", says the professor. As Mumkin opens his eyes half , he sees a bunch of students standing looking straight away at him.

"Join the team Mumkin quickly, don't stare too much, think much or feel much,join them, follow instructions quickly and walk 6.4 meters to join the group" says Prof George.

Mumkin stands up, walks straight towards the direction where other students were standing and looks forward towards the class after joining them. People were staring at this whole group. Mumkin is still figuring out what actually happened. He looks at his left side ,and sees Pamela smiling at him.

Prof George(facing towards the class):These young boys and girls from your class(total six including Mumkin,Pamela,Joy,Dominic Fred and Kate) will explain the implications of reinforcement theory which I explained just now. Joy, why don't you start enacting, Mumkin and Fred will accompany you. Kate,you act as a teacher. You all need to reflect how reinforcement theory is helpful in two behaviors through enactment.

All five of them form a small standing circle at the corner of the class and start discussing. Mumkin is still confused. The class seems disturbed as the students start prattling.

"Quiet everyone.The next time you will be in their place as I want to foster equality. All need to be given fair chances. The ones who are talking are prompting me to ask them to go up on the stage and reflect upon reinforcement theory" says Prof George.

Fred: Hey ,I was actually sleeping ,so can anyone explain the task.

Other Pamela explains the task....

Pamela: we have two behaviors, positive and negative, we need to act it out in the classroom. For good behavior students are rewarded with chocolates but there is extra homework related for bad behavior. So quickly let's decide the characters .

Fred: Okay, let's decide the character!You're Pamela right? Pamela, why don't you be the narrator as well as the teacher. I'll go for positive behavior and Kate can be with me .Dominic and Joy can be for the negative behavior. We got this man...Let's finish it off, and give rest to the old man. I hope it's ungraded as I'm quite bad at role plays(laugh).......Seriously man this is too much on the first day of college.

Dominic, Pamela, Joy and Mary look at Fred for three seconds, nod their heads to show agreement and soon start discussing the role play upon agreeing to his plan.Soon Professor George asks them to come up on class stage to perform the role play but there enters a teacher Olivia Grants. Miss Grants had a very deep personality who doesn't speak but is a crackerjack in understanding students. Teacher of multicultural education who made thirteen years of teaching ,however looked to be in her mid twenties. Pinkish tone, brown eyes and brown hair with a lean body structure but quick in her moves. Few even suggest to stay away from her due to some unknown reason.From her appearance Mumkin finds her a considerate woman. Despite having a solemn face, Mumkin finds patience on her face; People whisper about her that she doesn't interact with students informally, and is an extremely strict teacher.

"(knocking at classdoor and making slight eye contact with Mumkin and others)Prof George, there's information from the administration team" says Miss Grants.

Prof Gearge goes near her and both start talking to each other in low voice, Prof George instructs Benny Peterson, the class monitor to take charge. Benny was a tall guy who was popular among the teachers of this college but no one knows the reason why it is so! Probably he has this aura of a serious student with spectacles which make him look studious. His classmate from mount Hill school also revealed that Benny was the headboy in his school days and best in athletics.

In the quiet environment of class, students start whispering. Pamela looks at Mumkin and stands up from her seat to sit next to him.

Pamela: You look serious Mumkin, do you also feel irky due to something?

Mumkin: Irked. Well, I don't know. I think I have seen this teacher before..

Pamela: Oh you mean Professor Olivia, do you know her? But is it not the first time you've come to Himbertown. You might have seen him during your selections to this course . But no one knows much about her except that she's not from a pure psychology background. She's a professor of Multicultural education.

Mumkin: I think you have good information about the school, how do you know so much about her?

Pamela: Stop hitting on a teacher Mumkin! There are plenty of beautiful girls in college,don't be such a himbo.

Mumkin: Hey no, I'm asking genuinely. There's some connection that I feel ,I have with her.

Pamela: You're nuts. By the way, it's my uncle who works in the school's administration department. He told me about everyone. You see, professors here are strict but they interact with all students except for Miss Olivia. She is very quiet but uncle told me that she's inconsiderate to students who break rules and get them punished. He also said that thirteen years back when she applied here to join University, she has always been the same. No change .

John: Did you take the name of your uncle? How many times do I tell you not to bring it in front of everyone?

Pamela: John, I told about your secret to Mumkin (giggling)

John: Pamela, please. You need not tell everyone about it.'

Pamela: John wasn't selected here on the first try, so he bribed my uncle with a box of black caviar and made a statement that he's in love with his daughter Stella, my cousin and for their future he must make it to this university , as they'll marry in future. Poor Stella, had to lie to her father as I requested her to do so. Uncle agreed as we believe that he loves caviar more than Stella(chuckles).That's why he accepted John's offer thinking that Stella is also in love with this nerd. He requested Bison Sabastian, our college trustee, to reconsider him for Business Management . But due to unavailability of seats in management John settled with psychology. When I told that it was all a lie to uncle he got exasperated, especially at John. But you see my uncle is a warm hearted person. He forgave us after we three seeked loads of apologies from him.

John: It was exclusively your idea, as she wanted me to accompany her in this University.

Mumkin: Oh, okay(unkempt)

Pamela hits John with her book and chuckles away...John(astonished) starts scratching his head and says, "stop Pamela,I'm not sure how to handle her hyperactivity. But she's good .I mean she's a ridiculously colorful girl who's good from heart".

Mumkin: We do have this thing in common.

John: Who ? You and Pamela? You look calm, not like her!

Mumkin: Not me and her. You and me.

John: No ways, I don't have a crush on Professor Olivia.

Mumkin: Me neither. I just had a feeling that I kind of knew her. I am talking about your interest in management courses. I am also interested in it. That's the common thing between us!

John:Oh I wanted to invest in manufacturing wa....wa...he sneezes.

Mumkin: You mean weaponry?

John: Nah! Nah! Nah!, I am more into investing in vessels and porsha artifacts ,you know owned by high class people .There's a lot of money in that. Probably I might become a billionaire in the future .

Mumkin: I have another dream of starting a weapons Business.

John: I get it. Probably you are inspired from your dad's Military background. Where is he posted now?

Mumkin: He's no more.

John: Sorry to hear that. I see you're carrying a military bag, you talk about your village soldiers with pride! Why don't you join Military?

Mumkin: My mother won't let me do that. It's a long story.

John: Alright, let's head towards reception or else Pamela will kill both of us for being late.

CHAPTER TWO

Explorations!

As they were walking towards the reception ,John offered to make Mumkin make him as his partner in business with a partnership of 30 percent first then changing it to 20 percent and tell how his middle class working father always put him down. His father always tells him not to dream too big as one day John will end up wasting all his hard earned money from the bank job. His father is a clerk in an old bank run by the government in Himbertown and his step mother is a housewife. Mumkin too shares that his father's martyrdoom has made his mother to upbring him with a lot of difficulties seeing his mother getting major emotional breakdowns.

They reach reception where Pamela grabs her brand new books of psychology and makes the two guys load them back till the classroom.

During recess time Mumkin, Pamela and John were sitting together waiting for Uncle Nelon.

Mr.Bidar Nelon has been working from fifteen years in this college, he is a good observant and knows almost everyone in the school. Be it a student or faculty.Or probably his job demands that. He is also the maternal uncle of Pamela. He's bald in the center of his head,a short heighted man who has a dimple on one side of his cheek and a long pointed nose. His big belly tells a story that his job requires him to sit on a chair in order to keep records of students and teachers precisely. He's one of the most trusted people of college and has received Best employer of the College award incessantly for five years. He's dedicated to college and believes to be a well wisher of students. Probably due to his graciousness, many students approach when their hall tickets for exams are blocked due to attendance shortage. He adds up the genuine certificates of sports or health so as to unblock their hall tickets due to which almost a hundred students could write their exams in the past. He's like an alarm clock who reminds students of their crises time and sometimes act 'sankat mochan ' for them,

Pamela: Uncle(runs and hug him)

Nelon: Pamela, dear child. I'm so happy to see you and your friends. Very pleased to meet you John(punching on John's arm playfully) Do visit Stella and her mother with friends for dinner this weekend.

Pamela: Uncle, I hope you remember that outstanding acting done by John and Stella to make you fool,so that John could get in there!

Nelon: You were involved too Pamela. I actually wanted to beat the hell out of him but soon I realized that it's the plan of all three of them,not only his fault as Stella was also involved. Forget about it Pam, stop pulling his legs. Poor John, I have forgiven him but now Pamela wants to dance on his head!

Pamela(coughing): Yeah uncle, I'll stop this fun, after all he's your future son in law.

John:You're a serious bully Pamela, you'll have to pay for it one day(earnest).

Pamela: John, I am just joking(holding his hand with both of her hands and slightly falling towards him in a childish way). Leave it John. Uncle how is aunty and Stella?

Nelon:They're doing fine. Your aunt enjoys her cooking and Stella wants to study something in Business.`

Pamela: In what area does Stella want to do business?

Nelon: I am not too sure ,but I think it's business in food!

Pamela: Well said uncle, she wants to do business in food and John wants a business in vessels and crockery stuff. Our future couple can run a restaurant well!(giggling).

After a slight slap to John on his shoulder,Pamela starts running towards the corridor.

Uncle Nelon laughs after seeing this, annoyed John runs behind Pamela but she shows her teeth making a monkey face that annoys him further. John attempts to follow her but she hides herself in the girls washroom.

Mumkin keeps looking for both of them to come back to the corridor crowded with students.

Nelon: God knows,when she'll grow up,still a naughty kid even after joining college.

Bell rings..

Nelon: Let me go to see them both, you hurry up to meet the principal and other members of the University. There is a meeting right now.

Mumkin: Only with me?

Nelon: No, not only you. It's all the students of the College.

He stands up in front of the entrance of the corridor and claps thrice to announce "All new students head up to attend the meeting in the Xavier hall."

New student: where's Xavier hall?

Nelon:It's that way, just behind the recycling building and there is Xavier hall in the block four ,third floor. Make sure you reach them on time or else gates will be closed and seats will be full. Even if you manage to get inside after being late, then learn to sit on the ground as you won't get any seat to sit. You won't want the first day of your college to look like that! Do you?

John comes and stands next to Mumkin. Pamela arrives and stands behind him. As John aggressively tries to hold her hand, she haphazardly says "save me Mumkin,protect me from this orangutan!". Mumkin asks both of them to stop as they need to go for a meeting . All three along with other students headed towards the hall. There's a huge paper recycling unit . There's fresh air blowing from the three banyan trees inside the unit ,like just in the middle. The recycling unit has thatch over it. Pamela peeps inside it and says "Is this a recycling unit? It looks like a junkyard to me. I mean look at all these machines! Isn't these machines should produce something marvelous out of waste, but I think they make good waste.".

John: For a second will you shut your mouth Pamela, can't you see it's a paper recycling unit! This is not a junkyard, these are machines that recycle paper and look to your right, can you see little cardboard houses? These are made after recycling paper. Once you color them ,they'll look more resplendent.

Pamela: Okay ,Mr. Erudite! That's the trifling thing to discuss, aren't you aware that we're getting late now?

John: Wait Pamela, I'll murder you and dig your grave in this paper recycling unit! Wasn't it you who started questioning the purpose of this junkyard, ahh(vexed) ,I mean recycling unit. You'll drive me nuts.

Pamela starts walking swiftly and turns back and says "Do all the planning of murdering me later, now's the time to reach the Xavier hall". She starts running, Mumkin and John follow her. John "I don't know why rags me down".

Mumkin :She's kind of playful,try not to take her seriously.

John: Haha. You took my words away. I've been doing that for a long time. Sometimes she acts weird.

Mumkin: You mean like a hypocrite?

John: Yeah!

Mumkin: She's just trying to put a trick on you.

John: That's a childish thing to do. Despite knowing what irritates me,she does it! One day,I'll make her taste her own medicine!

Mumkin: Haha,try let it go .Let's go!

As they reach the Xavier hall, it's all crowded with too many people. The trio chose the last row for them to sit, whereas the guard showed a baton, asking them to occupy the first few rows.As they look around, the other security guards are shifting other last seaters in the first few rows. Pamela chooses to sit in the sixth row where the access of security guards is minimal. John and Mumkin sit next to her.

There was a student who held the baton of a security guard "Tujhe pata hai mera baap kon hai?(you don't know who my dad is?)"

Guard: Tujhe vaadil kon ahet? (Who's your father?)Kon he re tera baap, bol na sale, kisne paida kiya tujh jaise sapole ko?(Tell me, who created snakelete like you?)

Students: How dare you talk to me like that?Huh? Vardi utarva dunga tera(I will get you dismissed from your job)

Guard: Tula majha uniform kadhayla of Miles?Tumi te kaise karte? Le tumi murkha(Miles to take off my uniform! How you'll do it, take this idiot).

The guard starts hitting the student with his baton ,the student howls in pain and other students occupy the seats within a few seconds.

A teacher arrives there and says "thambva raja(stop king)" to the security guard. "Follow what our guards say, or else they'll turn your life upside down! no matter whether you're the son of a billionaire (to the student)or a widowed mother(looking at Mumkin). Sarva tvareta base (all settle quickly)"

Mumkin gasps for a second.

Pamela:Asabhya stapha membara niye ki asabhya kaleja(What a savage college with savage staff member).

John:Shut up or else you'll get one savage from him.

Pamela:Mala konihi maru sakata nahi!(No one can hit me!)

John:Are,baghuya, surakṣa rakṣakala sema gosta sanga(oho, let's see, say the same thing to the security guard)

Mumkin: I don't understand what you both are saying, but you both seem to be augmenting again.

The security guard hits Mumkin at his back with his baton and says "Bola na chup reh(don't speak, shut up)". Pamela and John become quiet after that. They laughed quietly, keeping their hands on their mouths.

The principal enters and everyone stands up. He looks like a 65 years old man dressed in a plain gray shirt and black pants. He had a piece of paper in his hand which he handed over to Kimsu, the guard of the College.It was the welcome speech of the principal that he wrote thrice,not because he was a dolt or dullard. It's because he was a perfectionist and prescient who would never tolerate even a single mistake either from his side or from others. The trio are asked by Kimsu to get up,he tells Pamela to come in front and hands over a bouquet of tulips to her that is to be presented to principal Blacksmith. Mumkin and John sit back at their seats. There are more than five hundred other students in the hall. Principal Henry Blacksmith reaches up on stage, he checks the microphone first "Check 1,2,3....3,2,1..... 2,1,3.... 2,3,1.... 3,1,2 ......check .....you give the last combination....who knows? Many of you might be saying 'Oh no....I don't know anything.....Because I hate math....haha, how many of you do not like math?'

Many students raise their hands to express their dislike whereas Pamela raises both of her hands to give confession that she hates it double. Mumkin has been a huge fan of this subject. According to him math is used for managing money, handling finances, understanding cooking, sports etc.Especially the business and finance part of it he regularly reads magazines, newspapers and journals of it.

Principal Blacksmith: Good morning everyone!

Students reply to him murmuring.

Principal Blacksmith: What, didn't eat breakfast? Be loud , come again!

Students reply again to them in comparatively high pitch now!

Principal Blacksmith: The question that was posed is from math. Math is like a goldmine, the one who knows it is as smart as a whip!Person with math knowledge will be able to solve any problem in life like a pro. All my dear students who have joined this year, first of all I would like to congratulate you. This is one of the top colleges of the world. It's the dream of many students to join here, build their lives and finally leave the college making a big impact in the field of research, technology and innovation . We have produced successful people from all fields. Our alumni as scientists, musicians, engineers, doctors and businessmen etc are all flourishing in their fields. Our motto 'Faith and hard work' has made many students go from rags to riches .This year has been an auspicious year for us as we have a total 550 newcomers . Every Year 400 was the limit. As requested by our very able teacher Professor Olivia, the management has increased 150 more seats. You have been here after tough competition. Hope you will respect your decision to join this College. Ensure that you make good use of this time. A degree is a treasure for you to survive in this world. Also ensure that you keep the people happy who hold a great standard of trust in you by completing your degree. Make use of all resources and we wish to see you as great psychotherapists ,scientists, artists, doctors and managers etc. in future. I wish you all great luck. Hope you achieve all your dreams and make your parents and loved ones proud. All the very best...Also there's one new committee to be made . Please ensure that you all take part in it. It's open to all students however my special expectations are from the first years to take part in it . This is a request from an old man aged 76 years with 20 years of experience in college teaching.``

All are shocked to know about his age as he looks quite twenty years younger than that. He has served a few years in corporates after his retirement from the Military. He was also involved in the wars for almost thirty years where he got commissioned at the age of 19.

John whispers in ears of a boy sitting next to him "To khupa goda manusa ahe ase(he seems to be a very sweet man)"

The boy quietly says "hoya(yes)" .Both are hit by the guard at their backs saying "Bola na chup kar dono, mooh bandh rakho, dande khao tum(I told you both to shut up ! Take my beatings)"

Principal blacksmith "thambava(stop), eat your blood pressure medicines,students haven't joined to be beaten by you(to the guard). And students, keep quiet! Especially when I talk".

The guard takes four steps behind them and says "theek ahe sara(okay sir)".

Miss Olivia went to the stage, she called Pamela and asked her to go back after handling the bouquet which she gave to the Principal blacksmith. He happily received it but Olivia seems to be indiffeRent. As Principal Blacksmith gets down to occupy the first few seats .

Olivia: Prof Caleb William teaches developmental psychology , Prof. Rustin Henry.... statistical psychology, prof Rasko George.... behavioral psychology, Prof Alexander Keats..... research, prof Angola Kinman...... counseling and prof Rehman..... administration and teaching clinical psychology. Prof. Jaquiline Gomes teaches Sociological Theories, Prof Gretsha Jones ..... religion and Society and Prof Xiang Zin .... political sociology. and......(continues names of teachers and corresponding subjects in psychology for next few minutes).

Then she takes names of ninety eight teachers of other departments like mathematics, hotel management, Medical research etc.

Olivia: You are supposed to know the names of your faculty. No student will take leave without notification. If taken, with genuine reason ,take signature of pre and post leave permission from faculties. Once entered college, bunking any class the entire day is actionable. The set of non negotiable rules are: roaming in campus with no purpose is punishable, no plagiarism in academics and playing with practical instruments during practical sessions is prohibited, follow the formal dress code ,misbehavior on the side of students is considered as a serious offense,students need to keep an eye on notice board,especially on the circulars regarding examinations, placements and scholarships, ninety five percent of attendance needed to write term examinations,home assignment and tests are to be completed on time either graded or ungraded, parking of vehicles need to be made on parking stand , follow class schedules class, no taking leave after class, proper behavior to be displayed in classroom,hoteliers are expected to follow rules ,maintaining decorum of class(for next 8 minutes students are warned about the basic rules that need to be followed).

Pamela whispers in Mumkin's ear "What a boring teacher with a boring lecture".Then she turns towards John and says "nirupoyagi college(useless college), my fees are fully wasted here". In return John replies "oh hoshiyar bai,guard ke dande khane ka bahut shawk hai kya?(oh smart girl ,are you passionate of getting hit by guard)"

Mumkin signals Pamela to keep quiet by keeping his finger on his lips doing "shhhhhh".

Pamela: I've arrived here to learn, not to waste my time! What's wrong with everybody here?

The guard comes near her to warn 'Shanta mulagi(shut up girl)'.

Pamela:(To the guard) Ok uncle.

She whispers in Mumkin's ear "My father still has the marriage option open for me. He says if something pressures me ,be it in College studies or a future job, his doors will always welcome me. The restaurateur guy is also a sweet person. Actually I am the only child,the most pampered one!"

John: (whispering): I am also only child, but most tortured one!If I ever go back to my dad's house ,he'll treat me like a peice of shit!

Panela: My dad beats his chest with pride,when he introduces me to others. Mumkin, what about you?

Mumkin: I don't have one.

Prof Olivia finished her so-called speech that had just information about the college rules and faculty information. Professor Rehman on stage.

Prof Rehman: What's up babies. Yes babies you all are,when it comes to learning. A wise man once said ,if you think you lack knowledge ,you actually build it after acknowledgement as you avoid ignorance. So be a knowledge seeker. I am professor Rehman, you can call me Reyh. I am from the department of counseling. My job is to keep you students happy and teach you guys exciting ways everyday,especially when to deal with so-called firecrackers that explode in their life. Me and my colleagues,we are always there in your entire College journey .You are most welcome to stay in touch even after college. You can always visit the mindspace activities beside the auditorium .Welcome students to this lovely phase of your life called college.

The caravan of speech lasted for the next four hours.The trio started to sleep as they found it way too boring. The fall asleep sitting posture. With the sudden sound of a bell, they wake up seeing everybody has gotten up and people are starting to leave. They follow the que. That day Pamela and John went to their respective hostels but Mumkin was asked to sleep in an open area of the college's hostel corridor as he hadn't paid any hostel fee that was not part of scholarship. He makes his fat bag as his pillow ,as he covers himself with a bedsheet like a baby, he doesn't find this citation difficult. There has been a time in his life where he had to actually sleep on an empty stomach with mosquitoes especially on the hospital floor as his mother's health wasn't that good. She had to go through a cervical biopsy. Her mother's health improved after that,however Mumkin was just seven years old at that time .Today he didn't think the same way as he thought when he was young, this time he didn't question himself why he had to sleep in the open as he knows that money is the issue! This time the sleeping is more comfortable ,probably he is in deep sleep. He hears a heavenly voice 'Wake up sir, you got to come with me!' .There's bright light all around. He tries to open his eyes, rubbing them slightly to discover the College guard Kimsu standing with his torsch flashing on his face. The guard closes his torch and reiterates 'Take your bags sir, you need to come with me'. Mumkin is still breathing fast ,no wonder why and where the guard wants to take him.

Mumkin: What happened? Can you put the torch off?

Kimsu: Oh sorry(turning off the torch light). You can sleep with me.

Mumkin: With you?

Kimsu: Yes, just for today! From tomorrow you can go back to your hostel room.

Mumkin: Room? But I can't avail hostel facilities for now!

Kimsu: No sir, a room has been allotted to you in the hostel.

Mumkin: Who allotted the room?

Kimsu: I don't know.

Mumkin: How come, I still don't get it, do you know that I come under hostel fee offenders?

Kimsu: I don't know all that. I am just following the orders.

Mumkin: Who gave you the orders Mr. Kimsu?

Kimsu: My senior, the security supervisor of College. For now come with me.

Mumkin and Kimsu go to the guard dormitory. There were few guards,still in their blue uniform chit chatting at one o'clock at night. Three guards were sitting on a round table and drinking whisky,talking about all their experiences-their villages, wifes, childRen, cows ,properties and murders etc.

There's a huge man in his black and white night suit, he tells Mumkin to sleep in any one of the bedrooms and his hostel fee has already been paid by someone for him.Kimsu reveals that that huge man is the college's security supervisor. Mumkin sleeps in a relaxed way with this question in his head i.e. 'Who paid his hostel fee?'

CHAPTER THREE

The secret

The next morning, at 7:10 AM Miss Olivia walked through the way furiously, Mumkin saw her and was walking behind her quietly with a goal to head towards the class. He walks slowly to be behind her. She looks back suddenly and sees Mumkin and other students behind for a glance over them and looks forward. During that time Mumkin gets overwhelmingly serious and prepares himself to greet her. But she walks away within seconds near the subject head for the English subject meeting room. As Mumkin had to reach his class on time, he takes double size steps and starts to rush towards his class and suddenly slips over a shiny object, quickly balances himself and looks down at his shoe where the object is stuck. It was a pilot green leather pen. He thinks of two options, one is to keep the pen with himself and second is to give it to school security so that they can place it in lost and found items. He found the first one stealing which is unethical according to him. He goes with the second one but later as now he has to be in class. He rushingly decides to keep the pen in his bag. He opens the topmost zip of his olive green bag and is about to keep the pen inside it. But as his eyes go to the shining cap of the pen, he finds Commander Chamburt carved over it. It was astonishing. The surname on the pen belongs to him. He thinks once if it's someone's prank on him. Like Pamela trying to make April fool out of him, but still it's the month of May. He guesses if someone planned the carved pen as his birthday gift but still how insincere the person is to lose the birthday present here in the corridor with so many students might have stepped on it. If it wasn't Mumkin, someone else might have picked it up. In that conundrum with questions in his head, he rushed towards the classroom and quickly kept the pen in his bag as the class was about to start.

He finds John and Pamela waiting for him in the class.

Pamela: Mumkin, you're just on time. Five minutes, you would have missed your attendance! Where did you sleep last night?

Mumkin: I got a place at the guard's dormitory yesterday.

Pamela: I'll ask my father to pay for your hostel fee this time, which you can pay later once you get a part time job here in college.

Mumkin: No..actually, I can't do that now...

Pamela: Don't refuse, it's not a favor....I think you didn't hear, you'll have to pay back...haha...But ya if you have bad financial constraints in future, I'll request my dad to let you off. After all you're my close friend(pulling Mumkin's cheeks and pouting)

Mumkin: Thanks, but someone has already paid my hostel fee for this year.

Pamela: Awesome! Be careful with your bag's zip. it's torn. Your pen is lurching out.

Mumkin realizes the down part of his bag's zip is actually torn, he takes out the pen and tells Pamela that his surname is carved on this pen which he found today.

Pamela: If you have your surname on it then I think it belongs to you. In place of returning it back in the lost and found items, you better keep it to yourself as a memory. Also it's just a pen, not a big thing, so keep it with yourself!

John enters the class and comes near Mumkin.

John: Thank god! You reached on time. Don't know whose class it is, but late offenders have to pay heavy fines here. Also People have bet on you. Look at Ren and Janny our seniors, they both were saying that today also you'll be late. They know what happened in the first hour yesterday with you, that you were fifteen minutes late for the first hour. But they lost the bet thankfully. Now we need to head towards the ice cream parlor after college as Ren will pay the bill for three of us. You see it's a punishment for you Ren. Perhaps a blessing in disguise for us.

Pamela: That's good news John...Just cfan't wait till afternoon. If rules weRen't so heavy in this college, I would've bunked by now. Probably might have been playing 'you blink you lose' with my boyfriend.

John: You don't have any boyfriend to play it.

Pamela: I think I can't have one here .Especially when I have a dodo friend like you John, no guy will come near me.

John: What did you call me? A dodo!(frowning).

Mumkin tries to change the topic after seeing Pamela again trying to irk John .

Mumkin: Perhaps ,I've got an allotment for a hostel room. I'll shift there by today evening. So I will be early from tomorrow onwards.

John: Oh yes? Then we can be roommates! We'll request Mr.Nelon about it and see if there's a possibility!

Pamela: Really John? You still have the guts to talk to my uncle with eye to eye?(sarcastically)

John looks pissed off and Pamela chuckles.

Ren arrives with Janny.

Ren: You can't have any boyfriend Pamela in this college,no matter how beautiful you are(looking into her eyes), it's not because John is dumbo but Professor Olivia being a vulture who feeds up on spotting couples ,killing the love between them through fines and impositions.

The direct eye contact with Ren left an impact on her.

Janny: Yes, rightly said Ren, one needs to know how to behave in her class. After all, she does her job. It's the couples who get outrageous with her sometimes.

Ren and Janny are second year students. They are in separate courses but they love each other a lot. Janny is sort of a nerd but way too hot. She has beautiful long hair, with a thin body and long legs. Ren loves her more than she can imagine. In case of any fight it's Janny who gets out of the relationship and it's Ren who pulls her back and apologizes despite any reason for the fight or even if Janny was wrong. For example, Janny always ignores Ren when she has her physics practicals so that she can study and get good grades .Still if she gets nineteen out of twenty ,she blames him for losing one mark,just like being obsessed with full grades. She gets angry at him and he apologizes even without knowing where his mistake was. Janny loves this about him, he buys her the most expensive gifts of the world like a diamond necklace, fancy restaurants stay during weekends and gifts her everything that a twenty years old can rarely afford. He's from an affluent family background blessed with extra money floating in the house. But this couple break up on a temporary basis more than the number of seasons in a year but still reunite as Ren has an attachment which he calls love in his heart for Janny .

They both met for the first time at the admission counter of College.Ren fell for her deep brown eyes, he saw her again on the morning of their first day orientation and he proposed to her on the second day of College when their classes started. It took two days for Janny to say yes to his proposal and become his girlfriend.

Pamela:I heard that both of you lost the bet to John.

Janny: Not me, it's Ren who lost the bet. In psychological terms I say it's positive reinforcement of keeping such bets. You already knew that you would lose it, Ren.But still just to take me to the ice cream parlor ,you kept such a bet even knowing that your intuition always goes wrong. Next time these newcomers will again encourage you to keep such bets with you as you've mastered in losing them. Everytime they get free ice cream and snacks.

Pamela: Excuse me, I'm not an ice cream lover so whatever you said is applicable to John .Applicable to Mumkin too he likes ice creams .But not me!

Ren: Everyone, my bet was not to check Mumkin's arrival. I mean who's concerned about that?He sort of looks like a Military guy with that olive green bag who's disciplined enough to be on time in class. You guys are just lucky today to get ice cream treats from me. But my darling Janny understands me so deeply. In fact I wanted to lose the bet to win her back. I want to take her to her favorite ice cream spot. Look Janny, please can we spend some more time together after the ice cream treat to others, can we go for a movie? I am sorry for whatever happened last time.

Janny: Ren, last time when we went for a movie, we had a fight over the choice of movie .I don't want to fight anymore with you. I'm only here with you as my practical exams are over three weeks ago. This time I lost one mark due to the movie as you spoiled my mood.

Ren: But Janny, the movie we watched was last monday and your practical exams were three weeks ago, so exams were already over before the movie.

Janny: So you think that I am lying?(snivel)

Ren: No, I am not. Just stop crying Janny!

Janny: For now, I won't speak a word to you now!

Ren: Hey Janny,please don't cry. I will not say anything that will vex you! I love you so much. In Fact the movie out there is about making love which you will like, I'm sure. Or else we'll always watch movies of your choice from now onwards. Come on, Janny ,let's go. (expanding arms and moving towards Janny)

Janny hugs him.

Janny :What about them(pointing towards the trio). Pamela, Pumpkin and Ron?

Ren: I'll treat them to ice cream as I lost the bet, from there onwards we'll head for the movie! Do you guys want to join us for a movie?

(Janny hugs him and they are both smooched and petted. Ren touches her at her back and forehead and closes his eyes and starts rubbing his cheek with Janny's cheek)

John goes near both of them and blasts at Ren saying "I am not Ron, it's John and he's Mumkin not pumpkin. Tell Janny your girlfriend Janny to take our names correctly".

Pamela: Also, we're neither interested in your ice cream nor movie!

Ren: For the movie, never mind,you three can carry on but for ice cream you will have to come as I lost the bet.

Pamela: What if we don't want to come for ice cream also?

Ren: You can't say no!

Pamela(exasperatedly): Yes, we can't say no as you are our senior and you're trying to rag us.

Ren: Yes, rag you three in a friendly way. Come on guys I am that cool senior who is inviting his juniors for movie and inceream. Not making you three dance naked on your table, that's what ragging is.

Pamela: You can't do that chindi chor! Complaint about (what complain and with whom?)? You're a sample to be kept in the biology lab.You're like a chui mui ka paudha.(You're like a sensitive plant).

Pamela: Shut up, now I will really do that to the principal.

Ren starts laughing and says "Haha, to the principal? Go now only".

Pamela looks distressed and her eyes are watery now. Mumkin taps her shoulder.

Mumkin(whispering in Pamela's ear): Relax Pamela, just don't react to whatever he's saying. He's just trying to show that he's our senior and we need to obey his orders. Just ice cream today after that we'll get away from them.

Ren was still smiling at Pamela after her emotional outburst. He was kind of admiring the way she's standing up for herself and her friends. Janny held his hand and they started hugging each other again.

Janny(moving away a bit): I love you. I think we need to leave now for our classes .

Ren(getting closer to Janny and hugging her): I hate this separation.

Pamela whispers to Dompin 'They need to join the drama club!....separation....weee weee weee(mocking)'

Raphael: oh gosh, you both are here, you know who is going to come to take junior's class? It's Professor Olivia. Stop hugging and move apart otherwise it's a problem for both of you. As they both were listening to Raphael,there enters Professor Olivia to the class

Prof Olivia: Move apart Janny and Ren. This is the fifth time you are spotted doing this act in class, that means you still haven't understood the meaning of the no hugging rule in class. Again a strict action will be taken like (pause) restigation, which you have both been before twice on the same matter.

Ren(rankled) Oh gosh miss Olivia, you have no idea of the meaning of love. You're like a wax statue. Due to your non bumptiousness, we've never seen you appreciating it, at least don't stop those who do so. What a vulture you are!

Prof Olivia: You both will receive your restigation letter for being a rule breaker. Shortly you'll have a meeting with the principal.

Janny: Oh no Professor Olivia, we're sorry for breaking the rule . Please ,just don't do this. Third, restigation will affect our degrees. Could you please reconsider it? Please(she pleads joining her hands).

Ren: Baby don't have to request her.

Janny: Shut up Ren. It'll all be because of you. I'm no longer with you .

Ren; Because of me. And you're leaving me again. You don't have to be scared of her and don't say 'I'll leave you !'It breaks my heart.

Janny: Seriously at this point,you're not concerned about the degree Duh.(going near Ren and whispering in his ear), Say sorry Ren to escape third restigation. My dad won't appreciate my resignation and our relationship. He thinks that I came here to study not to flirt with a guy.

Ren:Seriously I don't care what your dad thinks and we love each other, so why are you saying 'flirting'?

Janny(whispering to Ren): Yes Ren,love not flirting. Just stay humble right now you fool. Don't act as if you're going to ask for a hand (marriage) from my dad.

Ren(whispering to Janny): One day, I will.

Prof Olivia: We'll deal with you both in the Principal's office, and return back to your class .

Ren and Janny start moving towards their respective classes.

Prof Olivia: pick your cognitive psychology book before leaving (pointing towards Ren but looking straight firmly).

Ren: Oh ,yeah miss. I appreciate that....

Prof Olivia: (firmly stops Ren from speaking more by showing her hand)

Janny already left and Ren picks his book and runs outside the classroom. He follows Janny and hugs her the third time saying "Don't worry ,I'll fix everything." He kisses on her cheek and runs towards second year psychology class.

Prof Olivia: Hand up those who've done multicultural education before?

38 students raise their hands out of 50.

Prof Olivia: Any incident where multicultural education got its importance. Miss Gages, can you answer?

Anita Gages: Multicultural education is about educational reforms ,so that equal educational opportunities can be provided to all members of society irrespective of their ethnicity, race ,color and economic status etc.

Prof Olivia: Unsatisfactory answer that reflects definition of multicultural education whereas the question is regarding incidents of multicultural education. You will get zero if this question is asked in the exams. Mr.Chamburt, answer!

Pamela: Well the incident I recall is when .....

Prof Olivia:Stop Miss Brown!Are you Mr. Chamburt ? No you are not. Kindly keep attention to know who is called to answer. Mr. Chamburt ,answer the question.

Daniel: Pamela is protecting Mumkin as he doesn't know the answer. I think they both are close enough, way too close .Professor Olivia, you need to punish these two love birds too just like Janny and Ren(he buches fingers of both hands with tip touching each other).

Prof Olivia: Oh is it? Mr. Stone(referring to Daniel Stone) it looks like you have done mastery in understanding people ,but this is a multicultural class not behavioral psychology. Or I call you an astrologer trying to pair up people. Better start answering the question if you know the answer.

Daniel: I .....I actually don't know as I am from a non multicultural background.

Prof Olivia: Get ready to run through the gauntlet. An empty cloud makes more sound.

Pamela: And your mind Daniel is filled with cotton candy with garnishing of straw

Everyone laughs

Prof Olivia: Silence everyone. Miss Pamela, only when asked!

Evening when all classes are over, while going back home, Mumkin, John and Pamela run through Janny and Ren.

Pamela: Janny and Ren hope things are fine with you both.

Ren: Woah, I didn't expect that from you! I thought you would be angry with me.

Pamela: After attending Prof Olivia's class I am determined to be friends with seniors and tolerate their ragging too.

Ren: Interesting. Why so?

Pamela: To borrow notes and book recommendations of first year multicultural education as she seems to be a hitler in strictness. I am concerned if I'll pass her paper.

Ren: Now I get it . You don't ask me. My girlfriend Janny is a brilliant student whereas I haven't written even a single page of notes till now.

Pamela: Then keep going Ren.

Ren: Stupid girl. Seniors can't rag you, instead you'll rag them.

Pamela: So you think that I am smart....is it?

Ren: Not smart but opportunist as you wanted to be my friend for a purpose.

Pamela: Then call me go getter not stupid person.

Ren: You talk a lot,how poor Mumkin and John are tolerating you?

John: Ren, you will slowly understand her !Believe me she has hell lot of potential to irritate people than you saw today. By the way,what about restigation? Did Professor Olivia give you unchasticised?

Ren: Who is Professor Olivia? You mean the love killing vulture? Never. She is very earnest in equating breaking of rules with punishment. But you see, my uncle Bison Silver is on the trustee board, so he handles well(wink one eye while talking to Janny). The principal with Prof Olivia had to show white flag.

Janny: Oh Ren that's why you're my favorite darling. You saved both of us.My astute babes!

Janny: (Pointing towards the ice cream parlor)Ren, the ice cream parlor is there , they sell great ice creams Raspberry Ice Cream,Coffee Ice CreamCaramel Ice Cream and my favorite strawberry ice cream. They might have some new flavors too. Take me to that place, today I am in a good mood!

Pamela whispers in Mumkin's ears "Why is she acting like a phool Kumari or the president of this country?"

Ren: Let's go, join us now juniors(pointing towards the trio- Mumkin, Pamela and John)

John: Oh definitely. For me, chocolate ice cream. Pamela, you better not eat that as it might affect your six packs.

Pamela: Shut up John and stop fat shaming me. I am not chubby, I am curvaceous with an alluring figure.

John: Look at yourself in the mirror. Brass and gold have diffeRences!

Pamela : Shut up John(she punches him on his shoulder).

Ren: I like the way you carry yourself so confidently Pamela, keep it up(blinking eye towards Pamela).

Pamela: That's what you are saying Ren, I want to hear the same from John as well.

John: Please don't mind Pamela, learning psychology from you has taught me to enjoy every moment in life. This seems like a fun moment when you are irritated!

All laugh together on John's statement

Both John and Pamela stop at a shop where the gate has black shiny mirror like glaze in it. John looks at himself. He is tall, has a wrestler like body as his father was a part time wrestler for seven years in his youth through which he got a clerical job in Himbertown . His father took up the second job of door washer.It was the government's recommendation as he became alcoholic after losing so many matches. He has blue eyes,blonde hair and while smiling his eyes get filled with glitter.

Whereas Pamela is slightly opposite to him, a chubby girl who loves to wear oversized sweatshirts. She has black eyes and red hair with a perfect smile filled with innocence. The daughter of teachers ,she wants to be a psychotherapist and believes in humanity a lot. She dreams to keep others happy around her.

After looking at their reflection in the shop's gate, Pamela looks at John and chuckles, which was no surprise to John.

Pamela: You won't ask the reason for my laughter?

John: Not interested as it'll be some stupid reason.

Pamela: Shut up John! Look at your back.

Mumkin takes a look and laughs out loudly for a few seconds. He then takes off the posted sticker from his right butt, where it's written 'Asshole's spot! Hit it, ok!'.

John(slightly irked): When did you stick it Pamela?

Pamela: Morning first period, when you sat down at your seat.

John: Why do you do all that?

Pamela: Yesterday, near the recycling unit you said that I am a hypocrite to Mumkin. That's why.

John: Gosh, you're holding grudges and taking revenge for it from me.

Pamela: Ofcourse, an important business principle is that you need to know your competitors well!And nothing is free in this world, neither jokes nor insults on me. So 'agar mujhse teda meda bologe to main bhi badla lungi(If you say something unfair to me, I'll take revenge)'

Mumkin: Pamela, we understand that you got hurt when he called you a hypocrite but we still like you a lot, especially your bubbliness. Yesterday it was all out of playfulness. You actually became a hypocrite in that moment to irritate John.

Pamela:Is it?

Mumkin: I am not supporting John, just clarifying misunderstandings.

John: Yes,we're your friends Pamela, we would never want to disrespect you.

Pamela: I'm sorry for misunderstanding you, but the posted stamp prank was really fun.

John: Yes this prank has to be repeated.

Mumkin: But this time prank on you Pamela!

John:We'll write bold hilarious lines on the huge posted stamp- 'Miss curvaceous/ Miss Roly Poly, or this baby elephant's poop candies ' and we'll stick it in your hair. How does Mumkin sound?

Pamela: Please friends, don't do that with me especially on my hair, I join my hands and touch your feets(chuckling)

Mumkin: Okay, we won't do it!

Mumkin gives a shoulder hug to Pamela and John gives the same from the other side.

Pamela: So I think we're now close friends or rather best friends forever!

John:Stop talking stupid girl. There isn't something like a best friend forever!

Pamela: There is! But you don't know about it as you haven't experienced it. Mumkin ,what do you say?

Mumkin: Yeah ,probably .

They join back Ren and Janny and move towards the parlor. It is a huge parlor with a theme of Amazon rainforest, all walls are painted green with timber wood being used to make benches and tables. It's very cozy and cold inside. The ice cream flavors, as said by Janny, were just diverse in number.

Ren: Take whatever you want to eat juniors, I pay today. Especially you Pamela, I give you a double treat.

Pamela:No way.'I'm not an ice cream lover. I'd rather have coffee.

Ren: No, according to bet, it was ice cream .

Pamela:You don't have to pay for it.

Ren:Come on ,try this new flavor. It's amazing.

Ren hands over red colored ice cream cups to the trio calling in red velvet ice cream.

He takes it too and all cheers up together. But after the first bite, Pamela started coughing saying 'it's so spicy, I just can't have it'.

Ren starts laughing and he hands over a mug to her saying 'Here take your coffee,you need it after having red chili flavored ice cream'.

She takes a few sips, her nose and eyes are watery and red.

Ren:Sorry Pamela, it was a prank on you. We're having delicious red velvet ice cream, and you're having chillicious ice cream. Anyways you don't like ice cream so this flavor wouldn't have caused any distress to your efficacy towards ice cream.

After a few cups of coffee, Pamela feels better.

Pamela:I just love this ice cream flavor now. Can I have it more and please pay for it?

Ren: Are you kidding me?

Pamela: Yes, please.

Ren(puzzled): Sure.

As the waiter brings the chili flavor ice cream, others are focused fully looking at the waiter, Pamela and ice cream. As she takes the first bite, she seems to enjoy it. Others in confusion have their ice cream when Ren cries out as his ice cream appears to be chillicious now.

Pamela: Now you're tasting your own medicine Ren. Here you go(she passes her coffee mug to him).

Ren takes a few sips and Janny asks him 'Are you okay babes? You shouldn't have done to him Pamela'.

Ren: I'm fine babes, but you're really an ingenious person Pamela. How did you manage to exchange our ice cream cups?

Pamela: Indeed I am ingenious, it's magic through which I exchanged. Also sorry ya. Let bygones be bygones.

Ren: Sure girl!(with a smile)

Ren and Janny head towards the movie theater just after finishing their ice creams whereas Mumkin, Pamela and John were heading towards the market as Pamela wanted to buy a statistical psychology book. It was a busy market and near one corner of the street they saw their teacher Olvia with a man. As usual she had firm facial expressions but was talking to the man facing opposite to him. This time her face was turning more stern. After a minute, they both hid behind the pillars.

The trio are standing hundred meters away from them.

Pamela: I really want to know how Professor Olivia is in real life. She's damn strict but as they say every person has double faces and the opposite is outside their workforce.

John: What's there in your devil mind?

Pamela: I want to hear the conversation between them.

Mumkin: Let's go to the shop as we need to be on time at the hostel.

Pamela: Don't worry Mumkin, we'll reach on time. Uncle Nelon told me that she's unmarried. So is it her boyfriend?

Mumkin: You leave it as it is.

Pamela: There's something black in the lentils.

Mumkin: You're not going to get any share of that lentils either so let's go.

John: Yes, don't be an ax on the foot.

Pamela: I won't do it again, you guys will accompany me. Let's go.

John: I think she's really a narcotic who listens to herself only.

Pamela: Narcissist hota ha re pagal(It's narcissist you mad fellow).

Pamela goes near a chai tapri, where tea, biscuits and candies were sold. There were many people who were enjoying tea in mud kulhads in drizzling weather. She stands a meter apart from Olivia and the man turning her back. Mumkin and John join her too, showing their back side. She purchases three cups of tea. They start sipping and Pamela's ear is towards the conversation.

John: By god, I'm unable to sip even once. If by mistake Professor Olivia spots us, we'll be back in our houses. Also we need to be back in the hostel.

Pamela: Shut up John, Ren and Janny are also out. They'll be back in the hostel only at seven pm, at least an hour after us.

John: Don't be nuts! Ren has his uncle as trustee, if something happens he'll be saved by him. If something happens to me, my father is the first one to go after my life. Chappalein chaand par baja denge(my father will beat me with his slippers).

Pamela: Shhh....Listen man.

Prof Olivia: I still can't believe the surname is the same.

Silver: Uff why you're always hussy fussy for you students?

Prof Olivia: It's not any disciplinary issue. It's something else I am afraid of. It's the connection.

Silver: Sometimes you discombobulate me. You're very strict on children.

Prof Olivia: I am doing what I am supposed to do(stringency on face and arms folded). Also they're not childRen, they're students who'll attain adulthood in two to three years!

Silver: You can't be strict with Ren, he's my nephew.

Prof Olivia: Rules are to be obeyed. If for everyone then for Ren and If not for Ren then not for anyone. Set the committee and change the rule for all .After all ,you're a member on the trustee board.

Silver: Professor Olivia, you also know that it's a humongous process to do so.

Mumkin, Pamela and John are still standing and listening to their conversation. Pamela whispers slowly.

Pamela: So….he's the one….Ren's godfather, his uncle, Bison….trustee of college….That's a reason Ren roams like an oxe without a peg. His uncle is only Bison, what to expect from him.

Mumkin and Ren chuckle.

Pamela(whispering): Yar chai bhi khatm ho gayi par koi baat palle nahi padi(tea is also over ,still I don;t get it).

A man pushes Pamela due to which her teacup falls down and breaks. She whispers to the man 'Bhaiya, dikhta nahi hai kya,andhe ho?(Are you blind ?can't you see?)'

The man turns back and says loudly 'What madam ?', she again whispers to him 'age chalo,jagah do(move ahead give some space)'. He replies again loudly 'Ha to chal riya hu,itni haule kya bolti ho?(Yes I am moving, but why do you speak so softly)'.

The trio ignore the man as they again hear conversation between Olivia and Bison.

Prof Olivia: Last time, in a meeting when I sat next to you at the corner, my extravagant thing had gone missing.

Silver: Ofcourse Olivia, I am always there to help you out. What is it? A necklace or a ring?

Pamela(whispering): I knew it, there's something between Professor Olivia and Ren's uncle Bison.Look at their chemistry.

Mumkin: Don't judge so quickly….listen and then decide….

The trio listened again…..

Prof Olivia: Exasperated sigh. No Mr. Silver. Not that.

Silver: Trust me , I can provide you with anything: a diamond ring ,any jewelry and luxurious rides.(Breathing heavily) Anything. Tell me a necklace you want of precious metals? Just order Olivia .

Prof Olivia: Silver you know me for decades, still you say this(serious straight look).

She turns opposite to Bison just in parallel to the trio due to which they get alerted.

Silver: Oh come on, this is all what all women want. You're acting out I think(tempestuously). For many many years I have been trying really hard to win you over. Look, all I want is you. I want to celebrate you in my life, your presence does matter a lot in my life. I really want to see you covered with the rosy red dress, high heels, nice fragrant perfume and jewelry bought by me. All will be exclusive for you I promise. I dream of my nights with you in my bathtub with champagne in hand, making love and we never stop kissing for the whole night.

The trio look at each other embarrassed, Pamela's mouth opens and she astonishingly keeps her hand over it with a red face. Then she embarrassingly starts smiling at Mumkin and John .Then she chuckles and is about to guffaw.

Mumkin: Shut up now baba Pamela or else we'll become history!

John: Shhhhh…shameless girl(towards Pamela)

Olivia: Stop frivolous talks(piquelosly walks away), you trying for years! Is it? What was there with you in past years, I know very well(smirking)?

Silver: I need not ask you to let me off the hook as I am not guilty or a sinner. Just a slave of time.

Prof Olivia: The most freedomful thing is never bound by time, but gets attached to the fragrance of purity. You're not fit to smell it ! At least with me !Never.

Olivia walks swiftly and leaves straight away looking forward. The trio runs towards an antique shop and try to hide themselves . But it's all made up of transpaRent glass where their multiple reflections are seen. The owner of the shop enters and he asks if they want to buy anything. They answer that they are just exploring, so they are asked to leave immediately rudely by him so that they don't break any of their anique pieces. As they come out ,scared to be coughed by Olivia. They see a man weaving towards them. He calls them inside his shop and they meet a bookkeeper who looked in the mid fifties and has both a new edition and thrift book sold to them by passed out students. The shopkeeper treats them well and introduces himself as junior Amrisk . He tells them not to worry about the way the antique shop keeper behaved with them as he's generally rude with youngsters as there are some spoiled youths who steal from that shop or break his items putting him into debt. He says 'Also that shopkeeper only welcomes the elite or high class'. He tells them that his shop is seventy years old where he's been in the shop for more than twenty years. He got to know the names of Mumkin and his friends.

John: How do you know that we require a book ?

Amrisk: You look like you're from Himbertown colleges . Many students have come to my store .Every year they've been buying books for decades. I thought you might have lost your way. Which book do you need?

Pamela: Statistical psychology by Kristopher Lee. Do you guys want to buy something, I am heading towards the third floor?

John: Yeah, a Funtalogy comic for me.

Amrisk: Pamela it's 3rd floor ,2nd shelf , 2nd row from down with book number 184329.(Looking towards John) Funtalogy is for childRen. Do you still want it? Oh my bad you might be gifting it to a little member in the family(smiling).

John: No, it's for myself.

Amrisk:Really ,are you a psychology student?

John: I am but for a temporary basis..... So comic books would do for me....

Amrisk: Alright, it's at the 1st floor, child section, 2nd row-1284 is the book number.

John: Oh thanks, can you repeat the number(closing his eyes due to baffleness) !

Amrisk: Yeah it's 1284, 2nd row, 1st floor and he writes in a piece of paper. Michigin, do you want anything?

Mumkin: It's Mumkin. I'll have a weaponry business book.

Amrisk: Sorry Mumkin. We don't have such books in our collection as no one buys them. Your taste is quite diffeRent. You don't want psychology?

Mumkin: No I am not much into it(looking down and contemplating).

Amrisk: So do you like weaponry business books? That's not available these days in any shop here. Probably you can find something in archives in the basement.

Amrisk accompanies him to the basement and as Mumkin bends down the leather pilot pen falls from his pocket.

Amrisk picks it up and looks at it to reminisce.

Amrisk: Does this belong to you?

Mumkin: I got it today morning in college but the name astonished me.

Amrisk: It's from this shop . Twenty five years back when the war was about to start , we used to sell those pens exclusively to the Army. Only our shop was authorized to do so. I remember that there was a young man who came in this shop and bought this pen. He specifically asked to carve this name and paid a special price for that.

Mumkin: Who was it, may I know his name please?

Amrisk: It's been a long time Mumkin. I just don't remember.

Recalling the physique of his father from the photos and mentioned by his mother, Mumkin asked if the man had gray eyes, brown hair and 6 feet height and broad chest, like that of a military personnel.

Amrisk said that the person whom he is describing doesn't match with the man he saw. In fact that man was lean , short statured and had blonde or brown hair as he didn't remember the hair color. Mumkin pondered again and then both him and Amrisk went to Pamela. Pamela was searching for another Statistical psychology book and John was already there standing and reading his old love ,Funtalogy and giggling over the expression given by his beloved in the written form.

Pamela: What the heck...he's just not serious about psychology. John, take some books so that you can pass the exam.

John: No way, I am not going to read any thick ass book. Even Mumkin isn't buying any of our course books, why don't you ask him for that?

Pamela: He appears as a hardworking guy who'll pass. You appear heedless.

John: Shut up Pamela!

Mumkin arrives there.

Mumkin: Did you get the book ?

Pamela: Yeah I got it. I'm just searching for a book by another author in the same section so that it can be taken as a refeRence.

John: Hehe...awesome. "The rain never dances in criss-cross direction, as the flying umbrella would become it's dress ", what a joke .Hehe.

Pamela:What an idiot you are John!

John:shut the fuck up Pamela.....wain wain wain wain......

Amrisk: Oh John .Why don't you read a book like "The sages said this", "Biggest religion" and ``Infidelity's innocence" or something like " Generosity's multi sides " . Generosity's multi-sided side would give you more insight to mature as a psychologist. Normally boys of your age ask for 'The secrets to being a woman's man' or 'how to steal her and make loveblind'. Believe me, the book is available in the basement , I can give it to you at a minimal price or you can borrow it. It's one of the best selling books here as this is what boys come up to me for hitherto!

Pamela: He is not a bibliophile as he can't understand the language of any book other than the one he's reading right now. (eyebrow flash) we'll read books, the book one you mentioned Amrisk.

Amrisk: So are a cross sexual Pamela?

Pamela: I'm not. Why do you think so?

Amrisk: Because you're asking for the books which men and boys read.

Pamela: No no. I'm asking for the books you mentioned earlier. The one with the saying of sages and generosity's multi sidedness as it'll help me in becoming a better psychologist and probably a better person.

Amrisk: Ofcourse. I appreciate your love towards books. Devkali Neelghanti Paul is the name of the author.

Pamela: Haha....Devkali Neelghanti...What a funny named author. paren ko ya to Devkali rakhna tha ya neelghanti..... Dono ek saath mein make it grotesque(paren should've kept her name as either Devkali or as Neelghanti....together makes it grotesque). But have heard about her somewhere(starts to think to recollect while looking at a corner of her book in hand).

Amrisk: She writes books related to sainthood and humanity. But her books are not the best selling ones. Despite the fact that the modern time isn't very appreciative of such topics as people like fashion, food or business etc. I mean who wants to read about sainthood? But she still writes, not for money but for her passion. Her books have helped people become more mindful.

Pamela: You're right. People's tastes are different these days.Everyone is running after money and fame. But they do require a piece of writing that gives a peaceful mind.Authors and writers earn very less and some of them die out of poverty .

Amrisk: But this author is very diffeRent from others. She's a part time writer and from a well working family. She writes with vigor, you must read her books .

Pamela: all right,

(suddenly she's startled by a loud noise as John is still looking into the book and he starts banging the book shelf with laughter).

Pamela: Hold on John, what's up to you. The books might fall as the shelf is an old iron shelf.

John ignores her completely.

Pamela: Oh hello....Hero....oye raja....stop...thamba guru....(stop)

He still doesn't listen, he's still deeply into his book.

Amrisk: Stop John.

All the books start falling down one by one. Pamela cries out loudly but Mumkin pulls her immediately towards himself due to which she is saved before the book shelf was about to fall on her .All books are scattered and the shelf is in reverse direction.

John looks around and realizes about the mess that he created.

John:What happened?

Pamela: Don't ask that stupid question!Help out Amrisk in keeping these books back. Just because of you we'll be late for the hostel.

John: Gosh, if we start setting these books we'll reach the hostel tomorrow.

Pamela: Talk less and help Amrisk as it's just one shef that we need to set. Also say sorry to Amrisk for creating such a mess in his shop.

Mumkin and John help out Amrisk in erecting the shelf back to its position and John apologizes to Amrisk the same time.

Amrisk: Keeping the books back is now a humongous task . K. Jalty,come in and help in keeping the books back.

K. Jalthy is a worker working in Amrisk's shop for eight years. He is from a small village known as village Kami, where many people migrate in search of jobs. He has sunburn marks on his face.

Pamela joined them to help.

Pamela: She's weird and cold.

John: Whom you're talking about?

Pamela: It's Professor Olivia. Just look at that man , Ren's uncle and trustee member of our University. He's in love with her. He was crying for love but she's so hard hearted. Dam it.

Dompin: Who knows what's happening between them too.

Amrisk: Discern with kindness impending.

Pamela: Pardon Mr. Amrisk!

Amrisk: Thou shalt avoid type 2 error .

Pamela : Okay, still I didn't get it..

Amrisk: One shouldn't accuse someone of guilt until proven.This is what type 2 error says in psychological research.

Pamela: You know a lot about psychology Mr. Amrisk.

Amrisk: Yehi to mera style hai(this is my style!)

Pamela: Still Mr. Amrisk ,if I had someone in my life loving me so much, I wouldn't have even given a second thought in accepting that man.

John:Don't worry, you won't even get the first thought.

Pamela: Excuse me, what did you just say?

John: Who'll propose to a witch like you who keeps on clamoring.

For a second Pamela is astounded by his comment and is embarrassed deeply from inside. Because the comment reminded her of not being in any relationship till now.

Dompin looks at John ,holds his hand signaling him to stop talking rudely to her.

Amrisk: Dear Pamela, can you pass that book on?

Pamela: Sure. Pamela passes the book to Amrisk.

John finds an article inside a book that amuses him.

John: Woah guys, isn't it our University . Just look at the photos of 1935 batch students. It's probably the year we were born.

Pamela takes the article and reads it out:

"Strategies flabbergasted General of Military:

10 Dec 1935, Sunday, ten science students of Himbertown university astonished the military general Shaid Sankoter based on a blueprint of weaponry manufacture to thunderstrike enemy with a befitting reply. These individuals are given a choice to join the Army by the General where one girl and two boys are selected directly by him. The only girl to join is Miss Lidiya Cheriyan, appaRently she accepted the offer to go through the training and soon after that she'll be at the position of Commander "

Pamela: Wow, Lidiya Cheriyan....she must be the woman who broke the glass ceiling to join the Military.

Mumkin: Definitely. Isn't that interesting about the weapons manufacturing of the military in 1935.

The girl and the two boys who were selected by the General are the chef-d'œuvre. They really intrigue me to know about them further. I want to really read their mindset and what sort of resilience they had.They can be true inspiration to today's generation.

Pamela: For the first time, I've seen you Dompin speaking so much. Now I realized that apart from weapon manufacturing, Military resilience is also your interest area.

Mumkin: Nah…not really. I'm just into weapon manufacturing.

Amrisk: I can't forget that this group of students came here to buy books in our store. Probably some twenty years back when I was some twenty six, when I had just started to help my father in doing business here. Miss Lidiya Cheriyan was a young gorgeous lady , whom everyone used to get attracted to. Despite being grown by a single mother as her father sacrificed his life in the previous war!She was joyous, brave, kind and innovative. Two boys who were selected were Jonathan Williams and Tiger Watson.

John: Woah, hats off to your memory . The way you not only remember names of the two boys but your description about the girl is unforgettable. Gorgeous ,kind, young and joyous…

Pamela: It's twenty years back, she's almost double your age now! So stop hitting every girl …you are trying to be a ladies man.

John frawns at Pamela and she winks at him. Suddenly she turns towards Amrisk.

Pamela: I am amazed to hear this name. Really, Tiger Watson? The famous billionaire of the present time? So he has a military background too?

Amrisk: (hesitantly)He refused to join the Army training and instead he promised to work with the Army in field weaponry business .Later changed his mind and created his own industries and became a billionaire.

Mumkin: Woah, the weaponry business is also my area of interest too. Can you connect me with Amrisk for mentorship?

Amrisk: I'm not in connection with him anymore. As mentioned by Pamela, he's a billionaire….his connection with me is like a penny hanging in a diamond necklace which no owner wants.

John: Who are you talking about?

Pamela: Kabhi akhbar pad liya kar re bandru(read newspapers occasionally you dullard).

John: Chalte ban(keep walking).

Amrisk: I could see your interest Mumkin, the way you were searching for a book in weaponry merchandising!

Mumkin: I am just too passionate about it. Weapons play a major role in any war. The USA is the biggest example for it. They're needed for countries' protection .

Amrisk: Absolutely!

Mumkin: What happened to Lidiya Chriyan and Jonathan Williams? How was their tenure when they joined the Military to become leaders?

Amrisk: Indeed, they were a part of multiple military projects. At that time women weRen't allowed in the military.Lidiya was the first. Both worked like anthimg to keep the countries flag high.Unfortunately Williams lost his life during his first posting to Samwin City while fighting with local terrorists.

Pamela: I've heard about his name in my history book!

Amrisk: Yes, he is considered a war hero. Both Jonathan and Lidiya made huge contributions to our country.

Mumkin: Awesome(surprised). Lidiya, just some nineteen years old college student, had become an important part of the military. Isn't that amazing.

Amrisk:Yes. She played a major role in training troops and even served outside Himbertown. She became a prominent public figure back then. She even visited this shop multiple times after joining the Military to grab a few nuclear science and geography books.

Mumkin: What happened to her during the war? Where is she now as none of us these days know about her. Her name is not even mentioned in history books!

Pamela: Agreed. In fact they mention the group of women who joined the Military but no one has ever heard about Lidiya. It's this article discovered by John which is telling a different story.

Amrisk: Well during the war time , everything including the military shuffled due to which the attention of the media also changed. From then on no one knows what really happened to her.

Pamela: Is she dead or alive? So that we could meet her.

Mumkin: You mean she died in war? And what's this military shuffle,hearing it for the first time?

Amrisk: No Mumkin ,it's not die ,it's martyred in war, which I think she did not…. The Military shuffle was the time when the Military of Himbertown changed its rules and became more secretive and got itself away from the media.

Mumkin: If she was such a great leader then why didn't she reach a top rank?

Amrisk: No idea,some say that they haven't seen her for a long time in Himbertown.

Pamela: Do you think she hid herself or ran away to not become part of war as few youngsters did this to evade going to the war front? Is that what happened to her too?

Amrisk: Nope,that can never happen. She's just not of those coward types !She bravely fought with her troops and made almost all missions successful. She was becoming an important hero and leader of mission after mission. Every faculty and student spoke about her in College at that time.Taking inspiration from her contribution.

Pamela: Then why don't we see her name anywhere in the history books?

Amrisk: It's said that during wars ,she was trauma stricken due to some incident. Trauma was taboo back then. Media intentionally was focusing on her ,there was a large political involvement too. As they thought that a trauma-stricken soldier would bring embarrassment for the country . There was some misunderstanding in public due to which the military took steps to shuffle to protect soldiers. This kept the trust of the public in the military of Himbertown.

Mumkin:That's really sad and silly though to not include the name of someone who did so much for this country.What's wrong if the person is trauma stricken? I wish I knew her. We could've done something for her, especially people like Pamela who is a budding psychotherapist.

Pamela: Exactly .

Amrisk:Haha. You have good intentions but don't worry Mumkin. No one knows anything about her. I think you all need to leave. It's 5:56PM , you need to reach back by 6:16 PM to your hostels. Better be on time (Smiling warmly).

Pamela: Oh yes, we'll see you tomorrow. Wish if we could clear all this mess that we've created today(looking at books on the shelf still on ground). It's all shit created by John(lightly hitting on his head).

John: I already said sorry so control your hands Pamela.

Amrisk:Okay....You guys don't fight...better keep going towards the hostel.

Mumkin looks at his watch and then at Pamela and John. He clenches his lips to indicate that they're getting late .The trio start moving outside the shop.

Amrisk: Don't worry K.Jalty will assist me and this will be finished quickly. You all three are kind souls.

Before leaving Dompin returns back once and tells Amrisk that they'll talk about this topic tomorrow as well. He especially wants to know about Lidiya.

After they leave, K Jalty hands over a cup of coffee to Amrisk .

K. Jalty: Why didn't you tell them everything?

Amrisk: They still have time to know about it and it's my loyalty too . They're young chaps.

Mumkin and his friends reach the hostels late, where the warden named Atrik Bloom was waiting for them.

Warden: You three are six minutes late, where have you been? What made you reach the hostel right now? Do you know about the rules of University? What will happen if I tell the authorities? Do you know what authority does about late comers? What kind of punishment does it give them? That's all your school habits, now I'm more interested in knowing from which school you belong to before joining our prestigious Himbertown University? Are you three from the same school? Your discipline issues suggest that , doesn't it? Name your school too! Before that anwer, Why are you late(loud and exasperated)

Pamela: (whispering) So many questions all at once! I don't even remember anything apart from the first and last.

John(whispering):Then you answer the first and last question.

Pamela: (whispering to John)Shut up John! Miss Bloom, we went to a bookstore to purchase a statistical psychology book. There it got a little late as the book suggested by prof Henry wasn't available in Brigget's wayside. Thus we had to enter inside to find it. It took a hell lot of time for us to get the book!

Warden: Don't use Miss Bloom ,it's Mr. Bloom (angry) Your reason sounds real. But the rules are ultimate.

John(whispering): He has long hair and a female voice with no facial hair. For a second I was happy to know that the warden was this hot female in red pants and black shirt..

Pamela(whisering):Yeah me too(chuckling).

Warden: Now it's your time to meet Prof Henry Hashtik, the discipline manager. He will ensure that you three are kept under control.

The warden took them into a narrow lane where it was completely dark and entered a room that resembled a store room with jumbled tables and chairs kept inside. AppaRently there isn't right now at this place.

Prof Hashtik: Who's there Bloom ? Did you find some other rule breakers?

Warden: Yes Professor. These three monkeys are six minutes late to reach the hostel.

Prof Hashtik: This is University, the famous Himbertown University. If you three assume that you can break any rule to show off being sangfroid to your other friends and classmates then you need not cook fancy pot pies(low voice). What's the reason for your delay (loud and frightening voice).

Pamela(shaking): Ah, it's it's , we we , we went to buy...bo book book.....

Prof Hashtik: Not you Pamela. I want them to answer. Your friends who always seem to be the quietest partners in crimes.

John: Yeah , we went to buy the book Mr. Hashtik.

Prof Hashtik: Enough modifying truth. Warden you leave. Thank you for bringing them here as they will be given impositions of extra work.

Dompin:But we're speaking the truth.

Prof Hashtik:Double imposition for using abusive tongue.

The warden leaves from there,Prof Hashtik keeps looking at the trio moving at his neck back while walking along the warden. Pamela and John are just cluelessly staring at Mumkin.

Pamela:I don't get it! Our Mumkin, who rarely speaks, just spoke a line and Professor Hashtik made a ruckus out of it.Very unfair. Double imposition!

Prof Hashtik comes back swiftly and makes bad eye contact with them which intimidates Pamela.

John(whispering):Ye budhe cha cha kya karane ki tayari mein hain?(what is this old uncle trying to do?)

Pamela:(whispering): Khatru dikh rahe hain(he's looking dangerous)

Mumkin: Both of you,don't worry ,I am there.

Prof Hashtik: Come here you three,take your chairs(pointing towards the pile of newspapers kept on tables). Now arrange them in date wise order.

John: Looks easy (smiling with confidence).

Prof Hashtik: Wait! Wait! The pile contains newspapers from 1883,all scattered.You've to ensure that each is arranged in order by 11PM. And don't forget to add 1946 newspapers in alignment.

Pamela: But Prof it's not possible to complete this humongous task in just three hours and why are we doing so? What's the use of it Professor?

Prof Hashtik: Miss Pamela, that's all up to you three. If you can't complete the task today then you can come tomorrow to complete it(smirking). Also it's required for our research . We are specifically focussing on articles based on our University. So you see that it's important.

John: But eleven pm, isn't ten pm the time to go to sleep?

Prof Hashtik: Taking away one hour of sleep is the rule for late comers. I can't help you here. But there's a shortcut to this! Instead if it was in my hands I would've made it for five hours of punishment at least .

John: Oh really? What's that professor?

Pamela:What a douchebag!

Prof Hashtik:Pardon miss Pamela, did you call me douchebag?

Pamela:Oh no no professor.I just asked where the garbage bag is?

Prof Hashtik: Why do you need that?

Pamela: We don't want to create a mess here with torn damaged articles and dust from the newspapers.

Prof Hashtik:Good girl. Here it is(pointing towards the corner of entrance). I make your imposition easy. As quickly you complete the task as quickly you can go to sleep(laughing).So hurry up young college students.

Pamela: (smugging)Okay professor.

The three sit on the chairs and Pamela divides the newspapers into three parts, where John doubts if on his side the pile is more ,so he exchanges it with Pamela due to which she exasperates. Mumkin quietly and patiently was doing his work.

Mumkin: Can we have a few white sheets of paper and sketch pens?

Prof Hashtik hands over the requested items to the trio. Mumkin makes a list of newspaper dates vs important headlines connected with the college.

Pamela: Gosh it's too time consuming and Mumkin is going one step ahead by writing an extra list of information.

Mumkin:This will make work organized and neat.

Pamela:Gosh, don't become an idiot like John. Just finish the work quickly so that we could go to sleep by 11.

After hearing this John holds on for a minute, keeps his hands on his waist to look at Pamela with questioning eyes. Pamela tries to cover up saying that 'Don't give me that look John, I am just joking, isn't Mumkin putting in too much effort?'.

The trio get back to work. Prof Hastik start drinking his alcohol near fireplace and singing"O sunny day, you take me away, I'll call my darling , sunflowers farms we'll show us the way, O sunny....O sunny, O sunny day,O sunny day(loud tone that shakes up the room), you take me away, I'll call my darling , sunflowers farms we'll show us the way".

Pamela:Pagal ho giya hai re buddha (the old fellow has gone mad).Aise ga riya jaise newspapers se iski darling bahar nikal ke ayegi(he's singing as if his darling will come out of the newspaper).

They kept on keeping the newspapers in order till eleven pm and Prof Hastik slept during that time.

Pamela: (Clearing throat) Professor,Professor Hastik it's eleven pm,can we leave?

Prof Hastik: (Threshold consciousness) who, who are you three, what you're doing here?

Professor wakes up and stands up and runs towards them with his cane, due to which they get horrified.

Pamela:My god, by god...he's running towards me.

Mumkin:Pamela, move towards the dustbin's side, exit from the door.

Pamela runs to the dustbin's side and professor Hastick is behind her, he eventually reaches near her and lifts his stick to hit her and she,closing her eyes, shouts out of pain....But he's still standing with the stick held high.

Prof Hastik: You youngsters are really sneaky. Just look at your pale faces.

Pamela:(Exasperatedly) Gosh! I thought you almost hit me with that nasty stick. Can we leave now(hands joined towards Professor Hastik)?

Prof Hastik: Oh yes yes! For what you're waiting.Leave. Are you clear with the instructions?

Pamela: Yeah , we need to come back tomorrow to complete the task.

Prof Hashtik: You can leave(professor starts drinking the wine near the fireplace and sings his old song).

The trio say goodnight to the professor and move towards the Loyola Hall where the ground floor was a mess and the first floor was a washing area. Next to Loyola Hall there was another hall named Franlinfin that was a hostel for boys and Saint Mary's Hall next to Franlinfin that was a hostel for girls. The trio move to their respective hostels. Mumkin and John are roommates.

CHAPTER FOUR

The tattoo removal!

The next day they attend the classes with swollen eyes. Mumkin wrote crooked shaped words in Professor WIlliams class , when Pamela asked for his notebook she wasn't able to identify even a single word. She says 'In developmental psychology class ,you've developed a new language!'.After the first four hour they were having lunch in the cafeteria when Ren and Janny visited them.

Pamela: Ren how do you see Prof Olivia?

Ren: I already gave her this nickname 'vulture, the killer of love'.

Pamela: But do you think she's actually got to do something with love?

Ren: No, not interested! I just don't like her.

Pamela: You need to know about it Ren...listen...

John interrupts Pamela in between.

John: Shut up Pamela, do you want to try the chili ice cream of Ren again?

Pamela: No ways.

Ren gives a high five to John and they chuckle. Mumkin was just sitting and looking at them with a faint smile. His eyes go to the cucumber orange salad kept just next to Ren. As he was looking at the cherry tomatoes, he discovered Janny constantly staring at him. In a muddle he takes his eyes away from her and starts smiling again at John and Ren who are teasing Pamela saying 'This time it'll be coffee with poop garnishing for you'.

Pamela: Shoot man, you go and have your exotic flavors. Mujhe baksh do(leave me alone with hands joined together).And how can you say something gross when all of us are having lunch?Gross you're!

Mumkin starts eating his lunch with a gross face.

Guys, let's eat fast as we need to head towards the classes. Before that I'm planning to take a quick nap.

Pamela: Of Course Mr. Sleeping douche, what can I expect from a dolt sleeping panda!

Mumkin, Ren and Janny look at each with big eyes, others startled and start chuckling over Pamela's comment on John.

John: What did you say? Wait,let me tell you who's a dolt panda.

Pamela runs away from there , John stands up and runs behind her, he holds her hand, takes her to the Dunkin doughnut shop and makes her purchase two chocolate doughnuts as revenge for calling him the 'dolt panda'.

He returns back and shows the doughnuts to others calling it a 'sweet revenge' .They go back to their classes and after the classes as they were heading towards Prof Hastik's room they were stopped by their dear friend at the back.It's Benny Sabastian.

Benny: Guys, wait. Why are you all in such a hurry?

Mumkin: Oh it's some urgent work given by Prof Hastik.

Benny: What work is it?

Mumkin: It's arranging the newspapers in order.

Pamela: yes, organizing those newspapers that have been kept disorganized by uncle Hashrik for centuries.

Benny: Sure carry on.Do let me know if you need any help from my side. Also just wanted to inform you that the selection for the committee is next week. So be ready.

Pamela: What committee is it Benny?

Benny: Well not aware as no information yet about that! They have some selections first and then the orientation about the committee's work or vice versa. I mean no idea!

Pamela: Very strange and puzzling. Isn't that first the orientation happens and then the selections? How are we supposed to know what work we have to do?

Benny: Well I asked a few stakeholders and they all say that it's a very secretive committee and students aren't supposed to know about it or else it be considered a rule breaking!

Mumkin : Who were your stakeholders?

Benny: Well I asked school officials, counselors and senior students!

John: When it comes to rule breaking, for everything they have rules.

Pamela: And they have tough punishments if the rule is broken. We'll thank you Benny ,we'll see you tomorrow.

Benny: You're welcome! I'll see then. Bye.

They all are heading towards Prof Hastrik's; they see Ren and Janny again sitting on a mini wall.

Ren: Hey shall we all go out for a music concert today evening by The Glassy Sapphires? What do you say guys?

Pamela:(hurriedly) I love the music concert by this band but as of now we're in a hurry.

As Mumkin, Pamela and John surpassed Ren and Janny but Mumkin asked them to stop for a minute and returned back to them.

Mmkin: Ren, do you know about the committee?

Ren: We'll have multiple committees in the University. Which one are you referring to?

Pamela: The secret committee!

Ren: Well, it's a new committee to be formed this year only and no one knows much about it, even its name isn't decided, except one thing, getting in there is an uphill battle. But I can talk to my uncle for your commendation Pamela! Do you?

Pamela diffidently looks into her books and walks away saying ' No thanks, I don't want such recommendations'.

Ren: Woah, she has a lot of attitude man .She's a sutli bomb(jute twine bomb).

He shouts at Pamela saying 'Wait girl Pamela'. She replies to that while moving forward 'No need Ren, I understand what you're thinking right now'.

Mumkin and John look at each other where John says 'We need to follow her up! See you guys later' . They run to reach near Pamela.

Janny: Ren!(covetously), what were you saying to her?

Ren: Nothing Janny, just trying to help her out as she's desperate to be part of the committee .

Janny: No need! You've no idea about these types of girls. She's not even thankful that you tried to help her out.

Ren: As you wish darling. Tell me what else you want my majesty?

Janny: I want that(pouts at him)!

Ren: Yeah, that's my girl! Lovely.(holding her hair softly)

He pulls her down behind the mini sports wall and they kiss.

The trio reached Professor Henry Hashtik's room where he was reading his newspaper and had kept fruit pastries with him. The three wished him good evening.

Prof Hashtik: Good evening. You three at 5 PM today! For what?

Mumkin:Professor, it's the work which we have to finish today?

Prof Hashtik: Oh great. You all are kind enough to help me out! Come come, just grab pastries for yourself(smiling) All three doubtfully look at each other's faces.

While Mumkin and John are standing still, Pamela whispers to them saying 'What's wrong with this old uncle. My sixth sense is saying that he's out of his mind' .

John(whispering): You only think shit! He's just trying to be friendly . By the way, those pastries are making me hungry.

Pamela: Chup karja bhukkad(shut up you hungry person).

Prof Hashtik: Come on! These are fresh pastries from a countryside organic fruit. You must taste them. Now quickly grab your favorite ones. Zaedy got me - It's peach, pineapple, raspberry ,mango and strawberry. Oh he didn't get chocolate today!

John asked in a dubious way

John: Are you sure that we can taste these?

Prof Hastik: Oh of course these are not poisonous. Come on eat or else I'll hit you with my cane.

Mumkin started chuckling.

Pamela(whispering): Stop laughing Mumkin, we have no idea where it might us to.How can you forget the way he was about to hit me with his cane yesterday?

Mumkin and John the pastries and start eating. Pamela dubiously makes an exasperated face at them. She looks slightly irritated.

Prof Hastik: What's your name, you , you tall guy. Do you study at the same University here?(pointing towards Mumkin)

Mumkin: It's Mumkin! Yes we three are from the same University and same course…..psychology course.

Prof Hastik: What ! Four of you entered the room, now I see only three .

Pamela:(whispering) I think he's some eighty years old .So….

Mumkin:(whispering) He might be having Alzheimer's. Crazzy.

Pamela: That's sad! But I hope today he behaves well like an eighty years old delightful grandpa.Not like an annoyed old man who is after the life of his students.

Mumkin:He appears to be a sweet person today.

John: That's right. Let's finish eating faster and complete the pending damn work.

Prof Hastik: Yes boy, just pass the wine from that shelf to me.

Mumkin goes near the down shelf and takes out the wine written: "The most intoxicating varuni sakha. Drink and forget the world"

Mumkin passes the wine to Prof Hastik and he pours it in his glass. As he takes one sip. Something happened to him. He lays himself on the ground,throws his hands and legs into different directions and starts crying like a baby. The trio go near him and try to pacify him .

Pamela: Professor Hastik,are you okay?

He continues behaving the same way.

Mumkin: It 's all after he drank this wine!

Pamela: Gosh, this is worse than any punishment. He's behaving like an infant!

John: Is he having seizures?

Pamela: Let's go to call a doctor.

Mumin: Just stop, look at him now.

All of sudden Professor Hastick stops crying and speaks.

Prof Hastik: What you are doing here, didn't you people finish the work of putting the newspaper pages in order? How long will you take as your punishment is not yet over? You three stole my pastries(angry)?

Pamela:(whispering)My gosh. He remembers everything(awestruck).

John: What a chameleon!

Prof Hastik hits Mumkin and John with his stick and they shout out in pain.

Pamela: Professor ,we came early today to do the work. We promise to complete it by today. And the pastries! As we arrived ,you only offered us ,I hope you recall it.(low soft voice and her voice drops as she finishes explaining).

Prof Hastik: Well Pamela and two of you dullard boys, as you know students, this work involves finding articles wherever the university is involved from the past eighty years of its formation.

Pamela: Professor, then this article would be of great information we suppose!

Pamela handles the article taken from Amrisik's bookstore to Prof Hastik!

Prof Hastik: What's this?

Mumkin: It's about Lidiya Cheriyan ,Jonathan Williams and Tiger Watson, the students who were from our University and especially Jonathan and Lidiya,they joined the Military as commanders and played a major role in various missions. Isn't it a great professor? We definitely need to include their names through this article as they are prominent motivational figures of our University to be remembered.

John: Yeah Professor ,I too think that this article can be included .(giving high five to Mumkin and Pamela). We got it from the shop while we went to buy a book,due to which we are punished today. I think you must consider now reducing our punishment.

Prof Hastik: What did you say,(He puts the spectacles on and reads the article).

He looks a bit nervous now.

Prof Hastik: From where did you get the article?I think I must give another imposition to you three.

Pamela(frightened): Another imposition, why sir? Regarding this article, it's from the book store , the UAS bookstore, deep inside the market.

Prof Hastik: (exhales)I know that store.

He throws an article inside the fire work.

Mumkin:(astonished) Prof, why did you do that ! That's a crucial article. It has military information in it and the name of crucial students of this University whose names our present students must know!

Prof Hastik: Shut up!

Pamela and John agree to Mumkin saying that 'you shouldn't have done this professor'where he tries to take the article out with the help of Professor's cane but the article is half burnt.

Prof Hastik: (loudly)You morons , listen carefully. Sit down on your chairs. Complete the work and leave quickly. Also the one who will take the name of this person will have to pay a huge fine!

Pamela: You mean fine for taking Lidiya Cheriyan's name?(whispering) This old uncle is again changing his chameleon color!

Mumkin:(blue in the face)Huge fine for what professor? We don't get the rules of this University. Even if one is truthful they're changed according to the teacher's wish here.You tell me, don't you think an old missing student and the martyred student need to be given importance? Why are you behaving like a baddie?

Pamela poops her eyes out at Mumkin saying 'Man, are you waiting to spend your entire life in this junky room completing impositions? Just calm down!'

Prof Hastik: Learn to follow the order Mr. Chamburt and Miss Brown .Sit down at your place. Complete the work and leave.

Pamela (whispering): Phew.... This moody pensioner didn't hold your collar this time Mumkin.

Pamela and John asked Mumkin to sit down and they took their seats . They Start doing the task at five twenty five. But this time, prof Hastik was keenly observing them ,his eyes were at their work just like staring at him restlessly and drinking his wine.

Pamela: Dadu to idahr hi nazre gada ke dekh rahe hai(Grandfather is just staring at us constantly).

Pamela hides two articles in her blouse and they are about to complete the work.

John: We finished professor. All done(with his thumbs up he's smiling).

Prof Hastik: Finished,is everything from 1880 till date of 21 June 1952?

John: Yes professor.

Prof Hastik: (Smiling) it's nine fifty two pm and you finished all tasks. Great! You all can leave now. Your imposition is over.

John(whispering): Thank god ,he's letting us go early. Probably he's scared of our Mumkin's anger!

John gives a fist bump to Mumkin and they smile at each other.

Pamela(whispering): Both of you, stop this drama right now, and try to leave as soon as you can before he can catch hold of you for another imposition!

John(whispering): You're overreacting Pamela. We finished our work so just chill!

As the trio prepare to leave from there, Professor speaks up in a loud and abrupt tone!

Prof Hastik: Remember that no one shall ever take that name anywhere.

John :Definitely professor(his hands are on his waist).

They come out of the room and enter the dark gallery.

John: What do we do by taking her name? They (referring to Lidiya and Jonathan) might be his students when he was a young professor. If he doesn't give a fuck then why do we bother!

Pamela: Seriously, he burnt that paper fully, I got so angry .....

They hear the sound of Prof Hashtik from behind. It's the loudest this time!

Prof Hastik: Wait! Miss Pamela, wait! Turn around.

Pamela(frightened like a thief is going to be caught): Pa, Pa professor. Yes .(stuttering voice).

Prof Hastik: You seem, you seem a good observant.

Pamela retains her calmness and answers back.

Pamela: Yes profesor, I think so that I observe well!

Prof Hastik: So did you check the work done by your friends ? Is it fine?

Pamela: Yeah sure. I'll do it now.

Pamela gets back in the room, Mumkin and John were stagnantly watching her go inside with disappointed faces, she holds her head for a second, blaming her friends for not leaving expeditiously.

Prof Hastik: Gentlemen, you both can help her in rechecking her work.

Mumkin and John too enter the room.

John(chuckling): From dullard boys we became gentlemen for him. Again the chameleon changes its color!

Pamela: It's not a college but a zoo. He's a chameleon, Professor Olivia is a vulture to Ren and his uncle is Bison! Their stupid rules of impsoitions will turn us into stressed lab rats.

All three take one and half hours to recheck each other's work and then leave after wishing the professor good night.

While they were leaving, the professor called them imbeciles but this time it wasn't unexpected from a moody person.

The next day Principal Henry Blacksmith arranges a meeting with Prof Hastik, Prof Olivia, Bison Silver and Prof Caleb Williams regarding the committee selections in the college staff room.

Principal Blacksmith: The committee dates are to be set for students. The selectors are coming from outside to select exclusive students from all over the college. Ensure that maximum participation takes place and real talent comes out.

Prof Hastik: Yes Principal. You worry not. All rules will be followed.

Silver:(smirking and looking at Olivia) Professor, ensure that rules are equal for all as I can't compromise with any discrepancy with any student.

Olivia keeps head high but looks down sighingly for Bison's hippocrity.

Olivia: That's your concern Mr.Bison as students who are relatives of powerful people are most likely to be favored!

Prof William: Of Course Mr. Silver and Professor Olivia, rest assured. Things will be according to planning

Principal blacksmith: I do trust my team .So shall we conclude the meeting?

Prof Hastik: Wait, Principal, I called you yesterday around eleven twenty midnight to report an important issue.

Principal Blacksmith: Oh yes! Very important Hastik. I'm becoming old like you,so I'm forgetting things. Thankfully you remember, despite your age . Surprisingly you remember(focusedly) as you're heavily drunk too, I think(chuckles). What a blessed person you are that drinking removes your alzheimer. Nevermind, as it's extremely important information.

Prof Hastik: Initially I got stuck to discover about it but I burnt the proof of it in the fire.

Principal Blacksmith: Yes yes, clever they are. Three students from the first year of psychology viz. Mumkin, Pamela and John know about Lidiya Cheriyan from an old article found at Amrisk's shop. We need to keep this secret away from anybody here.

Olivia and Williams have a sudden serious look on their face with a bit of nervousness.

Principal Blacksmith :Olivia, Williams and Hastik ensure that this information gets buried under the ground and is never revealed. Mr. Bison, we need your help too as it's important to protect the school's stature and keep one impeccable despite mud being tossed at once in the past.Be it anyone Bison.

Silver: Of course, I will always keep your words Principal. I too have deep connections and relations in this matter.

As Bison speaks this out, Olivia gives him a glance and looks down exhaling. He smirks at her.

After the class Mumkin along with Pamela and John reach out to Ren inside the ninth floor in an empty Philosophy department. As they reach there, they find Ren waiting for them.

John: Ren, hi. You're alone today .

Ren: Oh yeah, Janny wanted to read some stupid book from library which is not my place to spend time.

Pamela:Ren, listen I am sorry with the way I spoke to you .I need your urgent help!

Ren: No madame, I'm not here to serve you.

Mumkin: Pamela, could you please take a step back. Ren please, the request is from behalf of me and John.

Mumkin tells everything to Ren of how they found the article in the UAS shop about Lidiya Cheriyan and how Prof Hastik threw the paper on fire.

Ren: Why is this lady so important to you? What did you tell her name? Lidiya right?

Mumkin: Yes. She was a student here and after all a soldier who commanded very well, but no one knows about her! Professor told us not to take her name ever.

Ren:If the professor said, then there must be some crucial reason.

Pamela:Professor Hashtik isn't the right person to decide over the reason.He has diseased mind

Mumkin: Don't understand,why so much ignorance towards them? No one knows where Lidiya is ,but they deserve the tribute.

Ren: Who knows it's ignorance or something else.

Pamela: Look. (Showing the article) ,it's in 1936, where Ren, your uncle Bison who was a student in University, is standing with Lidiya Cheriyan, Jonathan Williams and Tiger Watson. I actually stole this article yesterday night from Prof Hastik.

John: You did what? Insane girl, if you were caught he might have taken strong actions against you.

Ren: So this sulti bomb is damn cool too.That's brave task to do, keep such thefts up. We'll appoint you as an official thief of college(winking an eye).

Pamela: Shut up. I'm not a thief, I stole it . And you see John ,it's an important article, since Ren's uncle is standing with them. Ren, why don't you ask your uncle about it?

Ren: Wait, did you take the name of Tiger Watson? He's my uncle's business partner. He can give some clues too.

Pamela: Amazing Ren.(giving high five to him)

John:(Irked) Pamela, read further. What's written in the article. We can get some clues from there.

Pamela: I can't as it's blackmarked by ink including the face of Lidiya Cheriyan. It's like we're solving a puzzle with pieces of articles. And now the next piece is missing. Duh!

Mumkin: I have an idea. We can find the next piece of it at the Amrisk shop I think.

John: That's a good idea. Let's go today to his shop after classes .Of course we need to return back on time by six fifteen pm.

Pamela: Not today! We are invited for Prof Olivia's extra hour after University normal timings for practical experiment.

John: Oh yeah, bunking Miss Olivia's class is like inviting an intentional trouble which can have grave consequences!

Ren: All the best with you three for Miss vulture's class(exhales) .Mr. Watson is also arriving for dinner tonight at home. He might give some clues about Lidiya.

Mumkin: Do ask him about his business in weaponry.

Ren: He isn't into it anymore. In Fact he has business in real estate, stock market,running educational institutes etc.

They say bye to Ren and head towards their classes and Prof Olivia enters.

Everyone stands up to wish except this a girl named Piya who was doing her nail polish .Olivia walks till her table. It was her first day in college. Olivia goes near her.She holds her nail polish bottle.

Prof Olivia: Where do you put it?

Piya(blowing air on her nails): Of course on nails.

Prof Olivia: It's to be applied on lips.

Piya: What! No way, it might give a burning sensation if applied on lips causing damage.

Prof Olivia: Burning sensation? Is it?

She takes the nail polish and puts that inside the Piya's water bottle that's filled with water in three fourth She shakes it well!The nail polish is submerged in water

Piya stands still realizing it's the bolt from the blue.

Prof Olivia:Will this reduce burning sensation now? Take your nail polish out and apply.

Piya:You're mad!

Prof Olivia:Your mind is clad for not attending orientation where rules and regulations of college were discussed.No makeup in class.

Piya stands downcastedly.

The students in the class are more intimidated now!

Pamela wants to change the name of Olivia from vulture to terror. Olivia takes the class of multidisciplinary education, where ninety percent of the students are sitting in class not out of interest but due to fear. Pamela whispers to Mumkin 'She's a real battle axe'.

Mumkin: What do you mean?

Pamela: She's a virago! The way she behaved with Piya, gosh...No one wants to be treated like that.

Mumkin: Yes,you mean Prof Olivia.that had to happen as Piya broke the rule!

Pamela:Gosh,why are you supporting her?

Mumkin: Prof Olivia a perfectionist and breaking rules in front of her isn't putting your legs on ax. We could've made Piya aware about the obsession of college with rules.

John: Yes, especially putting nail polish in front of her is just that's stupidity .

Mumkin: I too don't like Prof Olivia's classes but making multidisciplinary education a beauty parlor is not that cool!

Pamela:Mumkin,you'll speak like this as you're a military guy, discipline lover.. Today you both are sitting on an opposite boat to me supporting Olivia. I like her multidisciplinary classes but behavior wise,our teacher, she's a bitch.

After their classes get over the trio decide to head towards Amrisk's shop.

Ren takes Janny for a dinner party at home where his uncle Bison Silver and his business partner Tiger Watson arrived. Ren himself serves champagne to them. Tiger Watson is a Billionaire and owns almost half of the industry in the city. In the cordial environment when everyone is juggling with their Champagne glasses,the bottle of champagne falls on ground and breaks from his hand.The glass splatters all over. The maid starts cleaning it. He gets another champagne bottle.

Ren: You both are alumni of my University! I feel proud after seeing you .

Watson: Indeed! Silver, what do you say?

Silver: I feel proud too, you see from being a student and then coming to the position of trustee and reaching heights in business .Well all success wishes to you partner!

Ren: Great to hear that. I saw an old newspaper and I found a photo of you both!

Watson: Probably you might have seen the media praising our business achievements. There have been many articles like that for more than a decade.

Silver: Rightly said (laughs loudly and gives cheers to Watson . Then swirls his glass of champagne).

The champagne is shining golden,Ren is looking at their swirling glasses and after that at them!

Both Silver and Watson have appreciated each other's company since their college times. Ren is just waiting for them to take the first few sips so that he can give the correct description of the photo .

Ren: No uncle. It was with Lidiya Cheriyan and Jonathan Williams. Along with three more students who were helping the military during projects.

Watson: What? What did you say? Lidiya? Is she alive?

Silver: Hold on young man! Listen, take my card and take your girlfriend Janny to the most expensive restaurant in the city. Why are you wasting your time on irrelevant questions?

Watson: Silver, let the boy ask. Yes, Ren, what do you know about Miss Lidiya Cheriyan(precariously)?

Ren in confusion looks at his uncle and Watson as they just now are in small argumentation.

Ren: Thank you uncle for offering the card but me and Janny want to have dinner here with everyone. Probably tomorrow we might go(taking Silver's card). And Mr. And to you Mr. Watson this is what my question is! Who is Lidiya Cheriyan?

Silver: Why waste time? Go now. Look, she's waiting for you in your room. Enjoy your time.

Ren: We already enjoyed it !

Watson: Wait Silver, let me clear the doubt of Ren. Lidiya was a fugitive soldier who betrayed the country. Isn't that embarrassing (scowling). And Jonatha, he was one bootless person. Both were my fucking classmates!

Ren: (Dismayed) Really, was she a fugitive and Jonathan was a bootless person?

Watson: Of course. I can tell more of Lidiya's underhand deeds.(exasperated). Jonathan died in a military skirmish. Why are you asking about them suddenly?

Ren: Just out of curiosity from the very old newspaper I saw.

Silver(suddenly standing up): Ren, I need your help in finding my garage keys inside the guest room. Can you help?

Ren: Ofcourse uncle.

Silver: Then stop looking at me like an owl and start helping. Excuse me Mr. Watson, I'm a little worried if Ren has misplaced them.

Silver takes Ren inside the guest room and he holds his collar tightly, his face looking vexed.

Ren: What uncle, what happened, why are you angrily holding me like that?

Silver : Listen up young man, never ever take Lidiya's name again.

Ren: But she was a bad soldier ,that's it.

Silver: Ren, she was a student of our college and I am on the trustee board at present. What Watson said all about Lidiya is absolutely true because it's the information from the news articles that were published at that time. But we never know reality. As per I know about her she was an amazing human being and I loved her completely.

Ren: You loved her too?

Silver: Adored her. Promise me that you'll not talk about her ever again, whether it's for good or bad reasons. Same for Jonathan Williams.

Silver: Keep it confidential for the University's prestige and keep this name buried in the ground.

Ren: I promise uncle,I will never ever take their name again.

Silver: Chalo futoo(leave now)

He gives Ren a fist shake and hugs him before they come out of the garage.

They rejoin the dinner party where the serving includes balti curry,fish and chips, bangers and spaghetti bolognese,fish pie and mouth watering apple crumble with chocolate brownies for dessert.

There was all porsche crockery with golden flowers printed on it. Tiger Watson was eating spaghetti at lightning speed.

Whereas the trio that day had gone to attend Miss Olivia's class. The class is quiet, just waiting for the calm before the storm. Piya, one of the fashionable girls in the class, is wearing a simple gray shirt and black pants with a bun, she's just making a face like a rotten eggplant just counting time in her watch. Every moment seems to be very heavy, they just want this hour to be over. Especially Prof Olivia's cold calling to students to answer in class is making them study multiple times before every multidisciplinary class . This is making them ready for questions of a null exam.Why null?, as the subject that Olivia is teaching doesn't have any sort of exam at the end!

Pamela: I loved multidisciplinary education classes but while asking questions from others, Miss Vulture doesn't give me the opportunity to answer.

John:You're a grubbing grave sedulous!

Pamela: And you are jokingly ridiculous.

Benny Sabastian enters. He tells everyone to keep quiet as some authority figure is coming for inspection of class. But there is a familiar face with another person.

Atrika Bloom,the warden who just a day before took the trio to Prof Hastik for punishment after they got late from the book store. As they say ,the person's mouth burnt with milk, will sip buttermilk with a spoon. The trio is the most watchful among all to not to break any rule as they're the first one to face any imposition. There enters the class Prof Rustin Henry. Seeing Bloom, Mumkin and Pamela they show nervous expressions on their faces . Pamela keeps her back straight and takes out her notebook,keeps her click pen on a page and starts looking at Prof Henry. John looks at Mumkin and Pamela with edginess. Pamela whispers to John not to worry and take a deep breath, exhale and relax. As John follows it, he feels more hysterical in first breath and then feels calmer when he exhales.

Klis Mahn and Laila Sim,they both sit together at the second last bench of the class and are fellow classmates of the trio. Klis Mahn is more interested in knowing about the teacher rather than the subject, especially because he finds Prof Olivia's strictness attractive. Students find him both playful and weird. Whereas Laila Sim looks like a party girl. She probably has tattoos of her ex-boyfriends on her arms, waist and neck .People know her as the 'Tatty girl' because those tattoos aren't out of fashion but out of passion and obsession she had with her past relationships that she couldn't overcome till now.

Klis Mahn tells Laila :if I was born in Prof Olivia's era, I would have made her my girlfriend.

Laila softly smiles at him and her eyes are covered black due to her thick curled eyelashes.

Pamela giggles after hearing it whispering to herself 'What a psycho! To choose Professor Olivia as his girlfriend'.

Klis Mahn imagines what kind of students she would be!Perhaps way too traditional, who's compliant with all instructions of teachers, would be wearing long full sleeved gowns as she does it today with a single tight plaited hair. He tells Laila that he likes such sober and traditional girls with a little anger outbursts in the name of discipline.

KIis Mahn: What happened to Miss Oliva, is she not coming today?

A fellow student named Christopher speaks up.

Christopher: Woah, that's cool.Anyways she was taking an extra class that wasn't in the time table. So what for now, can I leave? Gotta hang out with friends!

Few more students in class get exhilarated after hearing him and start packing their bags.

Bloom and Prof Henry move uptil classroom podium.

Bloom: Shut up all! Be ashamed of yourself. A professor has entered a class ,you already have plans to bunk !Christopher(loud voice).

Whole class becomes quiet.

Bloom:Miss Sim, ask this Christopher sitting next to you to keep his mouth shut!

Laila Sim:Yes sir(little tense now)

Bloom:Look around,there are three reprimanded souls in this class. Take their guidance of consequences of any miss behavior. Mr. John ,please tell the class about an anecdote of yours and your friends! Before you waste more of my time,Prof Olivia, had to leave for another meeting with the Principal. So professor Henry will deal with a bunch of you nincompoops. Professor you can take over!

Bloom leaves.

Prof Henry: Good afternoon everyone or I rather say it evening as it's going to be 5 O' clock in the coming fifteen minutes. Also a little introduction about myself. I come from Monus Capasi village near the south of Naples. My education was from Philosophe University France, where I got a scholarship to do a specialization in psychotherapy from Sycho Bright University in India. I hold experience of sixteen years. Since I was a student like you, I give you full freedom to ask any doubts and present your point of view without fear. Keep your mind open like a parachute.

So today we'll have a practical session on hypnosis! What do you think about it?

All students remain quiet and then Pamela raises her left hand, looks at professor Henry to take permission to answer. Professor allowed her, whereas there were five to six other nerds like her who also raised their hands and they started murmuring in excitement to answer the question.

Pamela:Professor hypnosis is an induced state of consciousness in which a person apparently has no control over one's action and becomes responsive to the person who is hypnotizing. It's an important form of its use in therapy, typically to recover repressed emotions or memories due to which the behavior of the person who is being hypnotized improves to allow modification of behavior.

Prof Henry: Excellent miss Brown, well explained. Can someone tell who introduced hypnosis?

Gracy Mers is a fellow classmate known as the girl with long red curls.

Gracy Mers: I don't know if I'm right but I read it in my Psychology class in school that James Braid introduced it.

Prof Henry: You're very bright Miss Mers. Can you tell whether this dude is a psychotherapist, researcher or something else?

Gracy Mers: Well, I need not be sorry as I answered right. But I do not know about James Braid's profession. Probably he was a psychotherapist.

Benny Sabastian: (raising his hand) I can tell professor! Modern hypnosis was introduced by a physician in fact who was called Mesmer, Austrian by dysentery. He believed that there exists a fluid that is invisible to the person taking hypnosis and the therapist which he named as mesmerism or magnetism. The term hypnosis was introduced by Scottish surgeon James Braid, the person in a particular state of sleep called trance.

Prof Henry: Well done! You've just mastered this subject dear Sabastian. Mesmer introduced Mesmerism and James Braid coined this term. Mr. Stone, would you like to add something here.

Walter Stone: Professor, it's a controversial subject though!

Gracy Mers: I agree with stone.

Prof Henry: Yes Mr. Stone and Miss Mers. Controversy is that, the sole purpose of hypnosis is to modify the behavior of the subject and enhance their well being. By subject I mean the person who has arrived for hypnosis. But sometimes it doesn't work at all with few subjects. We're more concerned if it can be more helpful to healing people. Let's do an experiment today. I would like to invite the quiet people as I strongly believe that they have beautiful minds filled with ideas and deep experiences. Mr John, would you like to step forward to become my subject?

John with jitter steps on the podium and prof Henry arranges a sofa with the help of college staff members and asks John to lie down.

Prof Henry: Mr John, I want you to inhale and exhale and look at an imaginary triangle on my forehead.

Prof Henry titillates John from his head to check with his hands slowly slowly. He constantly takes his name and asks him to relax.

Prof Henry: Relax John, relax John, relax John....

He repeats it until John falls asleep.

Prof Henry: John, what do you see there?

John: I see that I'm in a spacecraft inside space. Yes. It's beautiful, it's dark blue but glittery everywhere.

Other students are chukling in the class and Prof Henry shows his finger on his lips to ask them to keep quiet.

Prof Henry: What are you doing there now?

John: I'm working out to prepare myself for the wrestling match.

The students along with Mumkin and Pamela laugh together. Professor Henry whispers again 'quiet all of you'.

Prof Henry: What else are you doing?

John: Reading!

Pamela whispers to all 'No ways, he can never read good!'

Prof Henry smiles at Pamela, and then he looks back at John.

Prof Henry : Reading which book?

John : My comic, love it. They've come to meet. When they hug they tingle a lot.

Prof Henry: Who has come?

John: Comic friends of mine- Shacha, Mindi, Lillibun and Gaspy. She came in a silver frock of stars. She's just as beautiful, but she's quite......

Prof Henry: Who is she?

After hearing this, Pamela's pupil enlarges, she feels a strong rush of oxytocin and dopamine. Her pupils dilate and pulse is running twice the speed. The gulps out of nervousness and her cheeks are red.

John: It's Stella! She's confident, compassionate, thin and has extremely beautiful eyes.

Pamela finds it bolds from the blue, her face is completely red and she's exasperated and feels a sudden slight pain in chest like John is stabbing her chest.

Prof Henry: Are you in endearment with her?

As Pamela tries to close her notebook, her ball point pen falls down, due to which suddenly the class looks at her, including Prof Henry. Her eyes are watery and Prof Henry gets the clear message that she has feelings towards John. He titillates the legs of John and gets him out of hypnosis.

Pamela is heartbroken,where she isn't interested in connecting with her environment anymore. This happens with her all the time when things do not go according to her choice. She believes that those living near her must always love her. After all, she considers John as her best friend. Although she always mocked and hit John but from inside she had an intuition that he deeply likes her. Her teasing is mainly sometimes to get him on track by proposing to her but now she realized that her mind was always in a land of dreams. She once mentioned her liking towards him to a few of her close friends.

Laila goes near Pamela and says 'I'm feeling sorry for you Pamela,you'll be alright soon (looking at Pamela)'. Pamela and Laila are both best friends and roommates.

Prof Henry: Okay students. So now ,I can claim the power of this technique. Isn't wonderful to cure patients where they speak out from their heart. We still have eighteen more minutes.Mr Chamburt, please come up to the podium. Mumkin moves up to the podium and follows instructions of Prof Henry and goes into a hypnosis state.

Prof Henry: Mumkin, what do you see?

Mumkin: It's a function of my school where the song is played.

Prof Henry: The song is regarding what?

Mumkin: It's about father's day. Fathers of other children have arrived. My father is not there . Seeing this, my mother is sobbing while hugging me and remembering my father.

Prof Henry: How do you feel Mumkin?

Mumkin:I miss him, I wish to spend time with him. I have no idea how it is to be with a dad.Wished we played chess together and he helped me with my homework during school days. My mother is dealing with prolonged loneliness. I would not mind him even giving me backlashes as I love him a lot as his son.

Prof Henry: Talk about your father Mumkin. How do you see him ?

Mumkin: Filled with courage, passion to serve the country and ready to follow any order of his senior ,make any mission successful. But he left me too early! I miss him.

Prof Henry: Mumkin, your father has come to meet you from heaven now. What is he saying?

Mumkin: He is not happy with me. But he was hugging me,he kissed my forehead. He's regretful to see the financial burden on my family, my unhappy mother and non contributing to me.(a tear drop off his eye)

Prof Henry: He's asking you, what do you do to make him happy?

Mumkin: J..J.stuttering(University bell ring)

Mumkin comes out of hypnotic state suddenly at the University due to the sound of the bell.He looks very nervous now.

Prof Henry: Don't worry Mumkin. Everything is fine. You did very well. Just calm down.(murmuring profoundly and leaving the classroom) I'll ask the Head staff member to not ring the University hourly bell, especially during my class .

Pamela, John and other students come near Mumkin. Few of them are exhilarated.

Eva Johnson, a fellow student, hugs Mumkin.

Eva: I never knew that your quietness had so much to do with.

Pamela: Yeah, you never speak about your family and remain quiet but today it's revealed.

Mumkin: What happened? I don't remember anything! Why do my eyes get wet?

Pamela: You got vulnerable today. You spoke about your dad, it was heartwarming that's why you cried. It was a voice from your unconscious mind which makes you miss him so much.

Pamela helds Mumkin's hand to help him stand up and walk away along with a few other classmates leaving John behind. John is confused but soon Benny Sabastian tells him everything that he said in a hypnotic state.

John: I always thought that I loved Pamela but I never confessed to her worrying about her rejection as a friend! And I can't believe that I spoke about Stella. What can it mean Benny?

Benny: I don't know brother but Pamela looked disappointed.

John runs towards Pamela and Mumkin, and tries to talk to Pamela.

John: Pamela, I never knew of what I said. I'm not even aware of it(nervously).

Pamela: Fuddu(stupid), why are you saying this to me!

John again tries to explain. Pamela stops at him and looks at John.

Pamela: It's okay John. It's not your fault to take the name of my cousin Stella! Today golden almonds delight ice cream from your side for Mumkin and coffee with doughnuts for me.

John: Why so, taking the name of Stella isn't that grave mistake that I have to empty my pockets!

Pamela: It isn't that grave until I tell my uncle Nelon. Shall I?

John: Alright(vexed). We'll head towards the ice cream parlor after this....

Pamela, Mumkin and John, all three head towards Amrisk's shop the next day, soon after attending the classes. Before they tried to look for Ren to know about the conversation between him, his uncle Silver and his uncle's business partner Watson, but they didn't see him in school that day.

As they reach Amrisk's shop, he tells him to wait outside on the bench as the shop's cleaning is taking place. As he doesn't come out after thirty minutes, they themselves enter the shop, but they didn't find him. K. Jalty informs him that he has left for his home from the backdoor of the shop without leaving a message for them to leave back to their hostels. The three of them return back to the hostel disappointed.

John: Don't understand why Amrisk left without meeting us.

Pamela: He might be in a hurry for some work of his own.

Mumkin: Yeah maybe.

The next day too they didn't find Ren, they tried to look for Janny too. But they hear from other seniors that the two are on leave, especially Ren isn't well after the party at his home.

The next day Mumkin sees Ren in the boy's washroom.

Mumkin: Ren, how do you feel now?

Ren: What will happen to me?

Mumkin: Alright, nothing! So did Tiger Watson and your uncle Silver Bison reveal something about Lidiya Cheriyan?

Ren: Oh yes, you'll be amazed to know!(surprising facial expression)

Ren informs everything about the conversation between him and uncle Bison and his business partner Watson. After hearing the information Mumkin is startled and soon after the classes he decides to head towards Amrisk's shop . He shares the same with Pamela and John but they are also unable to gulp the new truth they hear from Ren's mouth about Lidiya Cheriyan and Jonathan Williams .

Pamela: Gosh, Lidiya is a military fugitive! Just can't believe it.

What came out from Pamela's mouth accidently about Lidiya was coming true. After the classes they head towards Amrisk's shop as he's the only person who can clarify all their doubts. Today also the same cleaning process is happening. K Jalty is present but Amrisk isn't seen. The trio inquires about him from K.Jalty who in return with a grave face says that he doesn't know where Amrisk is .

Pamela: Ise konsa saap sung gaya?(What wrong happened to K.Jalty?)

Mumkin: The first day he appeared to be sweet but now he's acting weird.

John: Yes, he's sort of ignoring us.

Mumkin: I know where Amrisk would be now! Follow me friends.

As Mumkin reaches the end of the last book shelf , they see Amrisk trying to escape from them while he was moving towards the backdoor to get out, but he is astonished to see Mumkin , who ran from bookshelf to back door within seconds to confront him.

Amrisk: Oh Mumkin (sweating). You're too quick. Which book do you want? I'm in a hurry. K. Jalty will help you.

John and Pamela, reach there too.

Mumkin: We don't want any book, but we want to know more about what happened to Lidiya?

Amrisk: Lidiya!Who's she?

Pamela reminds Amrisk of the conversation they had about Lidiya Cheriyan when they came to his book store viz. UAS for the first time.

Mumkin: Why did you lie to us about her?

Amrisk: I never lied! What you're talking about dear Mumkin.

Pamela and John are also sternfully looking at Amrisk.

Mumkin: You said that Lidiya Cheriyan was a brave soldier, but it turns out that she was actually a fugitive .

Amrisk: Oh for god sake don't call Lidiya this! She was brave, very brave. But things didn't turn in her favor. (Amrisk look at them with disappointment)

Mumkin: But this is what Mr.Tiger Watson said to Ren, our college senior where Watson happened to be Ren's uncle's business partner. They know each other.

Amrisk: I cannot tell you more than this!

Mumkin: We request you Mr. Amrisk to stop dramatizing the facts as all this is getting messier in our heads.

Amrisk: Don't get me wrong, this is what I know about Miss Lidiya. Few years back she used to come here to buy books and I found her exceptionally nice with her conduct. I can't hear anything about Miss Lidiya, especially the old strategies of the press where they cook up storms to grab attention. We can't talk about things here outside. You better come to my home on Sunday .I need to leave for a very important task. K.Jalty, get these kids a cup of coffee with chicken puffs. Please excuse me, I have commitments.

As Amrisk was moving out of his shop from there, he returned back for a second with an earnest face.

Amrisk: You three do get selected in the committee.

Pamela: So can you tell us about the committee? What is it all about?

Amrisk: No,oops .I just actually don't know.But have just heard about it from some student who came here to buy books that there's a committee selection next week . But I will be highly glad if you three become part of it. You know these are some golden opportunities of life ,which might land you successful careers. I'm sure you'll learn something from the committee. Better head towards your hostels, before that finish your coffee and puffs. Also whenever during selections if you get anxious,just remember"don't you know yet it's your light that lights the world ". Warm wishes to your selection in committee.

Amrisk says goodbye to them and leaves from there. The trio had snacks and coffee while having a small chat.

Pamela:Guys, why was he giving so much of an explanation about the committee with a bizarre look.

Mumkin: He was in a hurry today just like yesterday!

John: And that quote, he said, was kind of out of context.

Pamela:I know it's a quote by a philosopher Rumi, who was born in the thirteenth century in a middle eastern country.

Mumkin: You're an encyclopedia!

Pamela:Thanks(winking her eyes).

John:I don't get the quote!

Pamela:Never mind,for a dullard like you no quote can work.

Pamela hits John with her book and chuckles after that.

John:Stop it !

Pamela: It's 4:20PM, let's go to the movie theater for a short movie.

Mumkin:What is the movie all about?

Pamela: It's a psychological thriller movie for twenty five minutes.

As they were heading towards a nearby movie theater, a man in a hurry strikes Mumkin, he is very nervous and has blood in his hands and he's holding a purse . There's turmoil in the market and they realize that a woman has been robbed and stabbed due to which she's in a critical state. Mumkin and John realize that the man with whom they collided is the culprit . They run back to catch hold of him and spot him at a distance of two hundred meters from them. Mumkin runs like thunder ,jumps at the thief and hits him on his hand due to which the knife falls off. He punches the thief on his face and John pushes the thief towards the wall leading him to hit the wall and faint. The police arrive there. And Pamela rushed towards the profusely wounded lady,tearing her frock,putting the cloth on wound to control blood and with help of nearby people, the lady was hospitalized by Pamela. Both Mumkin and John reach the hospital. The doctors inform the need for blood as the lady's wounds have caused high loss of blood. The three get their blood test done where Mumkin's blood group matches the lady's blood group. He gives her the blood. But it's already six thirty in the evening. They're late to reach University hostel.

They rush towards the hostel and John gets the idea to jump through the University's backyard wall in order to avoid punishment. Mumkin jumps down the other side of the wall and Pamela was sitting on John's shoulder's to cross over. Mumkin was waiting to help Pamela on the other side. Pamela crosses too, as John was about to cross, suddenly a shadow appears due to a lamp post in the backyard. It's a lady dressed gray .As they look at her face, it's Miss Olivia who is just coming after attending a meeting with Principal, Prof Williams ,Prof Hastik and other members for the upcoming committee selection. Olivia catches them red handed for breaking the rule of coming late.

Prof Olivia(fusiously): You three want to break the record by coming late. Just look at your dirty clothes. Now before the principal arrives here, leave towards your hostels, I'll ensure that you get a better lesson compared with your first punishment. This time you'll cry out tears of blood.

This the first one on one interaction of the trio with Professor Olivia. The trio are more like rhinoceros that are thick skinned .

Pamela speaks up 'You have no idea what happened with us professor!'

Prof Olivia: I am not interested in knowing your ice cream parlors, pizza parlors and coffee houses stories!

Pamela:No. Not that.

Prof Olivia: I am not interested in knowing about your sexual encounters of you three.

Pamela: No ways Professor, not that either.

Pamela now keeps her mouth shut and the trio leave towards the hostel, guard Max of University arrieves. He tells Prof Olivia something and shows her direction. She walks swiftly towards the Chevrolet car and Max tries to walk behind her trying to match her speed. She sits in it and leaves quickly as the driver drives the car away.

The next day,college students had to come there for an extra class. It was a Bunch of students who wanted to join the committee. Prof Olivia wasn't present in Xavier hall where all students are seated and the principal with teaching staff is sitting in front of seats. Prof Williams came up to the podium.

Prof Williams: Dear students, we have committee selections next week, I request Principal Blacksmith to come up on the stage and guide you further.

Everyone stands up as the Principal goes up on stage.

Principal Blacksmith: Dear students, I am glad to see the large number of students who want to be a part of this so-called "secret committee". We have the name of the committee but it will be known to exclusively selected students. As many of you want to know what is demanded to get in the committee, there are three things:"true rationality, true words and true actions" . This is the sole basis of selections. There are a set of tests through which you will be going through. Each test has stages. A good performer will get into the next stage or else it'll be eliminated from the committee. The committee will choose these students. The reason orientation is after selection is because selectors are from outside University and they want to select students on their own way. Keep your mind strong if you really want to try as the tests have fitness as one of the criteria. So sports teacher Kinen Zuna will train you from tomorrow till next week until the selection starts. You need to fill the form of declaration that selection is from your free will and if any unfortunate event occurs, the University is not responsible. Be it any injury or loss of life. You are given a choice to appear or not before the selections. But remember the most threatening situations bring the best in us and facing them requires bravery. All the best students.

He gets down off stage.

Pamela (whisper):What pastime they're doing. Can't they tell what the committee is all about?

Mumkin: They're not going to say a word I think!

John: Yes ,all they want us to do is get selected.

Prof Williams tells the students to collect their self declaration form and informs them about the instructions of the form. He gives them the next day's time to fill and sign the form. Also he tells them to collect their sports gear and check it before going to the field the next day. It's already five forty five pm ,so Mumkin and his friends go to the hostel.

Pamela reads the self declaration form in front of Laila which says 'I certify that I am ready for the committee selections both mentally and physically. In an extreme misfortune event, even death, I am solely responsible for it. '

The next evening they gather near the sports ground where sports teacher Kinen Zuna makes everyone run eight miles with tough exercises like jumping jacks, side planks ,lunges and squash repeating them seven times with ten sets each. After the exercises ,few of the students change their mind of not appearing in selections as they find it tough. Pamela is one among them .She starts moving along with the quitters when she's been stopped by somebody whose hand is on her shoulder. She looks back and it's Mumkin.

Mumkin: Where are you going, fugitive?

Pamela: I don't think I can really do it Mumkin. I mean, I'm chubby and today these exercises made me realize that I have been a couch potato my entire life till now.

Mumkin:Wait wait....don't call yourself that. Face the next stage of selections.

Mumkin asks other students who have given up so easily to come back and try for the next stage .He starts clapping both of them together ,saying 'Good job guys, stay back . Today was tough but you can sustain the next stages of selections as well. So fill up the declarations and give' John and Ren join him too as well.

Due to which the trio submit their self declaration form along with Ren and other students. By the end of the day most of the students sleep in their dining hall like the day never happened dreaming themselves involved in tiresome exercises, some asking for water and some wanting to sleep with their girlfriends and boyfriends to get rid of pain.

The next day too, after classes students had to go through the same fitness routine. But this time ,after forty five minutes Prof Williams interrupted. He gave the next task to students who have submitted their self declaration form. Now the task is to fill up another form that requires their biodata in a structured format. Indeed it was an intense form that required the knowledge of family members, occupation of family and ancestors, history , income of family, the city from which the students belonged to, population density of the city and the information about their schooling, hobbies, grade obtained, any backlog and participation in extracurricular etc. By evening Mumkin and John were stopped by Pamela where she had to prepare them for the class test of social psychology as there was an upcoming test of it. The whole week the aspiring committee students were occupied with tasks and events prior to appearing in the real selection process. Only Sunday was free. Mumkin decides to visit the hospital to check on the injured lady. Pamela and John accompany him. They buy flowers. As they reach the hospital they find from the nurse that someone from the family of the lady has taken her back to her home. But a note has been left by her for them. As Mumkin reads the note"Life can take any turn but angels do exist. Thank you for hospitalizing me on time, giving me blood and saving my life. Please do visit me at this address". The address is written on the back side of the note"134/ 4, street 8, Haffotin Town,HT158 ".

As the three decide to visit the lady whose name is mentioned as "Isabella Martin" in the note. They suddenly notice Bidar Nelon, Pamela's uncle, coming near them.

Nelon: Pamela, Pamela(smiling and walking towards her)..What are you doing here in hospital on sunday with your friends?

Pamela tells everything about the incident that happened on Tuesday and how they saved the life of the lady. Now they are planning to give a visit to her at home. When Pamela asks Nelon of his reason for visiting the hospital,he informs her that he has come here for University work for the upcoming event. On enquiring more, he tells that he is collecting extra first aid items and the University is hiring the hospital nurses in case of a medical emergency during committee selection.

Pamela:Oh goodness, I don't know what they'll make us do now!I think it'll not be a surprise if few of us ever return home in one full piece.

Nelon laughs and tells them that the first aid kit is just for injuries and emergencies. Not to worry. He appreciated their will to be part of the committee upon receiving their declaration forms in his office. He tells the trio to sit in his car as he wishes to drop them to the lady's address. He drives for the next twenty minutes and stops at a place which looks very familiar to Pamela.

Pamela: Uncle but it's your house!

Nelon: Yes dear, your Aunt and Stella will be surprised to see you and your friends. I promise to drop you all after meeting them .

Pamela : Sure uncle thank you. Also I am very sorry on behalf of me and my friends that we couldn't visit your family due to a frenzied schedule.

Nelon: Oh no dear, don't apologize. I know three of you have been a part of committee selection fitness practice conducted by Kinen Zuna. It looks like a tough row to hoe!

Pamela:Indeed! It's difficult to get selected.

John: It's like catching clouds in a mosquito net as we do not know what committee is all about.

As they enter the house, Stella and her mother hug Pamela and say hello to Mumkin and John. The house of Mr.Bidar Nelon is a middle class house with a beautiful flower vine of red and blue color covering the front of the house excluding the gate.

Stella feels a little embarrassed and nervous in front of John.

John: Hi Stella, how's everything with you?

Stella: Hello John. Things are great with me!

Pamela: Let me introduce you to Mumkin..Mumkin Chamburt. He's studying with us.

Stella says hello to Mumkin. Mrs Nelon too greets Mumkin and John. She gets back to her kitchen and brings back mashed potatoes, roasted chicken and fresh cranberry relish. Stella helps her mother in serving food to others on the dining table and soon after that they enjoy the meal together.

John: You know Mumkin is from a Military background?

Mrs. Nelon: Amazing, I'm pleased to hear that. My father too was in the Army . We got posted to many towns and cities like Binnaguri, Meerut, Srinagar and Pathankot....

Nelon: Honey , do tell me about the horse incident.

Mrs. Nelon: Ofcourse. When I was five, my father took me to an animal regiment for horse riding. As I sat on the horse, it ran as quick as flash and I jumped off from there. When I opened my eyes, I had a temporary memory loss where I refused to recognize my own father.(chuckles)

All start laughing . Later in the evening,Nelon sits in the front seat of his car to drive .Mumkin, Pamela and John join him just after saying goodbye to Mrs Nelon and Stella. Pamela was about to hand over the note on which address is written but he requests her to read it for him.Pamela reads the address.

Nelon: This address sounds familiar. Can you read it again dear?

Pamela: Sure uncle it's"134/4, street 8, Haffotin Town,HT158"

Nelon: Are you sure you wanna go there?(As he was speaking, his smile was fading away,he gives grave look)

John:Why what happened Mr. Nelon?

Nelon :Haffotin, it's the place where Miss Olivia lives!

Mumkin: Really?

Pamela: This week we were caught by her breaking a rule.

Nelon: This is quite a populated area so chances are rare that she catches on to you. But be careful kids, if she catches you again,the trouble will increase as she might set up an inquiry to rusticate you three!

Pamela: College mein rusticate nahi hue to kiya hi kya(if you haven't been rusticated in college then you have not lives the college life)

Nelon: It's not that simple darling. Once you get rusticated ,the monitoring on you will be so extreme that even a miniscule mistake will cause you another rustication. This not only includes discipline rules but low scores in academics too. Third, will make your life hell as your jobs in future will be at stake. So be heedful.

Mumkin: Sure Mr. Nelon.

John: Yes, agreeing with you Mr. Nelon. Pamela stop being a scallywag!

Nelon drops the trio near the house number 134/4 and street eight . He drives from there to another place due to important administrative work of the university . He was arranging writing material for test takers. In between Pamela tries to get more information about the committee.

Pamela: Uncle, this committee, isn't that weird that it's been set after a week of college. I mean why not on the first day itself?

Three of them reach house number 134/4 and knock on the door. It's opened by a middle aged man.

Man: Hi, how may I help you?

Pamela: We are actually here to visit Isabella Martin.

Man: Are you the ones who actually saved her?

Pamela: Yes ,we think so(awkward smile).

Man: Oh, hi . Oh my goodness. Deva svataḥ ala(lord himself has arrived).Please come inside, I'm Lucas Blaze. I'm the caretaker of her as well as the house.

Pamela: Yes, not only god, we have one satan too(pointing towards John).

John: Shut up you devil's granny.

Lucas laughs off after listening to their conversations saying 'You guys are kids.....chote bhagwan(little lords)'.

Pamela turns at John and Mumkin and makes a displeased face towards them as Lucas calls them little lords. She imagines herself as a cute little devil wearing red with horns.

He makes them sit on a comfortable sofa in a room which has a beautiful chandelier on the top of the roof. The house is quite big with a lot of paintings, pottery and artifacts . The walls are colorful with hanoi flowers painted on them. Each corner was breathtaking as if one had entered an art museum or gallery.

Lucas: Please do tell me what you would like to have from strawberry, chocolate , blueberry or apple flavored pastries? Tea or coffee(standing with a notebook to take down their orders)

John:(promptly) for me chocolate pastry .I would not shy away from trying apple pastry too.

Pamela: (lightly with a light slap on John's thigh and whispering)John! We have come to visit an injured person who is in the healing phase, not to eat away at their house.

John: Aaaooo(whispering out due to light pain)But he is the one who is asking us,I didn't order him pastries!

Lucas: Sure. I'll be right back.

Pamela: Shame on you John. Why don't you learn something from Mumkin.

Mumkin is quietly looking around with a calm face.

Pamela: He's a complete gentleman.

John: No ,not that he's a gentleman. It's because his stomach is full as he ate at your uncle Nelon's place.

Pamela: Don't lie, I saw you too taking huge servings of main course thrice and desert four times.

John: You're a blind I think. Although I took those, I could eat none as your cousin Stella was just admiring me through her constant stare.

Pamela: Not admiring, she might be thinking who this hungry soul who hasn't eaten for centuries. Also don't make false stories. Stella was working in the kitchen all the time with her mother,you petu(hungry).

Lucas goes to the kitchen and returns back with two chocolate and apple pastries. Pastries looked mouth-watering and John couldn't stop but started eating .

Lucas: Kids, soon Miss Isabella will be arriving here. She's feeling better. I was on holiday that day, due to which she herself went out to buy her arts and crafts material .This unfortunate event occurred. Wish if we both were together,this wouldn't have happened.

As the trio were listening to Lucas, someone arrived on seeing whom John gulped out and found it difficult to eat .His hand started shaking after seeing her.

All three stand up in a thunderstorm.

John: Prof Olivia, what are you doing here?

Olivia: Wow John, don't you think the question has to be reversed? What are you doing in my house?

John: Prof Olivia, are you Miss Isabella?((whispering) as I recall Isabella was injured, but Prof Olivia looks absolutely perfect,in fact she's looking Junoesque.

Pamela:(whispering)John, Keep quiet! How can you make such a brainless claim?

John(whispering): See, kya pata inke ghar ka naam Isabella ho, hota hai logo ka(Her home name might be Isabella as some people have it).

• 43 •

Pamela(whispering):May be,

Mumkin:(whispering): Guys shut up, we're in a lion's cave now !

John: And the lioness is just in front of us(referring to Olivia)

Prof Olivia: John! Is the effect of pastry that your mind is disillusioned now? I am not Miss Isabella. Isabella lives with me. What blunder are you loose cannons planning today here in my house without permission?

Now the trio are able to connect dots where that day when they were caught by Prof Olivia, she left immediately because Isabella Martin, the lady who was attacked and robbed by the thief is related to Prof Olivia, probably her sister who is married as the surname is Martin. That day, when the trio were crossing the wall, hearing an unfortunate event with Isabella, Prof Olivia left them there itself asking them to leave to their hostels in order to visit her in hospital .

Lucas arrives there suddenly from the kitchen.

Lucas: Miss Olivia, they've come to see Isabella!

Prof Olivia: How are they knowing Bella?

Lucas: They are the ones who hospitalized Miss Isabella that day when she was attacked. Police mentioned that two young college boys helped Police get the thief arrested.

Prof Olivia:(tongue tied with earnest face) You three, come here.

The trio follow Olivia where they enter a small garden with orange trees and grape vines . It is covered with vivid spring flowers like sunflower, poppy,lobellias, portulaca and roses. There are three benches in the garden and one lady is sitting and writing. There is a puppy on her lap on whom she's embracing affection. She is Isabella Martin. She's a thin woman in late thirties sitting on a wheelchair wearing a peach colored gown . She isn't moving much as she hasn't recovered completely from her stab injury on leg on the day of attack. She has a gracious look on her face .

Prof Olivia: Bella, someone has come to see you. Drink your mug of milk with medicines(pointing towards the mug kept on the tea table) and go to rest on time. No work for more than thirty minutes!

Prof Olivia calls the name of Lucas where he arrives before her quickly within a few seconds.

Prof Olivia: Lucas,ensure that the routine is followed .Take care of the house and give Bella medicines till i come back.

Isabella: Sure(tries to stand up).

Prof Olivia: Don't stand! You're not in the condition to work.

Prof Olivia leaves.

Isabella: Are you three the ones who saved me on that unfortunate day?

Lucas:Yes Miss Isabella.

Isabella: I hope you could reach the correct address without much trouble.

The trio introduce them to Miss Isabella. Isabella shows artwork that includes her paintings on pots and walls. She says that only four of them live here including the mother of Prof Olivia. In free time she likes to do this artwork. She also takes them near the drawing room rolling her wheelchair where Pamela is astonished to see familiar books.The names are"The sages said this", ``Infidelity's innocence" and " Generosity's painful side".

Pamela: Do you also like reading Devkali Neelghanti Paul's book?

Isabella: Of course(looks at the trio for a second,smiles and then looks at the painting made by her of Jesus Christ with mother Mary.She then goes near an easel and touches it.)

Pamela: Have heard from a friend that she's an unhonoured writer despite writing useful stuff.

Isabella: Damn it! What an incompetent writer!

Mumkin: Amrisk said that her content is connected with sainthood and humanity.Humanity is over and above all vocations. According to me this writing style is of high worthiness .In fact I admire such writers!

Pamela sees eye to eye with Mumkin.(Isabella smiles at Mumkin and John had gone to the garden due to his disinterest in arts and paintings)

Isabella: I have many photocopies of these books.

Pamela: Why are you keeping so many photocopies?

Isabella:I don't know. Lucas brought them.

John was playing with Isabella's puppy . As he throws the ball in a direction, it hits the wall destroying a few hanging rosemary vines . The ball hits a pencil holder kept near the easel due to which items containing pen ,pencil and paint brushes are scattered.

Pamela(shouting): John,pagalu(mad person). If you stay here for more than one hour, you'll convert this beautiful house into an earthquake hit place.

John: Don't shout so badly at me. It was all an accident.

Pamela: This accident might not only rusticate you from the college but also from the world as Prof Olivia will kill you!

Pamela scolds John for his casualness and both start to keep the items back. Pamela finds a signature stamp named "Devkali Neelghanti Paul" . Pamela moves towards Isabella to inquire about it. She wants to know how the signature stamp of writer Devkali Neelghanti Paul is in Isabella's pencil Stand .

Pamela: How is this signature stamp in your house?

Isabella: What can you guess from it?

Pamela: Does Devkali Neelghanti live with you?

Isabella: Kind of. Actually I am that writer.

She is astonished to know Isabella's revelation that Devkali Neelghanti Paul is Isabella's pen name. The trio are surprised to know that Isabella is one who is the writer of the books mentioned by Amrisk.

Pamela: Miss Isabella! May I know why you did not mention about you being the writer Devkali Neelghanti Paul despite mentioning that we like your writing style ?

Isabella:It wouldn't have made any difference how much I owe you three what you've done to me by hospitalizing me on time . Thank you very much!I request you three to not reveal my pen name to others as I believe in anonymity.

John:Sure,probably that's a reason for so many copies of these books in your house.

Isabella: Yes, I give these books to various colleges and universities as they're using them in curriculum for philosophy. I don't want to write for money!Probably that's why I'm unable to make that much money.

They agree with her intention of writing and appreciate it. She discusses various topics with the trio from their interest areas like philosophy, psychology, business and politics.

John couldn't stand the discussion for too long and he entered another room where he sees a huge three dimensional model.He gets curious and inquires about the meaning of the landform mountains, island and vegetation.

Pamela: John, stop asking stupid questions. It's just an arts model. Since when did you start becoming a deep thinker?

Isabella:Well, this is not in the syllabus for me.

Pamela: What do you mean?

Isabella: I mean that….I actually don't remember what this model is all about!(looking tensed)

Pamela: That's fine, but why do you look so tense ?

Isabella: Who's tensed?

Isabella: No, not tensed…(awkward smile). I forgot about it(pointing towards the model….but I know it).

Mumkin: That's fine. Being a writer doesn't need you to be well grounded in everything.

Pamela: Especially at the minute grass landscape like this in which insignificant people like John can only take interest.

Isabella's eyes were down in doubt when Prof Olivia and Lucas entered the room.

Prof Olivia: It's a famous Konigsberg bridge problem. Bella, don't do more than what's needed.

Lucas: Yes, she needs to take that rest now.

John: Can you explain this more of this landscape thing Prof Olivia?

Prof Olivia:(explaining with help of a stick)This landform model is about a medieval German city that lay on the sides of Pregel river.At the center there are two large islands which are connected to each other and the river bank with seven bridges. So there was a mathematician who later became the mayor of the city who got obsessed with these islands and bridges. He asked one question about which route would allow someone to cross all seven bridges without crossing any of them more than once.

Mumkin: So do we need to think of a solution to this problem?

Prof Olivia looks emotionless gazing at the model. With her stern face she does a light blink directing them to think of a solution.

The trio think for a few seconds.

John: One can fly airplanes so the problem won't rise!

Prof Olivia: Did your ancestors raise this city? Try not to forget that it's a medieval city with no airplanes invention at that time.

John: Oh yes sorry.

Pamela(whispers to Mumkin): How rude Prof Olivia is (vexed).

She gives them a few more seconds to think but they don't come up with a solution.

Prof Olivia: If you think hard then you're a fool .

Mumkin : Why so?

Prof Olivia: The problem has no solution because it is impossible to do so!

John become irritable on hearing her answer to an impossible problem. By seeing John, her face turns even more stern, then she explains,

Prof Olivia: This led to the invention of the mathematical branch Graph Theory in mathematics invented by famous mathematician Euler who named this as Geometry of positions. Lucas, you continue.

She leaves from there.

Lucas takes out a cardboard which had a drawing of circles ,lines and dots which he called a simplified graph of the Konigberg bridge problem. He further explained to the trio that to cross the bridge one needed to remove any one bridge in this three dimensional structure.

Lucas: You know what,in reality too, in world war two, where the bombing was done that destroyed the two bridges of Konigsberg.

The trio are astonished to see the amount of knowledge the servant of Prof Olivia has. Normally they do household and a bit of administrative work. But this was just as rare as a four leaf clover.

They appreciated Prof Olivia's knowledge in multi disciplines . Her likely sister Isabella whom she calls Bella is creative too. Lucas further gave them more such examples that made them brainstorm. They enjoyed their time with him.

When the time arrived for them to leave, Mumkin and Pamela asked for a few books written by Isabella to broaden their horizon of knowledge .The books were brought by Lucas from the store room where extra printed copies of her books were kept. Lucas is an all rounder. He's the driver of Prof Olivia too. He drops the trio in Prof Olivia's Chevrolet car ,due to which they reach the hostel on time. Lucas drives them till University where they reach at five forty five pm.

Upon reaching the hostel,they went to their rooms. When Pamela enters the room,Laila gives her a few packets of green tea that she got from her paternal grandmother's home as they own farm lands doing green tea cultivation. With a steamingly hot mug of green tea and peanut butter cookies Pamela starts reading "The Sages Said This". Laila is sitting on her chair. She's looking outside the window. It's raining heavily. She squatted down. Her eyes are just on the droplets that are falling from the gray sky ,hitting the ground and diminishing. With a huge thunder, she squatted down on bed and tied her hair into a bun. She inclines towards Pamela and picks up one peanut butter cookie.

Pamela: It's too sweet!

Laila nods her head in agreement ,takes a bite of the cookie and then she keeps it half eaten on her table lamp. She looks at Pamela's face who's just engrossed in reading.

Laila: I'm just not feeling happy. The weather is gloomy. What are you reading?

Pamela: It's a philosophical book.

Laila: Can you read it for me too?

Pamela: Sure.

She read it out for Laila synopsis of book"The book talks about various ways a human being lives and develops, the perspectives that he develops through those experiences and which way is best in order to attain liberation and how one can live life following few rules to serve maximum to humanity. The book also made connections of human psychology with philosophy and salvation. It consisted of experiences of anonymous people who are working into various jobs around the world in the best ways from various vocations like social work, journalism ,defense and medicines etc. These people believe in considering the whole world as one where they enjoy culture ,people and render their help to the needy through their profession,ultimately forming a community known as 'the humanity ambassador' . The ones who are given help are made self-sufficient and when that happens, they join the community by helping others the way they were helped. Human salvation happens when good karmas are more than sins. The liberation of soul leads one to it's dissolution to Brahmna where suffering and happiness is all the same. Yet keeping this idea in mind the ultimate goal of this community is to help others rather than achieving salvation."

As Pamela was reading the book, Laila too got completely involved in listening to what Pamela was reading.

Pamela:Now I understand why this book is a flop. It lacks practicality.(closing the book)

Laila:This book is useful for depressed souls like me.

Pamela:Oh is it! I was planning to go to sleep, but I'll read it further for you.

The book had magnanimous quotes from Bhagwat Geeta, the hindu holy book. The five quotes read by Pamela were:

1. "No one who does good work will ever come to a bad end, either here or in the world to come"

2."It is better to live your own destiny imperfectly than to live an imitation of somebody else's life with perfection."

3."The peace of God is with those whose mind and soul are in harmony, who are free from desire and wrath, who know their own soul."

4."He who has let go of hatred who treats all beings with kindness and compassion, who is always serene, unmoved by pain or pleasure,"

5. "He who experiences the unity of life sees his own Self in all beings, and all beings in his own Self, and looks on everything with an impartial eye."

After reading thirty seven pages of the book, the hostel room's door knocks. When Laila opens the door, it's the warden Bloom.

Bloom: What's going on? You two are still awake? Trying to break the rule of no activity, only sleep after eleven pm. It's eleven ten, your lights are still on! Do you know the punishment for this? Shall I inform the authority? Which school do you two belong to? Your school rules are not applicable here!

After listening to warden Bloom, Pamela realizes that he is again questioning the same way as he questioned her last time with Mumkin and John when they came late to the hostel for the first time. She gets apprehensive of the punishment they might get now.

Pamela: We're very sorry Mr. Bloom. We'll just sleep now. It was the problem of mosquitos that disturbed us from sleep so we woke up again.

Bloom checks the room where he claps multiple times to kill mosquitos,he runs behind and stumbles upon bed legs and falls down in a funnier way that makes Pamela and Laila chuckle quietly . Then he calls the guard and asks him to put a mosquito killer coil in the room. He switches off the room's light after Pamela and Laila go to bed.

Pamela slept off and Laila was acting to sleep.

Laila reflects on the quotes that Pamela read out from the book, she extravagantes her thoughts about the guys she dated till now. She feels that she was lollygagging .She hated the guys she dated as they either cheated on her or they didn't want her presence in their lives as they found her depressed and uninteresting .Whenever she got a tattoo of their name, her trust was shattered as they all broke up with her after that .They all rejected her, leaving her in tears. Although at one point she thought of partying it out. But that didn't work well for her either as the effect of alcohol had no effect on her, leading to disruption of her peace of mind and low self esteem .However this book is changing her vision towards life.It is a different book as it stands out from her romantic collection of books. She never had any acquaintance with any philosophical books. Within three years of dating , she could never sleep peacefully. But today after hearing quotes, her hate is getting converted to forgiveness .She felt as if all pain that was accumulated in heart was gone now, feeling light from inside. She sleeps sweetly as if some spiritual power has held her on its lap.

Next day arrives, it is Monday.Another circular has been passed where Wednesday is the day from which the selection process of the committee starts, stating that it will take three to four days to complete the selection process. There won't be any class for students not appearing in the selection committee .Mumkin, Pamela and John are going to Majestics room to attend a session of counseling and therapy to be conducted by Prof Rehman. Majestics room is specially designed in a circular way. The center is the place where Therapy session is conducted by Prof Rehman and his team.Whole room is dark except the center place. The students sit around the circular seats. There is a camera that takes photos of the session automatically.Prof Rehman is the one who designed this room. He is a tall, handsome man with coffee brown eye color and dusky skin tone.

As the trio reach Majestics Hall where Laila Sim joins them. As they sit at their places. Prof Rehman arrives with his team. He introduces himself and his team members. As usual, he appears to be a friendly professor and his team contains senior students of psychology. Ren is also part of his team. They don't see Janny there.

Prof Rehman: Dear students, counseling and therapy is the core of Psychological studies. A counselor and a therapist needs to have certain types of characteristics. They need to be compassionate, excellent communicators, open minded ,genuine and patient while dealing with their client. With this a strong therapist and client alliance is built. Now Ren will be a client and I will nominate four students of Junior grades to Counsel him. We will reflect at the end which among the four students displayed the above mentioned qualities and is more suitable to become a therapist. I would like Eva Johnson,John Greze, Benny Sabastian and Pamela Brown to act as therapists one by one. John ,would you like to try your hand at it? Remember the theoretical aspects that are taught in class while doing the role play of a therapist.Case is that Ren suffers from low self esteem and he has issues in gelling up with people.

John whispers ,'I don't know about his esteem issues, but his gelling with others is a fuck sometimes due to his extreme high ego'.

Pamela chuckles and says 'Truly said John ' in return.

John goes near the center of the Hall where Ren is sitting . There is a table in between therapists and the client's chair .John sits on the therapist's chair and Ren is sitting on the client's chair. The conversation between them starts.

John: Hi , may I help you?

Ren: Yes, I don't feel good these days.

John: Hmmm. You don't feel good! Why

Ren: I don't know. I just don't feel good about myself.

John: You're a gray colored eye guy. Probably you're between average to good in your looks because you're tall but thin. I guess bodybuilding and wrestling will make you look better and you'll feel good about yourself after that. I feel good because of my fit physique.

The whole class frowns after John's comment on Ren. Ren himself gets a little disappointed from John.

Prof Rehman: Come back John. Not good!A therapist's role is very important in a client's life. Any bitter comment can do more harm than good. So no judgment on the client's appearance.(Looking towards class and holding the shoulder of John).John's comment on Ren isn't much appreciable. But I think if you practice more ,you'll understand better ,which will in turn make you a better therapist John. Better performance next time John. Eva Johnson, it's your turn.

John goes back to his seat .Pamela was constantly smiling at John and he was just looking a little lost. She tells Mumkin that whatever John said to Ren gave her a lot of emotional satisfaction as Ren has been mean to her .Mumkin tells her to ignore the mean comments of Ren as he isn't mature enough.

She says 'okay' to Mumkin while locking her hair behind her ears ,twisting her lips that shows her reluctance in agreeing to Mumkin.

Eva comes and sits on the therapist's chair facing Ren. The conversation between them starts.

Eva: Hi ,how are you?(smiling)

Ren: I don't feel good these days.(sad)

Eva: How do you feel?

Ren: I feel bad about myself and I think people don't like me.

Eva: Why do you think like that?

Ren: I don't know,I just feel like that!

Eva: Hey don't worry(she holds her hands with Ren's hand). I'm always there for you. Don't feel bad about yourself. Don't think that people don't like you, as I like you. You seem like a nice guy! In Fact we can go for a date after therapy sessions! (excited)

Ren is speechless and he starts looking at Prof Rehman with a slight smirk.Prof smirks back.Other students start laughing.

Prof Rehman: Good try at starting , but touching a client or asking them for a date is unprofessional. A therapist needs to deal with clients in a highly professional way. Students, better not ask for a date on the first day of meeting your clients . Eva, you can do better. Pamela, you can take the place of Eva.

Eva goes back to her place. Pamela comes and sits on the therapist's chair facing Ren. The conversation between them starts. Firsty she lifts her left eyebrow up and makes her lips twitch again. Ren lifts both of his eyebrows in irritation. After seeing a cold war between the two through facial expressions, Mumkin says 'Professor, I think we must start or else we'll lose time'. Professor Rehman, upon agreement with Mumkin, asks Pamela to start.

Pamela: Hey ,how are you?(her face expression suddenly changes from irritated to smiling)

Ren: I don't know,I'm not feeling good.(sad)

Pamela: Oh I'm sorry to hear that. I'm here to listen to you. Tell me how you feel?

Ren: I just don't feel good about myself. I think people are not liking me.

Pamela: I completely understand .Relax . I will count three, we'll inhale and exhale together. Why do you think people don't like you?

Ren pauses for a moment, he looks at Pamela's face that is filled with serenity and sincerity .Whatever arguments and fights they had before, there isn't any trace of it at all. He feels trust in her .There is a high amount of trust.

Pamela: You can always take your time and open up.

She remains quiet and there's silence all over the hall. Everyone's eyes are on both of them.

Ren: I think because none of my relationships were successful in the past!

Pamela: You believe that your relationships weren't successful in the past that makes you sad. Isn't it?

Ren:Yes.

Pamela: Since when are you feeling like this?

Ren: It's been a long time. You won't understand.

Pamela: I am sorry that I don't have a similar experience as yours . There's an experience that I want to share with you. Probably we both can connect through that.May I?

Ren: Sure.

Pamela:I have few childhood friends in my life, whom I still miss and wish to see . They are no longer part of my life. There are various reasons for that . Their families got transferred to different cities, few have their own lives and few just ignore.I understand the pain of not having the people around whom we loved once.

Ren: Hmmm.

Pamela: Coming to your side of the story, can you introspect what can be the reason for your relationship being unsuccessful?

Ren: I guess,mostly effort comes from my side. They stay for sometime and leave afterwards.

Pamela: Sometimes we need to find the right person. You were in a relationship where probably the person was not right for you. Although you made the effort, they were probably always on the advantageous side .A relationship is based on trust where the feeling of taking advantage doesn't come .

Ren is now quiet, he is very comfortable with Pamela's therapy. There's a pin drop silence in the hall as the therapy looks very real! Prof Rehman talks in between.

Prof Rehman: Well done ! Pamela, you have the right approach of therapy and you displayed compassion, genuinity , good communication and you were openly listening to client's problems. But remember that the right example has to be given as the relationship between a couple and that of with friends is a different thing!.

Pamela: Thank you professor. I'll work on my weak areas.

Prof Rehman: Sure, you can modify the weak areas to improve areas.

Okay everyone, we'll learn about the three types of counseling in the next class. Benny we'll have you first to roleplay as a therapist as today you couldn't get this opportunity due to lack of time .Others will also get similar opportunities soon in my next sessions.

Prof Rehman leaves from there. The class is over. As the trio are in the corridor going to attend the next class, Ren arrives there and says hello to Mumkin and John, but makes slight eye contact with Pamela almost trying to ignore her completely. Laila praises the role play skills of Pamela and she tells her to quickly leave towards the market for her tattoo removal and she displays her excitement towards reading the left out chapters of Isabella's book.

They attend the academic classes for the rest of the day and evening they move to the ground along with other students where sports teacher Kinen Zuna prepares them for fitness for the upcoming committee selection. After the practice, Mumkin and John go back to the hostel ,whereas Pamela and Laila go to a shop near the University for a tattoo removal appointment. John is tired so Mumkin alone goes out to the hostel to buy shoes for himself during selections as his present shoes are torn. As he purchases the shoes, he sees Pamela and Laila there .

Mumkin: How are you both doing here?

Pamela: Just came for Laila's tattoo removal.

Mumiin: These tattoos look cool, don't they? Why do you want to get them removed?

Laila: I want to get them removed. They're like baggage from the past which I am still carrying.

Mumkin remains quiet.

Pamela comes up with the appointment, that is next week. Removal of these tattoos will free Laila from her baggage as she believes to live a more meaningful life.

Mumkin :I never chose psychology because I was into this subject! But you can always share with me if you have any past experiences that still haunts you.

Laila darts crying. She tells him everything, about her relationship failures and with her heavy nostalgic emotions she hugs him! Her trust issues with men are dealing with depression deeply. She expresses her desire for a boyfriend who would constantly hug her, make her feel secure and kiss her whenever she's anxious.

Laila: Infact, I am aware that the surgery is going to be a really painful one but I am still ready for it!

Mumkin gives her a shoulder hug in order to calm down her aggravated emotional state. Later three of them drink a latte coffee. As they stand up to move back to their hostels, Laila sees an old friend of hers named Jack who invites her for a hard drink. She numbs for a second then refuses him saying that she isn't a party animal any more and wouldn't prefer to drink!

She wants to go with Pamela to read the book that is transforming her to live a more fulfilling way. As the trio get back to the University they get back to their respective hostel rooms. Laila takes the book from Pamela and reads aloud the quotes that Pamela had highlighted last time when she was reading it for her. Laila finds them cathartic. Soon Pamela reads ten more pages before eleven pm night and they go back to sleep.Now Laila sleeps with no regrets and she wants to wake up with a peaceful mind. As Pamela sees Laila who's having a new born spirit, she starts writing a letter to Miss Isabella, sharing her experience and showing gratitude for the way the book improved Laila's life. Soon they reach the University to attend classes. This time they are left early as from tomorrow is the Committee selection.

CHAPTER FIVE

The toughest selections ever!

It is 23 September, the day of committee selections. Laila wished them luck before they left the hostel and she stayed back as she couldn't apply for the Committee which had strict rules on no tattoos for candidates who are applying. There are six hundred twenty four students in total who are reporting in the University grounds occupying their chairs classwise. Mumkin, Pamela and John are sitting there too. They had to come well groomed with only one pen in their hand. All students had to ensure that they didn't carry any watch, handkerchief or any other accessory. Principal Blacksmith enters the ground and facilitates everyone to keep quiet and soon the selection starts. The students are asked to check under their tables, they find chits consisting of different numbers written on both sides with pink and green color each. Principal tells them to choose the number written on the pink color side, follow group leaders and keep the dual colored chits safe. As pre directed the sixty leaders including Benny Sabastian's group the students based on their numbers. Each group has twenty students. These groups are taken to thirty one different halls of the University, where testing will take place. Mumkin and John are now in two different groups. Pamela is in a group with Benny and Ren. In each hall, there are well groomed people who don't belong to the University as they haven't seen here before. In the hall where Mumkin is sitting, a Classy man enters, goes to the podium and gives instructions. In all halls consisting of twenty to twenty one students, instructions given are the same. When a classy person goes to the podium, tell them to sit according to the roll number allotted on the green side of the chit. Mumkin's number is 207, John is 330 and Pamela is 128. The students are instructed to unseal answer sheets when instructed. They are given a sealed question paper that has hunderend questions to be done in sixty minutes. The instructor instructs to write roll numbers and unseal both question paper and answer sheets and start writing answers. Mumkin observes on the top right side written as "Unique Association for Success(UAS)", he quickly realizes that the writing material is from the Amrisk's shop. He goes into deep thinking. He recalls the day when Amrisk was busy, probably it was because he was trying to provide the University with writing material for an upcoming exam. But he doubted why Amrisk didn't give this info to the trio when they reached his shop that day. He suddenly gets out of his thoughts and he remembered that the time was running out, he quickly opened the booklet that contained twenty aptitude questions based on analogies, classifications, reasoning and mirror images, twenty each questions based on general knowledge, basic science, mathematical skills and puzzles.

Students were rigorously solving questions, most of them struggling in mathematics and science as they have humanities background and Science students struggled with general knowledge. Few struggled with aptitude. Few finished the exam and they were asked to shut their mouths and wait by the examiner upon asking to leave early. As it seemed that there's very few minutes left or time was already up, then the Examiner rang the bell and asked them to lift their both hands up, stand up, move in que and leave the room. Mumkin, Pamela and John met each other. Pamela tells them that like criminals they've been asked to lift up their hands and walk. This college is not just a zoo but a prison too. John replies that 'Yeah, zoo where violent animals like you Pamela take admission to learn humaness through psychology'. Pamela lightly punches John on his shoulder indicating him to shut up.

Along with other students they move out, where they are served coffee and hot dogs. As the trio are standing in que, the discussion happens.

Mumkin: How was the test? For a moment I thought I wouldn't be able to complete it!

Pamela said that she did all hundred questions and John did some ninety of them. Still skeptical about his performance, Mumkin tells Pamela and John that he thinks he won't be able to make it in the next round. Ren, Benny

,Fred and Daniel join the trio too. Fred and Daniel are self assured with their selections. Benny doesn't share any thought , instead he snatches Pamela's hotdog, takes a bite and returns it back with the purpose of teasing her. As Pamela sees Ren, he makes eye contact with her, turns back after taking his snacks and returns back to Janny who isn't taking the committee selection test but she has come to support him. Suddenly John comes in front of Pamela, he asks her to move away from a big wolf spider . Pamela shouts out loudly and takes three steps backward, loses balance and is about to hit the ground when John holds her hand and lifts her up. Mumkin steps on the spider and kills it finally. They hear an announcement.

Prof Olivia: All, return back to your seats now. Quick or else it will be taken as rustication from the committee selections.

All students return to their seats. There comes a gentleman with spectacles from the committee selection team who introduces himself as Philip Hielmaster .

Hielmaster: Good morning, ladies and gentlemen(crowd wish him back). So feeble, who all missed eating the snacks?Was prof Olivia the reason for speaking so feebly as you are scared of her?

The crowd laughs and Prof Olivia standing on the left side down the podium gives a quasi smile for half a second and becomes unresponsive again with a stern face.

Hielmaster : I'm going to announce names to students who made it to the next round of the committee based on an intelligence test. Those who don't need to leave university quickly as per directions of the committee. The selected ones will be guided by respective leaders. The people who are selected for next round are- Jim Gua, Manasa, Lilly John, Benny Sabastian, Diha Azan, Alax Pitruda, Pamela Brown, Kiki Won, Bessy Thomson, John Breze, Palkunia Johnson, Ren, Alacia, Bravoz Woodsmith.......

Many students didn't hear their name and got a message from Hielmaster that they weren't selected.This included Mumkin and Fred . As Mumkin was moving back to the University he got various thoughts that it might be a mistake , a miserable mistake where Hielmaester might have announced the names of unselected students as selected, thus reversing the order. He feels as if he has missed an opportunity. He goes to the canteen of his hostel and buys two lemon balm tea. He heads towards the Prism tower which is the longest tower of his University. This is the first time when he isn't having his friends John and Pamela with him.They both made it to the next round. After reading the top he finds Janny there. She recognizes him and tells her that she isn't in love with Ren. She considers Ren as an immature guy who is emotionally and physically dependent on her. She doesn't find her future with him . In Fact she is with him due to his affluent family background. She wants to be into journalism. Ren's endearment has enslaved her. She further tells Mumkin that she doesn't want Ren anymore. She goes near Mumkin and her eyes get filled with tears and she gets closer further where Mumkin can feel warm air blowing through her exhale. She is about to kiss him, but Mumkin takes a step back, says sorry and leaves. He hears an inner voice that Ren is his friend who loves Janny, letting Janny kiss him is actually perfidy on Ren. Mumkin leaves the place.He finds Laila in front of the hostel .She tries to communicate with him, she goes near him and holds his hand.

Laila: Mumkin, I want to talk with you.

Mumkin: (Leaving her hand) Sorry Laila, now.

He takes the sideway of Laila and starts moving in the direction opposite to her. She stops him

Laila:I know it's Mumkin, that you couldn't make it in committee . That is why you're sad and seeking alone time. Fred told me about you and him.

Mumkin stops, moves back to Laila.

Mumkin: Yes, I wanted to be there in the committee. I'm disappointed that I did not make it.

Laila: Don't worry , you can try for selection next year if they conduct selections. Who knows what the committee is all about? It can be a futile committee too.

Mumkin: No idea if such selections will be conducted again and a committee will be made for it! Indeed I believe that it's not futile but a paramount. That's why selections are so tough! Majority of the students couldn't make it.

Laila takes Mumkin to a shady place in the park where the red, pink and yellow roses are blooming and colorful butterflies are flying. They both sit there under a banyan tree.

Laila: You know Mumkin, these colorful butterflies are actually transparent . They are not two legged but four legged. This is the reflection through the multi miniature scales, due to which we see colors. Do you know how many days they can live?

Mumkin: Probably a few weeks.

Laila: Yes ,four weeks . But that doesn't make it debilitated, through pollination butterflies become predominant in the ecosystem. Its colorless wings aren't weak but strongest as change of its behavior can flip and change the ecosystem's egalitarianism. That's the power of a butterfly! What can be the potential of this six point two feet tall and seventy three kg boy with his brain power of around one thousand three hundred seventy grams.(pointing towards Mumkin).

On hearing Laila Mumkin starts chortling of this new transformation. How an introverted tattooed girl in class who once was addicted to alcohol parties is now a motivator in his life . She is interpreting human existence, their strength and probably making Mumkin fall in love with her. On asking this, Laila reiterates about the book that Pamela reads for her written by Devkali Neelghanti Paul . Mumkin too recalls that he hasn't seen the book due to his over ornate routine from the past three days. She tells him the meaning of Brahmana and various quotes for salvation of human beings. They both discuss the human brain, the speciality of human organs, the bewilderness of the Universe and Mumkin shares his dream of selling weapons through the Armed Forces for the first time with Laila. She provides moral support to him by saying that she trusts his abilities. Then they go back to their respective hostel rooms after a kiss between them. Mumkin assures himself that he will read the books given by Miss Isabela to him .He also plans that he will exchange the books with Pamela once he's done with reading.

On the other hand the selected students are just one twenty in number selected for the next round of committee selections. Pamela, John, Ren and Benny are feeling bad for Mumkin and Fred. Hielmaster tells them to go back to their respective hostels and arrive tomorrow morning at 8 AM for the second stage. As John enters the room, he sees Mumkin sleeping with his hand placed on the book which is kept on the table.John wakes him up. They chit chat and then John leaves the room to get a fever medicine as he is feeling febrile. Mumkin opens one of the two books written by Devkali Neelghanti Paul which is the same as that of Pamela``The sages said this". He reads eleven pages of it and could make connections with Laila's contentment. Mumkin understands that the part that Pamela called boring is actually healing Laila. He appreciates Bhagwat Geeta's quotes and closes the book on twenty third pages. He then keeps this book on table and picks up the second book just to take a glance of it, as he decides that he makes a plan that he will go out with John after reading a little from the second book. As he opens the book, he finds that it's actually not a book. In Fact it's like the written notes of someone. As he turns the pages and moves to the first one, he realizes that it's a diary entry named "ALORA DIARIES". Mumkin assumes that the book has mistakenly come to him. He glances through it.

ALORA DIARIES

10 June,

"There faces were worth watching ,when they saw me sitting and gaping upon them wearing the dog's leash. From the fire of my eyes itself they got to know that the leader of the student council is revolting against the notice of the University to make Uniform necessary. Almost three fourth of the University students are rebellious , after all we're not school students. And finally kudos to this knockout girl, yeah I'm referring to my brilliant idea that the whole shitting plan of University to control students and make their lives excruciating is in vain. From now onwards till forever, no student in Himbertown University would ever have to wear the Uniform! This all drama I created wearing my bra and panti only with that 'Fuck off uniform written ,we're not dogs' written on our flag of protest. Every professor and principal were just gazing at me. But this time there was a handsome man who was just looking at me as if I'm acting immature.

14 July 1934, 11 AM, As I walked through the corridor I realized a group of students working on some sort of plan. I peeped in . They invited me to be a part of a chemistry project. A project that is envisioned to make our military stronger. I straight away said yes! and joined the team. I don't know much about the military although my dad was in it whom we lost when I was a kid. I joined this programme because I know that my intellect will be stimulated,along with that I'll get new resources for Chemistry experimentation. I don't know where I'll be heading with this project.

Today working wasn't easy as I wore a crop top and pants . With a little more cleavage, others found it difficult to focus too. Swear I need to be less fashionable to work here"

Few pages of the book were torn. There was inconsistency in writing.

25 Aug,

"It's going well! Project's plan is riveting.I have in fact very similar people. We are a team of ten students working. They made me the vice president of the project. Probably they find me highly intelligent! Haha. Not just that Alora, it's just that I'm gifted with passion to work deliberately in this field. Blueprints are made, soon we'll start with a project. I am going to U.M.B.A.S. book store. It's Unique MIlitary Base Association with Students. The shop is specifically designed to collaborate students with the Military to prepare them for war. Probably I might find something which can help our project to grow at a fast pace as the Government is hinting that in future we might face a war due to fast progress of our country.I don't care about war, but I do care about becoming the best scientist. Yeah but I will not shy away from standing with the country during war, the way my father did!It's like a single arrow hitting two targets. Both country's need and my ambition "

16 Sept ,

"Wook man. I searched a lot and finally discovered four books that have specific mention of what the military requires. I wrote a letter for the same to the Military. Soon there will be personnels from the Military and other students from separate courses who will be joining us in the project for guidance and assistance. And Alora the most lively part of today is Amrisk, he's the bookseller. I've spoken to him. He mentioned that he recently joined his ancestral business and they provide all books, especially to the books related to the military. He will further assist me in searching for good books in the Military. Indeed a very helpful person, I appreciate his helpfulness.The best thing about his shop is the black coffee and doughnuts that he offers exclusively to me whenever I visit him. My tummy is filled with that. I am lying on my bed with a cozy blanket. Very sleepy, good night Alora . "

20 Nov,

Soon Mumkin smells that this book is mentioning Amrisk,Military and some project of college students with collaboration of Military personals. He recalls that the story is kind of similar to the batch of 1935 students that the trio found in Amrisk's shop.They were also selected in the Military due to a similar project. He is excited now to know more or written more in the book, whether the dots he's trying to connect are making the right sense or not. He straight away reads the other pages.

30 Dec,

" The day was full of events . Two more people from different backgrounds joined us .Jonathan Williams and Tiger Watson. Tiger is a student from the engineering branch.He is brother of professor William, the one in psychology . He's a funny guy, who became friends with us as soon as we met him. The other guy, Tiger Watson, he's in Business Management. He seems high at intellectual level as he answers most of my doubts. He has a good knowledge of the Military . He says that there's a business with the Military that his family is in. He is an extremely rich person ,but he doesn't interact much with people. Reason is his arrogance! He was quite rude when Leisley asked him out for coffee after work. Weird guy, I mean who refuses by saying "I like coffee of bottle gourd flavor which no shop can provide. Coffee with you in your fuckin dreams!". We'll hope he helps us in making the project complete as not only Leisley ,he's rude with the majority of the other people. He sits in one place and doesn't want to contribute much until I approach him for doubts ."

19 Feb,

"We're making some amendments in the project as we think that the capacity of rifles can be enhanced to eight bullets as compared to the present capacity of five bullets. This is one of the innovative projects as it will actually enhance the capacity of our soldiers too. We're doing the modifications. Amrisk is proving concerned books with knowledge of the same and finally he gave us special writing materials, especially the leathered pen that can work for at least ten years without refilling them . Very useful in making continuous notes. He gave me a pocket diary that is portable. When I tried to pay him money for the stuff, he refused by saying that he considers me as his friend and he won't charge any. "

29 March

"Jonathan Willaims , Tiger Watson and I have been selected to prepare a chemical at a certain price. We three went out today for a coffee so that we can discuss our plan after work. Jonathan is really good at catching ideas but Tiger doesn't seem to be interested.I don't understand why he has been put up in this project? He's highly egoistic, I mean although he has great knowledge and ideas of projects but the heart of a person should matter too. He has a very antisocial personality. He takes everything so seriously and gives an exasperated look at us whenever we laugh at any joke. But at the coffee shop the time was spent intellectually between me and Jonathan. Tiger ignored him completely and answered my two questions. I want to sleep with a light heart now. Let me appreciate that the drizzling in the evening before arriving at the hostel made my mood happy . Work and student life are in balance."

14May

"Tiger ,as he came today in the room where I was experimenting with Jonathan, he threw away the beaker . He tore an empty page of my notes and after snatching my pen from me , writing on the notebook wrote "Come to my place right now!" . He tore away the page ,gave it to me in my hand and snapped his fingers on my face. The first thing that comes to my mind after seeing his behavior is what an obsessive wild man he is. Am I a slut that he's calling me to his place? Apart from clearing my doubts, he spoke just once till now in all discussions I had with him and Jonathan. He just spoke about his successful business ,money and flounting on his ancestral property. Not only me, everyone sees him as a shallow person. I had to say no to and feel sorry for that. He got really angry , bangged the door and walked away. He looked frustrated. I felt that his proposal can never be love ,in fact it looked like he's demanding something else...... Poor Tiger, I wish he gets someone better than me as I don't feel anything for him and can't take his tantrums. Now with this behavior ,I would never date him my entire life even though he's the last man on earth."

26 July

"None of us can believe what really happened today. General Alexander of Himbertown came today. He really liked the idea explained by me. Of Course my best friend Jonathan also has a huge contribution here.As we displayed our final rifles with increased capacity of bullets, lightweight and advanced chemical formula, he appreciated our work. He kept an option for the three of us to join the Military. I mean seriously man? Who would refuse that but Tiger did! It's a blessing in disguise .Who would like to work with that creep? At the start of the project I was concerned about fulfilling my intellect but now working in a team with the Military personnels has taught me that Military projects are far bigger than my intellect . In Fact both are related. Jonathan and I are excited to join the Military. Woohoo"

17 Aug

"The first day of the Military is unfamiliar. As I recall, my mother always missed my father who sacrificed his life for the country during war . I was just three years old. I'm sure Alora, dad must be proud of me. Just the day before yesterday I realized that history is repeating. Who knows , I might become an important part during the country's emergency! My blood is just driving up the wall for it. I'm excited to meet trainers ,and will do everything to keep my mom and family happy. Will never put down my dad. Just going to sleep to wake up tomorrow,timing is antithetical from hostel timings . Hostel's life was full of freedom, no one to do surveillance, we didn't have warden there. But here there are always two or more seniors who check on us. I thought joining military would be like turn up for the books"

17 Sept

"Alora! I can't write....I just can't because the schedules are packed, morning four am till night eleven pm is all continuous work, I and Williams entered the military training. It's the toughest training in an extreme way. There is one senior who wants to harass me.He forcefully bent my head in dirty rain water on the ground,I still don't know the reason for doing so. But I think he believes that I'm not fit to join the Military as I'm a woman. I'm worried till what extent he'll go! I am the only girl present there. Yesterday he made me do forty push ups in heavy rain. I feel lonely but I'm hopeful to become a good soldier. There are many good things here if we ignore him".

27Oct

"I was going for a break in between training, that same senior stopped me, he asked me to bend down . He was carrying a cane through which he hit trainees. He hit Williams, Joshua and Brian about ten times in each leg. They were crying loudly in pain. As he was about to hit me, I found myself already crying, drops of sweat irritated my eyes and I could read his name on his name plate as AJ Handon. He hit me in the knees after that he said 'For what hell a woman has entered the Military? Fuck'. He kept hitting my knees until they bled profusely. I couldn't speak much as it was really traumatizing. Things turned blur for me, still he didn't stop. Williams told me that he stopped until I was on ground and the sand on earth turned red. Nurse Samantha came to put ointment on wounds and she brought me back to consciousness . Still there wasn't any action taken on beating me like that as none of us can raise our voice against the seniors in the military due to

the hierarchy."

1 Nov

"Jesus, on the third day of training we had rifle practice. I am able to do almost everything but drill parade, oooops, it's one of the most difficult things to do. Probably the most strenuous one, I'm not coordinating that well with six to seven feet tall fellow male trainees. They all blame me for their bad contingent formation. But I want to stay here and prove to others that women are not liabilities but the biggest assets. So far I have understood that here respect is not not given for free, it has to be earned. I will not give up, no matter how much I have to suffer in this training.``

4 Nov

" I had to climb a rock today , but my two feet long hair opened, I lost my balance and was about to meet a mishap. There was a new officer who called the rescue team at the right time through a whistle. The team held my rope and brought me down.Other men trainees with me got exasperated too. He's that officer only who saw me rebelling against the college uniform code. I though he hated me because I was rebelling as a feminist wearing my innerware only, but he actually saved my life. Commander Handon angrily took out his rifle and pointed towards me. He said he would shoot me right away. As I was about to get shot by him something good happened.As I shivered in consternation ,this officer who's supposed to be AJ's friend came in between. He's endearing, the way he wished me"Hello lady, you probably are the only girl from Himbertown University to do the training of the Military to support the armed forces. Proud of you. How's it going? " . I was still tepid. As I was about to say something, Commander Handon pulled his rifle back, he introduced this person to my male batchmates as his fellow commander cum batchmate Charles Chamburt, who has come back to train us after ten days of holidays. AJ Handon , in front of everybody, warned me that if I make such a mistake again, then his rifle will drink my blood away! What a crook he is."

After seeing this name Mumkin is dazed. Charles Chamburt is the name of Mumkin's father. He wants to know now, who's the author of this diary. For a moment he speculates it to be Isabella, as she mentioned it before to Mumkin , Pamela and John in their first meeting. Now he's convinced that the diary belongs to Isabella who is only Lidiya Cheriyan. So now, Prof Olivia's related person Isabella, who probably is her sister, is only Lidiya Cheriyan for which the trio and Ren have been inquiring for a long time in this entire world.He thinks that this is the biggest enlightenment of the world. But there were many more yet to come in reality.

He wants to read more but he doesn't realize that it's ten thirty pm, he looks to his left side and finds John already sleeping there. He keeps the diary back and turns off his light and goes to sleep.

The next morning is the selection process again. Mumkin and Laila wish luck to Pamela, John, Ren and Benny with the selections , after which the two go out of University. Laila sees the various flamboyant wine shops due to which she gets out of her impulse and starts running towards the shop on the other side of the road before she collides with a wheelbarrow carrying garbage. Mumkin runs to reach out to her to help .He holds her hand and lids her up. The person with the wheelbarrow also fell down with his wheelbarrow. He calls Laila an idiot and says 'Are you drunk?Can't you see and walk'. Upon which she replies 'Not yet, but was about to get drunk'. Mumkin chuckles on hearing Laila's answer. Seeing garbage scattered the guy further admonishes Laila,Mumkin firstly defends her by asking the guy to use wise words while interacting with ladies ,but he also asks for an apology on behalf of her as she was the one who collided with the wheelbarrow inorder to get drunk. He helps the guy in keeping his garbage bags back and gives compensation in form of a little money from his pocket money due to which the guy gets happy and leaves from there .He leaves the place by holding Laila's shoulder as her knee is injured to provide her with support. He takes her on his lap where they leave for the University clinic .

Warden Atrika Bloom sees both of them . He comes in front of Mumkin who's breathing heavily as Laila is on his lap.

Bloom: Where are you both going? Why are you going like this? Why is it in your lap? Are the newly formed couple of college? Don't you know the rules of college? Do you have any idea if I should tell Prof Olivia? Do you know what punishment is given to couples in college?

Mumkin whispers in Laila's ear: Have you seen monkeys with cymbals? Once you plug in the key, they keep playing the cymbals. Warden Bloom is like that monkey toy.

Laila chuckles.

Bloom: You didn't answer my question. You think I am a fool to stand here. What do you think of yourself? Don't you know that you're in your first year only? Are you trying to compare yourself with other students of other colleges? Don't you know how undisciplined they are ?

Mumkin : Sir, you can ask these questions later, she's my aunt's daughter and was injured as she fell down on the road as she was running after the candy van to buy candies. We aren't couples as she's technically my cousin. I'm just trying to be kind with her.

Bloom: Put down your cousin right now! Don't hold her like that after all she's your cousin, I'll get a wheelchair arranged . You both wait.

Bloom leaves from there.

Laila gets angry at Mumkin saying 'Oh, so I am your aunt's daughter, your cousin's sister and you're trying to be kind with me! Really(enraged). You're a liar Mumkin, I hate you(blows her cheeks in anger)'.

Mumkin lifts her again and says 'darling ,I had to lie to save ourselves. Also everything is fair in love and war, be it a lie'. He holds her cheeks with his hands and pampers her with love,seeking for forgiveness.

The nurse applies the antiseptic dressing. He drops Laila till her room in a wheelchair and tells her to take care of herself. Then he goes back towards the shop of Amrisk. During the way, he is connecting the dots . Questions that are coming in his mind are- Does Amrisk know about Mumkin's father? Who is Lidiya Cheriyan? The confirmation whether if Prof Olivia's sister Isabella and Lidiya the same person, why Amrisk shop's name is changed from UMBAS (Unique Military Base Association With Students) to UAS(Unique Association with Students), why didn't Amrisk mention about providing material to the University for Committee selection?

As Mumkin was near the University gate he heard John's voice. As he turns back ,he sees John running towards him. He tells him that Principal Blacksmith wants to meet him as he is being pushed for the second stage of committee selections. Mumkin gets astonished with news, on inquiring further John tells him that he doesn't know much about Principal's decision but heard someone near office saying that one staff member of college eyewitnessed that Mumkin ran behind the thief and got him caught by Police on the day while they were returning from Amrisk's shop. This might be the reason for his recommendation into the second stage. Both Mumkin and John head towards the principal's office.They were asked to wait outside. Warden Bloom takes them inside the Office room, which is a fully furnished room with trophies and medals of achievement . Mumkin and John wish morning to Principal Blacksmith.

Principal Blacksmith: Good morning young man, do you know why you've been called here?

Mumkin: No sir.

Principal Blacksmith:Apparently today the game of probability favored you Mumkin, it was your roll number that came out from six hundred twenty three students for one vacancy. You can leave now. Join others for next round selections . All the best!

Mumkin couldn't believe what he heard just now, as till now this was his luckiest day. He has never been that lucky in anything even including ticking the right answer in multiple choice questions of exams. Since morning the day has been great for him,in the beginning he got to spend time with his girlfriend Laila. He also made it to committee.

As Mumkin was listening to Principal Blacksmith, he was stuck to find the photograph of his father with Principal blacksmith and Professor William. He couldn't ask Principal Blacksmith as Warden Bloom comes to take both of them outside the office. After leaving from there, Mumkin feels that he doesn't want to be part of committee selections just based on luck. He believes in his abilities but John tells him not to think in those terms and calls him "estimable ". The duo reunites with rest members selected for the second round of committee selections. Pamela congratulated Mumkin upon his arrival . Then Philip Hielmaster arrived with Prof Olivia,where she asked all students to assemble in Gandhi hall. It's a huge hall painted with green and light green colors with symbols of The rainbow. A rainbow peace flag, the broken rifle, the white poppy, the 'V' hand sign and a big painting of Mahatma Gandhi displaying peace. The students were assigned random numbers on a chit of papers and they were made to sit in an arrangement according to the numbers allotted. Mr. Hielmaster steps up on stage and addresses students about the second stage.

Hielmaster: Dear students, as you have come to the second stage where the number is twenty two now from six forty five. That shows how deserving you all are! Congratulations to all of you for making this far in selections.

Now let's start with the next test, which is based on psychological testing . There is a battery of tests based on human behavior. Mr. Bloom ,please circulate the answer sheets to students.

As Warden Bloom circulated the answer sheets, it was again of Amrisk's shop. Mumkin recalls visiting Amrisk's shop after the second round of selections. Mr. Hielmaster further addresses.

Hielmaster: You will not write anything on the answer sheet until instructed or else it'll lead to your disqualification. A question paper will contain three parts starting with writing a paragraph about yourself for around five hundred words. The second part has completion of sentences, the third part is see, think and wonder based on patterns observed. You can comprehend these patterns into anything you see and imagination is all up to you. Frame your understanding and give a conclusion based on that. Time given is half hours for each. After the bell rings every half hour, move on to the next part. Ensure handwriting is clean. Our psychologists will check the test but assume Prof Olivia is correcting,or without correction ma'am will disqualify you. So write neatly(sarcastically), show trepidation!

Everyone laughs.

Mumkin is a little skeptical with the question paper pattern. Pamela sees the test more as an English test as it has sentence making and paragraph writing etc in the first page.

Hielmaster rings up the first bell to give indication that the test has started.

Mumkin, in the first part, writes about his family members. He writes that he belongs to Ranidetro village where it's rural area based on farming and dairy products. He mentioned about his father whom he loves the most and misses him in his life. He writes about his desires that he had if his father was alive i.e. of going fishing early in the morning in his village's river, polishing his shoe and his father making him sit on his shoulder while returning back. He describes his mother as a serene breath after suffocating tiredness of work. The family of three eat together under a tree while having woodfire cooked fish with rice afternoons, followed by muskmelons.The sugar granules on them are enhancing the taste buds of his mother but his father is disgusted. Still eating quietly. He mentions his dreams of building highly sufficient weaponry to armed forces as his father always spoke about weapons. In the next two fifty words he mentions about the details of his education, his favorite cuisines and his reading habits. He further mentions Isabella's books and how consistent reflection from those is transforming lives of people. He writes about John and Pamela, where both always accompany him. Pamela is a curious cat who brings various life puzzles to solve like the mystery of Lidiya Cheriyan. He also writes about Laila as a new friend in his life who is a supportive and caring person. He writes about his future plans of discontinuing the subject of Psychology and doing a management course next year.

After that the second bell rings giving indication to start with the second part of the exam. Mumkin opens the booklet of sentences like I am in love with a girl who loves someone else I will……., I see an accident , I will….., senior's girlfriend for me is …… biggest promise I have made to someone is ………, I am guilty of……The thing that I hate the most is ……all these fill in the blank sentences are making upto fifty questions. Mumkin starts completing all the sentences as I am in love with a girl who loves someone else I will move on to explore other venues in life and wish her luck, I see an accident call ambulance ,hospitalize and ensure least loss takes place, senior's girlfriend for me is Madam senior, biggest promise I have made to someone is helpful to all and good human, this is promise that I made to my father, I am guilty of nothing , The thing that I hate the most is traitor trying to harm country's peace……

Mumkin keeps on writing the similar sort of responses upto thirty nine when the bell rings for next round. Still there were thirteen sentences left incomplete by him. Mumkin opens the third booklet that contains patterns. It was just dots. He connects them as the dancing dots- belle dancers, people going for picnics in mountains, girl making gift wrap for her lover ,giving a farewell party to seniors and making super technological rifles. He writes the above things in almost twenty pictures before the bell rings .

John writes about himself as the guy who loves to workout. He tries to be a cool dude but dull in studies. He likes modern girls but from inside he wants a girl who loves him deeply. His world revolves around love. The second love of his life is his starting own business and he hates when other people discourage him in doing so. He wants to live life happily with his wife in future and wants to give her a protected life.

After his introduction in the first part, in the second part of sentence completion his answers are metamorphosed into different directions from his introduction. John writes- I am in love with a girl who loves someone else I will buy that girl gifts and win her to steal her away from her boyfriend, I see an accident help in controlling situation , senior's girlfriend for me is attractive or unattractive based on her looks, biggest promise I have made to someone is to not to lie to her, I am guilty of probably making mistakes as I never took help from anyone in knowing how to impress girls so faced various rejections .The thing that I hate the most is reading any book apart from comic .... In the third part he connects the dots with various comic characters doing different things, food testing, stories of movies, children singing songs etc.

Pamela in her introduction writes that she calls herself the lover of this world as she loves every single thing that she might find fun. Like being with children, or on the beach or blowing bubbles from the soap solution. She loves her parents a lot . She believes in the power of healing of every broken thing. She wants to help as many people as she can through her counseling. She hates violence and condemns people who do it especially when there is rape, murder and sexual assault on women and children. But becoming the victim of one of those is her nightmare as she's scared to confront her perpetrator. For her, the perpetrator is evil who not only harms physically but steals the soul away forever leaving a life spiritless.

Whereas Pamela completes the sentences in following way- I am in love with a guy who loves someone else I will give him freedom to make choice, I see an accident will help in giving the first aid by calling for help , senior's boyfriend for me is senior, biggest promise I have made to someone is to nurture people around me ,always, I am guilty of not being able to help a friend through counseling completely ,unfortunately he committed suicide, The thing that I hate the most is sitting idely and doing nothing.... In the third part of the test i.e. connecting dots, she connects the dots while imaging dots as characters that have different ailments with their mental health and she is the center dot which is helping them out for their mental well being .She imagines that the dots are giving her movement therapy, counseling and being a nurse.

Other students too wrote their answers - I am in love with a girl who loves someone else I will give up upon her, fight with the guy,love her more, kill her....., I see an accident i will ignore, I can't see blood, help in call police, give painkiller.....senior's girlfriend for me is senior's girlfriend, beautiful, ugly in comparison to my girlfriend, not matching that great with senior, crazy girl.... biggest promise I have made to someone is to be loyal, make up love everyday, bring money to my family, help in orphanage, drink milk everyday...I am guilty of betraying religion, cheating on my girlfriend, drinking too much late at night, wasting time,stealing hearts of girls, being too good..... The thing that I hate the most is exercise, submitting assignments, someone gaslighting me ,ugly people.....

There were a number of responses written by all people. After the second stage exams the students headed to have their breakfast. Mumkin was just thinking about meeting Amrisk and continuing reading the book given by Lucas that suggests Isabella and Lidiya are the same person. He isn't concerned about his selection in committee for the next stage as if it's death after death then there is no more death. Because he already has seen the rejection in the first stage. So a second rejection will not matter much. All the answers he wrote were his candid responses. In the dining hall Mumkin, Pamela and John are sitting together. Pamela was just getting worried about the result of selections for the next stage . While having breakfast she drops off her spoon in a hurry. As she tries to pick it up, Mumkin picks it for her and she shows her palm to take it from him. But he keeps it away.

Pamela(feeble voice): Mumkin, can you hand over my spoon back to me please.

Mumkin: Pamela, why do you want to use the spoon that has fallen down on the ground? Don't you think it's dirty with germs?

Pamela: Oh yes, it just completely went off my mind. Let me get a new spoon for myself.

Mumkin: Here(giving his spoon to her), you take this. I will drink soup directly from the bowl.Wait, where is your soup?

Pamela: Thanks Mumkin, but I don't think I need a spoon as I forgot to carry my soup from the cafeteria. I just bought sandwitches.I think I need to go back there to get my soup bowl.

Mumkin: What happened to you , you look not that confident as usual!

Pamela: I'm just nervous with my selection.

John: Oh gosh Pamela, for heaven's sake don't be like this. Look at me, whether I make or not in the committee, I'm enjoying my breakfast. You too enjoy it . Don't be a cry baby as it's making me uncomfortable to have food.

Pamela:Why are you feeling uncomfortable?

John: Because you're getting too emotional with selections that's making me also nervous now. So stop it right away.

Pamela feels more disappointed.

Pamela: John I'm not doing it intentionally. I don't feel like eating now.

Mumkin: Okay, Pamela, I understand what you're going through ,but chill. Be like the colorful bird that we see in you everyday. Enjoy your breakfast. John you too, calm down. It's the way she's feeling and she can't deny it.At Least that much I have learnt from our psychology course.

Pamela and John chucke over his last sentence.

The trio eat their breakfast fast and Mumkin assures both of them that the result will be in the favor of the trio only.

As directed at the previous stage everyone is asked to assemble in Gandhi hall again. Hielmaster enters the Hall. He addresses all.

Hielmaser: Hello ladies and gentlemen. So congratulations to all that your writing was readable by our psychologists ,that has been successfully assessed. However there are six of you who made it to the next stage.Let's start with reverse order. These eunoia are -Zeena, Rose, Ren, Pamela, Bessy and last but not the least Mumkin Chamburt. Pamela takes a sign of relief, Mumkin and Ren were unaffected .

Mumkin was deeply thinking about notes in diary after Hielmaster left the stage. He felt a sudden excitement thrilled with anxiety where he got curious about the next stage of committee selections as the diary of Lidiya might give some clues. His thinking is diverted now ,more focused towards the selections. Benny and John are disappointed as they don't hear their names. John says good luck for the next stage to Mumkin and Pamela before he leaves from there kiddingly saying 'You scared me ,but you yourself made it through selections. What a masked girl you are Pamela!'.

Hielmaster: Those selected will have to come after two days on Saturday for the next stage of selection. Good luck to those who couldn't make it. Don't get disappointed as this is not the end but just the beginning. We have our own requirements for the committee.Unfortunately the selected ones will only come to know what the committee is all about,so don't have any regrets in your heart. Should you have? Naah...

Prof Olivia orders everyone to disperse and takes a look at the form handed by Hielmaster. She discusses something with him. While everyone is dispersing ,Mumkin swiftly walks and runs towards the gate to reach the Amrisk's shop. After reaching there, he finds him keeping the books with K.Jalty. He looks at Mumkin,adjusts his spectacles that are on his nose and then welcomes him to get inside. He finds that Mumkin looks tired.

Amrisk: Oh hello Mumkin. Long time, I haven't seen you three for a long time. Where are Pamela and John?

Mumkin: Hi Amrisk(breathing heavily). Was occupied due to committee selections. Pamela and John did not come today.,as in I haven't informed them of me coming here.

Amrisk: So you came alone, leaving your best friends behind!

Mumkin:Yes, I have important work with you .

As Amrisk looks at Mumkin's eyes he finds that his eye lashes are heavy .

Amrisk: Ofcourse. I am always there for you dear. Sit here. (he slightly slides today's newspaper towards Mumkin and starts pouring coffee in a cup).

Mumkin: You're amazing, Amrisk.

Amrisk: Why you're saying it....for the service I give when you visit me...is it?

Mumkin: Yes.

Amrisk: I do it for almost all my customers as they're special to me.

Mumkin: That's not the only thing that makes you amazing.

Amrisk: Then what is it?

Mumkin keeps quiet, his eyes are still heavy and tired.

Amrisk: Mumkin ,I understand that you're rigorously involved with committee selections that's why you look tired. Here you go, drink this black coffee.

Mumkin: Thank you.

Mumkin takes the cup of black coffee from Amrisk. When he takes the first sip, he finds it extremely bitter. So he leaves the cup there itself.

Mumkin: The coffee, it's kind of bitter today.

Amrisk: I've got it made strong....I knew you needed it.....but didn't know that it'll be that strong that you'll leave the cup just after the first sip.

Mumkin: Sorry about that, I can't drink it completely as I prefer a mild taste.

Amrisk: No problem. Is committee selection still going on?

Mumkin: Yes, committee selection is just going on.

Amrisk: So how is it till now?

Mumkin: Me and Pamela made it to the next stage!

Amrisk: Oh congratulations to both of you(giving a shoulder hug to Mumkin).

Mumkin: Thank you sir.

Amrisk: What about John...Didn't he make it?

Mumkin: Unfortunately not!

Amrisk: Where he might have gone wrong?

Mumkin: No idea.

Amrisk: A guy who reads comics can't make into sophisticated committees like these.

Mumkin nods his head in a mixed way, to show his both agreement and disagreement with Amrisk.

Mumkin: I want to ask you something very crucial. I hope you'll not hide anything as it's regarding my dad.

Amrisk: Of Course Mumkin! I ain't sure of your dad's connection with me, but I'm always there to help you. Go ahead(picks up the cup of coffee and starts sipping).(He moved his eyes away from Mumkin staring at the newspaper).

Mumkin: Is Lidiya Cheriyan and Devkali Neelghanti Paul same?

Amrisk: I don't know Devkali Neelghanti Paul in person .

Mumkin: Still, at least you know Lidiya right!

Amrisk: Yes. What you want to say.

Mumkin: Is Lidiya ,Isabella and Devkali Neelghanti Paul, all three the same person?

Amrisk: Wait, what? So many names you took at once, it's very confusing ,don't you think?

Mumkin: Yes ,but can you resolve this mystery?

Amrisk: I know Lidiya, the girl from your College who joined Military. Devkali Neelghanti Paul is a writer. But now who the hell is this Isabella?

Mumkin: Isabella is Professor Olivia's sister.

Amrisk: You're making things too complicated. Listen to me, you focus on plans to make your business in weaponry. You seem unfocused.

Mumkin: No, I don't think that I'm unfocused.

Amrisk: I used to think John is only into women. I didn't know you too are!

Mumkin: Not at all, sorry to say I respect all women, but the ones I am referring to are middle aged women, probably of your age. By no chance I can be interested in them.

Amrisk: So what women are you interested in?

Mumkin: I have a girlfriend ,my classmate.

Amrisk: Let's discuss her then....why are you asking about these middle aged ones?

Mumkin: I want to know more about Lidiya.

Amrisk: I already mentioned about Lidiya that no one including me knows anything about her. She's past for everyone. Better not talk about her,Prof Hastik might have told you the same.

Mumkin: How do you know that Prof Hastik told us this? How do you know the information about the meeting among teachers and students of our college? Don't you think it's all happening inside the college, how that information reached your shop?

Amrisk stops sipping coffee, he keeps the cup back on the table. K. Jalty tells him that a new edition of Educational Sociology is kept on the second floor's third book shelf but Amrisk stops him by telling"we'll discuss this later Jalty". Now Amrisk is looking at Mumkin freezed.

Amrisk: You're asking questions like your warden Bloom.

Mumkin: So you know about all of them, right?

Amrisk: Yes, Professor Hastik came to this shop and he mentioned this incident -that you , Pamela and John reached University late after visiting our shop when you three came here for the first time!

Mumkin: Is this the only truth? How about providing the writing material for committee selection? Why didn't you tell the three of us about it regarding the same?

Amrisk: Oh Mumkin, that was because Committee selections were to be done in a secretive way by the University, so they requested me not to mention anyone regarding the same.

Mumkin: Is it? What about Changing your shop's name from UMBAS (Unique Military Base Association With Students) to UAS(Unique Association with Students)?

Amrisk: Yes Mumkin, that's true that till 1943, we had collaboration with the Military in our shop for war purposes but ours is not the only shop! There was another shop which closed in 1942 ,which was also helping the military in their research and providing writing material to the students. Why are you asking about it? How is this all connected with your father?

Mumkin starts believing what Amrisk is saying as it's matching with events in the diary but he doesn't wish to mention about the diary of Lidiya Cheriyan. Mumkin looks at Amrisk and starts sipping the black coffee.

Amrisk: How are you sipping the coffee that you find strong?

Mumkin: It's alright. I'll finish this cup at least

Amrisk:You're a determined guy. Now what's there in your mind ,tell me frankly.

Mumkin: It's just anything about the military that intrigues me about my father. It refreshes my imaginations with my father.

Amrisk: I understand Mumkin for how much you loved your father. There's something that you're not telling as the conversion of UMBAS to UAS was done in a confidential manner. You were a child at that time. I don't know who gave you this piece of information. Be vigilant to not to share this with anyone as still there are traitors who want to pull the flag of Himbertown down.

Mumkin: Traitors? Who are they?

Amrisk: Like every country has patriots and traitors. We too have people who want to hamper the country 's growth and destroy peace. Now don't ask me more than that, as I'm not entitled to share this information to a teenager for security reasons. Indeed we worked with the Military and I am proud of it too Mumkin. Anything pertaining to the Military I can't share.

Mumkin is fascinated by the words of Amrisk. Upon inquiry by Amrisk , Mumkin shares his experience of how luck which never favored him actually made him luckiest today as out of some six thirty students, his name turned up to sit in second stage becoming twenty second member and ultimately he made it to third round.

Amrisk congratulated him again. He shows him the new collection of books regarding weapons that he ordered specifically for Mumkin as requested by him in their first meeting. He gives him three books regarding weapon technologies, business management and techniques of winning wars with technologies. Mumkin leaves back to his University as it's five thirty in the evening. K. Jalty comes near Amrisk and they have a crucial chat.

K.Jalty: I tried to divert his attention by interrupting you, he knows so much.Principal Blacksmith needs to be informed about the same.

Amrik: Thanks Jalty. I have no idea about the source of this information . Yes, I will inform Principal Blacksmith again about him. Especially about his knowledge of Lidiya and Devkali Neelghanti Paul.

K.Jalty:During the committee selection process, thankfully we informed Principal Blacksmith about the way he , John and Pamela helped Isabella in saving her life. He deserved a second chance at least in psychology testing.

Amrisk: Yes, he was right that luck favors him the least. It was his own kindness that made Principal Blacksmith recommend him for the second stage after we informed him. I am going to meet him again today to inform about today's conversation with Mumkin. He will have a better plan.

K. Jalty: It will as you know the mastermind of all this can never fail in her plans.

Amrisk: Yes, she's moving the waves in her direction. Things will always be the way she wants them to be!

Amrisk wears black hat, coat and sunglasses . He heads towards the University to meet Principal Blacksmith.

Mumkin further goes to the hospital to purchase bandages for Laila's injuries. When he reaches the University, he meets Laila and Pamela. Pamela was changing Laila's knee dressing and Mumkin put bandages on it.

Pamela: Mumkin, are you hiding something? It's been a long time that you haven't interacted openly. You're always in a hurry!

Mumkin : Haha. That's not true(amicably). I am just occupied these days. Did you finish reading Devkali Neelghanti Paul's book?

Pamela: No not yet. Just finished half of it. I too got a little occupied with selections.

Mumkin: Did you find those books as a book or you found something else?

Pamela: What do you mean?

Mumkin: Is her book like other normal books?

Pamela:(befuddled) of course it's a book! What else do you expect from it?

Mumkin: I mean, something peculiar about the books!

Pamela: Not peculiar. The book is slightly boring for me. But Laila likes that ,that's what is peculiar.

Laila:I got it! Yeah Mumkin, these aRen't just books but guides for life. That's what you're asking!

Mumkin:Yeah, I got it. I need to leave for important work given by professor Rehman. Will see you two later. Please excuse.(Mumkin realizes that the books given to Pamela by Lucas are just the published books of Isabella, which doesn't have any information similar to the diary possessed by Mumkin related to Lidiya Cheriyan.)

Mumkin walks towards his hostel room.

Pamela: I don't understand. These days he's behaving bizarre.

Laila: I don't think so. I've been seeing him like this since the time I have known him personally.

Pamela: He used to spend a lot of time with me and John before. But nowadays mostly in his room at the hostel. I 'm concerned about this sudden behavior.

Laila: Probably, you know him since the beginning of class. And you're better at reading people.

Pamela: There's one more reason for his change in behavior(chuckling).

Laila: What's that?

Pamela: Why did he put a bandage on your injury madam?You're a sweetheart for him!(teasing)

Laila: No...ways.

Pamela: Don't lie. You've hypnotized him in your love.

Laila: As you said hypnosis, let's go to a hypnosis therapy workshop.

Pamela: Good idea. Where is it happening and when?

Laila: It's going to happen next week, four days- Monday,Tuesday, Thursday and Friday evening 5 to 6PM.Also, It's by Prof Rehman.

Pamela: Good initiative by Prof Rehman. I'll ask John and Mumkin if they want to join us. Most probably they wouldn't.

Laila: Why won't they join?

Pamela: Because both took psychology forcefully!

They hear a voice"I'm interested to join. Psychology can sometimes be fun". Pamela recognises this voice. It's Ren's voice. As she turns back. She finds Ren smiling at Laila and then he looks at Pamela. The eye contact he makes with her is as deep as she could see layers of brown black colors with sparkles in his eyes. She's speechless to say anything to him as she recalls back that he's been ignorant to him for a long time. She recalls that before a few days he was ignoring her.

He comes near her and starts talking to Laila.

Ren:(laughing) Not in this birth.Just sarcastic. I mean seriously Laila, you're going for that stupid therapy?Not coming for today's party? I'll make some arrangements with the help of my uncle so that you can sneak in.

Laila: No Ren, I just don't feel like being part of anything like a party. I want to live life in a more fulfilling way!

Ren: Party girl what's wrong with you, did you take drugs? What about those tattoos?

Laila: I want to get rid of all past memories that hamper my growth.

Ren: Wait wait...fulfilling, growth and tattoo removal. What's up with you ! Seriously, you don't wanna come?

Pamela: Ren she doesn't want to come. Don't put her into peer pressure. You need not influence her by doing something that's blocking her growth. Stop it!

Ren: I'm not talking to you . Mind your own business. (irked)

Laila: Ren,Pamela is just trying to help me out.

Laila walks away towards her hostel. Now Ren and Pamela are the only ones left near the quadrangle. The sky is blue like blue nightingale's feathers are covering it slowly. Ren turns his back towards Pamela and starts moving away towards the University's exit gate.

Pamela: Ren , why has your behavior towards me has become like this?

Ren: Like what?

Pamela: Before you always teased me and now you are ignoring me.

Ren: What ?

Pamela: It's only after Prof Rehman's therapy class that you are getting more irritated by me. Please answer.

He starts moving quicker but hears her whimpering . As he turns back he sees her face turning red and tears rolling down from her eyes and nose as she is sobbing.

Ren: Stop crying Pamela. You're an overthinker ,there's nothing like that.

She continues crying more. He goes near her. He tells her something due to which her sobbing stops.

Ren: You see, I love my girlfriend Janny very much. During the counseling session of Prof Rehman, the way I could connect with you, I could never do that with any girl including Janny.

Pamela: What do you mean?

Ren: Your serenity and innocence was unavoidable for me. Coming close to you was like losing Janny which I can't imagine even in my dreams as I love her the most. That's why I was impertinent with you and I ain't one responsible for it.

After saying this he starts walking towards the University exit gate. As his image was getting smaller and smaller, she was given a shoulder hug by someone very familiar. It's John who consoles her .

John: Buddy , why are you crying?

Pamela: Nothing John, just like that!

John: Come on, you tease me just like that, I'm seeing you crying after a long time. So please stop!

John again gives a quick friendly hug to her. He covers her with his jacket,and she feels very comfortable .

Pamela: how come you're so caring suddenly?

John: You made it to committee.

Pamela: So I should treat you with an ice cream ,right?

John: Not ice cream!

Pamela: What do you want John?

John: Convince your uncle to recommend me for the committee, like the way Mumkin is recommended by Principal Blacksmith!

Pamela: Shut up Ren. My uncle rarely gets a chance to interact with him.

John: Do something .Please.

Pamela: Okay ,I'll put a word to him. Let's go to the hostel before we reach late.

They both move towards their hostels.

Mumkin enters his hostel room and starts reading Lidiya Cheriyan's diary again.

"Just don't want to give up Alora. Training looks like an impossible mission. If I give up and return back ,probably forgiving myself will be most difficult. My mother,despite being a widow of a military officer, told me to boldly complete the training and prove my worth. I'm the paramount person here as all eyes are on me. If I complete the Military training successfully, it'll open the door for other women to join the Military. But here everyday is a do and die situation for me. I remember my selections.The first day was intelligence testing which was based on verbal and non verbal questions, I'm ain't good at abstract. I practiced many books borrowed from Amrisk and made it to the first round.The second round of psychology which I never studied being a science student seemed like climbing a battlefield but somehow I connected the pattern, had positive affirmations in subject and through this the second stage was like a cake walk for me...............................But initially all the psychology rounds seems to be very ambiguous. I mean what do I write when I have to connect the dots. Whatever I wrote was naturally coming in my mind like a research student creating an antidote for a disease, a college student teaching dance to her batchmates due to which they win the competition and a housewife beautifully decorating her house to accommodate her guests etc. I don't know how they passed me after I wrote all this shit"

As Mumkin reads this he realizes the same pattern of examination is followed in committee selection- Intelligence test and psychology test. Same questions regarding writing a paragraph about oneself, completion of sentences based on vague incomplete sentences . For psychology it's making connections on the dots presented on paper and writing interpretation. He realizes that the pattern of selection of Lidiya in the Military and the committee selection is just the same . Now to read the next line things might become crystal clear, he anticipates that the committee can be somewhere related to Lidiya Cheriyan. To train candidates for the military at the position of commander. This thought revolved again in his head and now there's a strong adrenaline rush in his body. He's getting warmed up with these thoughts running in his head. He tries to read further but is feeling jittery to focus.. He lies on his bed, takes a deep breath and again picks up the same diary to read further steps .If his anticipation is true then he'll have the upper hand over others to be a part of the committee as he will know what will happen in the next stage. He decided to share these secrets with everyone to provide everyone the level playing field.

As he reads through the books Lidiya mentions that the next stage before her selection into the Military is the interview process that lasts for four hours.

"Alora, I wasn to recall an incident before I was asked to join the Military. It was a mauldin experience. I was asked to arrive at the placement room early at 6:30AM.I wore white silhouette . As I entered the room, I was asked to sit down. There was a senior from the Military who was there to interview me. He looked at me for a second and then asked me to take down my seat.He was rude in his tone. I was asked at least twenty questions pertaining to my name, occupation, place of birth ,time of birth, what I like about my name, who kept it, what is famous about my place and what problems I see at my hometown, how can I improve those problems...So many questions that it was difficult for me to keep questions in order and recall them all, but I got the idea that the sole purpose of these questions is to scare me away,of course which I won't be as my name is Lidiya. Lidiya Cheriyan. As I answered around nine out of twelve questions, he asked me to recall back the questions that I've left. I recalled two and answered them on the spot. Then he asked me counter questions from my answers provided to him with respect to the solution of problems in my hometown. I told him women aren't taking up the leadership roles there, he enquired why , I answered patriarchy .He requisitioned me, why is it so? I remained confident and gave him the evidence with respect to unequal pay, job segregation, upbringing of women, gender roles, examples of operation by Military where not even a single woman was involved etc.After my answer Alora, he asked me how do I unroot the patriarchy if I see that as the main problem? I answered him by joining the military, my life will be a chronicle to uproot patriarchy. I don't want women to be either treated as slaves or masters, but give equal treatment where women aren't superior or inferior but indistinguishable, as we all are human beings. Then he asked me further questions regarding my father, what was his role and rank in the military, how I lost him, what was age at that time,how my mother coped up with it, number of siblings I have, what did I do to bring my family to stability etc? All these questions were certainly hysterical for me, but I answered them with firm belief in myself that bad experiences in my life build my strength mentally as I am Lydia. He asked me if I compromised anywhere in my life to meet the daily needs of my family.I answered that I can compromise with daily consumption but never compromise with my values .And needs....needs get fulfilled when one is passionate in life. Another question ,why do I want to join the Military? Is it because I want to give a lesson of feminism to the Military?I answered by saying that keeping up a country's pride is larger than any personal goal. He further asked me to explain my answer. I explained by giving various records where our country had to face many challenges and war-like situations, where both men and women contributed directly or indirectly. Especially when the economy of a country went down, it was both genders who enhanced it. I made a mistake there. Not only both genders but third gender too which contributed. He asked me further about my education project, why did I choose it and how can I contribute to the military through that? After my answers all questions ended.Then he asked me to leave by wishing me the best. I can't forget the propitious day when the Military called me to get trained before joining, giving clear indication that I cleared all stages as I was an honest and learned person. My joining letter made my mother proud. It was all two days after my interview was over."

Mumkin anticipates that for him and the other five candidates selected for the interview is the next round which is going to happen after two days. The next two days, classes are to be attended by all students of college including the ones selected for the next round of the committee. He tells Zeen, Rose, Ren, Pamela and Bessy to meet him after the class near the exit gate ground, under the banyan tree at four thirty pm. After they assemble, Mumkin wants to address them. John arrived there too just to accompany Mumkin.

Mumkin: I have called you all so that you can prepare better for the committee selections. As yesterday, I was walking through the corridor to meet Prof Rehman, I heard someone saying that the next stage will be extensive interview where questions asked will be based on your choices of getting into committee, information about my parents, my name, occupation, place of birth ,time of birth, who kept it, liking and disliking that you may have, what is famous about my place and what problems I see in my place, how can you improve those problems and did you compromise anywhere in your life to meet the daily needs of your family? ....So you have to confidently answer those questions. There will be many counter questions too regarding the same.

Pamela: Haha. The way you are speaking Mumkin, you sound like Warden Atrika Bloom. Is he alive or has his ghost entered your body?

Zeen: Really? Why do you think we shall trust what your ears say? I better inquire about this to Prof Olivia.

Pamela: Trust Mumkin . He's a good guy and there isn't any harm in being prepared for something.

Rose:I agree with Mumkin and Pamela, if he has heard about it then it might be true.

Bessy: Zeen there isn't any point in inquiring from Prof Olivia. Ultimately it might lead to our resignation from the next stage of committee selection.

Ren isn't bothered with what Mumkin says ,but then he stands there to get more ints about the committee selections. They all leave their places . The ones who believe Mumkin start preparing for their interviews which might be the next stage of committee selection. The next few days they attend the classes and meet up for three hours from two thirty to five fifty in the evening. They all discuss their small details and give feedback upon their areas to ameliorate.

Pamela:I'm Pamela, I want to get into committee because I want to be a support system for all in whatever I do. My parents are very supportive towards my goals in life. Being an only child ,I am pampered the most but still I have a soft corner for everybody in this world because I can feel the pain of people. I did my schooling from Christ School.I was born in Himbertown's western part. And I don't remember the exact time but it was Saturday morning around four twenty.I like my name as it means sweet, it resembles me as I've always been sweet with people hitherto except for a few people in my life. One of them is John who's a good friend of mine. We tease each other. Although what

I don't like is when people take my winsome nature for granted and try taking advantage. My dad kept my name. My place ,I think it's famous for its river, well planned city, greenery, cuisines like raspberry pudding and wheat champagne etc. Problem in Himbertown can be the crime that is increasing due to unemployment . I think providing quality education, frequent policing, strict laws and of course more jobs can really change the situation. Also these days mental illness is getting common. I want to help people regarding the same. When it comes to compromising with my values ,I ....I (a sudden sobbing),I did it once. I slept with my ex boyfriend, where my parents do not know about it.They trust me a lot. Hiding this from them is like agony of mind. I ...(weeping continues)

Everyone is astonished after hearing this . Not because she isn't a virgin but the way she's taking it on herself like a taboo.

Mumkin goes near her and gives her a shoulder hug.

Mumkin: Don't get worked up!

Ren looks at Pamela and Mumkin and then he looks at her bracelet Pamela is wearing. The stars shaped design is moving, it's shining more and making a pleasant noise.

Rose: Yeah, Pam. This is very normal. I too have parents who don't want me to date multiple people at one time. I still do it, it's my life and after all this time I have four exes.That's not cool according to my parents.

John: Exactly, not a big deal. Just a hiccup. Also you took my name in your interview.What a child you are!

Zeen starts scoffing at Pamela.

Zeen: Really, why Pamela?You will never grow. i think even after sleeping with your ex boyfriend you didn't mature? Trust me ,I can do it better (wicked laugh).

Zeen goes near Pamela and holds her back tightly and she's feeling intimidated with being timorous.

Pamela: Stop it!

Mumkin moves Zeen's hand away from Pamela and John goes near Zeen and punches him on his face due to which his nose starts bleeding.

Mumkin: Shut your damn thing, rascal. Get out of this place.

Angrily Zeen leaves the place.

Situation is quite pensive.Bessy and Rose comfort Pamela. They give her a water bottle . She drinks water from that. After six to seven minutes they rejoin the group. Mumkin tells everyone to reflect on what Pamela answered.

Mumkin: What you don't like can be anything else,saying things like you don't like when people take advantage of winsome nature, that's an undeveloped answer. You can also say the name of a movie or food that you don't like. Like, I don't like bitter gourds!

Bessy: Well, it's a natural answer from my point.

Mumkin: But it's going to cast questions like when people take advantage of yours, why you let them do that and why do they do that etc? You see, it's gonna be chaotic for her to answer such questions.

Bessy: Agree as ultimately one needs to appear confident in one's abilities.

Mumkin: Also you can still hide your dating history as it isn't required! It can also show intense emotions. Remember the selections are for Mi.....secret committee. Who knows what's their demand. So let's be prudent to be confident and avoid hassleness. It's just like a selection that happens to be someone's body guard. One has to always show a strong side of oneself. This is what I heard near the end of Prof Rehman's corridor.I think we shall move to Bessy. Shall we?

All agree and Bessy starts talking about herself. Bessy is a brown skinned girl with beautiful curly hair, her eyes are big with thick eyelashes.

Bessy: I am Bessy Jonas. I apply to this committee as I don't know anything but I look for opportunities. Basically to explore and grow myself. My father is a weaver and mother is a housewife. I have a family of five members with three younger siblings. But in my life I not only want to support my family,but I want to do something great. I was born on the Island of Brijko. I like my name as it means god is bountiful. I'm a very religious person.I like everything in this world. Something that I dislike is wasting food. I wish the world was with zero poverty so that no one had to sleep empty stomach. My grandmother kept my name. My Island is famous for its beach, sea food ,culture especially folk dance and cuisines. The major problem at my place is poverty but we are still highly effective people who use the available resources from the environment to sustain our livelihood. It can be reduced through education, skills development, infrastructure development and big countries can also invest in my country. When it comes to compromising with anything in life , I believe one needs to be ardent in protecting one's traditions and beliefs .But be open minded too. One need not compromise on the above but one can always be diplomatic in making the right choice.

People clapped after she spoke. They mentioned that she is to the point, genuine, practical and her answers show a practical approach towards life. They all discussed their answers and Mumkin was just listening to them to give them feedback to improve their quality of response. It was six pm when Mumkin's turn came. He could only explain the meaning of his name and his passion for his hobbies that includes reading war books. Chamburt is the surname adopted by his great grandfather as they climbed mountains to provide food to village people in Ranidetro village in ancient times. Warden Atrika Bloom came in between his speech to order everyone to get back to their hostels.

They all leave back to their hostel at six three pm and Mumkin decides not to read the diary further as he feels tired and wants to go fresh for tomorrow's selection process. At one point he feels he might miss something very important regarding the selection ,but by not reading further he doesn't have energy to check or overcome that intuitive feeling.

The next morning all of them wake up early as they believe that it is their interview today. That included Zeen too. They all are wearing formal uniforms. The three boys are dressed up in their formal pants,shirt,coats and ties whereas the three girls are wearing formal skirts with full sleeved shirts.It is the third stage of the selection process . All six of them assembled on the ground.Six of them are feeling jittery and anticipating except Zeen who is invigoratingly confident.They are also hiding this important information that the third stage of the process can be an interview. Prof Rehman tells the students to relax as he finds tightness in them. Hielmaster enters with Prof Olivia.

Hielmaster: Good morning everyone! Welcome to the third stage of selections. This is gonna be tough though!

Zeen: I know what this is all about. Just an obtuse interview. Mumkin leaked the information that he heard in the corridor. What a traitor!

Hielmaster: Ooo, that's why you six are dressed so fancy!If what Zeen said is true then your dreams are just magnetic Mumkin. Zeen you too are filled with lovely fantasy as you just now said something about the obtuse interview and traitorhood etc. Did you ever try writing fiction? You'll do great. Believe me.(smirks).

Zeen is atwitter now! Mumkin with Pamela, Ren and other two candidates are too bowled over as they realize that it's not the interviews that'll happen.

Zeen: What do you mean as I am zero percent interested in writing fiction?

Prof Olivia(loud voice): Quiet everyone. Wait for further instructions.

Hielmaster:Thank you Miss Olivia. Interview is never a part of committee selection! Gosh,you guys are just dumb asses.

Pamela raises her left eyebrow and looks at Mumkin as Hielmaster calls them dumbasses.

Hielmaster :Now, without wasting time, run towards the field. Further directions were given there.Five of them assembled near ground running , they were breathing heavily and Hielmaster arrived there after two minutes. Pamela reached ground after him.

Hielmaster: It's a test of intelligence quotient and mental stamina. You're already trained by your teacher regarding the same. What do you see in front?

Mumkin: There's a huge rock with a trophy at top around forty feet from ground.

Zeen: All I see is the shining trophy.

Hielmaster: Okay. Anyone else?

Bessy : A mountain.

Hielmaster: Alright. Your task is to get that top trophy. Can anyone tell its height?

Mumkin: It's forty three feet tall.

Hielmaster: Why that answer ?

Mumkin: The protrusions in the form of small rocks attached are at a distance of two to four feet on the rock. So that'll make up to forty three feets in total.

Hielmaster: What's your name gentleman?

Mumkin: Mumkin Chamburt.

Hielmaster: Yes, what Mr Chamburt said is logical. Remember your mission by using the available resources from that store room(pointing towards the store room attached to the College's sports department building). After completion of the task ,come back to this position, reflection will be done to know the purpose of the task . Results will be announced after that.

As all six of them run towards the store room they find items like rope, fragile wooden stairs of two feet, two feet long log, harness and net. As they check further all these items are just in pairs. Mumkin thinks that just in case one item breaks, another one can be used for backup.

Mumkin: Let's all of us be circumspect while using these items as the number is limited only to two.

Zeen: What do you mean by "us"? It's a competition.I will win. Always. You losers!

Mumkin: Nevertheless, reaching alone to take the trophy is a hardship! We need each other to complete the task. I believe it's teamwork that wins.

Zeen: Shut up you unfastened ! A winner always walks alone with pride(holding the stairs and rope)

Zeen runs with stairs and ropes. He set up the stair near the rock, climbs on stairs and helds first protrusion. Mumkin and other four people- Pamela, Ren, Bessy and Rose take the left material near the ground. Mumkin sets up a stair near a rock at a distance of around five feet from Zeen. Ren climbs on the stairs. He holds the protrusion. Pamela makes a knot with rope and ties it with a log, Mumkin handles the log with a knot attached to it to Ren. Ren climbs the next protrusion around four feet away from the first one easily. However the third protrusion is further away. Mumkin gives Ren the idea that to go to the third protrusion, he needs to keep the log between the second and third protrusion. Ren does it which forms the bridge . He climbs over that temporary bridge and reaches the third protrusion from the second. Now as soon as Rose tries to climb the first protrusion to provide harness to him, the stairs break. She's falling backwards where her head would hit the ground. Fortunately Mumkin and Bessy swiftly provide her support ,holding her through their hands due to which her body turns forward hitting her knee. Meanwhile Pamela also turns her body towards Rose to provide her with the support.

Pamela :Are you okay Rose?

Rose : Yes I am.

Pamela: I think your knee is bleeding.

Rose: Yes it is. The injury is minimal as Mumkin and Bessy gave support at the right time but still I don't know if I can climb again.

Mumkin: Don't worry Rose, you take care of yourself. Pamela, you go ahead.

Pamela: Sure.

Mumkin: You sit on my shoulder as the protrusion is broken now.

Pamela starts giggling.

Pamela: Isn't that awkward that I climb on your shoulder Mumkin?

Mumkin: When you have the right intentions then it's not awkward! Let's do it quickly as we're losing time.

Bessy: Yes, do it Pamela, or else I will climb his shoulder in your place.

Pamela: No, I was just kidding. I will go, Mumkin, just bend yourself.

Pamela sits on Mumkin's shoulder ,Ren passes the log back to Pamela. She ties the harness to the log and lifts the log up . He quickly wears the harness and makes a knot of rope which he ties to one side of the log. The length of the log is smaller to reach the next protrusion. Ren lifts the log till the next protrusion and he gives it a push due to which the knot of one side of rope at log gets fixed to the protrusion.The other side of the rope he ties to his harness and takes a tarzan swing to reach that protrusion .Mumkin starts clapping for Ren's successful efforts to reach the forth protrusion. Other hand Zeen is climbing a second protrusion copying the method of Ren. He keeps the log in order to make a bridge after joining the second and third protrusion and starts to climb it to reach the third protrusion, but suddenly his leg slips and he is losing his grip.His left knee is fixed in log and right leg is in the air. He cries out loud for help. Mumkin goes near him and asks Pamela and Bessy to hold the net as a preventive measure to avoid injury in case Zeen falls down. Pamela is hesitant but Mumkin convinces her to ignore what Zeen did as he looks in trouble which is life threatening.

Mumkin: Zeen , just take a deep breath. Try standing up, then balance yourself and take three steps back. You'll make it to the first protrusion. That's safe.

Zeen: I can't . I just can't. My heart is pumping very fast as I look down.

Bessy: It's not that high. Some nine feet only! Why isn't he able to come down?

Mumkin: Hold on Zeen. Keep your grip on the rope strong.

Zeen loses his grip and falls on the net held by Mumkin,Pamela and Bessy. Due to his overweight the net gets torn and Zeen straight away falls to kiss the ground. Along with him, his log ties with rope also falls down. He cries out loud in affliction. The two nurses wearing white frocks arrive out of nowhere and take Zeen with them on a stretcher.

Pamela: Where did these nurses come from suddenly? It seemed like a scene from a movie!

Mumkin: They might have kept the staff in case of a medical emergency .

Meanwhile Ren looks stuck on protrusion forth as his shoelace is stuck to a nail on rock. He isn't able to move further and is feeling dizzy. Mumkin takes the stairs ,log and rope of Zeen. He makes the arrangement of stairs to climb up, move to first protrusion, uses a log, rope and knot for climbing first,second and third protrusion with techniques of Ren, ultimately he reaches to the forth protrusion where Ren is standing. He unties his shoe lace. Mumkin shows him the way to climb up. But Ren looked a little exhausted so Mumkin took the lead. He starts climbing up one protrusion after the next where Ren follows him. With the support of Ren's hands, Mumkin reaches the top and takes the trophy. The duo climbs down smoothly in a back fashioned way from top to lowest protrusion with the trophy. Pamela and Bessy happily clap for both of them.

The five gather on the ground. Hielmaster comes there.

Hielmaster: So let's reflect! Why did you get the trophy?

Bessy: It's presence of mind because when Ren was stuck, Mumkin went to help him.

Hielmaster: What else do you see?

Pamela: What Zeen did was wrong! Even after knowing the fact that each item is only two,still he took half of the materials with him.

Hielmaster: So what happened after that?

Pamela: He fell down as he wanted to do things alone seeking for self victory.

Hielmaster: Good answer! He believed more in competition than cooperation. Rome wasn't built by a single man, it required a full team. Is there anyone who thinks they could've done the task alone?

Everyone remains silent for a second and then Bessy says no, followed by Pamela and Ren saying "no sir".

Hielmaster: Alright ,hope he learnt a lesson and you follow like this to have a balanced combination of presence of mind and heart! Keep it up .Your team did a good job!

Prof Olivia: Have your snack break, arrive back to know the results.

Hielmaster: Wait miss Olivia, before that I have a question to ask them!.....(silence) What do you think the committee is all about?

Bessy:Is it about making us better professionals?

Hielmaster: Think deeply .

Bessy: Yes, making us better counselors, business professionals and theater artists etc. Is it?

Hielmaster: No not at all! Carry on for your snacks break.

All five reach the snack counter, they are handed cheese tomato pasta, muffins,jelly and chocolate milk. This time they also have arrangements to sit and eat. They eat heartily and strike upon interesting conversation.

Bessy:So stupid of Zeen. He didn't think before becoming a joker in selection!

Rose: Yeah, I saw him as a hoaxer who got tricked down by his own actions!

Mumkin and Pamela are eating muffins and listening to them. Mumkin asks Pamella to pass the sugar vessel. As Pamela does so, he adds a spoon of it in his chocolate milk and mixes with the well. Few drops are stuck on his right hand, he wipes it with a tissue with his left hand.

Bessy: By the way, I have heard a lot about Zeen.

Rose: He has a really bad attitude. The way he treated all of us was like a peice of shit .

Pamela: He was behaving like a self conceited person!

Rose: Yes yes, as if he knows everything.

Bessy: Still whatever wrong he does, he's always able to get out of it!

Rose: I don't know much of his wrong doings but I've heard that he was caught carrying weed in his lunch box.

Pamela puts her hand on her face and says 'shoot, how wasn't he rusticated then?'

Rose: Who can rusticate him, no one has that level?

Pamela: No but, even if we come late to the hostel we're given an imposition of five days. Right Mumkin?

Mumkin and Ren are quietly having their food and getting bored in the conversations of ladies.

Mumkin replies in one word 'Yes'.

Pamela: Ya...Then why isn't he rusticated permanently for carrying weed , that too in a tiffin box?

Bessy: He has powerful people backing him!

Pamela: That's why his behavior of entitlement, is it?

Bessy: Do you know he is nephew of whom?

Pamela: No...I'm in first year, I don't know much about the seniors.

Bessy: Do you know Rose?

Rose: No, I don't.

Bessy takes a muffin, puts peanut butter over it and takes a bite. She chews and speaks simultaneously.

Bessy: T...Th(coughing).

The muffin enters her windpipe and she feels choked...Pamela, quickly asks Ren to pass the water jar. As she is waiting for him to fill the glass, he directly goes near Bessy and passes the glass to her saying 'Tiger Watson'.

Rose: What?

Bessy drinks the glass prompt and feels better .

Bessy: Yes, that's what I was trying to say. He is the nephew of Tiger Watson.

Pamela: Tiger toh, he's your uncle's business partner. Isn't Ren.

Ren: Nah, I'm not concerned

Pamela: Okay....(whispering to Bessy and Rose)...He's not less self conceited than Zeen.

They both quietly chuckle after listening to this.

Bessy: Tiger Watson! He's a good friend of our trustee, Silver Bison.

Ren: Mr. Watson is our family friend . He's a nice man.

Bessy: Oh yes, you Ren, you're the nephew of our trustee. Alas, pompous like Zeen is the nephew of a good man like Tiger Watson.

Pamela: I understand now, this is what feeds his delinquency

Bessy: Rightly said Pamela, that's why he is so imperious!

Mumkin: Let's leave this matter here. Hope Zeen recovers quickly. Let's hurry up, Prof Olivia asked to come on time!

All of them reassembled back at the same place . But this time there are seats for them as well as eighty other seats for guests. This wasn't there before. It was all arranged during the time of their break in a bullet train manner. Slowly all guests including faculty members ,student union members and staff members including Pamela's uncle Bidar Nelon arrived there and occupied the seats. SIlver Bison and Tiger Watson also arrived.

Prof Rehman enters, goes on the stage and addresses all sitting guests.

Prof Rehman: Good afternoon. Firstly we would like to thank Mr. Hielmaster for trusting our students for committee selections and giving precious time .It was a strenuous process to screen twenty two out of six hundred and then selecting four members after it finally. The lucky four will be announced by the Principal blacksmith.

Prof Olivia is not present there.

Prof Hashtik in place of Prof Olivia handed a file to Principal Blacksmith while he was climbing up to the podium.

Principal Blacksmith: Good afternoon everyone. Our students have always made us proud. They have been part of various committees. Those involve sports, cultural ,educational reforms, well being etc. When our students have been selected for exclusive projects, that has been a proud moment. This is another such selection which is unique in its own way. This is a salient but secretive committee. The intelligence testing, brain testing via psychology and group compatibility helped in selecting four of you. Also the effort of the team is appreciated in the last stage, helping the fellow student in saving his life and preventing mishappening. Now you all might be wondering what this committee is all about? Again as its name is.....It's a secret committee. The selected ones will get full information about the committee's work. The ones not making it here need to assume that their forte lies somewhere else but we appreciate their efforts. The committee is kept internal as the work or problems related are internal. So the lucky ones are-Ren ....People clap. Tiger Watson shouts"Congratulations Ren. Now next will be the turn of Zeen I know".

Principal Blacksmith: Second is Bessy, third is Rose and forth is Mumkin.

As people clap, Tiger stands up and looks infuriated!

Tiger Watson: Principal Blacksmith, why Zeen's name isn't there?

Principal Blacksmith: He couldn't perform well in the last stage.

TIger Watson: I paid five thousand pound to get him a seat in committee.

Principal Blacksmith: Selections are strict. Your money will be refunded to the person to whom you paid a bribe.

Tiger Watson: Nonsense you took a student through a lucky drawer in a second round! Isn't that dereliction?

Principal Blacksmith: Absolutely not. He (referring to Mumkin)is not selected on the basis of grace or being a super intelligence chap but due to his bravery in saving the life of a woman . Giving him another chance was worth it! He nailed it .

Tiger Watson: Bravery, is it? He made it through a lucky drawer.

Principal Blacksmith: We lied to him and everybody here(adjusting his spectacles). The lie is his selection through the lucky drawer, but he and his two lovely friends- Pamela and John rendered their help in saving the life of a young lady . All three were recommended by committee members to appear in the second stage! Unfortunately John couldn't make it to the next stage, still the committee's decision is reserved in choosing the right candidate at the right time.

Tiger Watson: I'm not here to listen to some benevolence lecture or you being pastoral care to Mumkin. If the committee can change its decision to choose John in future, why don't you take my nephew into consideration?

Principal Blacksmith: Because he's ill mannered.

Tiger Watson: What ?repeat!

Principal Blacksmith:He's ill mannered .I'll mannered like you(smirk).

Tiger Watson: Bloody heck! You'll pay the price of it, you old codger. I wanted my nephew to be the chief of this Secret committee.His name as Zeen Watson was supposed to be published in newspapers, thus enhancing my reputation in public. He's not even made to this stupid secret committee. "They spilled water on my plans".

He wears his black sunglasses back and looks at Bison, holds his collar for a second saying "you! Slothful,so-called best friend". Bison tells him that he can't help as it isn't in his hands. Tiger Watson leaves from there disappointedly.

Principal Blacksmith: Congratulations four of you. Fill up the forms and instructions will be given by Hielmaster. Mr. Bloom escorted the winners to Rama Krishna Hall.

CHAPTER SIX

More secrets revealed

Bloom escorts three of them to a huge hall with pictures of Krishna, Rama, Seeta, Hanuman and various other Hindu mythological lords .Messages of Bhagwat Geeta written all over in Sanskrit language. Only Pamela is able to understand.

As they look around they see -

dehino'sminyathā dehe kaumāraṃ yauvanaṃ jarā|

tathā dehāntaraprāptirdhīrastatra na muhyati||

na jāyate mriyate vā kadācin

nāyaṃ bhūtvā bhavitā vā na bhūyaḥ|

ajo nityaḥ śāśvato'yaṃ purāṇo

na hanyate hanyamāne śarīre||

They hear a familiar voice from behind them. It's Hielmaster.

Hielmaster: It's written in Sanskrit in case you do not understand.

Pamela: I know how to read and interpret the Sanskrit language.

Hielmaster: I am roman catholic, same as you Pamela. All these are from Hindu Mythology. Since you four are fortunate to join the committee, you need to be highly observant about the various cultures .Through this you will have a deep understanding about the purpose of the committee.

He read two shlokas written on the wall

"dehino'sminyathā dehe kaumāraṃ yauvanaṃ jarā|

tathā dehāntaraprāptirdhīrastatra na muhyati||

Meaning is -Just as the boyhood, youth and old age come to the embodied Soul in this body, in the same manner, is the attaining of another body; the wise man is not deluded at that."

Then he looks at another shlokas and in that excitement he reads another shlokas

"na jāyate mriyate vā kadācin

nāyaṃ bhūtvā bhavitā vā na bhūyaḥ|

ajo nityaḥ śāśvato'yaṃ purāṇo

na hanyate hanyamāne śarīre||

The meaning of it is -The soul is never born, it never dies having come into being once, it never ceases to be. Unborn, eternal, abiding and primeval, the soul is not slain when the body is slain.

Now you must be thinking , why am I telling you this!"

Pamela: We're clueless. I hope the committee isn't about philosophical or religious work, Mr. Hielmaster. If that is the case then I am the first person to run away from here. I'll leave the committee.

Bessy whispers in Pamela's ears.

Bessy: You're not the first one to leave the committee. In fact I'll be the first one to do that.

Ren: I'm leaving right now! Philosophy and shit . It's not my area to claim fame.

Bessy: Then Zeen and Rose are luckier to not make it to the committee right away! So much hard work we did just to know that we're here to prepare pamphlets of philosophical teaching.

Hielmaster: I heard this word for the first time from her.....Aaaaaa(keeping his palm on his forehead).... that person ....she's your warden.....

Pamela: Is it Warden Augustina?

Hielmaster: Nope! Who's she?

Pamela:She's a warden of the girls ward.

Hielmaster: What I'll do with her? Tell the name of that warden! Before sometime she was near the podium when Principal Blacksmith was giving his speech!

Pamela: It's not she...is he...So it's not her name but it's his name...probably that's what you're asking for. Are you talking about Warden Atrika Bloom?

Hielamster: Okay...Yes Mr. Bloom....I always thought that he's a lady! Yes ....so what does he call you people?

Pamela: Don't know about others but for him I, Mumkin and John, we three are rule breakers!

Hielmaster: Rule breakers is a decent word ....but all four of you here are 'Nincompoops'....

Pamela: But why?

Hielamaster: Without my instructions, you're creating your own interpretations! Now shall I give my instructions?

Pamela:Yes sir.

Hielamter: Pamela, you're the most talkative among four of you. What about the three of you?

Mumkin, Ren and Bessy also agree to Hielmaster.

Hielmaster: My name is Colonel Hielmaster. I am in the Army working as a behavioral therapist and a trainer. You can definitely call me Mr. Hielmaster. Ensure that from now onwards you learn to conceal all information that you receive . Including my name and your role in this committee . This committee's philosophy is depicted through this hall. This hall's blueprint was given in 1936 by a student like you who also joined the similar committee. She is Lidiya Cheriyan! There were few other prominent members too where late Rama Parmeshwar was spiritual trainer of University. He was the creator of the committee's philosophy.

Pamela: We know about Lidiya Cheriyan, people think she's a traitor.

Hielmaster: (cackles) You'll come to meet her today afternoon! For now fill up the forms of your basic information declaration.

Mumkin remains silent as he knows from the diary of Lidiya Cheriyan that Devkali Neelghanti Paul, Isabella and Lidiya Cheriyan are all the same people. For a second he is hesitant to talk about it. The doubt is that he has it ,Isabella is still recovering with the injury from the attack and she's in a wheelchair. Isn't that too soon for her to come here in college to visit them?

They all fill up the forms of their basic information and sign the declaration of agreement to join the committee from where students will be further selected to work with the Military .The exception to them was Ren who is hesitant as he is in Business Management.

Hielmaster: Junior Bison, why aren't you signing the declaration?

Ren: I don't think that ever in my dreams I would want to join the Military!

Hielmaster: So what will you do?

Ren: Business.

Hielmaster: God! I asked what will you do right now with the declaration, seriously you four are nincompoops?

Ren looks at him with anger in his eyes.

Hielmaster: Keep your good looks, especially those eyes with red wine filled in them for your girlfriend Ren.You don't have to impress me with those as I am a straight guy.

Ren remains silent looking at the declaration form in anger. Hielmaster gave him time to think about that contribution to join the Armed forces through his business skills. Mumkin, Pamela and Bessy fill the forms and return back to their hostels as they need to return back to the hall by noon at 3:30 PM. Ren goes near his uncle's office in college.

Ren:Uncle Silver, I don't want to be part of this committee.

Silver Bison: I am happy that you want to back out Ren.

Ren: Uncle why are you happy?

Silver Bison: Because I know that the area of your interest !

Ren: Yes. It's to join your business .

Silver Bison: After your selection in the committee, I too thought the same , You're my only nephew, how can I let you join the Military.

Ren: I am surprised that uncle, you too know about the secret committee which is all about the Military! How do you know it Uncle?

Silver Bison: Some amount of funding is from my side too in this committee. The committee doesn't have any aspect of business in it .Due to this your learning in your interest i.e. Business will stop!

Ren: That's why I am so concerned.

Silver Bison: And another thing is the adventurous life in the Military! I'm concerned about that too.

Ren: Did you say adventurous? I want to live an adventurous life uncle, I am all in to join the Military!

Silver Bison: Halliluah. Within a second you changed your mind from doing Business to join the Military. But be careful,the mission of this committee is paramount, so the risk factor is also high.

Ren: It makes it even more interesting.

Silver Bison: I know you're a young blood ,so you like adventurous things.

Ren: Uncle I'll fill up the declaration and submit it as soon as I can.

After giving a head hug to his nephew, Silver Bison leaves from there.

Mumkin goes back to his hostel. He enters the room but doesn't find John. A fellow hostel mate tells him that he has gone to a wine making workshop to learn how to make wines.

Mumkin finds this as a good time to go for a quick nap. He dreams of himself with a lady wearing black gown with a black headscarf on her head.There's a marigold smell all around. She's facing the opposite of him. She looks kind of familiar until she turns towards Mumkin . It's Prof Olivia, who is actually chuckling gorgeously looking at the flowers . It's probably the rarest of the rare moments on earth. It's all a beautiful background with sunny days and colorful flowers. He wakes up by saying that the dream was bizarre as she is just way too rude ,opposite to how he saw in his dream. In reality, not even her sister Isabella might have seen her chuckling like that .Anyone would get happy seeing her smiling like that. He sees at his wrist watch and it's already three fifteen noon. He quickly wears his shoes and collapses head to head with John, he tells him that he'll see him in the evening and runs towards the Rama Krishna hall. On his way to Ramakrishna hall he's not able to find the hall anywhere.He got jittery as he was getting late. This time he goes near warden Bloom's office and doesn't find the hall there either. Principal Blacksmith's office is just next to Bloom's office. As he peeps in there ,he finds various military officers sitting together in full Uniform . There was a senior personnel in between. There wasn't any mark of the hasleness college life inside the office as everything was so well maintained. He doesn't find even a single college professor inside the room! He was just looking at the hygiene and discipline of the room when Principal Blacksmith kept his hand on his shoulder.

Principal Blacksmith: Mumkin, what are you doing here?

Mumkin: I am searching for Ramakrishna Hall. I am lost.

Principal: You need to remember every detail from now onwards! You've got to play a crucial role in the committee selections.

He calls the guard Kimsu and gives instructions to take Mumkin along with him. He shows Mumkin the way towards Rama Krishna hall.

He enters where the room is completely empty and dark with only one light on near the stage. Before he could ask anything from Kimsu, he turns around and sees that Kimsu is not present. He shouts "Hello, Colonel ,I'm Mumkin". He hears back a sound saying". Yes Mumkin, come near the stage, towards the left, find the staircase. Follow it and come down". Mumkin moves near the stage and to the left he finds a staircase ,which he climbs and on his right side he finds curtains covering painted walls, he goes towards the right side and finds the second staircase heading down. He climbs down the round wooden staircase and reaches the basement with a huge space filled with white light all over. He takes a second to adjust his eyes and then looks in front, where Pamela, Bessy and Ren are sitting in a circular fashion with Colonel Hielmaster. He is wearing a service dress with medals and commendations on his left side. He is wearing a peaked cap with a cane in his hands.

Hielmaster: Come here Mumkin, have your chair. You three will get to meet ex Captain Lidiya Cheriyan. She will tell you three about your roles.

Pamela: Ex captain. Is she retired?

Hielmaster: Well, she is and she is not.

Pamela: What do you understand by your mixed answer?

Hielmaster: Stand up you lady!

Pamela: Who? Is it me?

Hielmaster: Yes you! Don't you know how to talk to seniors? You need to address me as sir not as 'you'. Now sit. She sits down with her head down.

Mumkin secures the position on the left of Bessy, next to Bessy is Pamela and next to Pamela is Ren.

Hielmaster: There comes Lidiya Cheriyan. Welcome Miss Cheriyan.

As Mumkin, Bessy, Pamela and Ren turn towards the direction pointed by Colonel Hielmaster, as they look there it's a long hallway filled with whitelight and a shadow starts appearing slowly. As the shadow gets clearer, they find Professor Olivia arriving there. They all are shocked to see that their teacher Prof Olivia is only captain Lidiya Cheriyan . Mumkin is especially shocked and confused to discover that Lidiya and Prof Olivia are the same person. The diary named Devkali Neelghanti Paul is written by Prof Olivia and not by her sister Isabella. Thus all the books written by Devkali Neelghanti Paul are actually written by Prof Olivia. Isabella is completely out of picture now!

Prof Olivia addresses everyone. This time she appears more strict with them.

Prof Olivia urf Lidiya Cheriya: I am ex Captain Lidiya Cheriyan. For those who know or do not know, people sometimes call me a good human or a traitor. I'm none but a soldier, an uplifted or upgraded version of a so-called normal person. Coming to the crux of this committee, it's name is Learning to Guard. Once selected you will be trained . Training involves a routine. Morning to afternoon University classes. Continue training in the evening. Training needs to be done hiddenly. Know your forte and weak areas. Choose the stream wisely or else you'll be put in these areas accordingly. Best wishes to complete the training successfully so as to become an integral part of the Military.

Complete information sharing is tomorrow. Any questions?

Mumkin: Prof Olivia, I mean Captain Cheriyan....

Prof Olivia: Call in educational terms, speaking half information leads to crucial hiding from others. This prevents delinquent habits i.e. title-tattle.

Pamela looks very confused based on the statement of Prof Olivia.

Mumkin: Yes, prof Olivia.

Mumkin raises his left hand to clarify a doubt.

Prof Olivia: Mr. Chamburt, speak up.

Mumkin: Will they provide uniforms after training gets over?

Prof Olivia: Question will be answered tomorrow. Anyone else?

Everyone remains quiet .

Mumkin again raises his left hand to ask a question.

Prof Olivia: Second time questioning, time allotted- 3 seconds!

Mumkin: I want to meet you in person, when will you be free?

Prof Oliva: Meeting will be arranged at the right time.

Mumkin: Sure.

Prof Oliva: I assume, today's information is clear.

Hielmaster: Captain Cheriyan, you're Prof Olivia for them, they're panic stricken from your presence.

Prof Olivia: They need to get out of this intimidation in order to join the Military!

Prof Olivia leaves the place.

Hielmaster: I'll see you four tomorrow at four thirty in the evening. Take rest, be fresh .Fresh like sunflowers. Especially you Pamela.

Pamela: Yes sir.

Hielmaster: Be a sunflower, not a leech sitting on that!

Pamela: Sure sir.

Hielmaster(While leaving): Bye.

Bessy comes near Pamela and says.

Bessy: I didn't know that leeches sit on sunflowers. I thought insects like butterflies, moths, spiders and ladybugs were sitting on it.

Pamela:It doesn't matter what sits on a sunflower, ultimately he called me a leech.(her right eyebrow is raised).

Bessy:Doesn't matter! At least he didn't call you a botfly.

Pamela: Why are you saying so?

Bessy: A botfly doesn't sit on a sunflower and is more dangerous than a leech. Let's leave things here itself. I am feeling hungry. Let's get out of here.

The two ladies go out of the hall near the cafeteria to grab some snacks.

Mumkin and Ren stay back. Ren doesn't say a word to him and is constantly staring at the white light hallway through which Prof Olivia had arrived.

Mumkin: Did you submit the declaration form?

Ren: Yes. Why are you asking?

Mumkin: Just wanted to know.

Ren:I submitted it before you arrived here.

Mumkin: So you are going to join the military leaving your Business Management course,is it?

Ren: I do.

Mumkin: Business will get you more money than a military job.

Ren: I don't care about money. I got everything in my life through my uncle Silver whose earning is in Billions. It's just that….(he again stares at the while light hallway).

Mumkin: So what is it ?

Ren: The adventurous life in Military.

Mumkin: I see!

Ren: What's your motivation?

Mumkin: I always wanted to do business in weaponry, so probably this is my gateway to fulfill my dreams.

Ren: No ways. You have to imagine how tough military life is!

Mumkin: What do you mean?

Ren: My uncle knows few military officers. The truth is doing business while in the military is like cooking tapioca without fire! There's no time.

Mumkin: Why is it so?

Ren: There's no time in the military!

Mumkin: But I believe if you desire something good,you always reach a fruitful outcome.

Ren: Let's see how much your beliefs and philosophies sustain in the Military.

Mumkin smiles at the harsh comment of Ren. John arrives there along with Pamela and Bessy. He congratulates Mumkin and at the same time brings a red velvet cake for his best friends Mumkin and Pamela. He invites Ren also as a gesture to celebrate their success. Laila joined them too. As they cut the cake ,Laila hugs Mumkin warmly to congratulate him. After that John , Mumkin and Pamela hug each other in a circle of three as a gesture of luck to Mukin and Pamela.

Pamela: This is unfair.

Mumkin: What's unfair Pamela?

Pamela:They should've included John too in the committee. I wish both of my best friends were part of the committee.

John: What best friend? I'm not your best friend.

Pamela kisses John on his cheek out of happiness, saying 'Yes you are!'.It was a little shocking for him. For Pamela the kiss was out of a childish act but for him ,it bloomed pink heart bubbles filled with love.

John rubs off the tinch of saliva from the kiss off his cheek. He was just feeling something deep and warm. His cheeks were turning red. Pamela tries to kiss Mumkin also on his cheek but he stops her right away saying 'He also considers her as his best friend but he would preferably be kissed by his girlfriend Laila only.'

Ren takes a piece of cake and leaves the place quietly while eating the cake simultaneously, he looks back and says 'Pamela can never grow into an adult and laughs off' . Mumkin and Pamela start sharing their experiences with John till six pm.

Pamela: John, it was good that you didn't make it in the last stage.

John: Why are you saying so?

This time John's pupils are deviating as he's finding Pamela really beautiful. Her eyes are more shinier, cheeks are more pinkish and there's an irresistible glow on her face.

Pamela: Last stage was all about teamwork.

John: So you think I can't work in a team.

Pamela: No...not at all. I mean ,it causes injury to Rose , Zeen....don't ask about him.

John: Why what happened?

Pamela: He not only got injured physically but proved to be a lunatic person. Do you know he's the son of Tiger Watson.

John: Alright....But why did you make this statement that I shouldn't be a part of the last stage of selection?

Pamela: There are two reasons. First is it requires a lot of physical effort to climb the protrusions on rock .

John:When it comes to physical fitness, you need to be worried about it because I am fitter than you.

He looks at the slight belly of Pamela which is bulging out. She gets a little conscious. His comment also disappoints her ,she feels that John is rude to her, behaving like Ren.

John: What;s the second reason?

Pamela: It's professor Olivia, she's only.....

Mumkin interrupts her in between saying......"Pamela ,look at that colorful bird flying there(pointing his forefinger)".

Pamela: Where?

She starts looking in the blue sky at various birds and starts laughing saying 'they're really beautiful . But which one are you referring to?'.

Mumkin: Professor Olivia was the teacher incharge for today.

He tactfully hides the information that Professor Olivia and Lidiya Cheriyan are the same people.

John: Woah.....if it's Professor Olivia then who wants to be part of the committee? even if the committee was a non secretive one! She's like a leech that will suck away all your blood.

Pamela: Don't say leech. Hielmaster called me that.

John: He appeared to be a sweet man...why would he call you that?

Pamela: Because he is our senior in committee it seems. He's coronel in the Mi..(Mumkin interrupts as she's about to say colonel in the Military).

Mumkin:He's a colossal man....Pamela asked him too many questions due to which he called her leech ....He's a cool and sweet man..

John: Yes....Pamela is a nerd when it comes to studies....he gave her the right name......Pamela I have one suggestion for you.

Pamela: What?

John: Don't ask so many questions from people....look your mind is unstable now!

Pamela: Why is my mind unstable?

John: You're calling 'colossal man' as 'coronel in the Mi'. Your tongue is slipping today a lot, Mumkin is jumping in all between to save the conversation between me and you,so that it makes some sense.

Pamela:Don't call me unstable.I am disappointed,....first Hielmaster called me leech and now you're calling me unstable.

John laughingly says 'The way you kissed me on my cheek, it was a leechy action as still my cheek is hurting'.

Upon hearing this Pamela irritatedly punches John's shoulder, to which he reacts saying 'Uiiii, that hurts'.

Pamela: I'll give you one more punch on your nose if you call me a leech. Leeches suck blood ,my punch will take your blood out from your nose automatically.

Mumkin and John laugh on hearing what Pamela says. Mumkin tells her to calm down . The trio start to return back to their respective hostel rooms .When John was ahead of them, Mumkin is still few steps behind. He whispers in the ears of Pamela.

Mumkin:Pamela, try to keep things in the committee meetings itself.Do not reveal anything to any other non committee member like John.

Pamela: Why what happened?

Mumkin: Girl, you need not reveal any sensitive information like -Professor Olivia is only Lidiya Cheriyan, Colonel Hielmaster being in the Military and any a to z information pertaining to the Military.

Pamela: Sure.

Mumkin: Yes, these were the instructions right by Professor Olivia, or I better call her Captain Lidiya Cheriyan. Remember when she was saying to me 'call things in educational terms, speaking half information leads to crucial hiding from others. This prevents delinquent habits'.

Pamela:Yes ,I remember her saying that alien sentence. What did she mean by that?

Mumkin:She meant that we need to call her Prof Olivia not Captain Lidiya for others. We need to give people half information about the committee. Spreading any information can be delinquent.

Pamela: Okay, I'll try not to share but John is my best friend you know and I find it difficult to hide things from people whom I regard as close to me!

Mumkin: Miss, you need to hide the committee information irrespective of how close you are to anyone.

This was the first time when Mumkin was slightly rude with Pamela as he wanted her to be a little more self-controlled when it comes to keeping any information about the committee..

Pamela: Sure, I'll not rant around from now onwards.

Mumkin:Alright, let's go to our hostels.

They both move towards their respective hostels. Upon reaching John went to sleep whereas Mumkin starts reading the diary with more of curiosity as now he knows that Professor Olivia is only Lidiya Cheriyan ,the owner of this diary.While reading, he looks up at the ceiling of the building to ponder. He reflects that he has kept all the extra information of the diary only at one place i.e. In his mind . Not revealing it to any other person, even Lidiya Cheriyan aka Prof Olivia doesn't know that he had a hint of knowing that Lidiya is the owner of this diary. One thing that was questionable is, why are the selections done at Lidiya's time different from that of his time. It was a long interview for Miss Cheriyan but for Mumkin and five others, they had to face a group task of some twenty minutes. While everything before the last stage of selections remains the same. In hope of discovering more, he decides to read further. As he reads he realizes that the selection is done in Lidiya's aka Olivia's time was different. The committee's name was 'Join the mIlitary',there was nothing secretive about it.But this time it is a secret committee.

Mumkin finds that Lidiya and his father became comrades along with Jonathan William. Where Lidiya and Jonathan were trainees, Charles Chamburt turned out to be their best instructors. He mentored the duo for rock climbing and weapon training . He saved Lidiya from harassment.

"Commander Charles Chamburt is someone whom I admire the most. He's tall ,handsome and a kind person. One day I was called by AJ Handon. It rained heavily that day. I ran to reach his office on time.As I entered his room, he asked me to look down .As I looked down on the floor, his loud and infuriating voice scared me. He said"Bastard, not on ground ,on your shoes". There was mud in my shoes. Probably it happened as I was running near rainwater while coming to his office. He ordered me to bend down. He hit me twice with his cane. As I cried in agony, I heard Commander Chamburt entering the room with a luminous smile .He's the coolest person. He was chuckling about an incident that happened outside. He punished the soldier who came a day late from his holidays. The punishment he gave was to enact the role of a joker on corps day, due to which the person had to now decide which joker dress he'll purchase and from where. Jokingly Chamburt said, choose it quickly or be ready for the quarter guard. This sentence made everyone laugh including commander major Chamburt. But as he entered her room,his smile disappeared.He got serious after seeing me and AJ Handon. AJ Handon hit me a third time in front of him saying "these three for your left dirty shoe and other three will be for right". As he raised his stick, Commander Chamburt stopped him saying "I have better punishment for her. Let her polish shoes of herself and her batchmates with waterproof shoe polish. By this she'll learn the ultimate lesson of the importance of neat and clean shoes in a soldier's life". Handon agreed to that and ordered me to polish the shoes of everyone in my batch. It's a tedious task. Although it's better than the beatings and harassment of AJ Handon. I'm shocked as Commander Chamburt could've saved me from both punishment and beatings. I had to spend three sleepless nights polishing everyone's shoes. "

Reading the diary further, Mumkin realizes that although Lidiya was a pretty lady, still she wasn't aware of the demeanors of parties in the Military. He guided her for that too.

She writes "Allora, I just can't believe how thankful I am to him. He's just a great person.Today was my first party in Military. He was supposed to guide all junior trainees. As we were ready with our formal attire, we were getting inside the military vehicles to reach the party area. But he stopped me saying that I am not wearing the right one. I was wearing a yellow colored frock below the knees, which I am not supposed to ,as yellow is a forbidden color for all junior trainees. He took me on his bullet bike to the Military wives shopping complex. He bought a red frock above my knees . As I wore it, he said to me 'You look so perfect junior'. One military wife was shopping, she too complimented saying that I looked very pretty. It was six thirty in the evening, we were supposed to be at six forty five at the party. He rode bike so fast that I had to hold his waist and close my eyes. Strong statured man with masculine face, still his smile when I held his waist was adorable. I too started blushing after that. He dropped me near a tree, where the military vehicle that came to pick us up earlier arrived. It picked me up. Jonathan was already there. We arrived at the party on time. Everyone praised me for my dressing style. Kudos to my senior Chamburt"

Mumkin realsies that his Lidiya was not just a junior for his father but probably more than that. The next incident in the diary substantiated it. She writes "Allora, today things came up to my basic human need. We are in a jungle training camp, there's all men all over. I wanted to relieve myself and take a bath. They all could do that in an open area but me being the only girl, I didn't know how to manage and openly say what I needed. But commander Chamburt came like a savior for me as usual. He arranged a small tarpaulin cloth and made a tent-like structure, arranged two buckets of water. He stood there till the time I was inside the tent taking a bath and relieving myself. This made me feel really protected. Evening I was feeling cold even in my training uniform . He gave me his black leather jacket that gave me comfort at night. I consider him as my hero"

It's all written in the diary. She writes further…

"Alora, we've come for a camp for ten days. Two pieces of good news. First good news is AJ Handon is not there with us and Commander. Senior Chamburt is leading the camp. He's an amazing teacher. Filled with intelligence and wittiness. Morning after our run we had a stretching exercise session, and we were ordered to clean up the area. We all were in pairs. I was with Febin Paul, where both of us had to collect medicinal plants. I saw a beautiful flower of a big size. As I called Paul, he wasn't aware about it either. Commander Chamburt came to check our work and he laughed when I said "The red spots and opening on that big flower resemble ..something like a cushion where little angels come to rest ". He said " The flower's name is Rafflesia. It's a corpse flower which kills insects that can die trapped in it . If you go closer, you smell rotten meat. It doesn't resemble a fairy's house by anysense. Haha. Since you both discovered two of them in camp, these flowers are quite rare, so I name your two flowers as "Rafflesia Cheriyan and Rafflesia Paul ". When I replied back to him that Rafflesia is a common name for both flowers. He then scolded us after that as we've wasted time doing unwanted chit chat. But while leaving he gave me a different name. He called me Devkali Neelghanti which are names of two different flowers. Well I do not know the reason for him calling me this, but he is addressing me through this name, nowadays".

"I've been chosen for a crucial role. Commander Chamburt wants me and Jonathan to supervise the manufacturing of inner jackets that are bullet proof in huge amounts. There is anticipation that we might be at war in upcoming years and we need to be prepared for it. Commander will be supervising us in that! He holds expertise in weaponries manufacturing. I ordered ballistic nylon. It was supplemented by plates of fiber-glass,ceramic, titanium, steel and titanium etc.I am taking time to ensure each product is meeting what was envisioned for it. Commander Chamburt is meticulous, he told me that every successful piece of equipment will lead a step forwards towards acting as bulwark. We both spend a lot of time perusing each step starting from conveyance of raw materials to manufacturing of the final bulletproof jacket. Just for a break he took me to a sunflower field. He called me there along with Jonathan and three other trainees. He conducted a barbeque party. The sizzling sound and aroma of barbeque getting cooked was just mouth watering. He fed me barbeque by his own hands and shook his hand with me upon successful completion of one third of work. We raised a toast of joy. I'm extremely happy to be closer to him!".

"I sent Lucas, our Regiment servant, to Amrisk's shop. I want to give Commander Chamburt a pen on his birthday. I specifically asked Lucas to carve 'Charles Chamburt' on the pen. His birthday is going to be one week after, i.e. on 15 of February ,but I'll give him the pen on 14th of February. You see, it's valentine's day. It will be like a subtle proposal from my side to him ".

"Today is 14 February, as I went to the office of Commander Chamburt ,I didn't see him there. I was getting restless not seeing him in his office. Every morning when we, the trainees run five kilometers as a part of our fitness routine,we cross senior Chamburt's office. Well, a glimpse of it makes my day and if he is present ,it's like seeing a saint in paradise. In this whole place,this only 10 cross 10 feet office of Commander Chamburt is heaven or else, the whole military training is like hell. Senior Chamburt is like medicine on deep injuries or I better give him the name of a healer. Until now he hasn't confessed his love towards me,this always confuses me. Why is he taking so much time? But his actions, they make always show his deep love towards me. For example, taking me to the Military shopping complex to buy me a new dress when I wore the wrong one for the party, saving me from getting harassed from AJ Hondon physically through his stick and reducing my punishment to just polishing shoes, making a tent like structure so that I could take bath and relieve myself and standing there for my protection until I completed it. And giving me a totally different name Deevkali Neelghanti.....All these things make me feel that ,he got some stuff in his heart for me. But I think he's just shy to not tell it. But I will take the lead. I will tell him how much love and respect I hold for him in my heart!

Jonathan knows that I love Commander Chamburt or my love 'my senior Chamburt'.Upon my request, Jonathan inquired about the same from seniors. Where is Senior Chamburt right now? They revealed that he's been sent for an important mission that involves fighting with a misanthropic group near Hambgit next to Ranidetro Village. Commander belongs to Ranidetro, so he has a better idea about the terrain of that place. Being a half soldier who has completed one year of training, I know that Commander is a desirable person for this mission. I just wish and pray for his well being and welfare. O lord, wherever he is, please ensure he's safe. My senior Chamburt will always succeed in every mission. I know that . My heart says that. I completely trust his capability not only as my life partner but also as a Military officer. He will raise the name of the regiment to prestige. I just wish him good health . I promise, whenever he comes back, the first act of mine will be to propose to him with this pen ".

Mumkin realizes that the pen on which his father's name has been carved belongs to Lidiya Cheriyan urf Prof Olivia. He also realizes that it was Lucas who bought the pen from Amrisk's shop, whom Amrisk was recalling that day.He's also astonished to see that Prof Olivia who is so indifferent ,distant and kind with students was once a person filled with love, admiration and passion towards life. He is curious to know what transformed her today as a completely different person who is rude and despicable for others? He reads further.

"Allora, I am expressing my feelings with you after a long time. It's been four months. I haven't seen commander Chamburt. No news of him has come from anyone.I miss him a lot. Tomorrow is the day of completion of our training. I wish he was there. I swear the day I will see him, I'll hug him so strongly that I won't let him go anywhere. One or two kisses from me to him will be like cherry on cake to make him realize how this distance between us affected me till now. I just wish to be posted near Hambgit Village.I'll request Paul to find out the information about the first transfer of me and Jonathan as he's been working in the transfer section of the regiment. Paul is just two years senior to us but he's a very friendly person. He considers me as his younger sister. I don't know anything about cooking. But during the traditional festival, I tried to cook sweet rice pudding with nuts and fruits. I think I added too much sugar. Nobody liked it .People were throwing away their full bowls of my pudding. Except for one person. I remember that I invited Paul also but he loved the pudding. From that time he licked his lips and he craves for my pudding . So if he does my posting work i.e. giving me the first posting near Hambgit, I'll definitely cook and serve him the pudding with exotic nuts like walnuts and cashews. I'll remember to serve him hot"

"God listened to my prayers. When I spoke to Paul if he could fix the posting of mine to Hambgit village. He surprised me by saying that me, Jonathan and Paul, all three of us are posted in Rakoti Village which is just near Hambgit. Oh lord, long live Paul. When I offered him the idea of a pudding party, he refused saying that day when he tasted my pudding, its taste wasn't that great because it wasn't too much of sugar, but too much of salt that caused people to dislike it. It was actually not sweet pudding but salty pudding… When he revealed that, My mouth was literally dry at that time that how stupid I am to add salt in place of sugar .But he told me that he ate it ,as he always praised my effort in everything. This is to keep my morale high during training as I am the only girl here. He sees me as his younger sister. Well thank you so much Paul for being so supportive. After my senior Chamburt,you are the second person who gives me such enormous support here. I am very happy with this news. This time, when the same pudding I'll cook ,Paul said, he will add the sugar. Haha….I can't wait to see Commander. "

"Today is the pipping ceremony of mine, Jonathan and other fellow trainees. I am the first girl to be a part of the Military. They are planning to put me into the various upcoming operations. This is indeed the best part. Another thing is, isn't that a great experience when your mother comes with your younger sister for your commissioning ceremony. Today is an auspicious day for us. Now I am second Lieutenant Lidiya Cheriyan. My honorable dear father, late Brigadier John Cheriyan would be immensely proud of me. The one and half year of rugged training paid off. This prefix of Lieutenant, not everyone can get it. Few lucky ones selected can only join the Military. Indeed. "

As Mumkin tries to read the further sentences, he's utterly confused…It's very difficult to read for him. Few sentences are like graphs on a heart rate monitor. Still he tries to read the further sentences to get some meaning. He feels the need of a handwriting reading expert to read this sloppier handwriting.

"Alora, just another blood thumping day for me. It's my first mission……………………lovely………all green…………………(non readable handwriting). We're heading towards Rakoti village in a military bus. I'm writing while the bus is moving. My handwriting is just like jalebis…. We're fully dressed in camouflage uniforms,all………………(non readable) with heavy rifles and ammunition. We three are the ………plethora…………(non readable handwriting) of these eighty seven men. Paul and Jonathan are heading the…………………… (non readable handwriting) team with thirty soldiers each and I am heading the Charlie team which is the quick action team consisting of twenty six plus one soldier including the driver ……(non readable handwriting) in the ….(non readable handwriting)".

"I'm writing all this after the mission…..Gosh, my hands are shaking while I am writing. What I experienced today, it happens in the movies. We were heading towards the Magenta Mountains which are famous for a jungle of magenta trees. The name also signifies the bloodletting of convoys by miscreants. These miscreants have gotten on the nerves of local people. They loot and dominate them with their local guns and weapons aries. The crime rate is high in that area. There isn't any law and order as the local government has given up its administration two years ago. The minister of Magenta Mountains was overthrown ,evicted and murdered at that time. Localites are like orphans. These miscreants are out of control, so our government of Himbertown, i.e. My town, the Military, has decided to solve this issue. I am part of this mission, very passionate to give miscreants the kissing reminder that it's their time to be evicted,just like a farmer plows out poisonous mushrooms from his farming. Today my quick reaction team gave a lot of love to the miscreants. What happened was while our convoy reached near the Magenta mountains, there was a sudden boom sound that we heard near the Grayish Cale pass. I alerted the quick reaction team to be ready with ammunition. I scrutinized using three sixty degree cameras where I found that there's a group of miscreants hiding in the bushes just ready with their rifles to conduct an attack on us. God knows how they got to know that Himbertown Military is taking the charge to evict them. But since they know it now, we'll ensure that they regret knowing it. As it is their death day. I told my troops to fire in the air continuously, behaving as if they were fearful, untrained soldiers with low morale. They instantaneously shouted crying out in pain shouting loudly 'Wo's ther…Who is there, I kill you'.They did so for the next twenty minutes,when firing done by troops was at peak. The next ten minutes the intensity of firing came down as few of them stopped firing . Just after three minutes, troops shouted 'It's over...ammunition is over'. The miscreants took a few steps near our truck in a benefit of doubt that we're done with the ammunition as we created a fake notion in their minds. In reality the bullets fired in the air by our troops were fake. We had enough ammunition to stand by the place at least for the next two days. This time with minimal bullets and two Mk1 grenades we managed to kill eleven of them, capturing four alive. We took them in our custody. Taking them to the quarters in Rakoti village. Through our unique interrogation method ,we wanted them to reveal some information. First meeting was between the Military and miscreants to get the information, second to know their family details ,wives,parents, children and develop friendship to interrogate them in order to get complete information about history, geographical locations and reasons for their cruel acts etc. Still if they don't open their mouths then we use the least used and least preferred method i.e. their faces and our hands....Sometime the method has an upgrade in it...their backs and our belts....Or something more rigorous than that....Well ,I don't want to write more than that. Jesus, they were unforthcoming in starting but as they were ......I want to openly write here.......As four of the miscreants, they were beaten till death until one member spoke that these miscreants belong to a huge malefactors organization ,that is preparing to create bloodshed starting from small villages and towns. Magenta hills was one of their targets. The reason is they want to create fear in the minds and hearts of people. They want to make the government of the state powerless by taking over these small villages and towns by either overthrowing the local ministers ,assassinating them or joining hands with one or two odd chicken miniter who are corrupt and bribelovers. They want to take financial,geographical and political power on the state....Well another crucial information is,this group isn't born naturally . There isn't any genuine reason for its birth like poverty or any incident of injustice that might have triggered its formation .These miscreants are paid by someone known as Watson. Infact, they are headed by him. As the miscreant was revealing the information, I was jotting down all the paramount places ....I ended up creating a map using all the information... Ultimately this name, Watson, got stuck in my head.

I've heard about this name before. But I can't recall it back. Who is Watson?I asked Jonathan about this. He slapped my head softly reminding me that Tiger watson was the guy involved in doing the research with the Military. He was also from a business background. And now I was able to connect the dots very well. Each and everything including the fact that Tiger Watson was also about to join the Military but he refused ! He was also a kind of weird guy who would never talk anything else except his show off of his riches. Way too arrogant, but sometimes his ideas were good. Probably it's been five years since I left the University that I completely forgot about that guy. My mind is or it can be the washing of the old memories as everything in life is happening at its fastest pace. Tonight I ain't able to sleep. The question of connection between Tiger Watson and this leader Waston made me laugh at night. Tiger was, although arrogant and a bit showy but ultimately an uncanny student of Himbertown University who contributed towards the country through his involvement in a research project that happened two years ago. He indirectly served the nation. It will be an obnoxious idea to even give a thought of this leader , Watson is anywhere connected with Tiger Watson. There are many people with the same surname ,so the probability that the two people are anywhere connected can be completely mutually exclusive. For a second the thought of what Tiger Watson would be doing now came to my mind, promptly I remembered commander Chamburt. If he knew that our first mission came out as a success, he would be really proud of me. Day after tomorrow I will go to Ranidetro to explore the place . My destiny allows, I'll meet my senior Chamburt ."

"I've just gone to the local market of Rakoti Village, we bought three boxes of Turkish delight sweets and a portrait of Gautam buddha. This is for the family of Commander Chamburt.I don't know much about him as he never revealed anything till now . This is the most general but beautiful gift anyone can give. Indeed. I just can't wait to see him. Jonathan and Paul will accompany me as they were also students of Commander Chamburt. They want to meet him. I asked them if they wanted to give him something...so they laughingly said that instead of giving something to commander Major Chamburt, they would have dinner at his house. They bought a jacket together to give to him."

"It is the day to explore Ranidetro. We're traveling through a Military jeep, it's a beautiful small village. I feel the inner desire to unite with each and every glimpse of this place. All I see is my senior Chamburt everywhere. I fantasize him being a shepherd with his sheeps , a cobbler fitting shoes, a shopkeeper selling handlooms and a sweet seller ,giving sweets free to small children. He's everywhere....just smiling at me. When I come to reality ,I see it's not him but the people of the village Ranidetro who are so sweet and smiling. This place has a different fragrance of marigold flowers. The Weather is slightly cold but still manageable. Most of the roads are under construction and people of the village aren't rich enough to own vehicles. Most of them are either walking or on a cycle or in a bullackart. There was both excitement and nervousness as I'll be meeting my senior Chamburt after four years.My plan will go according to what I have decided, i.e. once we see each other, I'll run towards him, tightly hug him and shower him with two kisses on both sides of his cheeks followed by a lip kiss. I'll propose to him there itself with the pen on which his surname is carved. It is the same pen that I made Lucas purchased from Amrisk's shop. Yes it was 15 February, four years back when I wanted to give this pen to my senior Chamburt on the occasion of his birthday. His birthday is on 15 February. We'll, guys propose to girls with roses and a ring. I'll propose to him through my pen as he should know that his Lidiya is only one in billions and she is unique. Now we are entering the farmland of the village, it's rice and mustard cultivation all over. We asked the people of Ranidetro about the house of Commander Chamburt, where an eleven years old boy became our guide.His name was duggu. He sat in our jeep and took us to a place. There were three houses in isolation where he pointed towards a specific house of what we're looking for. It was a huge mansion painted white all over, with two Porsche cars outside it. There were two security guards on the main gate with a huge lawn in which there was cultivation of tulip flowers. As we entered the place, there was a beautiful young woman with green eyes and long hair soaking wet clothes. I am sure, it's the younger sister of my senior Chamburt. Someone was saying that he has a sibling. She was wearing a crimson color frock with a peach color scarf. If she is his sister, then in comparison to me, she's too pretty. Look at her eyes and long for her . But due to my Military training and involvement in various missions,my skin is filled with marks and pimples. My hair has changed its shine,now it's all brown like a muddy color due to sun damage. I've cut it short too. It resembles a pancake. But I am still very confident that my senior Chamburt will love me irrespective of changes in my hair or skin. So ,Jonathan went near that lady. He asked her "Excuse me ma'am, do you know about Commander Chamburt, is this his house?" She replied that we aren't asking the correct question. It was a bit confusing for her I think.She asked Jonathan to leave. We think that the teenager has taken us to the wrong place just to get a free jeep ride. I am stopping to write as I need to inquire about the scene between the lady and Jonathan."

"I went to see what's happening between Jonathan and the lady . She mentioned that she lives in this house .She told Jonathan to 'the correct way of addressing him is Commander major Chamburt not Commander Chamburt as he's been promoted two years ago'. I became joyful after hearing about this propitious success that we are in the right house. I wanted to request her to take all three of us to him. It was an awkward communication between me and her as I knew one day she'll be my sister in law as I am one twenty percent sure that she is sister to Commander Major Chamburt. A sister is the third person who is happy about a man's success. The first one is his mother and second is his wife, which I am going to be to him in the upcoming future. This is how conversations happened between me and her when I reached near Jonathan:

Lady: Will you introduce yourself?

Lidiya: Hi ma'am. I am Captain Lidiya. They are Captain Jonathan and Captain Paul. We are juniors of Commander Major Chamburt.

I extended my right hand for a handshake but she stood still. She was silent but there was a faint smile on her face. She asked us to follow her.

I requested Paul to bring all the gifts that I purchased yesterday . He did that and as we entered the hall there was an old lady. The lady introduced her to be Commander Major Chamburt's mother. Now I met my mother in law and sister in law....It's the time to meet my husband. Haha. The house inside was like an ancestral house with huge rooms and wooden furnishing . Floors are smooth like a mosquito will slip and shine like flower carvings on roof's reflections could be seen on them. We were made to sit on a sofa in one of the rooms. There was a vass on which laughing buddha was painted. There were yellow tulip flowers kept inside it with their stems going inside the vass. I wondered if the flowers were kept with or without water to maintain their freshness.I wished to go near it, but I kept myself in self control. Next to that there were two peacock feathers .One was completely embedded in the wall, probably through glue and the other one's tail was slightly attached to the embedded one, it was swinging to and fro due to air. I wanted to fix it too. But I kept myself calm, waiting for my senior Chamburt to arrive in the room. My heart was thumping. We were served with tea"

"Just didn't know how to write,guts seems to have gone to the market to buy eggs . Now, I am in the guest room ,peeping outside the window. Those who drink and smoke need to be put in prison as they have this bad habit to reduce their pain in life through bad addictions.I always stayed away from it. Just wondering if there can be other ways to reduce pains .Being straightforward, what happened was ,as we headed towards the first floor, we saw Commander Major Chamburt injured on his knee and head. He was lying in bed. As she woke him up saying honey ,look who has come to meet you?'That made me intuit that the lady is actually not Commander Major's sister. To my horror, he held her hands together and kissed them while lying on his bed. He said to her 'baby, give me a kiss'. In return she asked him to wake up as we had come to meet him. He opened his eyes and gave a broad smile to the three of us. The question that I had in my mind was when did he marry? As during our training he wasn't married. For a second I felt betrayed. How can he forget me? Since he left Himbertown, he never looked back. All I had was false hopes to reunite with him. If I knew that he's married, I wouldn't have waited so long. Although he is my senior and I cannot go beyond my limits. I wanted to hear if it's true from his mouth that this lady is his wife for confirmation. He welcomed all three of us saying 'Oh my god, is that Lidiya ,Jonathan and Paul or shall I call you Rafflesia Lidiya and Rafflesia Paul, haha(chuckling). Honey(looking at this lady),they're my trainees and Lidiya is the first woman to be trained in combat. You three will reach very high positions . It's the feedback of your very first successful mission. I'm proud of you today(looking at Jonathan , then to me and Paul)'.

That's it, it was confirmed that this lady is his wife. He just introduced me as his trainee, just a trainee whom he called Rafflesia Lidiya once. He forgot the name of Devakali Neelghanti, that he gave me when two of us were left alone in one of the training sessions. My confidence is shattered now, as all the experiences that I had with him in the past, I mistakenly thought that it was love. It was not love. Probably, he was just trying to be kind with me. My bad that what I thought was love is just a delusion. At that moment in front of him and others, I kept a fake smile on my face. As I inquired him of how he got these bad injuries, he mentioned that it all happened just four months ago. He was posted to Habgit village which is filled with terrorists and traitors who are known as malefactors of Watson. These malefactors have their base centre for ammunition at Hambgit village. He was posted to carry out a mission to settle them there with peace talks but the leader of Malefactors who is under Watson provoked the terrorists to carry assaults on his convoy before he could reach there. As he got the message early morning that day, he alerted his team to defend and attack but due to the ratio of one is to eight of Himbertown soldiers vs traitors and terrorists, his team could defend very well but in attack part his team could draw tight boundary but failed to overpower them due to which he lost many of his men and got injured. He gave gratitude to his wife whom he called Mrs. Rima Chamburt' as a good nurse, who took good care of him and other soldiers along with twenty other nurses. He mentioned that his marriage took place just a month after he came to consciousness after a month of coma. People praised her work and diligence towards taking care of him, due to which he decided to marry her . After a short meeting, I took his permission to leave the place requesting for a washroom break.In reality, at that moment I felt confused of how to react . I found myself helpless. I truly loved Charles or my Commander Chamburt for five years, since the time of my training and today he's with someone else! I always contemplated myself, cooking for him, cleaning his clothes and hugging him tight when exhausted from a hectic schedule and making love at nights with him. Now all that belongs to this nurse Rima. My dreams are now lived by her. Initially I compared myself with her thinking that she is his sister. Now I'm comparing myself with her as his wife with an unaware mind that it's useless as I need to move on. Mind's logic shows direction but heart meanders in fantasies ,past and expectations .This isn't a good quality of a soldier. Oh lord, take away this bad jealousy and frustration ,change me completely to a tough person who can never feel any emotion like love again. I don't want to be withered again in my entire life like this. I choose not to fall in love again as I am afraid now to do so. But I salute Mrs Chamburt for remaining with Charles in his lowest point. Indeed she's a true soldier's wife. Probably Commander Major Chamburt always supported me in my lows in the past as my senior and friend but his wife Rima always supported him in his lows that is why she is his wife".

Mumkin realizes that Prof Olivia loved Mumkin's father before his mother Rima Chamburt, but she faced a heart break due to it as her love could never unite with him and she could never propose to him. Probably her contemplation is right, his father was just trying to be helpful to her as his senior. Or he was compassionately kind to her as she was the only girl in the Military to be trained at that time .In the past also his father, when he joined the military he was known for his kindness in Ranidetro village . Whenever his father came during holidays to Ranidetro, he helped the poor village farmers in the development of farming through coming up with innovative ideas of converting the kitchen wastes into manure and biogas,equipping the farmers with better farming equipment. This produced good results in farming. His second involvement was in the field of education, especially his emphasis on education of girls, low economic groups and their empowerment. He had huge ancestral property and farmlands. He was a philanthropist too. His ninety percent of the property got sold after his death as family and wife had to meet their livelihood .He was loved by everybody. It was not just his family but the villagers too always waited for him to be back from the Military through leave. Probably due to all these reasons he was kind with Lidiya too. Now Mumkin wonders the transition of bubbly Olivia into a sober abstinent soul. That's why she is so rough and tough in her life with almost everything. He reads further.

"Dear Alora, I have been ordered to live in Commander Major Chamburt's house for the next two days to share a report on our first operation and create our next action plan. Mrs. Chamburt cooks luscious meals, Jonathan guzzled into sumptuous chicken tikka masala last night. He was quite fidgety about his stomach since morning . He and Paul have left back to the quarters in the Rakoti village. He mentioned that he's been in poor health since late at night. Afterwards, I discussed the event with Commander Major Chamburt and prepared the whole report based on facts, reflections and valuable inputs given by him. I submitted it to him. We were making our plan of action to knock out malefactors and apprehend Watson, before they commit any other crime that impacts the capability of our Military. It was four thirty in the afternoon when I decided to accompany Mrs. Chamburt to the local market in order to help her out during dinner time. I don't hate her as she's my senior, instead I respect her thrice .This is part of estimable Military culture. We purchased chicken, dried thieme,pepper, lemons and garlic to cook Spanish lemon chicken.Well, I just don't feel like writing anymore.....(sketch of moons and stars on the page)".

" I am just dying from inside. Unable to express through writing. To my trepidation ,I heard unimaginable news from a runner who mentioned that Jonathan and Paul along with the driver faced a lethal bomb blast on their way. As I rushed to the hospital in Milil, a city near Hambgit in forty five minutes , Paul and the driver were declared dead by the doctors. Jonathan was highly injured where he lost his left leg.I squealed about the death of my sworn brother Paul and an important soldier. I was tumultuous for a second , then I informed their family members through making a telephone call. Made the traveling arrangements for them in military buses. Arranged a team of best military doctors to save the life of Jonathan and informed professor WIlliams ,made an arrangement for his travel to see his younger brother and pray for his soon recovery. All of the three families were devastated to hear this news. The deceased driver has his two daughters aged two and four and his wife in the family. There's no one else to take care of them in the family .I feel so angry and now the revenge will be taken. These bloody fuckin malefactors will be uprooted by me like goddess kali massacred rakshasas. I went back to Commander Major Chamburt's house in order to make a plan to thrash down the malefactors. Things will be handled more rationally now as Commander Major Major Chamburt has successfully handled such types of missions in the past ."

"Another three troops of soldiers are called. A team of commandos has been called with special devices to communicate and destroy this traitor group completely .The positions of commandos have been set up ,according to our plan they are present at five distinguished positions covering Hambgit village from five sides. Rantidetro , Rakoti and a nearby third village will provide support for extra troops and rations. In these three villages concrete, cement, rocks, woods and water supply is provided to construct permanent quarters for troops for a reason bigger than present mission. It is going to be done in another week. A local war has started, soon the soldiers from Himbertown will be asked to join the war. Commander Major Chamburt will be leaving after two weeks and today is 23rd of December . Our mission to eliminate traitors, it will take place on 25 december at eleven pm night! These are winters, we need to be extra careful, especially with the continuous supply of food and clothing supplies to our soldiers."

"Troops were alerted at twenty one forty seven am, the birth time of Paul.I am headed the first group of troops, we're all carrying heavy ammunition , fifty bullets each troop and wearing camouflage ,bulletproof jacket and helmet. Alora, you will be knowing what we upto now. We're going for this mission to massacre the malefactors. With minimal sound we made a black diamond formation of convoy with I being the trip leader. A fellow Captain of mine was a Trip End Charlie. I instructed them to start their convoy towards Hambgit village. I ordered all soldiers to be occupying their positions. To reach there, we had to cross the gates which we did with caution. Upon reaching near the obligated place ,we were at a certain distance from our target. With the help of binoculars I saw that malefactors have completely fenced the area with electrified iron rods. But we had to destroy this place as it is the center spot of bloody malefactors. To transgress the place, I had chosen eight out of twenty soldiers from our convoy and we wore clothes decoded by the security team to look like the malefactor's security. Full black pants and shirt ,face covered with black masks. We kept timebombs in our air jackets. Two espionage from the Military are working in the security section who helped us in infiltrating through mixing with the malefactors security guard's team. As eleven of us entered the eight storey building of malefactors,as pre planned we divided ourselves into teams,two each in an eight storey. We're well merged with other security personnels of malefactors ,still unidentified .Team one named Alpha went to the seventh floor . Team Delta went to the fifth and sixth floor, Team Charlie went to third and Team Romeo went to the fourth floor. Team gamma along with me,where I was code named as pii, we took charge of the ground, first and second floor . We planted our time bombs there. All of us including the espionages came out except Team Delta. As I used my binoculars to observe, I saw a man wearing similar security dress being thrown from the eighth floor, to our horror, it was our brother from Team Delta aka soldier Silvester Joy, he was murdered just in front of us .I could sense that they got to know our plan.I instantaneously ordered charlie to press the button .We blasted the whole building. Everything came to ashes in the next half an hour. I have no idea how,but suddenly Commander Major Chamburt appeared. He was just standing next to me, as I looked at him, his eyes were glittering with fire radiation falling on him. I was gritting my teeth for the loss caused by malefactors, especially the death of Silvester Joy. I felt exasperated but triumphant too. I lost Paul, unit driver and Delta. The terminus of traitors is this! Commander Major Chamburt, four years back, he alway kept his hands on my shoulders to calm me down whenever I was in any vulnerable state like this. This time, I kept staring at him, my shoulder was automatically, desperately moving to get his touch but after five minutes ,he looked at me with a professional smile and gave me a handshake for successfully completing the task. The happiness that he had in his eyes for me before is missing. My heart throbbed suddenly with pain. I said to myself 'Calm down Lidiya,just calm down'. Suddenly my Heart and mind were in conflicted state :

Heart:Where does the love that sparked in his eyes for me go away?

Mind: It no longer exists.

Heart: Why?

Mind: He loves someone else.

Heart: How can he forget me?

Mind: He found someone better than you.

Heart: But I can't do the same.

Mind: Why?

Heart: For me he is the only one and no one else can replace.

Mind: You're a bloody strumpet eyeing the husbands of others.

Heart: Mind your language mind. No, I am not a strumpet. I am not eyeing husbands of others. I know and have loved my senior Chamburt before Rima even entered his life.

Mind: He's not your Commander Chamburt, he's Rima Chamburt's husband now. Keep yourself and your eyes away from him.

Heart: Accepting that is a nearly impossible task to do.

Mind: So you better address him as Commander Major Chamburt ,professionally and husband of Rima Chamburt, personally.

Mind: Kick the bucket with one ml of water. You should be ashamed of yourself.

Suddenly I heard a voice that took away my attention while I was thinking and staring at my shoes simultaneously. 'You did a great job Miss Cheriyan, soon be ready for your promotion' said Commander Major Chamburt. I replied to him saying that 'it was all my duty Sir. I am not bothered about the promotion'. He said 'You've changed a lot'. For this I asked whether the change is good or bad. He remained quiet while I was at his disappointed face. As I had never bad mouthed with him. It was the inner agitation. After sometime he again said 'You've actually changed a lot'. I replied 'Commander Major Chamburt, the same applied to you too'. There was a smile on my face but bitterness from inside. I was smiling dirty as a hog with a broken heart inside. He looked at me with his eyebrows raised and then he walked away from there".

"The very next day I had to move to Himbertown due to the paperwork there. I submitted the report at 3 AM morning to commander major chamburt . He was a very dry person at that time. This time not even once he made eye contact with me. There wasn't any reply when I wished him this morning. I now realize my mistake. I not only lost my respect in his eyes as a junior but whatever friendship bond that both of us had till yesterday is tarnished now completely. I do feel guilty for not being able to control my emotions ,behaving impolitely with him.The effect of it is ,it was like I am talking to the robot. Soon after I wished him while getting out of the room, I went to the hospital to see Jonathan in a military jeep . Non commissioned officer Harry bought yellow roses on the way near and by three fifty am we reached Milil Hospital, it was all dark. I haven't slept for many days.Upon reaching the hospital, we heard the news from the doctor that unfortunately Jonathan is comatose and his right leg was infected. The doctors discussed that they might amputate it if infection doesn't stop. His elder brother, Professor Williams is accommodated near the Military Hospital quarters. I went to meet him. He and his wife fell on my feet upon opening the door of the house. As I sat on their sofa ,we had a very heart touching conversation.

Prof Williams: Lidiya, you were my student once. Dear when will revenge be taken? I can't see my Jonathan in this state?

I: recrimination had taken place sir. The full building containing malefactors has been destroyed.

Prof Williams: There is a lot of resentment in my heart.

I: I understand your emotions sir, it's natural to have resentment as our Jonathan is in an unfortunate state due to these bloody malefactors.

Prof William:I've been teaching in Himbertown University for the past ten years, I decided to not to have children. Me and my wife Greta devoted our life towards education.

Greta Williams: Yes, we don't have our own children, we adopted Jonathan.

Prof Williams: Jonathan is twenty one years younger to me.He was not only my brother but also legally my son. Seeing him in this condition is breaking my heart (whimpering)'.

I: Jonathan is a close friend of mine and he is a real fighter. I am sure he will valiantly be able to come out of this state.

With his eyes filled with tears ,he told me 'I hope no soldier's family goes through this. Our sacrifices brought us to this point in life. So inequitable(shrieking) '.

I showed him something due to which he sighed with relief to some extent. I got papers signed by him for the treatment and compensation of Jonathan. The best team of doctors are taking care of the treatment .I requested him to stay resilient. Similar papers for Paul's family and the driver's family have been signed by Commander Major Chamburt for the compensation to their families and education of the children. After reaching Himbertown, I'll get compensation papers done for soldier Silver Joy too. His family also has to be informed , his three years old twins ,wife and elderly parents will be supported by the Military. A specific amount of money ,with free medical aid and education to the families of late soldiers will be given. His family is residing at a distant place from Himbertown in the countryside. Brave soldier Joy played the most crucial role in our mission before he got martyred. I myself will give the late soldier's family a visit soon after reaching Himbertown. "

" Early morning as I woke up with a weird mewling sound. It was Lucas standing next to my legs and looking at my face during the break of day. As he just kept crying ,I changed my inquiry from soft to harsh. I said 'Lucas, nincompoop! You speak fast or else I shoot you.' The reply he gave slipped the land away from my feet. He said 'He's, he's(shrieking), he's no more! Mr. Chamburt's martyrdoom news(handing over the letter to me)'. I was completely dismayed! I snatched the letter from him. It was from Military headquarters informing that in a mission for the local war,Commander Major Chamburt was carrying out the search mission to destroy traitors hubs supporting enemy nations. He successfully completed the task but succumbed to injuries along with five men. The letter contained a military invitation to the funeral. I dressed up smartly with pride on my face and stones in my chest. Everything was numb. My world was paralyzed....Just didn't know how to react. What just happened? I'm emotionless. Lucas ,Isabella and I reached the funeral. I saw his wife crying ,holding his coffin in which his dead body is kept. I went near her,she hugged me and cried louder .I consoled her by keeping my hand on her shoulder. My face was sober and I was emotionless. I did the same with five other soldier's wives and family members. I too wanted to cry ,but I couldn't. I've made strapping obligations of uniform . After coming back home, I locked myself inside. Being a military officer I had to look like a strong person. The person whom I adored the most doesn't exist anymore physically. I tried to hug him in the air .My senior Chamburt is gone forever. I incessantly screeched till night. I couldn't sleep, and the next day was my duty. My head was aching. I couldn't stop crying so I slept off after taking a headache pill. After that I don't know what really happened to me.

The next day when I opened my eyes and found myself in a dark room. I was feeling suffocated. There was a weird smell of grass and mud. My eyes were paining and I was feeling very exhausted as if someone made me grind rice flour through a manual mill or I've been belted for five hours in my dreams while I was sleeping. My muscles were aching badly. I went to switch on the lights, but couldn't find the switch. I had a tingly feeling in my stomach as I had to go to my duty, I was getting late for that. In the darkness,I wasn't able to find any switch. I went near the door, to my surprise ,it was made of iron. I soon realized that this isn't my room as there wasn't any switch. My door is made of wood. I'm at the wrong place. I was extremely sure that I'd been kidnapped. Where's my mom, my sister Isabella and my servant Lucas. Are they safe? How in their presence, I've been nobbled. Suddenly the door opened,the light turned on, it was my sister Isabella in front of me. As I could speak anything, directly hugged me. She looked very nervous. She mentioned that we're at Prof William's residence. Jonathan Williams is no more, he is dead. As I stood up in surprise, she held my hand , as I compelled her to leave my hand and let me go .She told me to stop resisting and keep quiet. She cried more. I stood there quietly to let her explain herself. But before that I asked her why we were at Prof William's residence. Aren't I supposed to be at Jonathan's funeral now? I cried too as Jonathan was my best friend. But had to hurry up to be present at his funeral organized by the Military or else it would be breaching discipline of the Military to be absent from the funeral of a fellow soldier . A disciplinary action might be taken against me due to it. I told Isabella to stop crying and let me go there. There must be an official funeral invitation at my place. I asked her about it. She explained further that I'm waking up after five days whereas I thought I had just five hours of sleep.

She further said 'Sister, some antisocial group made the fake news that Lidiya Cheriyan is a fugitive as she didn't come for her duty on time for more than three days. This news is spreading like fire. It is there in all newspapers that the first woman to join the Military is the fugitive and a rule breaker. Tiger Watson and his lawyer raised a complaint against you sister,they requested the court to criminalize you saying that Captain Lidiya Cheriyan blew away the building in Hambgit Village killing innocent people. Yesterday this news was there in the newspaper. These two things are acting against you and people are agitated as they want justice for the killing of villagers in Hambgit .They have lost their faith in the Military. All stars are against you.'

I told Isabella that those in the building of Hambgit were not innocent villagers but the miscreants headed by the leader named Watson who is somehow connected to Tiger Watson. She told me that the Military is helpless too as there isn't any proof to prove my innocence .All reports that were given to Commander Major Chamburt by me are destroyed by malefactors as he was carrying them during the mission to hand over the combined report to the senior authority once the mission was done. There's outrage in the general public as the media also amplified the news of giving me names such as murderer, fugitive, rule breaker and terrorist etc. As I didn't turn up to court proceedings, I'm guilty according to the court as evidence given in court by Tiger Watson are against me.

Isabella added further in a whimpering tone that I can never go to my duty now as the order of court martial is being processed against me . I was perplexed. Court martial means getting removed from my job which is my passion. I thought then what is Lidiya's identity? I always identified myself as a brave military officer. Every morning before praying to god, I always prayed to my uniform which keeps my purpose of life alive. Other women look beautiful through their makeup and jewelry whereas my uniform makes me a thousand times more gorgeous that what I am in reality . For a second I thought I was losing my soul if my uniform was taken away from me. Isabella revealed the mystery that the headache pills were actually the sleeping pills that I had taken after coming from Commander

Major Chamburt's funeral. It was actually a drug that made me sleep for five days. This havoc was done through a conspiracy. How can a conspiracy ever happen in my house? It means that my house isn't safe anymore as some outsider replaced my headache pills with sleeping pills of high power !Especially I need to save Isabella as she is my cooperator. I whispered to Lucas the plan to safeguard Isabella by bringing another woman servant who would share the same name and age with my sister. She needs to be loyal. Let Isabella marry her longtime boyfriend. And what the heck is wrong with this Tiger Watson? Watson is an enemy of mine and the Military but why is Tiger Watson against me? Probably his business is connected with miscreants of Hambgit. As after destroying the building ,it might have created the loss ,that's why he's troubling me as revenge. Also how close is he connected to Watson?

Prof Williams, soon after Jonathan's funeral, came home to my room at his house after hearing the news that I came to consciousness. He told us that he and his wife trust that I am innocent and all rumors about me are fake, so he provided me and my family ,his house's basement as a place to hide. With the help of Lucas, Isabella and mom, I've been shifted here hiddenly. Our house is no more safe as it's the target of cruel Watson . "

"After reading the reports from Military headquarters about the massacre done by Watson, sometimes I wonder what Watson might look like! Probably he is like a deamon ,he has such a dark heart indeed to kill and torture so many people and destroying the peace and making people suffer!He must be having black horns on his head. If not then I will definitely insert them forcefully if I encounter him. Killing him right away".

This was the last page of her diary named Allora. Mumkin recalls that this diary is written by Prof Olivia aka Lidiya Cheriyan. She's living a new life with her sister Isabella and their servant Lucas. Prof Olivia has kept her identity hidden from others .

It's saturday where it's a holiday for all students. Mumkin heads towards prof Olivia's office. He knocks on the transparent glass door, she's signing some documents while sitting on a table.Her office is so well organized that it looks like a museum with a fully furnished cupboard in which files are kept making the pyramidal shape. Not even a single file is deviated from another even one inch. She looks so much focused on her work as if she's doing some 'sadhana'. She's sitting erect with her hands and shoulders broad .Her face is slightly oily and sweaty with her cheeks and chin shining. She looks at him for a second then recontinues with her work.

Prof Olivia: Come in Mr. Chamburt(while reading and signing papers). The complete information about the committee will be revealed tomorrow. Your arrival here is futile .

Mumkin: Miss, I wanted to return this to you!

Prof Olivia: Is it my pen or the diary

Mumkin: Do you know that your pen and diary are with me ?

Prof Olivia:Yes. How are these two things with you?

Mumkin: I found the pen on the second day when my college started. It had fallen on the ground . Regarding your diary, Lucas gave it to me by mistake.

Prof Olivia: My belongings Mr. Chamburt , who would know better? It was all pre planned to provide you with my pen and diary to make you more aware about your father,his contributions in the Military and the greatness that he had. It was done so that you can get out of the weaponry business mindset and fairly contribute where you're most required to contribute, i.e. in the field of Military.

Mumkin: I am completely astonished to hear this! Really?It was all planned, then, how did you know about our arrival at your house to meet Miss Isabella?

Prof Olivia:The day you visited Isabella, Amrisk was waiting for Lucas .Lucas had to go to his shop to hand over my diary. Since you visit Amrisk's shop often, it was planned that he will hand over my diary to you. Before Lucas could hand over the diary to Amrisk, he handed it to you directly as you with your classmates Pamela and John entered my house like unannounced guests. This diary had all details about the formation of the committee and reasons for its formation. In Fact it is my personal diary named Alora.

Mumkin: I am not carrying your pen now!

Prof Olivia: (stops signing the papers and looks at Mumkin), Mr. Chamurt, it belongs to you more than anyone else in this world.

A file fell down on the ground while prof Olivia was keeping it on a bookshelf nearby. As Mumkin goes to pick it up, she stops him saying 'don't pick it up Mr. Chamburt, that's not your work but mine'.

Mumkin: Let me help you .

Mumkin again bends down to pick up the file. Prof Olivia shows her hand to stop him.

Prof Olivia: Follow orders Mr. Chamburt.

Mumkin: Sure. I was just trying to help a lady.

Prof Olivia: I didn't ask for your help.

Mumkin: Sorry.

Prof Olivia: Your father did a lot of favors on me during my training to join the Military. These small tasks are not for you, as they have a bigger role to play. And this man's chauvinism will never stop!

She stands up and picks up the file and leaves the room! Mumkin keeps her diary on her table .He looks at the cover page for a second saying ' Alora! Dedicated to my bosom buddies'. As he looks outside her room seeing her walking swiftly with her brown gown blowing with wind, he contemplates her transition from a bubbly Lidiya Cheriyan who was curious about life to Prof Olivia who is quiescence with time filled with maturity and wisdom. He ponders what kind of person he will be when he attains her age? Will he be like his father?Or will he be like his mother? Or an aggressive military officer. He mumbles 'Life is really unpredictable, it transforms people ,where the change is like bullock carts changing ferraris!'.

The next day Mumkin along with Pamela, Ren and Bessy arrive at the Gandhi Hall again. It was all dark and in a dramatic way one light gets switched on which has white orangish color, Prof Olivia is seen just standing there.

Pamela (whispering) : Is it always planned or it just happens accidentally?

Mumkin: What?

Pamela: Prof Olivia's entry is always like a movie scene to me.

Mumkin:I have no idea about this ,but yes, whenever she enters this hall ,the lights turn on at a darker place.

Prof Olivia orders all four of them to occupy the first four seats. Ren keeps on sitting in the fourth row dismissing orders of Prof Olivia.

Prof Olivia: Four and one can never be equal. Both in real life and in mathematical terms!

Ren:I don't wish to move!

Ren hears a familiar voice from the dark and it's getting closer.There appears Silver Bison.

Bison: Ren, come on boy, respect Prof Olivia's order. You know that she's Lidiya Cheriyan.

Ren: Yes, the woman who was a fugitive soldier once. She can be your teenage crush, but for me she's a dumb person who betrayed the country!

Bison:Ren, hold your tongue young man!

Prof Olivia: Handle your nephew. There is a predominant task to be completed. I don't wish to waste time anymore.

Prof Olivia leaves from there with a raged face. Bison looks furiously at Ren and then goes behind Prof Olivia.

Mumkin: Ren, Prof Olivia isn't a fugitive soldier. In fact she's a dedicated officer who discplinefully followed all duties ,she gave her everything as a military personnel and proved her audacity through her actions!

Ren is startled and is staring deeply in Mumkin's eyes.

Mumkin: Trust me Ren, my father was her senior who trained her.

Mumkin gives the anecdotes of how professor Olivia conducted an ambush on traitors in Hambgit village when she was in service and in fact she was the first girl who was selected in the Military . She was also about to get a promotion and was supposed to be awarded with a Military bravery medal. But due to some conspiracy she was falsely declared a fugitive soldier.

Hielmaster enters the Hall with Silver Bison. They both were talking to each other.

Hielmaster: By the way Bison, your love for those dark rooms has been there since you attained puberty .

Bison: Stop it,not in front of my nephew!(his cheeks are now crimson).

Bison leaves from there

Hielmaster: I heard the conversation. If you want to ask something, ask me Ren. Mumkin's information is limited as the diary ended at an unfinished note.I have known Lidiya for more than a decade. The time she was made fugitive, the world disowned her. But her venerable actions towards military orders were apparent that she isn't a fugitive. I was five years senior to her. Mumkin, your father, was commanded by Brigadier Blacksmith at that time . He knew Lidiya through the eulogizing done by him after each successful mission that was completed by her. When Lt. General Blacksmith came to know that Lidiya with her family is hiddingly sheltered at Prof William's basement, he respectfully provided her the quarter to keep her hidden for two years where she wrote a few books under the name of Devkali Neelghanti Paul and her younger ,Isabella Martin who's my girlfriend right now, became a painter at that time. Finally after his retirement ,he became the Principal of Himbertown University and hired Lidiya as professor here. She changed her name to Olivia. Her identity is hidden from the world and with time Lidiya's case became a cold case with the Military's efforts after persuading politicians!

Pamela: That's the reason why Prof Hashtik burnt the paper to keep Lidiya Cheriyan's identity hidden!

Hielmaster: Absolutely!

Mumkin: Yes, I can recall from the diary that Captain Lidiya wanted to safeguard her sister ,that's why she hired a maid named Isabella who was also of her sister's age.

Pamela:So that day ,we met Captain Lidiya's servant Isabella, not her sister Isabella at her house. I see, it was her maid who was injured in the attack. Wasn't it like that?

Hielmaster: You're right, I'll add more to that.

Ren: I always believe that she's Professor Olivia, insolent who restigates students. As I was always kept out of reality ,I accused her of being a fugitive soldier but still trying to train us. After knowing the reality, I hope she doesn't throw me out of the committee for my behavior.

Hielmaster: You don't have to think like that Ren. Lidiya is an egalitarian person! But if you breach rules like kissing a girl in the Military,like the way you do it here in the University with your girlfriend. Then chances are you'll not only be thrown out of the military but also be quarter guarded for infinite time.

Ren: What ? Quarter Guard, means jailed for infinite time, is it?

Hielmaster: Haha, just kidding. Don't kiss your girlfriend when in Military in public. I'll give you one tip which I use all the time.

Ren: Please, go ahead sir.

Hielmaster: A guy like you who's disrespectful to majority of teh population on earth is calling me sir! So for that let me tell you the secret- when you want to kiss your girlfriend, kiss her in hidden places like near a corner or behind a tree. You won't be caught like that. Don't you watch movies?

Pamela guffaws upon the piece of advice given by Hielmaster to Ren. Both of them start to smile at her.

Hielamster: How are you Miss leech on sunflower?

Pamela: Don't call me that sir (showing tantrums).

Hielamster: Aww...Don't call me that sir(puffed cheeks making a funny face). Grow up toddler, your tantrums won't work in the Military .You'll have a tough time there.

Pamela: I will be the best soldier selected sir, I know that(saluting Hielmaster).

Hiemaster: That time will reveal.

As Pamela was saying 'How meeeee …….(mean)' , Mumkin interrupts her by raising his hand saying 'Sir I got to ask you something'.

Hielmaster: Yes, go ahead Mumkin!

Mumkin: What about miscreants? As in Captain Lidiya's diary ,she blew up the building. Is the problem of miscreants still there?

Hielmaster: Yes that's true that Lidiya destroyed the building but Brian Watson the mastermind in creating a military of miscreants. He mushroomed other miscreant groups in various villages. These miscreants are doing the demonic acts there. He's ruling them through his dark powers. Apart from that the Secret Agency of Military says that they're planning something appalling. He formed another organization with the motto to destroy the country's development and turncoat the Military .This is the main reason for forming our secret committee to elude their plan.

Tiger Watson is his son. He too supports his ideology. In fact he is his partner in crime. They aren't aware of the fact that Lidiya is still alive and is living as Prof Olivia! The whole university i.e. each and every member of University, including Ren's uncle Bison, always ensures that her identity is hidden from any outsider.

Mumkin: Why doesn't the government do something about it?

Hielmaster: Because Watsons are powerful as they hold thirty percent of business in the whole of Himbertown, probably more powerful than the government. There isn't any proof to prove them traitors. They are all whitecollar job givers. Yes,I reiterate, they're job givers of whitecaller not the job takers.

Ren:Yes, they are the rich of Himbertown and their business is also shooting up in the sky.

Hielmaster: It's a poisonous money from the business Ren. This money is going to train miscreants in their training camps. The people and the resources of the villages are exploited. Watson and his son are again filling up their pockets from those villages by making money establishing their dicating venture .

Pamela goes near Mumkin and whispers something in his ear and he seems to agree with what she said!

Pamela: We want to know how both the Isabellas are? Especially the one whom we mistakenly thought is the younger sister of Prof Olivia, that was actually her maid. We couldn't see her the second time. Probably due to committee selections and John is petrified with Prof Olivia. So we didn't get to make a second visit to Prof Olivia's house !

Hielmaster: I'm sure you're talking about Isabella Martin who lives with Captain Lidiya. Yes, refer to her as Captain Lidiya from now on when we are together. This maid Isabella is very intelligent. Lidiya hired her from the secret agency. The maid is fully devoted to her .She is well trained to act ,think and speak like Lidiya's sister, Isabella Grants who lives with me now. I'm sure she is doing well!

Mumkin: Is that a reason that when we visited the house of Captain Lidiya, Isabella was able to answer almost all questions pertaining to the house of Captain Lidiya, books written by and her family. I remember at one point she got stuck, i.e. during the Konigsberg Bridge problem, so Captain Lidiya herself handled the situation and then Lucas covered the rest.

Hielmaster: Ofcouse, she's just not Lidiya's maid but a resourceful and trainable woman. And Lucas, I love that guy. He's equal to the age of Lidiya and joined her house as her father's servant when he was sixteen. Since then he's been like the fourth pillar of Lidiya's family after her father's death.

Pamela: You know a lot about Captain Lidiya's family! Probably these secrets are revealed to us as we are trustworthy enough.

Hielmaster: Not just that. This knowledge is provided to train you for a mission to get ready in fight with miscreants!

Pamela: Cool.

Hielmaster: Hello miss toddler leech, it's not at all cool. It's a military mission not a pet show!

Pamela: Okay sir.

Hielmaster: Prof Olivia's aka Captain Cheriyan's techniques will make you equip better with unforeseen circumstances. However since I am an extrovert ,getting deflected from the topic is natural!(eyes wide open in excitement).

Pamela: Alright sir.

Hielmaster: Do you guys want to know how I and Isabella met?

Bessy: Sure sir.

Mumkin and Ren look at each other with a disappointment as both of them aren't interested in knowing about the love story of him and his girlfriend Isabella who is happened to the sister of Captain Lidiya,

Hielmaster: Infact, I am the most lucky man to have Isabella in my life. She's very simple and selfless just like her elder sister. Whatever was happening with Lidiya deeply affected Isabella. She couldn't take her sister being convicted as a fugitive by the public, infact when proceedings from court were going to court martial Lidiya, Isabella had a nervous breakdown!She went for counseling at Himbertown University's counseling professor as her ailment was increasing everyday, unfortunately he manipulated her,promised her of marriage,although later it was revealed that he came from a broken marriage and he manipulated multiple girls like that before in the past.

Pamela: Okay sir. But in starting you mentioned that , you call yourself the happiest man on earth. Why is it so as Isabella's story doesn't sound like a pleasing one to hear?

Hielmaster: Because Isabella completely broke after that ,So when I met her to counsel her through Lidiya, she just couldn't trust me at all. Despite the fact that she has trust issues, I took her to another female therapist friend of mine. It's been five years since we've been together!

He takes out his wallet which has Isabella's photo and he kisses it!

Pamela: What a great love story sir.

Bessy and Pamela look at each other's faces with smiles.

Captain Lidiya Cheriyan enters the room with a stick in her hand. There are two workers holding a map 50*60 inches, pasted on a wooden cardboard.

Captain Lidiya Cheriyan: Keep it here (pointing a direction in front of students).

She looks at Hielmaster.

Captain Lidiya Cheriyan: Colonel, I am just about to start explaining to them our action plan. Before that, Pamela will give the insight of new knowledge learnt from Colonel. Chop chop Pamela.

Pamela: We, we just learnt that your sister Isabella is his girlfriend. He got her counsel from his lady counselor friend and he loves.....

Captain Lidiya Cheriyan: Shut up Pamela! Colonel, another jest. When did you fall in love and marry my sister? Infact she is married to Prof Martin. What a fake story teller you are sir!

All including Pamela, Mumkin, Ren and Bessy are dumbstruck now!

Pamela: But he kissed her photo from his wallet!

Hielmaster takes out his wallet from his pocket and waves it in front of others. The wallet turns out to be empty with no photo in it. He just pretended to kiss an empty wallet!

Hielmaster: Alright everyone, Although at one point I had a crush on her, the manipulation part about both of them is not true. The professor didn't manipulate her but loved her truly that's why she's married to him, leaving my love as one sided. I told you this to lighten your mood!(dazzling smile).

Captain Lidiya Cheriyan looks serious but then she orders students to sit at their seats.

Hielmaster: Stop it Lidiya, don't give me that nasty look!

Captain Lidiya : Sir, a lie sounds ...

He interrupts and says

Hielamster: Shut up Lidiya, don't you start your preaching now.

Captain Lidiya: Yes sir. Look at this map. This map represents the various locations. You will be assigned roles based on the aptitude report generated during the committee selection process. Your training starts next monday . For three months you'll be trained here as soldiers. Then you'll be put into roles. You all need to be aware about the plan, look at the map!

Pointing towards the map, Captain Lidiya Cheriyan explains the meaning of various symbols associated . She decodes the symbols for church, hospital, police station and Military headquarters. These symbols look like mini drawings of triangular, rectangle and rhombus etc like shapes of a single inch on a map . She uses her stick to explain to them the roads connecting five places, including three cities and two villages viz Diewa ,Surae and Piklin are the names of cities . Marvo and Tonio are the names of villages . Pointing towards the thin ladder looking lines of varied thickness are the roads connecting these places .

Captain Cheriyan: The distance between Diewa and Marvo is 123 km, you'll be given a military jeep to travel, how much time you'll take?

Mumkin: 3.5 hours approximately.

Captain Lidiya :Others agree?

Ren: It's 3.75 hours precisely!

Captain Lidiya accepts Ren's answer and explains to them that all five places are of huge importance. She enthralls everyone by saying that they need to have quick calculation skills while planning the mission. It's not just presence of mind but strong mathematical skills that matters too.

Captain Lidiya: As every mission demands a work under high level of pressure, completion in a short time along with sharp mindedness is must. Diewa is an important Military base with an armory. Surae is 160 km away from Diewa with the facility of Military Hospital, troops , small armory unit and a small air force base. Marvo village ,210 km away from Surae is where Malefactors are trained by Watson .People of Marvo Village are oppressed by these malefactors, they're having catastrophe after the malefactors closed schools, imposed heavy taxes on the villagers which are dependent on farming and women are mostly illtreated as the malefactors are using them for their own benefits as slaves, prostitutes and entertainment purposes! Piklin is the city where Watson is presently residing which is 60km away from village Surae. In the village Tonio which is 290 km away from Piklin is the place where the mission will start. This village has trained youth of Himbertown Military to fight the injustice happening in Marvo village. The task of the selected committee members is to overthrow Watson's oppression in Marvo Village and hamper Watson's master plan by nobbing him from the city Piklin. There are two roads that connect Diewa and Surae, one unsettled road connects Diewa to Piklin, three roads connect three cities to Marvo and Tonio. Look at the map(moving the stick on roads and showing the connections on the map). Any doubt?

Ren: What's the time limit to complete this task?

Prof Olivia: Do calculate and let me know ,all of you.

Mumkin: If six month is training then, it's after seven months where we will take five weeks to complete the task- first week in traveling to respective places,second and third week in destroying malefactors, third week in establishing peace . Fourth and fifth week in reconstructing the Surae village.

Prof Olivia: Acceptable. The training is of short duration. The mission is an emergency mission. You all are assigned roles according to aptitude. Ren is in a complete combat role, Mumkin is in combat with arms improvise role, Bessy is in ammunition and arms supply support role .All of you are assigned roles. Is it clear?

All say "yes Captain" except Pamela.

Pamela raises her hand.

Pamela: There isn't any role assigned to me?

Captain Lidiya: Can others repeat the plan that I explained just now on map?In case you can then raise your left hand.

All three viz. Mumkin, Ren and Bessy raise their left hand and Captain Lidiya chooses Bessy to explain the plan. She explains the plan clearly.

Captain Lidiya: Now can you explain the plan, Miss ?(looking at Pamela)

Pamela: I can try but I just don't remember numbers and facts well!

Captain Lidiya: We know that. That's why you aren't into the main plan. You lack bravery and you have weak memory power. There are many things that make you completely redundant for the mission .

Pamela: Memory power I agree that I don't have a good memory power but bravery.....I don't think that I lack it.

Captain Lidiya: Reference is from one's aptitude test during the selection process of the committee.

Pamela: I...I get it(hesitant and sad). Then why have I been made part of this Military Committee if I am redundant for this mission.

Captain Lidiya: Your aptitude score reflects that you are a very humanistic and nurturing person. The military is going to train you for two positions- as a nurse and a counselor in the Military.

Pamela: I don't think I want to be a nurse. Counseling is my passion, not nursing.

Captain Lidiya: You have no choice but to follow.

Hielmaster: Yes Lidiya, this girl viz. Leech on sunflowers is irritating. Constantly she's rebuking my orders to learn the military atticates that you cannot cross question your seniors.

Captain Lidiya: Rulebreakers have no place in the military. She needs to be pulled out from the committee.

Hielmaster: No Lidiya. But she needs to see this as her last warning,

Pamela: Alright sir.

Captain Lidiya: Look at this map,calculate distances, discuss among all, suggestions in plan are allowed! 1cm=1km .Training uniforms will be allotted before you leave. Next time be prepared.

Captain Lidiya and Colonel Hielmaster leave from the place and then the discussion starts.

Ren: As of now I see on the map that there is a river with a bridge connecting Tonio and Marvo villages. As we start our mission at Tonio village, we can directly attack the Malefactors in Marvo by using the bridge. This will be 130 kms,shorter than the route if taken from Tonio-Surae- Diewa to Marvo as this distance is covering up to 400 kms.

Mumkin: Since Marvo is in complete control of Watson's malefactors, don't you think there is tight security at the bridge for people to enter from Tonio to Marvo? I'm sure that Watson and his malefactors are also aware that youth from Tonio isn't in the support of malefactors. As our plan will be apparent, they will be more alerted. We need to look for another way to reach Marvo. How about an underground tunnel from Pikling to Marvo?

Pamela: Is it Piklin or Pinkling?

Bessy: No idea, but let's not beat around the bush.

Ren: Agreeing to Bessy. Now from Piklin to Marvo, why not from Surae or Dieva?

Mumkin: Since Watson is aware about the Military base and Military facilities at two cities, he would be expecting any action to happen from these cities. I know it's riskier to do so but,

we need to give the enemy a bleeding nose under its roof.

Bessy:Yes and Pikling is 60km away from Diewa,so ammunition support can be easily provided. The job will be done quickly.

Mumkin and Ren agree with Bessy. Both give her high five. Pamela looks at Ren ,where he's looking at Bessy,kind of admiring her proactiveness.

Ren: After we overthrow Watson's rule, the second thing would be to send the troops from Pikling to Marvo. Once they capture the bridge connecting Tonio to Marvo, we can send troops from two ways.

Mumkin: An important resource we missed out! The trained youth of Tonio.

Bessy : Adding to Mumkin, the Military troops of Surae can be transported to Tonio in order to support our two groups! One is of troops from Diewa and the other are the trained youth of Tonio trained by our Military.

Ren: Confounding inputs Bessy and Mumkin!

Seeing the dynamism of Bessy, Pamela raises her hand in order to get herself involved more.

Pamela: I ...I ...I gotta say something!

Mumkin: Yes Pam, go ahead!

Pamela: After the malefactor's rule in that village is overthrown, we'll put the victims into rehabilitation camps.

Pamela finds Mumkin and Bessy listening to her carefully by making eye contact with her but Ren is least bothered as if he doesn't find it important at all!

Bessy:You mean Marvo village.

Pamela: Yeah, Marvo village!.

Ren: All that isn't prominent as of now and can be discussed later once the mission is accomplished.

Mumkin: (Looking at Ren)But I think we can include that too! That completes the whole plan. I believe everything we're doing is to save innocent people whose rehabilitation is needed immediately after the completion of the mission!

Ren: Alright brother. I need to leave.

Bessy: Early morning I saw Janny just looking for you.

Ren: Ofcourse, I need to meet her. She called me,she needs me the most right now.

Bessy: What if Prof Olivia comes back here.

Ren: (looking at Bessy)You tell her that Pamela's uncle Nelon, who is in the administration here, called me for a mistake in my documents(winks an eye).

Bessy: Yes, I will. But I thought you and Janny weren't together.

Ren: (chuckles) no ways. Look, people like Pamela can be accessible to all. Albeit, I am committed to Janny as Janny is a busy girl. So pardon me.

Ren leaves from there.

Pamela's eyes are now filled with tears.

Bessy: Sometimes he acts weirdly mean with you Pamela. Is there something between you and him?

Pamela: I.....I don't know what he keeps for me in his heart. But I have always kept good intentions for him in my heart.

Mumkin: Look Pamela, I know you are kind to him. But you see he's ignorant to you! Pam(keeping his hands on her shoulders). You deserve to be treated a lot better.

Bessy: Yes, you see how harsh he was with you. Just don't go behind someone who doesn't respect your feelings!

Mumkin:Cheer up!It's fifteen minutes more for the meeting to be over. We're going to meet John at Amrisk's shop. From there we'll go to a new shop!They sell the best milkshakes! Bessy you can join us too if you want.

Bessy: I would love to ,but I have plans with my boyfriend .

As Ren walks near the corridor,he sneaks into the University backyard by using University's basement way . He finds Janny waiting for him inside the student's club house. He goes from behind and closes her eyes with his hands.

Janny: I know Ren, it's you!

Ren: Janny, babe I really missed you all these days.There wasn't any time to talk to you as the committee selection kept us really engaged!

Janny: What's that committee all about? It's very secretive, I heard. Are you guys trained there as detectives to detect which person is breaking the rules of the University ?

Ren: Babe you heard it right! I ain't supposed to share any information ,but yeah our work is kind of similar to what you assumed!

Ren takes Janny for a movie and he takes her to her favorite ice cream parlor and then to an extortionate jewelry store. He extravagantly spends money on shopping for a diamond necklace, bracelets and a pair of gold diamond earrings . His driver arrives,they sit in their car and leave for his home . As Janny was sitting on her couch, Ren sat next to her ,held her hand and kissed her.

Ren: I love you Janny! You got something different from other girls. I like the way you balance your hotness with excellent grades in studies.

Janny: Ren, I want to tell you something!

Ren: Yeah(coming near her and keeping his chin on her shoulder).

Janny: We can't be together like this.

Ren: Janny, don't start it again.I'm already exhausted with the committee work. I'm here to spend some quality time with you.

Janny: This is what I don't like about you. You're into everything except your studies. This committee is a waste. You got all C's ,D's and F's. I know your uncle is a trustee here, but what about you Ren? You use his credit cards to pay for all your own bills. I just can't see where I will be with you in the next few years.

Ren: What are you talking about? You mean that I am not capable enough to keep your desires met? You think that I'm dependent on my family for all this(pointing towards the necklace that she's wearing that he bought for her)?

Janny: Exactly. Just look at your classmate Nick Lawrance, he is so promising! He always gets good grades and he has marvelous ideas of establishing his own business. I listened to him and it all sounds feasible. Although both you and him are in the same course of Business Management in University, still I see him always having a vision! And you.....I see you always being with me

Ren: Janny, why are you juxtaposing me with him? We two are different people.

Janny:Because he asked me.He likes me Ren. I want to be with him. We have many things in common including our grades and passion to succeed.

Ren: You know Janny, my parents died in a car accident when I was just four years old. From that time till now, Uncle Silver has supported me in education. The second person I trusted in this would be you.

Janny:I'm sorry Ren, I know you trusted me, but I can't trust you anymore. Look at Nick, he already opened his restaurant near the countryside of Himbertown. I can't give you a better chance than this.

Ren: Janny, just trust my abilities, I really promise you a stable future! Just a few more years.

Janny: No Ren, you're depending on your uncle. I need a person in my life who's doing better than me. I'm sorry but I just don't see that in you.

Ren: Alright Janny. Is this your final decision? You're leaving me for Nick as you feel your future is secure with him!

Janny: Yes.

She stands up and looks at the jewelry bought by Ren for her.

Janny: I will buy all this jewelry.

Ren: No, you can take all of it. No need to pay me back. Can you wait for a minute or two.

Ren runs upstairs to his room and returns back with all the gifts Janny gave him till now.

Ren: My driver will drop you in your house. Let's not meet again.

Janny: We can be friends ,if you want.

Ren: No ,I don't wish to be friends with a person whom I deeply trusted and loved. Our relationship was built on these components. Albeit, there isn't any relation between us. Good bye . I wish you luck and happiness in your new relationship!

Janny: I wish you luck too! Bye Ren.

Janny sits in Ren's car with all the shopping items with her gifts that once she gave to Ren. Ren was standing outside. As the driver starts the car Janny looks out .

Janny: Ren, I feel bad for you. But I just don't have feelings for you. You're a kind person. Thanks for today's shopping.

Ren: Bye Janny.

The driver drives away .Ren looks at his car and is heartbroken. His golden retriever dog comes near him. He sits next to it and breaks down into tears. He starts shouting the name of Janny loudly....So loud that his uncle comes near him to console by hugging him while he is sitting on the ground crying.

Mumkin, Pamela and Bessy leave the Gandhi hall. Bessy goes near the hot dog just outside University where her boyfriend of Irish ancestry arrived after five minutes. Mumkin and Pamela, wait near the school's artificial fountain . There arrives John with Laila.Laila gives a hug to Mumkin and Pamela. Pamela hits John on his shoulder lightly with her book.

John: Aaao(painfully) how you guys have been! What is this committee all about?

Mumkin: Dude, we're good! The committee kind of involves some sort of secretive work. How have you been? ?(Looking at Laila) Laila hope you are all right?

Laila: Yup, after seeing you both(referring to Mumkin and Pamela), the day has got better.

Pamela: Stop lying Laila, it's not both of you...In Fact it's seeing Mumkin your day has got better. What's there in seeing me?

Laila starts blushing. She and Mumkin make eye contact and she starts to blush more.

Pamela: Let's go out to Amrisk's shop, It's been a long time.

All four head towards Amrisk's shop. They find him setting up the library catalog with K Jalty.As they enter into his shop, he gets super excited.

Amrisk: Oh my goodness. What a pleasure to see warriors here. Truly content to see Mumkin and Pamela to be a part of the committee. Errr. Ren, welcome back to the shop. Never mind if you didn't make it to committee. The new edition of your comic is available. Here(throwing the comic at John which he successfully catches), go ahead and read it. Oh, we got a new guest here. What's your name, young lady?

Laila: Hello Sir, I'm Laila Sim.

John interrupts in between,

John: How do you get information about the University's committee selection, you're not even part of it. Before I wasn't bothered about not making it to committee, but after you called Mumkin and Pamela warriors, I'm filled with repentance now. Seriously, what's up with the committee that made them superstars.

Amrisk: Oh young man, cool down! Don't forget it's a bookstore. Students come here to buy books and share a word of conversation with me. One of them told me about how hard the selection process was and only a handful made it to selection. Don't worry. All students who visit my shop are warriors for me, including you. Come on, help yourself with cinnamon rolls and coffee.

All sit together on a round table with coffee and cinnamon rolls. Sequence follows Pamela, Mumkin, Laila, John and Amrisk in a circle. As usual, John grabs the roll and enjoys eating. He snatches half of Pamela's roll too. She shouts in return 'stop it Ren....I mean John' and hits John with her book on his shoulder.

Miss Laila, it's great to see at my shop. Explore the books of your interest.

Laila: Can I get books by Devkali Neelghanti Paul? I like her writing pieces.

Mumkin and Pamela stop eating and look at each other. Pamela whispers in Mumkin's ears, 'Captain Lidiya needs to write a few more books for Laila. Undoubtedly, those boring books are written by Prof Olivia or I call her what Ren calls her, vulture Olivia. Damn boring books, I don't know what Laila likes about those?'.

Mumkin replies whispering back, "Pamela, don't discuss anything here, we're supposed to keep things secretive".

Pamela: Mumkin, what's the issue of Captain Lidiya with me, why did she say that I lacked bravery?

Mumkin: Pamela, have good emotional control. Laila, Amrisk or any other outsider shouldn't come to know about anything. So keep quiet now.

Pamela: Mmmmm(murmuring)....okay

Amrisk: Miss Laila, you can check if her books are available here. As of now the author's writings are limited. I'm not aware of the reason why it is so.

Laila: Sure. I'll check books that aren't available with Mumkin and Pamela. Both of them have a few of her books. They are soothing when I read them.

Laila checks his shop and finds two more books written by Devkali Neelghanti Paul.

They do a chit chat with Amrisk. After half an hour all four leave. Mumkin walks with Laila and John walks with Pamela.

Laila: You see, there's something new I've learnt. Can you wait for fifteen minutes? I want to give you a surprise.

Mumkin: Sure Laila, well it's already five fifty pm. However I'll wait in the basement, if it turns out to be above the hostel return time.

Laila: Great!.

Laila hugs Mumkin. They move faster to reach the hostel.

Pamela and John were walking together, three meters behind Mumkin and Laila.

John: Pamela, you look sad. Aren't you happy with the committee work?

Pamela: John, it's ...it's not like that. I'm happy(sighs).

John: No, you're either lying to yourself or to me! I know you're a very irritating girl but today you look low in your energy.

Pamela: John...I have never felt this before. The more I try to get away from him, the more I'm getting obsessed with him.

John: Who's he, the unlucky man on earth?

Pamela hits John with her book.

Pamela: It's Ren.

John: But Pam, Ren is already committed to Janny. In Fact I see that he loves Janny more than Janny loves him! You see the intensity of their relationship, it's fluctuating and Janny is dominating it. He's just her biggest fan.

Pamela: I find Ren a perfect boyfriend. I wish I was at Janny's place. But he constantly ignores me and avoids even eye contact with me. Even when I gave my ideas during committee meetings, he was unreciprocated towards me.

John: I don't know what to say for your love which has zero chances of getting requited to you! Let me call Mumkin and Laila to give you some love tips.

John calls them both and he reveals Pamela's feelings towards Ren.

Mumkin: You need to realize Pam that relationships are built on mutual respect and attraction. You might be the world's most beautiful woman, however Ren's eyes are able to appreciate what Jenny has to offer, in that case, you're disrespectful to yourself as you're running behind a guy who isn't interested and respectful enough to even make eye contact or listen to your ideas. Think about it.

Laila: Yes. I know how it feels. Most of my past boyfriends were like Ren, that's why I am saying this that it's better to be single than to be in a relationship with a person who's unhealthy or toxic for you.

Pamela: John, I seriously need to learn to get away with this obsession. The more I want to avoid him, the more I'm getting to see him in the committee!

Mumkin: You need to introspect about what kind of person you want to date. Probably his ignorance is making you curious to know more about him, or you want a boyfriend who's emotionally unavailable!

Pamela: What? An emotionally unavailable person? Am I really doing it?

Mumkin: Yes, just look at yourself. You're finding his ignorance attractive. Tomorrow, if this person comes near you and talks on a regular basis, you might not be attracted to him any more. Probably he was friendly with you in the beginning and you saw a behavioral change afterwards, that's making you desperate to find the reason why is it so? You need to accept this Pamela that Ren isn't interested anymore and he already is committed to Janny.You need to get yourself away from Ren as he isn't for you.

Pamela:I'm not behind him, I 'm just can't take him off my mind.

Mumkin: I understand that . Don't worry. Focus on new available challenges and opportunities that you're facing!

John: What's up with the committee, you can tell me atleast of what's supposed to be done by you all!

Pamela: I'm sorry John, there's a strict rule that we need to adhere to not to spread any information about it. Mumkin and Laila, thank you so much for guiding me. It helped me to get a useful insight!

Mumkin: You're most welcome.

Pamela: I think as we slowed down while talking that's why we reached the hostel quite late.

Mumkin: I think probably. We're on time. Any help you need,me Laila and John are always available to listen to you and get you out of any situation, how matter how goofy it is. Good bye. See you in tomorrow's class.

Laila: Yes Pamela, we're there for you.

John: They are ,not me. I can't listen to your nonsense continuously!

They head towards the hostel. As John enters the hostel, he doesn't find Mumkin around. While Mumkin is waiting for Laila in the basement. It's getting late. He sees her hurriedly walking towards him with a white bowl covered with a glass lid of golden color.

Laila: Mumkin, here you go. I recently learnt cooking from a crockery book by Pamela. cooked cheese pasta for you by taking special permission from the hostel chef !It was indeed a secretive mission which is successful now.

Mumkin, twinkle fully takes the bowl from Laila. He takes a spoonful of it...and tastes it!

Mumkin: It's delicious, how many times have you made this before? You're an expert!

Laila: Really, thank you so much(hugging)I made it for the first time, I wanted you to taste it. I knew you would like it.

As Laila looks into Mumkin's eyes, he leans towards her, breathes heavily for his first kiss between them. It's the first kiss of Laila too! Laila laughs.

Laila: Mumkin, you look nervous.

Mumkin: Yeah, I'm just trying to....

Laila kisses Mumkin on his lips. His breath is stuck. She immediately takes a spoon full of cheese pasta and fills her mouth with it.

As Laila leans towards him for a second kiss, he holds her into his arms, Laila's eyes start blinking fast with her chest beating in anticipation of what's next going to happen, until they hear a sound of someone coming down the stairs towards the basement. They both are dumbstruck. Mumkin tells Laila to leave early as already they are half an hour late to be in their hostels. Laila requests Mumkin to meet her again here at the same place. He agrees. After saying goodnight to each other, they move back to their hostel buildings . Mumkin carries the cheese pasta cooked by Laila and eats it as his dinner. For him each bite was filled with a beautiful ,overwhelming and warm feeling filled with deliciousness. He took one hour to finish a small bowl of pasta as he took small bites. After interacting with John about the football that happened yesterday on campus, he tries to sleep. There was a constant flashback of his making out with Laila and he felt snuggy. This was his brand new experience that affected his daily sleep pattern.

The next day as Mumkin sits with Laila and Pamela is sitting with John. Prof Olivia gets inside the class. Everyone is amused to see her as it's professor Rehman's hour. She points at Mumkin and John.

Prof Olivia: Mumkin and John, exchange your seats! Pamela and Mumkin, stand up and meet me outside the class.

As they go outside the class , professor Olivia asks both of them to stay together from now on as Committee work requires its members to stay together like buddies.

Prof Olivia: Remember to reach the University sports ground just after your classes get over. A small delay leads to elimination from the committee or worse than that.

Pamela: What's worse than that?

Prof Olivia: And curiosity killed the cat. I know that this question will come from your side. Worse is the restigation from the University for being disloyal! Recall the declaration forms signed by you all!

(Prof Olivia leaves from there after giving a serious stare in the eyes of Pamela).

Mumkin is now with Pamela and Laila is sitting with John. Prof Rehman enters the class. He's with a beautiful woman who's wearing a frock of peach color. He goes up on the class podium and introduces her in front of everyone!

Prof Rehman: Hello everyone! Meet Miss Grace Norris,she's a guest lecturer for trauma recovery. If by any chance you have anything to ask or share ,you can reach out to her to seek help. She'll take class for four hours for you every week.

A guy in the class whispers to another guy friend 'Miss Grace is so beautiful ,everyone wants to be her trauma patient because looking at her beautiful face will cause fast recovery.'

Other guys agree with him and chuckle .

Prof Rehman: Quiet everyone! Miss Norris. You can go ahead to address your students.

Grace Norris: Hello everyone, as you know how climacteric it is to provide the right recovery from trauma at the right time. Trauma can be anything that puts a person into an uncomfortable situation that deeply distresses the person. Most of us, yes ! I'm using the word 'us' to share that, almost the majority of us suffer from trauma and we sometimes use the wrong coping mechanisms to get out of these. In this class of future counselors and psychologists, this area of study can not be forbidden. I've been especially called from University College of London to teach this specific subject. Now I want all of you to form a team. The person sitting next to you will be your partner from now onwards in trauma rehabilitation. No , choice isn't given to you all in choosing your partner because we want you to be able to learn to work with your classmates first for a few weeks and then partners will change. This will enhance your own skills to work with your clients better in future!

Alright let's get started.

She puts Mumkin and Pamela together, John and Laila together and those who are left out as they were sitting alone were put in a group of three. Seeing Pamela with Mumkin, John regretted .He wished he was sitting with Pamela. She is carving another gateway of fantasies in the mind of John. For him her selection in committee is an impressive thing. He cursed Prof Olivia from inside for changing their seats.

John:"Ren was absolutely right. She's a real Eris, goddess of hate".

Grace Norris: Apparently there are fifteen groups. You'll be assigned roles . These roles will be in rotation for the next three months. After which your roles and partners ,both will change. By this you'll be able to identify what major subject you can choose in your upcoming semester.

The list will be displayed on the notice board by today afternoon. Anyone have any doubts?

Pamela: Miss all seem a little lost ,so no one says anything.

Grace Norris: So I assume that either ,you all have understood everything or you're clueless about what is happening. Never mind. Things will be more clear by afternoon. Well, for now give the combined areas of your interests with your names in a chit of paper after discussing with your partner.

Students start discussing with each other in a pair group.

Mumkin: Pamela, what's your area of interest in psychology?

Pamela: Counseling may be...

Mumkin:Counseling to everyone or a specific group of people ,like counseling to children in school or to patients in hospital.

Pamela: I want to counsel everybody who comes across me! Especially free therapy sessions to the ones who aren't able to afford counseling.

Mumkin: Well, I'm not a big fan of counseling people as I just can't do it. For me sports or military psychology . Even business psychology is somewhere I want to work.

Pamela: I'm fine with military and business psychology as I'm not a sports lover ,so sports psychology is a big no for me.

Pamela, takes out a small chit of paper, writes Mumkin and her name on it, under which she writes their area of interest as 1. Counseling (Pamela) 2. Business (both) and 3. Military psychology(both Pamela and Mumkin).

Laila is talking to John...

Laila: Well I'm more into philosophy. Don't know whether psychological philosophy exists!

John: Well I don't have much idea about that. Let me ask Pamela .

John calls Pamela, but she doesn't respond as the class is highly noisy. He calls her name again, she turns back and sees John saying something. She doesn't get it as John and Laila are occupying the last seat whereas she's sitting on the first seat. She turns her back towards John as someone from the first row called her.

John: She isn't responding! I'll ask Benny .

John calls Benny, the intelligent dude of the class who's sitting on three rows in front of him.

John: Benny, is there something called psychological philosophy?

Benny: Yeah bro ,according to my knowledge there isn't psychological philosophy but there's philosophy of psychology . Also psychology was actually a branch of philosophy until 1850's or 1860's where I think in Germany it developed as an independent discipline. So psychology evolved as a separate discipline or a scientific discipline in the 19th century.

John:Thanks man, you're a genius! I asked for candy and you gave me a full box of candies.

Benny: You're welcome(smiling).

Pamela comes near them.

Pamela:I heard about the chocolate box. Where is it?

John: Dumbo, I meant to say that I just asked Benny to tell me something about psychological philosophy ,I mean about philosophy of psychology. But he gave me an A to Z information about it that I called a box of chocolates when I just asked for candy.

John takes out a chit and writes his name and Laila's name together in a shabby handwriting. Under that he writes- 1. Psychological philosophy . Laila suggests him to write that as philosophy and psychology. So after cutting psychological philosophy ,he changes that to philosophy and psychology.

John: Shall we write anything else? Let's ask Mumkin's group what they're into.

Laila: Well I think Pamela would have chosen counseling. Remember that day, the way she asked open ended questions from Ren, that was so natural for him. It was cool.

Benny: Who, Ren? Our senior,that handsome dude. He was kind of stuck with her questions at that time. Yeah , indeed it was awesome the way Pamela could understand him so deeply.

From inside John was envious of Ren as now he knows that Pamela has feelings for him.

John: Ren, how handsome he looks, we must not forget how bad his behavior is with others , in fact he's a bad boy.

Pamela: No I don't think so he's a bad boy.

John: Alright granny Pamela. Laila, let's write counseling in our chit too!

Laila:I ain't sure if I want to go for that particularly.

John: We'll, I want to go for counseling!

Laila: Really,but that day in the therapy session you pretended as if you didn't care about counseling at all! I thought business is your area of interest!

John: Who said? I like counseling and business is my second preference!

Laila: In that case, you can include both.

John was never interested in counseling, in fact he was pretty bad at it. Business was his first choice. However he wanted to work with Pamela as he knew that Pamela would take counseling too.In that case he'll get a chance to be close to her and keep her distracted by falling in love with Ren. He is mentally making plans to distort Ren's image in front of her!, That's why he wrote on chit their second choice as Counseling and third choice as business psychology. He somewhere had the fear of losing Pamela to Ren.

Grace Norris collected all the chits and was preparing to leave the class. John stood up and walked up to her.

John: Miss Norris, is there any chance to exchange our partner, if in case we two have common areas of interest?

Grace Norris: Yes there is. If in case the other two partners also agree then , yes you can work with the person.

John: Oh, absolutely, they won't have any issue. I'm hopeful about that! Thanks Miss Norris.

As Grace Norris leaves the office, John looks at Mumkin and Pamela. He was untroubled as if he's ready to conquer.

He goes near Mumkin and asks him to move outside the class as he has got something important to share.

As Mumkin comes out of the class, John puts his hand around Mumkin's neck.

John: Mumkin, you know how much I love Pamela!

Mumkin: I didn't know that suddenly your feelings for her spiked .Why don't you reveal this to her?Instead I see you irritating her all the time.

John: Nah, I'm afraid our friendship breaks. I remembered the first time I dated a girl, she was my classmate since grade one. When we started dating in middle school, we discovered that we're two different people who aren't compatible. Things got a little messy and guess what we aren't friends anymore, honestly we call each other friends but we're just two people who know each other well that we just can't be together. It's awkward man!

Mumkin: I see, what about Pamela?

John: She joined during highschool first year. I've been secretly loving her since then. I don't want to lose her. I irritate her as I want to grab her attention and I like when she gets crazy at me and sometimes she hits me in the process. In Fact I want to do my best to impress her.

Mumkin: So what's your plan John?

John: Let's exchange our partners. I'll pair up with Pamela and you pair up with your girl Laila. Pamela is concerned about Ren's ignorance towards her. This is the only time where I can support her emotionally and hopefully we fall in love .Get into a long lasting relationship, forever.

Mumkin: That's not possible!

Ren: What! Man you're my best friend and you're supposed to be helping me out. I took permission from Miss Norris. In Fact she told us we can exchange partners. What's up with you?

Mumkin: Pamela and I need to work together!

John: I've been observing the way you two are behaving with me ,since the time you two became part of the committee. It's weird man. Pamela also didn't respond to my doubt and you don't want to listen. Mumkin, do you both have feelings for each other? Is that true?

Mumkin: Oh no John. That's not true. You see Prof Olivia has given us crucial committee work, that's a reason for us being in the same team.

John: What's up with this stupid ca....

Mumkin interrupts John

Mumkin: No John, that's not stupid. In Fact when the right time will arrive, you'll feel that we're into something more important stuff that lies even beyond your imagination. As of now buddy, I need not reveal anything!

John: Alright bro. I've lost her completely.

Mumkin: If she's meant for you, she'll be part of life even if it may look an uphill battle to do so!Trust me John, good things will happen to you. All you need is patience.

John: I'm keeping myself patient Mumkin, I want her to be happy in life.Probably I must tell her about my feelings towards her. There's a new coffee shop that has opened.I'll take her there and express my feelings!

Mumkin: Brother,as soon as the classes finish,we need to join the committee meeting!

John: Oh, gosh, hell with that committee.

Mumkin:Why don't you tell everything now itself, like within the class brakes?

John: That sounds great. But I don't have flowers or chocolates to propose to her now. I'd rather not attend this hour, I'll go through the basement way ,buy the stuff and get back in the next hour.

Mumkin: Hold on buddy, if you leave class in between, you'll have to face principal Blacksmith, as it's against the University rules to leave class in between except in case of urgency.

John:Yes, urgency. You tell me that I'm sick, so I left the hospital.

Mumkin: Get going , hurry up! Return by next hour and all the best. All the best, man! I'm happy for you as you're trying for the right girl who happened to be your good friend .(hugging John).

The next hour begins. As Prof Xiang Zin came to teach political sociology. On enquiring about John, Mumkin tells him that John was having a light fever due to which he went to the nurse to take medicine. On the other hand John runs to the University Clinic which is next to the Warden Bloom's office. He finds the nurse there. He tells her that he is feeling dizzy and has had a bad stomach since yesterday. She makes him sit . She takes out her register and starts asking questions from John.

Nurse : What did you eat yesterday night John?

John: I had pasta,two plates of it. Since then I've been feeling sick.

Nurse : Don't worry John. I'm giving you tablets for your bad stomach and dizziness. (Nurse hands over the two tablets, blue and red in color. John takes them and looks at Nurse's face. For six seconds he looks and smiles at her until she asks him to eat those tables in front of her after giving a glass of water. John eats the tablets in front of the Nurse and leaves the clinic by giving the excuse that he needs to attend the next hour in class. He takes the basement way to reach near the market. After reaching he purchases a bouquet of red roses, dark chocolate box and Gourielli Moonlight Mist perfume .All this money he's been saving to buy a new towel for his gym workout. He got it packed in a sparkling pink color wrapping paper. He was feeling exhilarated as he had put all his delightful feelings in these gifts. He's one twenty percent confident that it will be yes from her side after all she considers John as her best friend or close friend.And what can be more amazing if a guy best friend becomes boyfriend of a girl. He hurriedly reached the University, in fact he returned back in just forty five minutes. He jumps the backyard wall of University, as there was a guard standing, he runs in flash and hides behind the tree and again runs near the basement soon when the guard turns his back. He rushes towards his locker to keep the stuff ,as in the next class break he plans on proposing to Pamela. When he's done with keeping his stuff within ten minutes of waiting inside the washroom to let Prof Xiang Zin finish the class. When he was near the washroom, he turned his back ,he could feel a warm hand touching his shoulder. In nerves, as he turns back, it's Ren.

Ren: What's up man? Why do your cocky face look so worried?

John: Hi, I actually bunked the class .

Ren: Why so man? You're with that book worm and self proclaimed counselor cum therapist girl Pamela right, how can you even think about bunking? She would never allow you to do that as you're a part of her group.

John: It's for a special reason man! I want to propose to somebody.

Ren: Well when it comes to love, I stop bullying my juniors at that time .All the best. I too have the same plan.

John: So you're planning to propose to Janny for your marriage with her? Aren't you?

Ren: I don't want to reveal anything. Certainly I am proposing today.

John: Bravo, let's go for it !

Ren leaves from there without saying anything.

The bell rings for the next hour . There's a five minutes break in between. John runs towards his locker to get flowers and gifts .He's mentally getting ready to prepare himself, he smells the fresh red roses and observes the water droplets sitting on them with red and pinkish glaze. He imagines Pamela's smiling face in those droplets which gives instant satisfactory warmth in his heart. As he gets inside his class with flowers and chocolates, he sees Pamela hugging Ren. She notices John standing .She comes near him.

Pamela: John, you know what happened..

She stops hugging Ren, holds his hand and kisses him. Ren says bye to her, he reaches near John, gives him a soft shoulder punch saying"Buddy ,I see you got a lot of stuff for your girl which shows you love her a lot, go for it." . Ren leaves the place.

Pamela: John you know what ,you were right, I need not run behind Ren. In Fact he came to me just three minutes before, went down on his knees and he proposed to me to be his girlfriend! And I said yes!

Ren leaves from there after giving her a lip kiss, Pamela is blushing looking down and smiling.

John is dumbstruck. He could see Pamela's merry smile. He posted a fake laughter expression.

Pamela: Red roses, chocolates and gifts. It's for whom John? And where were you in the previous hour?

John:Actually, it's a part of Ren's proposal for you. In Fact I was also a part of it. I mean part of planning to get all these things for you. These are from Ren for you as a part of his proposal.

Pamela: Really, you're a dork!(she pouches him on his shoulder). Ren should've waited to give all this stuff by himself. He's always in a hurry.

Mumkin came near both of them. Pamela was unwrapping the gift.

Pamela: It's Gourielli Moonlight Mist perfume. He knows that I love it so much!

Mumkin: What about Janny?

Pamela:Yeah, Ren mentioned that they aren't together anymore. Just yesterday they broke up!

Mumkin: Just yesterday! Isn't that too quick to propose to somebody new?

Pamela gives a despondent expression towards both of them.

John: Hey, never mind. We know that he's a cool fellow . I mean a hot and cool guy.

Pamela: What do you mean by hot and cold ?

John:It might have been easy for him to surpass the baggage of his spoiled relationship.

Pamela: That's what I love about him. He's actually an aggressive guy whose sarcasm is good.

John: You eat chocolates Pamela and big congratulations.

Pamela: Thank you so much John. (She holds his hands and gives John a friendly hug with a warm smile).

Pamela sits at her place and she shares and eats chocolates with her nearby girlfriends including Laila.

Mumkin takes John to the last bench. He consoles John who's shattered from inside. John starts weeping slowly.

John: I was afraid of losing her to Ren . But it came out true.

Mumkin: I'm sorry brother. My advice is to be patient in love. You'll find the right girl for yourself.

John: No, probably I should've been quicker than Ren as I met him near the washroom and couldn't realize that he's going to propose to Pamela. When he proposed to her, I was planning to do so during that time. But if she also has feelings for Ren then I'm nobody to come between them. Ren is a good guy. At Least Pamela likes his hot and cold behavior. He'll always keep her happy, always like the way he kept his ex girlfriend Janny. Pamela is desiring for Ren. He's very rich and resourceful who'll treat her like a queen.

Mumkin remains silent and sees the pain in the eyes of John. They hear a voice "Yeah, here he is ,catch hold of him!". It's warden Bloom who comes near John and holds his arm and collar. John resists it. The whole class sees the struggle between them.

John: Why are you holding me like that?What did I do?

Bloom: You've been spotted outside the University by one of our guards, bunking . The previous hour you bunked !

Pamela comes nearby and stands next to him.

John: No, I never bunked. I was sick. I went to the clinic. You can check the record from the nurse.

Mumkin: Yes Mr. Bloom, John wasn't well. Infact, you can ask Prof Xiang Zin, he took the previous hour. I myself mentioned to him about John.

Bloom: Shut up you half wit! Or else you'll be punished in his lie too for breaking the University rule! And you(pointing towards John), you'll be given the roughest punishment for trespassing a third time. Second time you were exonerated as you were part of the Committee selection process. You're done!

Warden Bloom tightens the grip of John's arm which starts hurting him further. John jerkingly moves his hand ,which loosens Bloom's grip on his arm .He thrashed him in a commotion and walks towards the door. But he couldn't walk more than twelve steps and fell to the floor. There's an upsurge that he feels in his stomach and starts vomiting . He realizes that it's the allergy medicine that the nurse gave him. He completely lays on the ground and sees black shoes .As he looks upwards, it's Prof Olviia standing. Bloom still tries to catch hold of him saying ' where you're running nincompoop?'.

Prof Olviia: Stop . Call the nurse now.

Bloom runs near the clinic to call a nurse and returns back with the nurse.

Nurse: Oh lord, you again. What happened?

Mumkin: He's vomiting after taking the medicines from the previous hour.

Nurse: Probably he took it on an empty stomach or he's allergic to the drug that I gave him.

Prof Olivia orders Bloom and the nurse take John to the clinic. They take John till the clinic.

Prof Olivia: Everyone, get back to your classes!

Mumkin and Pamela come near Prof Olivia to have a quick conversation.

Prof Olivia: I know, before you both request me to accompany John, let me give clear instructions, the University holds experiences of such kinds of cases for years more than your age. Inquiry of the event will happen as John was seen outside. Moreover ,the clinic has best practitioners to absolve any sickness .Be it indisposition of breaking rules!

Pamela: He had a valid reason for not attending class as he was sick.

Prof Olivia: Keep your focus in present class Miss Brown, the regulation committee knows it's job. Both of you ,be in my office after this hour.

Prof Olivia turns back and starts moving. Mumkin and Pamela also go in the class to attend Prof. Jaquiline Gomes class who teaches Sociological Theories.

After the class both Mumkin and Pamela go near the office of Prof Olivia. They hear her talking to somebody.

Bison: Olivia, come for dinner today evening.

Prof Olivia: I got a lot on my to do list.

Bison: There's no way you can refuse as it's an official dinner. Principal Blacksmith and other crucial members of the committee will be arriving like Principal Blacksmith and that man, your Military counterpart....Hielmaster.

Prof Olivia: Dinner is for official talk, I don't want any balderdash from you!

Bison: Ofcourse, Olive, Lidiya.....Or what do I call you my love? All predominant things about the committee will be discussed. Do come at seven pm tonight in a shining velvet billowy skirt. And keep your hair open. Discussion is official, but the dinner after that is candle light in dim light decorated with a beautiful chandelier on the roof.

Prof Olivia gives Bison a glower face.

Bison: Don't give me that scowl face. In all busy happenings of committee talk, the crockery will have Devkali flowers printed on them. It's another crockery business branch that I started on your first pen name. Whenever you feel, you can come over to my place and you can ask anything from me. You understand right, ask for anything(smirk). I promise to never put you down!

Prof Olivia:You're just a self absorbed man. Leave!

Bison: You sound strident. I love you so much and you just don't care. That's the issue with you virgins, you don't know any beauty of intimacy!

Prof Olivia: Just leave!

Bison leaves and comes out of prof Olivia's office . Mumkin and Pamela look at him hiddenly from a corner. His face looked exasperated.

As Mumkin and Pamela are still outside Olivia says to herself "You're just never doing well Bison. As you always say, 'I'll give you what I want!' Just a garrulous cloud you are".

Pamela giggles silently after Prof Olivia calls Bison a garrulous cloud.

Mumkin asks Pamela to be ready and he knocks on her office door of Prof Olivia. This time her office door has nothing, just white walls and a desk with a chair. The whole arrangement has been changed from the previous arrangements which had a fully furnished office. On the desk there are books and papers lying with a pen stand. There's a smell of white paint.. Her desk looks well organized.

Prof Olivia: Get inside you both.

Now Prof Olivia became Captain Lidiya for them.

John and Bessy also arrived there.

Captain Lidiya: Come in. All four you stand according to alphabetical orders of your name. Take these packages. There's a pile of well packed cartons behind you. These are your uniforms with other essential requirements!

Mumkin passes the box according to Bessy, Pamela and Ren based on their names written on the carton boxes. Bessy starts opening it.

Captain Lidiya: Learn to follow instructions. These aren't your Christmas presents. You aren't yet ordered to open and see what's there in the boxes. Keep the boxes down.

As they keep their boxes down, Prof Olivia provides them with their badges and name plates, according to their roles which are golden plated with different letters for each.

Captain Lidiya: Ren it's "C" for Charlie coded for combat role, Mumkin it's batch "A" for Alpha coded to arms improvise and combat role, Bessy it's batch "S" for Sierra coded to supply of ammunition and Pamela it's "N" for November coded to nurturer. Remember, all these items are to be kept hidden from any non committee member. Just after classes, today at four pm assemble in Gandhi hall without letting anyone know. Miss Grace Norris took class for both seniors(pointing towards Ren and Bessy) and Juniors (pointing towards Mumkin and Pamela). Has she done the process of class division based on the interests of you and your partner?

Ren and Bessy say yes. Pamela and Mumkin also nod their heads.

Captain Lidiya: Answer only yes or no.No head nodding. Keep stiff posture and zero head movement until ordered. What you wrote today morning was pseudo interest as you will be on a committee named as "water recycling committee".

Ren shows a slight disappointment on his face.

Captain Cheriyan: The Water recycling committee is actually a secret Military training committee. It's named so,in order to give other students a false notion. Only four of you are put under that committee, other students will assume that you four have gone to conserve and recycle water . In reality you will be given full time Military training from now onwards.

Bessy: But what's the meaning of full time training?

Prof Olivia: You're making a second mistake today. You haven't been asked to ask a question yet! Keep your mouth shut until asked. You all can go back to your classes. You'll get these items(pointing to carton boxes) in Gandhi hall by today evening. Check the fitting of uniforms.

Ren and Bessy leave for their classes .Whereas Mumkin and Pamela try to reach near Nurse's office,but Bloom sees them and tells them to return back to their classes by pointing his finger disgracefully at them. He also reveals that John will be in his class. So they do so. As they enter class they don't find John. Just after the class Mumkin and Pamela run towards the Nurse's office.

Mumkin: Madam(referring to Nurse), where's John, the boy who was vomiting for two hours?

Nurse: Oh that boy. Poor boy, he had some allergy with drugs so I gave him an anti-allergic drug.

Mumkin: Could you please tell where is he now?

Nurse: Yeah,Mr. Bloom took him along with him. He was saying that the boy has been taken back to his classes despite me telling him that he needs rest.

Mumkin and Pamela leave the clinic and rush towards Bloom's office. They see Bloom sitting on a chair inside his office.

Mumkin(hurrid and edgy):Warden Bloom where's John. He didn't come to the class in the previous two hours.

Bloom ignores them completely.

Mumkin: Please tell us, he's our friend and we want to know how he is! Or else we'll take this forward to Principal Blacksmith.

Bloom: He's at the right place where he's supposed to be!

Mumkin: Where?

Bloom: He's grounded in the University basement room for the next few days or perhaps an unlimited time. The place where there's no food,water and savage insects like bed bugs and spiders.

Mumkin: You gotta be kidding. This can't be happening to a University student. This is menacious.

Bloom: Don't disturb me, if you really wanna to know more, then ask Prof Olivia as she orders me to bring John to her office.

Mumkin: Gosh, Prof Olivia will not give answers to our questions.

Pamela: And we can't enter her office without her permission. Let's give it a try.

They run towards Prof Olivia's office but to their disappointment they find her office locked.

Mumkin: Pamela, why don't you ask Mr. Nelon, your uncle who is in the administrative staff.

Pamela: Uncle is on leave for ten days. He's visiting Holy Ship Place with aunty and Stella. It's our religious programme that happens every year. Let's go to Ren, he might help us out .His uncle Bison can find out.

Mumkin: Yeah ,let's go.

Mumkin and Pamela look for Ren but they don't find him anywhere. They eat their lunch in the cafeteria dolorously. Mumkin wants to tell Pamela about the love possessed by John for her. But he thinks ,if he does that now, Pamela might get agonized more or will be in a state of turmoil. This in fact might also create apprehension between her relationship with Ren which has just now started.

As soon as they finish lunch ,they rush to the class. However on the way to class, Mumkin observes that all of John is empty as if someone has looted it.

Mumkin: Pamela wait, isn't that John's locker? Why is it all empty? I think we need to talk about John to higher authorities like Prof Olivia or Principal Blacksmith.

They leave towards the Office of Prof Olivia but still it's empty. Even the principal Blacksmith's office is empty. They run and head towards Ren's class. They start inquiering from his classmates if they saw him anywhere. But no clue. After the classes they meet him bunking and smoking cigarettes with other guys in the junkyard cum recycling area of University.Mumkin and Pamela inform John to him.

Ren: Don't worry! No student till now has been punished like that. It's against the rules of the University. The rules of this University are strict hitherto, but punishment of grounding can't be given. John might have gone to the hostel. Did you check there?

Mumkin: No, we can't go now as we're already late. We need to head towards Gandhi Hall as per the order of Prof Olivia.

Ren: I'm one twenty percent sure of John's presence in the hostel, as of now let's head towards Gandhi Hall. Bessy will meet us there. She was about to meet her boyfriend .

All three walk towards the Gandhi Hall.

Pamela: Ren, darling ,we tried to search for you in your class, cafeteria and sports ground. But we found you smoking cigarettes?

Ren: So what? What's wrong with that?

Pamela: Smoking is injurious darling.

Ren: Don't mother me. Just be a good girlfriend.

Pamela: That's what I am trying to be, a good girlfriend!

Ren: Don't irritate me Pamela.

Mumkin: Ren, where are officials of the University?

Ren: Actually, I had to meet my Uncle Bison during the lunch break as today evening there's a meeting of officials for the sake of the committee. So Captain Lidiya won't be present today for us as she'll be going there.

Mumkin: Yeah we heard the conversation between Captain Lidiya and Mr. Bison. If she's not there then I think it's Hielmaster for us in the training.

Ren : May be or may not be. He's also a prominent part of the committee.

Pamela: Through conversation between captain Lidiya and your uncle ,it's very apparent that he loves her a lot. I mean what does he see in that cocky behavior which she shows towards him?

Ren: I always wondered about this but after hearing from Mumkin that Prof Olivia and Lidiya Cheriyan are the same people, I've realized my uncle truly loves her . It all started when Prof Olivia was a student here, my uncle was two years senior to her. He mentioned to me that she was the most beautiful lady with the kindest behavior. My uncle was a playboy who dated and cheated upon multiple women of his time. Few of them were friends with Olivia. She was very loyal to her friends and hated my uncle's deeds. Her loyalty,sincerity and kindness attracted my uncle the most. In the last twenty five years my uncle had three broken marriages, he visits brothels on rountined basis. Hielmaster in our previous meeting was mentioning the connection of dark rooms with my uncle ,he actually meant the prostitute houses, my uncle is a regular customer. He's a big womanizer and Olivia remained a virgin who never dated anyone in her entire life except him at once.

Mumkin: Really, she dated him? Then why aren't they together now?

Uncle Bison believes that they are soulmates .Thus he's ready to do anything for her. Whereas she believes that his sole interest lies in taking her virginity away. That's why she shows disdainful behavior towards him.

Pamela:Oh I see,I think your uncle is obsessed with her!

Ren: I also used to think this. As we see, there has been change in her behavior and personality since she faced many traumatizing experiences in her life, but my uncle's caring nature has been the same throughout for her after all this time. The issue is that my uncle just can't hide his desperation .The only thing that ruined their relationship was when she came here from the military to teach as a University Professor, Uncle propped her. They went on regular non sexual dates. She established her trust in him and was ready to marry him . But he didn't tell her the truth that he's already married. Two days before their marriage, his third wife somewhere met Prof Olivia and told her the truth that he's cheating on her with younger women and he's been frequently visiting brothels. That left Prof Olivia heart broken and being manipulated by uncle Bison. She lost all her trust in him. She never trusted him after that. My uncle's third marriage also broke and Prof Olivia was the reason.

Pamela: You mean, your uncle cheating on his wife at the time was the reason that his marriage couldn't be sustained a third time. I don't think Prof Olivia can be the reason for this broken marriage.

Ren: Whatever you say, my uncle is everything for me. I'll always be on his side. I've been seeing him in loneliness for many years.It's Prof Olivia's presence in his life that makes him happy. He says that he mostly takes out time from his business ventures to visit the university ,just to get a glimpse of Prof Olivia.

Pamela explores this brand new emotional side of Ren towards his uncle.

Pamela:But still ,I believe that Mr. Bison needs to respect Prof Olivia's choice.

Ren: Shut up girl, keep your free advice with you.

Mumkin realsies that Ren has been hot and cold with Pamela.

Pamela:Ren, I just remembered, why did you send John for all those fairy gifts like chocolates, red roses and my perfume. You could've gotten it by yourself since you wanted to propose to me!

Ren: What are you saying? Chocolates and perfume! Since you wanted me in your life that's why I proposed to you after Janny and I broke up. Nevertheless I don't know much about your favorite perfume or chocolates! It's only from today that our relationship started!

Pamela: I don't get it ,then why did John hand over that stuff to me ? I thought you asked him about my favorite things. Did he buy those items?

Ren: No ways, I don't know what you like and dislike.

Mumkin: Actually John wanted to propose to you Pamela!

Ren:Yeah I also met him before the third hour. I saw him with those gifts ,but I never knew that he's bringing all that for you!

Pamela: I ....I didn't realize that John is into me. Why did he lie to me about those gifts by you?

Mumkin overhears their talk. He comes to Pamela and Ren.

Mumkin: Because he didn't want to hurt you! When Ren proposed to you, you were on cloud nine. He didn't want to bring you down.

Pamela: Why did you hide this Mumkin from me?

Mumkin: Pamela,I realized that both Ren and you are into each other before John could propose to you.Imagine the awkwardness of revealing the feelings of John to you when you are already with Ren. I just wanted to hide it for the better of everyone. But you and Ren iself dug deeper in the matter.

Ren: Now you heard Pamela(vexed), that John is also into you. You might feel like a queen .

Pamela: What you're saying Ren . I consider John as my boyfriend, but I'm also shocked with this revelation.

Ren: Now you might be seeing me as just an alternative !

Pamela: Stop it Ren!

Ren: So,you're leaving me ?I knew it. This will be your decision.

Pamela: No Ren, not at all, why are you assuming such a thing? I and Mumkin are bothered about John,however that doesn't mean I am into John. Please Ren, I see a lot of hindrance from your side to keep our relationship even though it's the first day of your proposal! I don't know where it'll go!

Ren: So you mean that I am creating problems and I have hindrance in our relationship? You know what, you must be thankful that a guy like me who's six feet four inches tall, super rich and valiant is dating a girl like you . Holy crap! There can't be anyone comparable to Janny!

After listening to this, Pamela starts crying.

Pamela: You're mean Ren.

Mumkin asked Pamela not to cry as they reached the Gandhi Hall and tell them probably the Hillmaster might be waiting for them! He asks Ren to use better language for Pamela as he won;t tolerate his friend being treated badly by her boyfriend. Ren ignores Mumkin. He tries to console her by providing his shoulder to cry. Bessy joins them, as Pamela was crying ,she comes to know about what happened between Pamela and Ren through Mumkin. As they are standing outside the Gandhi Hall, she goes near Ren who's some eight meters away from Mumkin and Pamela. Bessy talks to him.

Bessy: Why you're so mean to Ren.Just today you proposed to her and you're comparing her with Janny.

Ren: I was just honest! She and Janny are so different. I mean, I gave her a chase to be my girlfriend and she already has a guy who's missing from the University in her love.

Bessy: Are you nuts? It's not an unerring thing of what you're doing! You're comparing your new girlfriend with your ex? Tell me what so intoxicating Janny had ,that you're completely ignoring Pamela's humannes?

Ren: Janny was just gorgeous, I still remember her perfume, her figure of hourglass shape and the way she treated me ,my presence to her never bothered her. What a confident girl with non clingy behavior. I mean Pamela is cute. Kind of chubby ,short like lilliputs in guliver's travel but she's way too emotional. I'm unable to handle her side. She has zero confidence in her abilities and it's like she's quite clingy She seeks attention and validation. I ignored all that and dated her as I don't want to miss Janny anymore after our breakup. But after John's plan to propose to Pamela, I'm just infuriated. You see Janny also left me for another guy whom she found rich and promising. Bloody hell.

Bessy: Oh lord! You're still not out of Janny.

Mumkin comes near Bessy and Ren.

Mumkin :Ren ,why don't you realize that you're in a new relationship now. Janny and Pamela are completely different people. At Least don't harm Pamela's esteem by calling her chubby and short. I know she's quite emotional but she has a good heart. She's extremely loyal and she won't leave you for anybody. Trust me. Infact trust her. Not even once she said that she wants to be with John, when she came to know that John was into him!

Bessy: Ren ,she's an emotionally deep person who cries on small things. You'll get depth from her. It means she isn't shallow like Janny, who'll leave you just for money and security in life.

Ren: Yeah ,I think you guys have a point. Although Pamela isn't like Janny, she's a bit of a weakling chicken but she's sweet. In fact her smile is gorgeous. I think I hold an apology for being such a crap!

Mumkin : Of course you do.

Bessy: For what are you waiting for?(cross arms towards Ren)

John goes near Pamela.

John: Pamela,I'm sorry .

Pamela: Ren, why do you act like that? I understand that you've been through a breakup, but why do downplay me for that.

Ren: No, I never tried to do it. I just spoke the truth about how I see things.

Pamela: Ren, listen to me. I find it bitter. I can't handle so much criticism. Your truth is making me inferior.

Ren: In that case heartfelt apologies. (Ren sits down on his knees).

Pamela: Janny was able to handle your theatrics but I just can't take it.

Ren: What do you mean you can't take?

Pamela: Ren, every relationship is based on mutual respect. I see you've given it only to Janny. You always praise her. In that case you're still not out of her . You can start your journey with me only if your mind is clear.

Ren: Clear.Huh?

Pamela: It means if Janny arrieves, you'll still want to be with me! You're not going back to her .So do you think you're ready for that ?

Ren: No. No Pamela. I think it'll be difficult to choose between you and Janny. In Fact I ...I choose Janny over you. As she left me, I never asked her to leave.

Pamela: But Ren, you need to get over her only then you and I are possible! Also I'm not forcing you for anything, you can walk off from this relationship right away!

Ren: Woah, I thought you're a clingy girl who would cry if her boyfriend ignored her, but you aren't! You seem to be strong minded here! At Least you and Janny have this in common!

Pamela chuckles.

Pamela: Ren, don't judge a book by its cover!

Ren: I choose Janny over you! My final decision.

Pamela: Go ahead.

Ren: Haha, just kidding. I choose you ,if you and I get very close.

Pamela's pupils are dilating after hearing this.

Pamela: Ren ,I want you to know about my past.

Ren comes near Pamela and whispers in ear of Pamela.

Ren: Fuck all, there's no time for all that. Listen my new girlfriend, you do what I say. Surrender yourself to me sweetheart.

She smiles after hearing the word sweetheart from his mouth for her.

Pamela: Ren, let's go inside as they've opened the doors of Gandhi Hall.

Ren starts moving inside the hall leaving her behind. She follows him. As they enter the hall, they see their sports teacher Kinen Zuna inside. He always wears a red cap. This time as he took off his cap, they saw that he's completely bald. But still he looked handsome! He has a tall posture with a fit body and a wide jawline.

Zuna: For what you guys are waiting there. Get in fast!

Pamela: Aren't we supposed to see Mr. Hielmaster here?

Zuna: It's Col Hielmaster not Hielmaster, miss! It's my turn to train you today !

Mumkin: Are you also from Military background?

Zuna. Me,military background. Haha, I always wanted to be a cricketer . I played at national level too but got an injury and couldn't play anymore. Now coming to your question Mumkin! This University is run by retired Military Officer Blacksmith, who ensures all rules are strictly implemented and each person is used as a resource to achieve the mission. In fact a new world record needs to be given to this University for producing the most trusted employees. Here forty percent faculty is aware of the committee's motto and history of Captain Lidiya, but they've kept their mouth shut vouching to take revenge of what happened with her and the death of each soldier who were killed by malefactors including Prof William's younger brother Jonathan's death. Do you know that Unique Military Base Association With Students (UMBAS) was formed by your father Mumkin?

Mumkin: My father really?

Zuna: It was your father's idea to choose students from University for Military training including choosing Captain Cheriyan. To provide these students with further support , your father recommended the Govt to do partnership with Amrisk's father, and that is why the name sounds UMBAS. As the time changed , to keep the identity of the University hidden the name was changed from UMBAS to UAS(Unique Association with Students). Your father was an extremely strategic person , almost in everything. However in finances and business ,no one could beat his ideas.

Pamela: Probably that's the reason that Mumkin has all his dreams towards business......He sometimes dreams of his father also doing something in business....

Zuna: Doing what in business?

Mumkin: Business in weaponry! Yeah I see my father in dreams testing weapons with me to protect the country from any attack or war!

Zuna: (Chuckles) So that's why you're always thinking about business! Family genes. But there can't be a bigger war when you have malefactors in a country who are creating against its own people. They killed Jonathan Williams and Febin Paul who were the promising students of this University. They killed your father. They killed thousands of people and are still active in Marvo village. It's the time to not let them take any other innocent life. Time to take revenge and stop them forever!

Mumkin clenches his fist in agony when Zuna reminds the murder of his father by malefactors.

Zuna: So this training is not just training. It's a recipe to make firecrackers, who'll crack down the whole system and free people from terror of Watson. As you are sitting right now, stand at your place, go to the ground, run till the last drop of sweat reaches the ground!

All four of them stand up and start running .They run the first five miles together, Pamela gets tired and her speed reduces after running half a mile, Bessy stops running eight miles in total and stops there ,she starts jumping to get her breath back. Mumkin and Ren are still running. Ren looks at Mumkin while running. All that is running in his mind is to beat Mumkin in order to prove to Pamela his manishness! He runs with his full speed and leaves Mumkin behind by twenty meters.

Zuna: This is how you take revenge on your father's murder Chamburt? Don't jog like a newly married bride walking in the garden on her husband's lawn. Run fast....more fast....faster....(putting pressure on Mumkin).

Mumkin gets majorly flustered and he straightaway doubles up with thrice of his average speed and surpasses Ren fifty meters. They run at the same speed. It's seven pm in the evening and they've covered twenty five miles. Covered in sweat as if they are drenched in rain heavily! But it was all their running that caused this havoc to them. Mumkin is still ahead of Ren, however he hears a sound as if it's an earthquake on the ground. Ren has fallen down on the ground, Mumkin double ups to run back fifty meters to reach out to him. Mr. Zuna comes with a bottle of water.

Zuna: Keep breathing Ren. It's just you're dehydrated after running more than twenty miles for the first time or after a long time. Give me a high five.

Ren isn't able to move. His eyes are half closed. Pamela comes near him and says 'Ren ,are you okay baby?'.

After five minutes he provides a glass of water to Ren.

Zuna: Well done boys. So this is how your evenings will go from now onwards. Girls ,run better next time. I want at least fifteen miles next time.

Pamela: That's unrealistic!

Zuna: Reality and dreams are all in mind(pointing his index finger towards his own head). So, if you think it's impossible then it will remain impossible for you Pamela! Impossible to attain forever.

After Ren gets comfortable again, he displays a few exercises after like quad stretch, hamstring stretch etc for ten minutes. He asks the guard to get inside with his trolley in which the boxes are kept. These are those boxes which Prof Olivia aka Captain Lidiya had shown to them. He gives them these uniforms and badges given by her.

Zuna: This is the only piece of uniform that'll be given to you in the entire training.

Bessy: Really ,the entire training? Then how do we manage with only one set of this jungle dress?

Zuna: Haha, it's not a dress, but a uniform. Regarding duration of its usage, I just mentioned it is just a punch as I am not your permanent trainer. Ask Captain Cheriyan about it.(silence)....If you have the guts to ask her. Also keep your uniform safe.

As they all say "Yes sir together", he instructs them to return back to their hostels with food packets wrapped tightly with brown paper. As they open the food packets, they find chicken curry and rice boxes .

Bessy: It just looks pathetic .

Ren: Seriously, running so much for this stuff!

Pamela tries it out.

Pamela: But it tastes good. Try it.

Bessy tries it.

Bessy: What's wrong with your taste buds! It's not appetizing at all.

Mumkin and Ren try it too, however they both like the taste. The three eat the food sitting on the stairs outside the gate of the cafeteria which is closed now, Bessy doesn't eat . Fresh air is blowing. There's a parlor palm plant which is swaying with the soft wind. It's all light blue . The clouds are creamy gray.

Pamela sits next to Ren.

Pamela: Isn't that so romantic Ren. Today's weather!

Ren: I don't know what you are talking about.

Pamela: I mean, look at the sky,clouds and cold air...After some time we'll be seeing the moon and stars too.

She holds his arm and hugs it saying 'I wish we could stay like this forever!'

Ren: What? Let me eat Pamela and nothing is permanent in life.

Pamela: What do you mean?

Ren: I mean we can't be like this forever.

Pamela gets up and says 'How unromantic you are Ren!'.

The other hand in the Bison's house the dinner is organized. It's one of the most aristocratic bungalows of thirty eight rooms. There's a big dining hall with blue, violet and silver lightning. There are curtains on the wall with expensive paintings and motivational thoughts. There are chandeliers on the roof with gold plated crystals. He welcomes all his guests- Principal Blacksmith, Jonathan Williams, Prof Hashtik, Hielmaster and Prof Olivia. It's a rectangular long table where Principal Blacksmith is sitting on the narrower side, Prof Williams is sitting next to him . Silver Bison is sitting on the other side. As Hielmaster wants to sit next to Silver Bison, he stops him saying "it's reserved for Prof Olivia ". Olivia unwillingly sits next to Bison and Hielmaster sits next to Prof Olivia. Prof Hashtik sits next to Hielmaster. There are delicacies and champagne on the table. They discuss the training of four students inside the armed forces campus and the progress plan status of it till now.

Principal Blacksmith: Prof Olivia and Col Hielmaster, how's Mumkin in training?

Hielmaster: You see, the boy is tremendously intrepid.He has a good heart and ambitious mind with loyalty towards his friends! A very humble person ,who's supportive in nature. Miss Cheriyan, can you tell more (eating chicken on fork).

Prof Olivia: He's been put in both combat and supportive roles .

Principal Blacksmith: Is he intrepid like his father? I'm sure the junior Chamburt will display all traits of his father, Commander Major Chamburt. Hope he's over with his business mindset of weaponry!

Prof Olivia: Training is stimulating! Soon he'll be over with his self seeking fantasy.

Principal Blacksmith: Haha, surely. What about our Silver Bison's nephew Ren.

Hielmaster: He's a big bootstrapper! Determined ,confident and speaks straight from the shoulder! Looks for undauntedly adventurous person.

As Hielmaster was saying this,Silver Bison started adjusting his tie to show how proud he is for the upbringing of his nephew Ren. He's smiling!

Prof Olivia looks at Bison!

Prof Olivia: Shows disrespectful behavior, dominating, has tendency to not to differentiate between cooperation and competition! And in personal relationships, he'll reduplicate his uncle's personality.

Silver Bison: Really Lidiya, like what! Of course, isn't that a great trait to be competitive ?

Prof Olivia frawns and then she turns her attention towards Principal Blacksmith.

Prof Olivia: He's been put into C for Charlie company!

Silver Bison: Yes, Combat role. It's not a surprise that Ren will lead and finish all tasks successfully! I think he's a superlative candidate among all four.

Principal Blacksmith:Surely, Amen! Let's talk about the bravado of girls. Tell me about Pamela. Isn't she the girl who's a keen learner and wants to be a psychotherapist?

Prof Olivia: She's an extra candidate who didn't display courage . Instead she has poor memorization, is sensitive,doubtful of herself and childish.

Principal Blacksmith: Then why did you take her up as an extra? We have a hell lot of students like her. She'll be more like a liability than an asset to us.

Prof Olivia: Because she has this extreme loyalty, sincerity, sacrificial and high compassion. A valued person who has a tendency to show extreme valor in face of dangerous situations. Sociable, helpful and trainable person! A kind hearted girl.

Hielmaster: She has been given a nurturer role.

Principal Blacksmith: Fine! I still expect more from her as it's a military operation not a motherhood competition.

Silver Bison starts laughing loudly whereas others have made earnest faces.

Prof Olivia: She'll be trained to be transformed to become the desired one.

Principal Blacksmith: What's Bessy upto?

Prof Olivia: Just like Ren and Mumkin, Bessy is brave, brilliant ,good at resource management and has an extremely good grasp of situations. She has good memory power in remembering facts and figures.

Principal Blacksmith: As expected,where has she been put up?

Prof Olivia: She's in a supply of ammunition.

Principal Blacksmith raises a toast of champagne "Sierra!". All join him. They all again start enjoying the delicious dinner with a variety of delicacies! As Olivia takes up mashed potatoes, Silver Bison stops her.

Bison: Stop Lidiya,try this. Waiter ,pass the special pie and bring the chicken stew here!

He offers pork pie and chicken stew. As he tries to put it on her plate.

Olivia: No need to worry about me!

Bison(whispering): This is especially for you! You see it has 24 carat gold leaf covering! Try this up, especially the top area of the pie. Come on .

He offers it again. But this time Hielmaster takes the Pie from his hand.

Hielmaster: Woah, pork pie. You know Silver Bison, your intentions are just to delight but you choose the wrong person! (putting a piece of pie on his plate and passing it to the Principal Blacksmith) .

Silver Bison's face is turning slightly red. His eyebrows are furrowed and lips are tense.

(Taking the first bite) Mmmm, it's luscious. Bon appetit. Ohhhh this gold leaf covering is just like cherry on top of cake!

Principal Backsmith:(taking a bite of pie): I completely agree. Delicious! Admirable work of your chefs Bison.

Bison: My pleasure in serving my guests! Thank you.

Within seconds the pie gets over as it gets passed to Prof WIlliams and Prof Hashtik. Bison looks at Hielmaster with infuriating eyes.

Hielmaster: (whispering) Don't look at me Silver Bison like that. You look like a real Bison who'll hit me with his red horns. I actually helped you out in not getting your pie wasted!As I said, you chose the wrong person for the right intentions.

Silver Bison: What do you mean by that?

Hielmaster: Lidiya is a vegan buddy, she'll not even smell your pie. Bon appetit!(chuckling and eating the last bite of pie with his fork).

Prof Olivia smirks while eating mashed potatoes.

Principal Blacksmith:Olivia Shift them from the present location to desired one. When will it be done?

Prof Olivia: Tomorrow eleven am, shifting will be finished.

On the other hand the four of them returned back to their hostels. Mumkin enters his room with hope that John might be there. As he gets inside the room through his door, he feels relieved because John is sitting near an electric heater, facing it . As he goes near him.

Mumkin:John, what's up man ! I didn't see you in class.

He doesn't get any reply from him.As he puts hand on John's shoulder, he gets ruffled. John wakes up from sleep, takes off his hoodie's hat. It's quickly revealed that it's not John but his college mate Stylin who has a carbon copy hairstyle,height and skin color and other body features as that of John .

Stylin: Bro ,you completely freaked me out! I was dozing off.

Mumkin: What are you doing in my room and where's John?

Stylin: I was feeling cold, so I thought I'll come to your room to get heat from the heater. Regarding John ,I haven't seen him since today morning at all!

Mumkin: But how did you manage to open the room, as it was locked?

Stylin: It was already open when I arrived here after classes.

Mumkin: It's bizarre.

He looks at Ren's almirah, all empty as nothing is there! It's like no one has lived in this place before. Mumkin tries to connect the dots as both the locker and the almirah of John are empty. But he's unsuccessful in understanding. Stylin leaves from there after two hours where they just talked about John's absence from the hostel room. Mumkin finds it difficult to sleep as his room mate is kind of missing and no one is concerned about it in University! He decides to meet Pamela for this and share the information of John and his luggage being missing from the hostel room too. He goes near the warden's room where there's one telephone. The person in charge was a guard. The guard looks at him in a cocky manner.

Guard: It's 11PM at night, what are you doing?

Mumkin: Need to make an important call?

Guard: Call to whom?

Mumkin: To my grandmother. She's really sick. I just can't sleep. She is the last elderly member left in my family, please!

Mumkin comes down on his knees and starts weeping.

Guard: Okay, wait I'll ask Mr. Bloom.

Mumkin: I already took permission from Mr. Bloom. He asked me to give you ten pounds.

Guard: But the call will barely cost 1 pound.

Mumkin: The rest you can keep, sir. Since you're working so hard at night to get us accustomed to hostel life. You are also away from your wife and children just like we students are away from our families.

Guard(frowning): I am unmarried. I have no wife and children.

takes the money from Mumkin.

Guard: Only one minute you'll get.

Mumkin: Sure. I'll appreciate that one minute of talking to connect with my grandmother!

He picks up the phone and dials the number of Pamela's hostel room!

Guard: Wait, I'll talk first.

The guard takes the phone from Mumkin and starts to talk.

Guard: Hello. Is it Mumkin's grandmother's number?

The next voice he heard was of a female guard of Pamela's room.

Female guard: Who? It's a wrong number.

Mumkin to Guard: Sir please let me talk. They don't call me Mumkin. They instead call me Mr. Brown.

Guard: What, do they call you Mr. Brown ? Why is it so!

Mumkin: Because I always loved brownies so that's why they named me as Mr. Brown.

Mumkin takes the telephone from the guard.

Mumkin: Hello this is Mr. Brown. I really need to talk to my family member Pamela .It's urgent, I need support ,things aren't fine with my health!

Female guard: Yes sir. Just a second.

The female guard asks counterpart to call Pamela Brown as there's a telephone call of Mr. Brown from her home.

Guard whispers to Mumkin

Guard: You call your Granny by her name, Pamela?

Mumkin: She's very close to me! Just like best friends.

Guard(nostalgically):I am happy to see the bond between you and your grandmother.

Mumkin: I am happy seeing that you are so understanding sir.

Guard: But why did you say that you aren't fine with your health? It's your grandmother who is sick right?

Mumkin: Yes sir. She is sick. I am proclaiming myself sick so that she should not feel alone that she's only sick. She needs to feel that her grandson who happens to be her best friend is sick too.

As Pamela is informed by her hostel guard, she get's horrified. She runs in a ruckus thinking there's some urgency in her family!Her father has probably fallen sick. She takes the phone from the female guard.

Pamela: Hello daddy! Is everything okay?

Mumkin: No, not okay. Relief is still missing! Even in the hostel, relief hasn't come till now .

Pamela understands it's Mumkin's voice.

Pamela: What Mumkin? What you're saying?

Mumkin: Don't act dumb Pamela. Relief is the second best friend of ours who's been missing since morning.

Pamela: Oh, now I get it. I am worried about relief.

Mumkin: Grand mother don't worry. But sometimes I feel, do you act dumb or you are dumb?

Pamela: What do you mean by that Mumkin?

Mumkin: Just keep quiet. I'm calling you from the hostel room with extreme difficulty. I appreciate the person in charge of his kindness(looking at the guard).

The guard feels good as Mumkin praises him! Pamela understands that the information is about John and keeps her calm after Mumkin calls her dumb.

Mumkin: Tomorrow Doctor DN Paul can only answer. I'm bothered. We need to know where the Relief is?

DN paul is abbreviation of Devakalai Neelghanti paul, who is professor Olivia.

Pamela: Yeah Prof Olivia will answer daddy this question. The stars dissolve at six like a matchbox gets lighted up . That's the time to search for relief!

Mumkin: Okay granny. Bye!

Both Mumkin and Pamela return back to their rooms after this fifteen seconds conversation, making the guards perplexed.

Mumkin, while sleeping, recalls the time he spent with his grandmother. Her warmth and old age with toothless mouth, wrinkled skin and dependability on Mumkin made Mumkin remember her who passed away four years back.

CHAPTER SEVEN

Worst training ever!

The next morning Mumkin and Pamela meet at six am outside the library after taking permission from their respective guards that they'll return the borrowed books from there. As they meet up, they decide to make a close team of trustworthy people that will be led by Mumkin so that they start searching for John in the University. Pamela will persuade Prof Hasktik as he should be aware as after rules are broken in the University, students are brought to him for punishment.

Mumkin: Benny can ask Prof Olivia about John as he's the topper of the class.

Pamela: Who else can you incorporate in searching?

Mumkin: Laila, Ren, Bessy, Jerry and Joseph. These people can search for John if we're not able to get any answers from Prof Olivia or Prof Hashtik. The search will happen in two phases. One will be right now and the other will be during lunch break if we don't finish searching all places in one go. Any now we need to find John . Bessy and Ren will search the University building for science courses and doctoral courses. Laila and I will search for post graduate courses. And Joseph with Jerry will search the basement, library and any other area of University where John can be present!

They wait near the main gate of University till seven am where they meet Laila, Joseph, Ren, Jerry and Joseph. Benny Sabastian also joins them to search for John.

Pamela moves towards Prof Olivia's office just to see it locked. She inquired about it from Prof Rehman who was moving nearby. Prof Rehman tells her that she's on special leave today as she's a part of the committee. She returns back to her class on the first floor where Mumkin and other five members are waiting for her. Upon her arrival they move to their respective groups . They just had forty five minutes to search as their first hour starts at eight am before they get caught by anyone. Pamela heads towards Prof Hashtick's room near the basement of University's entrance . The Other six members head to search the respective places.

On seeing Hashtick Pamela wishes him morning.

Pamela: How are you Professor?

Prof Hashtick: Good. Who are you ?

Pamela realizes that Prof Hashtick isn't drunk, which means he doesn't remember anything. Somehow she needs to give him the wine to make him recall the information!

Pamela: Sir my name is Pamela. I'm your student. We're doing research on the formation of wines . Few days back we made wine . I kept it there(pointing towards his cupboard). Shall we try it now?

Prof Hashtick: Sure bring it here.

Pamela goes near his cup board and grabs his wine bottle. It is the same wine bottle that she gave him the last time she was here with Mumkin and John. This wine recalled his memories.

Prof Hashtick takes a big sip of it and falls on the floor. He starts to shout and cry like the previous time and after twenty second he comes back to his consciousness!

Prof Hashtick: Miss Brown, what are you doing here? Don't you have to attend the first hour class?

Pamela: Professor , did John come to you ,for his imposition as punishment?

Prof Hashtick: You mean John Greza? No. One student came in making an insane mistake. So she's punished accordingly. I don't think John is her as it was the girl for punishment not a boy?

Pamela: Okay Professor.

Pamela leaves from there quickly and runs towards the corridor to inform Mumkin.

Prof Hashtick: Wooks John's changed too quickly from boy to girl in comparison to my wine's intoxication!

Joseph and Jerry go to the basement of the University but they find there nothing except for books, research journals and broken benches. They shout loudly the name of John but don't find anything there. Then they move towards the parking area of the University where horses, buggies, cars and motorcycles are parked,but John wasn't present there. They run towards the mini backyard of the University where the grapes are grown . There wasn't any point in searching there as they peeped through the wall they saw already two University gardeners were standing there. On the other hand Mumkin and Laila went to search for post graduate courses. They searched for psychology, hotel management, business and engineering department classes and labs . All empty except one or two early birds arrived thirty minutes early to their classes. Same was the case with Ren and Bessy. Within five minutes the halls and classes are now getting flooded with students. So all six of them return back to their class.

Afternoon they go for their search again. Ren and Bessy go to the building offering the Doctoral courses. As they climb the first five floors, they don't find anything. Now there isn't any chance that they can find John anywhere as the building where the courses of post graduation are offered has already been informally inspected by them. Now they move up to the sixth floor which is locked as above is the terrace with a big door and big lock. Nearby there are broken benches with artifacts. There are many distorted statues of bronze ,iron and marble. So there wouldn't be anyone.out there at that place. As Ren and Bessy start returning back to the fifth floor, they hear a voice. Ren stops .

Ren: Bessy, I heard something. Let's go back.

As they return back, she hears the voice again.

Ren: Bessy did you hear?

Bessy: No,hear what? I did not hear anything!

Ren hears the sobs again. Now he goes near the door and bangs it loudly.

Ren: Who's there? Who's there? John, are you locked in here?

After another loud sob, Ren is dumbstruck now! It's none other than his ex-girlfriend Janny who's sobbing on the other side of the locked terrace.

Ren: Janny, Janny . Is that you? I can hear your voice!

Bessy: Yes, I heard the voice. It's a girl's voice!

Janny(weeping): Ren, please take me out of here! It isn't my mistake. I didn't do anything. I just tried to defend myself!

Ren: Don't worry , I'm here(assertively).

Ren tries to hardy bang the door four times , it doesn't open. Bessy too pushes it. Ren has turned fully red . He takes the iron head of the big statue of a distorted man. He hits hard the few more times with it and the door breaks down. He runs towards the stairs leading to the terrace , where he finds Janny is sitting on a chair inside an iron cage,hanging above the ground some ten feets. Her hands, legs and hair are tied to the chair. She has one bruised eye and her left cheek looks swollen as if someone has striked her and after that she's been kidnapped here.

Ren: Janny, don't worry I'll get you down !

Ren climbs up the stairs to reach the horizontal rod to which the cage is tied. He makes his balance on the rod, walks twelve feet, with his full energy he rotates the wheel which brings the loose chain of the cage due to which it comes down. Ren opens the lock of the cage with a hair clip of Janny which he always kept in pocket after their breakup.

Ren: How did you reach this pathetic state?

As the door opens,Ren comes towards Janny and she reveals the name of his uncle Bison that he's responsible for her this state , before falling to his arms and getting unconscious. He lifts up Janny and rushes to take her to the nurse's room. But there guards of the University arrieve . They ask him to stay there himself and call the University doctor. Ren is disheartened to see Janny in that state and what's troubling him more is his accusation by her on his Uncle. Mumkin, Pamela and Laila arrived there . Pamela is completely envious of Janny after seeing Ren sad for her. She in fact feels a sense of merriment to see Janny's state but suddenly she thinks of the evilness of her thoughts and prays for forgiveness from God. Then she wishes for the wellbeing of Janny quickly . The recess time is going to be over, the guards order them to leave back to their classes and meet Janny later just when their classes will be over. He hesitates but guards forcefully throw him out. He walks away swiftly discontented. Pamela goes behind him but he asks her not to follow her. She walks backwards in order to be with Mumkin and Laila. Ren goes to make a phone call from the University's office. As the receptionist asks too many questions from him, he tells her to beware that he's the nephew of Mr. Bison who's the trustee of this University! The receptionist allows him to do so, but as he calls his uncle, his secretary picks up the phone.

Ren: Hello, Miss Martha, please give the phone to my uncle. Tell him it's his Ren. It's urgent.

Martha: I'm sorry ,he's in some important meeting. I can't enter his office now! Once he comes back, I will convey your regard to him.

Ren: Please, now I need him.

Martha: If in case it's that urgent then you can tell the message ,I'll inform him immediately once he returns back from the meeting.

Ren: (vexed) Alright, Fuck all. Fuck his office and fuck his secretary. Bye.

Martha:Sure. Bye, have a nice day. (She shuts the phone)

The receptionist was staring at him constantly.

Ren: For what are you staring at me like that?

Receptionist:It's the language that you are using.

Ren: Fuck you two recptionist.

Receptionist: Fuck you the entire time you are front of my eyes. Just double up mother fucker or else Principal Blacksmith and Prof Olivia will be there to teach you a lesson.

Ren: Yes I want to meet those assholes too. For now I am leaving.

Ren reaches his class ten minutes late. It was Prof Rehman's class!

Prof Rehman: You're late for the class, do you know what's the result of this act?

Ren: No ,I don't want to know. Your class right now is more than any punishment to me.

Everyone starts howling as it's a hullabaloo movement for them. Ren is known for his pugnacious behavior with professors too as the University trustee, Bison is his uncle. Hitherto, Prof Rehman was his most respected teacher due to the sensitivity he displayed towards him. Prof Rehman never expected this from Ren as he showed maximum sincerity in his class in comparison to all other teachers in the University.

Prof Rehman: I know that your uncle is a trustee here, but.....

Ren interrupts him in between,

Ren: I don't want to hear anything especially about my uncle now!

In his exasperation. Prof Rehman sees tears in his eyes.

Prof Rehman: Ren, you can sit on the last bench and put your head down. I can smell that something is bothering you insanely.

Ren: No, I am fine(heavy tone).

Prof Rehman: Don't worry Ren, we'll talk about it after the class.

Ren is still angry about what his uncle has done with Janny. He goes to the last bench and attends the whole lecture . Just after the bell rings and a five minutes break starts, Prof Rehman comes near him and tries to talk about the issue, but Ren keeps himself quiet and immediately runs away to the nurse's room. He finds Janny there lying on the bed and awake. He kisses her on her forehead and she tries to tell him everything that Nick Lawrence, the guy she was dating, took her to the University terrace yesterday after classes, however he was forceful with her and tried to harass her . In return she picked the bronze statue near her and she hit him on the head.

Ren: What happened after that ,how were you captured there?

Janny: As I tried to run away from there, your uncle came in with a guard. He pulled my hair and pushed me hard due to which I got this bruise on my eye. I don't know what happened after that as when I opened my eyes, I was in a large bird-like cage up in the air.

Ren now has an indignant feeling towards his uncle. He also recalls that he hasn't seen Nick in his class since morning. But he's also bewildered because of Nick.

Ren(muffling) : B..But...(heavy breathing) why Uncle Bison did that to you?

Janny: All I know is that Nick Lawrence is a third cousin to Prof Olivia, he mentioned to me that she's a godmother to him and she's been financing his education since the time he was born.

Ren realizes that it's all because of Prof Olivia, his uncle took up this big step.

Ren: I thought Nick is the nephew of Prof Olivia.

Janny: No ,infact Nick is her third cousin.

Ren: Don't worry Olivia, Nick and Prof Olivia will pay for their bad deeds. How dare they try to harm you?

Ren leaves from there towards his class promising Janny to meet later today. As he attends his classes, the University receptionist comes to his class informing that his uncle Bison wants to talk to him. Without taking permission from the teacher in class, he runs towards the receptions and picks up the phone.

Silver Bison: Ren, how are you dear, what happened, what is so urgent now?

Ren: Uncle how can you do this to my Janny, you know how much I love her.

Silver Bison: How do you know?

Ren: Answer my question Bison, why Janny was kept in such wringing condition! You know it's against the citizen fundamental rights law!

Silver Bison: Ren darling, not now. I'm sending my chauffeur ,come to my office and we'll talk there. I'm getting your half day leave approved.

Ren: No, ways .I don't want to see you anymore. I have to be with Janny now.

Silver Bison: Listen Ren . Sometimes the truth can hurt but no one can ever change it.

Ren: I will not come!(He keeps the phone in anger).

But as the chauffeur of his uncle arrieve, Ren sits in the car to leave, thinking in mind to give his uncle the last chance. After reaching his uncle's office he finds that the front door of his uncle's office is locked. He wonders where his uncle is ? But he hears the voice of uncle coming from behind the door of his office with his secretary and manager. As both of them go back to their cars, Ren gets out of his car and attacks his uncle Silver Bison by punching him hard on his face. He falls down on the floor and the driver,manager and secretary hurriedly come out to help him get up. His nose starts bleeding. The driver goes back in the car to take out the first aid. As his secretary and manager give Ren a vexed look, he starts running away.

Silver Bison: Ren, stop ...Just stop honey. My nephew, just give me one chance to explain. It's not what it looks like! Janny is lying to you!

Ren stops running, turns back.

Ren: Bullshit you are! First you hurt Janny and now you're reclining about her.

Silver Bison: Ren, just listen to me, I have proof of what I'm saying. Come here!

Silver Bison asks his manager and secretary to leave from there and he takes up the cotton to put into his nostrils to stop bleeding and lies down in the car. He puts bandages on his nose. Ren returns back and sits in the car of his uncle in the front seat with the driver. Silver Bison sits in the back seat. The driver starts to drive.

Ren: Where are you taking me? Janny needs me, I need to go back.

Silver Bison: Just shut up! You teenager, without listening to me, you hit me so hard. You're doing many such gaffes these days. Return my money card now!

Ren returns the money card of Silver Bison to him. In the next twenty minutes there is a verbal fight between the two and there is no sign of regret from the mouth of Ren. Bison stops the driver at a place, it is 134/4, street 8, Haffotin Town,HT158. Bison gets out of his car, puts on his black shade goggles and adjusts his tie. He tells the driver to open the car trunk. The trunk is filled with goodies including bath bombs, exhotic chocolates, essential oils,decorative rocks and incense sticks. He asks his driver and Ren to pick those up as his own hands are occupied with a bouquet of soft pink lilies.

Ren: No, definitely not Bison! What do you think?I'm a blockhead.

Silver Bison: Stop calling me by my name young man! Blockhead is me to give you everything you wanted, you spoiled brat. Pick these up with Hilbert(driver) and follow me. You got to be sentimental in the next few seconds.

Ren does what Bison says in an embittered way. The trio walks towards the house. Silver Bison ring the doorbell of a house.

Silver Bison: Ooops, I forgot to put perfume on! I think I need to go back to my car.

Ren: Stop, you already rang the doorbell.Someone might be anytime now. You behave as if you're preparing to go on a date with Prof Olivia or Lidiya Cheriyan.

Silver Bison: Have you learnt to read minds from someone? Probably it's when you started dating Pamela?

Ren: Are you serious?

Silver Bison: You're partially correct. I'm not going for a date with her, we'll hope that comes true soon! But we're going to enter Prof Olivia's house(grinning).

Ren: What the heck(gritting teeth)? Why did you bring me here? Till University and Committee it's fine. Truly, none of the kids at University want to be around her, not even in dreams hitherto! She's your love not mine(scoffs).

Silver Bison chuckles. The door is opened by Lucas.

Lucas: What a surprise,Mr. Silver Bison. Please get inside. Welcome to the other two guests too.

The trio enter the house and sit on a couch, Ren was looking around on the prepossessing paintings.

Silver Bison(whispering): Ren, this is all painted by my Lydia.

Ren: And I always thought she's only good at castgating others.

Lucas: Would you like to have the chicken pot pie?

Silver Bison: Later Lucas, I want to see how Olive and Nick are doing?

Lucas: Sure, Isabella is with Nick. You can go to meet him inside.

Silver Bison: Where's Olivia?

Lucas: She went to the nearby church to pray . She'll be back within half an hour.

Silver Bison: So, I will wait here until she arrives.

Ren: Why are you so mean to me? First you brought me to Prof Olivia's house and now Nick is also here(scoffs). You know what, I'm done with you.

Bison: You young people just have no patience. All this is for a purpose.

Ren: All these gifts and flowers are for purpose? What purpose? To get a woman for whom you've been craving for more than fifteen years.

Bison: Of Course what you said is right. But that's all for me. For you, something else is the purpose of being here.

Ren is vexed. As the trio waits he calls Lucas.

Lucas: Yes little Bison, what do you want?

Ren: I'm hungry . Get me something to eat.

Lucas: Sure, chicken pot pie, strawberry pastry,peach muffin, belgium chocolate brownies and coffee. What do you want?

Ren: Get everything.

Lucas gets everything. The trio ate and waited for half an hour after that. Prof Olivia arrieves.

Bison: Oh, Olivia. Looks like I got these goodies and flowers for you.

Prof Olivia doesn't take flowers from Bison and she asks Lucas to take the goodies and take a few of them back at home for his childRen.

Bison: Olive, you're very rude. That's for you . Not for Lucas.

Prof Olivia: I know that. What are you doing here?

Bison: I came to see you and Nick. How's your leg now?

Ren observes that Prof Olivia has leg splints on her left leg.

Prof Olivia: I'm feeling better.

Ren is bewildered. All of them head towards another room where Nick is sleeping with scratches on his face, his leg and arms are plastered.

Ren: (muffled)Wait, Janny hit Nick only on his head to protect herself. But he's injured at diffeRent places!

Prof Olivia: Great Ren, it's a great sample of being blind in love.

Bison:Ren, Janny did not not hit Nick in self defense. She hit him as we came to know about her truth.

Ren: What truth?

Bison: From the Intelligence report it was revealed that some student from the University is revealing a secret about the plan of the Committee and that particular student is close to committee members.

Ren: How sure that it's Janny.

Bison: We suspected a few students of the University. First is John, who's best friend of Pamela and Mumkin. Second is Laila, with whom Pamela shares a room and Mumkin likes her. We even suspected Bessy's boyfriend Larry, since he's working now and not studying anymore nor did he study from our University in the past, he quickly got out of our suspect list.We thought about Laila, but from her room it was found that she's just reading spiritual books and has a traumatic past .She's still struggling to get a good boyfriend, but finds comfort in Mumkin's company .Pamela is another kind friend to her. The last person to be suspected was Janny. From our detectives, it was found that Janny stole the book from Ren in which the plan of action during the training phase was written by him.

Ren: No ways! I did not realize it all, I'm not even aware about where the notebook is!

Silver Bison:That's because once you come out of University ,the only thing you have done till now is to spend time with Janny and take her shopping. Books, naaah! You get allergic from smelling them after classes.

Ren: Uncle Silver Bison ,stop it! I'm just dumbstruck now.

Bison: Yes, she was about to give the book to Watson's man,but we sent Nick to propose to her and get closer to her and get the book.

Ren: You could've asked me to get my notebook back from her by telling her truth. Why did you send Nick there?

Bison: Multiple reasons- You're part of committee training, soon you'll be shifted to a different place, you were blindly loving Janny ,so your emotions wouldn't have believed us and lastly it would've destroyed our relationship. It would have become like the way it was a few minutes ago. You started calling me Silver Bison instead of uncle.

Ren: Uncle I didn't know it would hurt you so much.

Bison:Ahh Ren, your uncle has been hurt by huge things in life(looking at prof Olivia), this is nothing. Nick dated Janny by flouting about himself,she broke up with you to get better things in life. He went to her house for family dinner and he got the notebook back from her. The next morning, the plan was to apprehend Janny for interrogation. Olivia dressed up as a guard to hide her identity and to arrest Janny. We couldn't do anything in front of the students, so Nick took Janny to the fourth floor in one of the block's of University. As Olivia arrived there as guard, Janny suspected her and Nick, she pushed Nick from stairs Olivia tried to protect Nick by trying to hold his hand while he was falling.Only Nick's fingers she could touch, she herself twisted her ankle in the process to protect him .She herself fell to the ground unconscious.Nick fell on ground too, due to which his leg and hand broke. He was crying in pain. I arrived there quickly with other guards to check the state of plan and of course I was worried about Olivia. Seeing Olivia in that stage infuriated me, so I ordered the guards to capture Jannu in the prisoner's cage, so that no student can ever find her here as no one goes to that place. There was a tussle between guards and her, during which one eye got bruised. She was given food ,water and a washroom facility as one guard was there to monitor her. Probably he didn't do his duty well and during that time you ,Pamela and Bessy freed her unknowingly without getting interrogation done. But still she's a threat as she might have already given a lot of information to Malefactor's leader Watson!

Ren:It's very difficult to believe this. My heart says that Janny can never do it.

Bison: Dear Nephew, I understand that you loved and trusted Janny a lot but the notebook was discovered from Janny's house. All evidence is pointing against Janny. She's a traitor.

Bison:Olivia, what about John ,where is he now?

Prof Olivia: John is an insane boy. Through a regulation management scout, it's revealed that Ren proposed to Pamela before John. There was a revelation that he bunked the classes and broke the rule of University to prepare for his proposal. His punishment was to go to the Military regiment and do guard duty for two days to learn a lesson. He was told to take his things with him. Few things ,just notebooks and clothing. But nincompoop took each and every material from his locker and room. He left people suspicious of him being a missing person. Bloom has mentioned to me hundred times that students are asking for him. You Ren, and Mumkin are searching for him like detectives. John is still doing his duty and will return back to University tomorrow.

Nick wakes up. He starts murmuring.

Nick: Aunt Lidiya, it all happened as I tried to overpower Janny when she tried to run away after seeing you. I ruined the plan.

Prof Olivia: Take rest and don't think too much. Regarding Janny ,she'll be shifted to a hospital where her painstaking interrogation will happen. Seventy percent of evidence is against her, if found guilty, she'll not only be permanently suspended from the University but also jailed for three years in Himbertown's jail.

Silver Bison: Wooks! Poor girl, this chastising is for betraying one's own people.

Ren: You mean going against the military is betraying the nation! Isn't that dictatorship?

Silver Bison: I would call it dictatorship if the Military was forceful on its people. Our military is honestly doing its job, Watson is trying to provoke people, and wants to establish its own rule . It wants to convert people into bonded labor like the way it's happening in Marvo village. Military and the government are trying to protect the lives of people and give them their basic rights. That's why the whole mission in Marvo Village is based on that. If the Military wanted to do dictatorship, not a tough assignment . You see ,Military is at each and every corner of our country, establishing military rule won't be a difficulty . But our Military is for people who work on morality.

Ren agrees to what Bison says. He sits back in the car and the chauffeur starts driving. Disappointed with the facts revealed about Janny, his car arrives at the University's clinic in the last hour. He plans to meet Janny and get her shifted in a hospital for better treatment as he still cares about her, at least for her health. Janny was also lying on her bed and waiting to see him when suddenly someone arrives with a bouquet of red roses ,whose face is hidden behind the bouquet.

Janny: Aww, I know it's you Ren!Thanks for the beautiful bouquet. You know that I love red roses.

Ren: No Janny, I'm here.

Janny sees that the person with whom she received the bouquet is someone else and Ren is standing next to that person.

Person behind the bouquet: Surprise Janny darling !That's me! After hurting Olivia, I've come here to tell you about the penalty of doing so!

Janny: Uncle Silver Bison, is that you? (piqued), I must not shy away from saying that because of you I'm in this state. And for the records, I never hurt Prof Olivia.

Bison: You viper, it was Olivia in guard's uniform .

Janny: Stop calling me such names(scorned). I never saw any guard. Instead I hit Nick, not Prof Olivia. She wasn't even present there. Ren tells your uncle to be mindful while talking to me.

Bison: Injured! The depth of injury is big,ten times more than your injuries. Nick is bedridden.

Janny: He had to be injured as he tried to force upon me, so I hit him on his head.

Ren: Stop lying Janny. Prof Olivia came there as a guard. Secondly Nick is injured on his leg,not his head.

Janny: I had turned towards the wall,I didn't know who was behind. I was just defending myself while hurtling, just can't recall where I hit him. I was traumatized.

Ren: Stop your self made chronicle! And Nick wasn't forcing upon you, instead he was just trying to get you apprehended for interrogation for sealing my notebook which he discovered back from your home!

Janny: (dumbstruck) Apprehension and interrogation! Let me clarify, I stole your notebook as I thought you'd written poetry in it for someone new you're meeting these days.

Ren: About whom you're talking about?

Janny: I thought you're cheating on me with Pamela, as both of you are part of the committee, you always kept that notebook close to yourself, once I asked you to show you refuse haphazardly and kept it back in your bag quickly. Remember on the first day of freshers, you told me that Pamela is kind of cute to you. You like the way she tries to show flares up with you. That's why I stole the notebook for reconfirmation to check whether you've written poetries for her or not.

Ren: So what did you find in the notebook?

Janny: Nothing, all scruffy work.

Ren: I can't write poetries as it isn't worth it to write for people who just leave you behind for better options.(looking at Janny).

Janny: Look Ren, we can try it all over again. You saved me, my love towards you has increased in a huge way.

Ren:Nick dated you strategically, I feel sorry for you. But I'm already with Pamela. I can't be with you again. I'm sorry.

Janny: I never knew that it's all counterfeit by Nick. But still can't believe that our love is over, we've done this many times before you see.

Ren: Not this time , as I'm no longer single .

Janny: Yes(dejected).

Ren gives Janny a friendly hug and leaves from there.

Silver Bison keeps the flowers near her bed.

Silver Bison: Flowers for you young lady. Apologies for whatever happened to you, especially the tussle between you and the guards. Of Course Nick's fake dating. It was perplexing as we thought you're a .....Never mind. You clarified everything, that's a big relief for us and of course thank you! Also this heartbreak won't last longer. Trust me, I've been heartbroken many times(winking his left eye). Look at me now, I am as fit as fiddle.

Janny: Uncle, can you convince Ren to be with me again?

Silver Bison: Sorry honey. You need this dose to know how inappropriate it is to leave someone you love for a better option especially if the second option is more resourceful!

Silver Bison goes behind Ren.

Silver Bison and Ren go back to Prof Olivia's house. Silver Bison tells everything to her, that Janny isn't involved with Watson, instead Nick's eagerness to capture Janny created a situation where she pushed him thinking he's forceful which made her an obvious culprit of their suspicion. Now the three ponder deeply which student is involved with Watson who's giving all secret plans to him. For a moment they doubt John.

On the other hand this is John's second night of punishment as tomorrow he has to return back to the University.The first day was very tiresome as his boss there in the Military made him work as a gardener, collecting all dry leaves, watering plants and brooming the lawn of eight kilometers. Food was just salted boiled potatoes with rice . It was a chicken sandwich and strawberry ice cream as an evening snack that helped him to survive the first day. Night although wasn't bad,as he got to be a part of bon fire with a glass of whiskey raising toast along with other soldiers in the name of country . Few sang songs of their separated lovers and families. Few sang based on being a soldier with patriotic feelings. John's anticipation of doing the guard's duty was wrong. Second day, he was asked to go for an early run of ten km where he ran just three. The rest of the ways he jogged and walked. After the breakfast of red beans with bread, he had to repeat his task as a gardener. Lunch was appetizing but there weren't any evening snacks. He was just waiting for the night, to celebrate the bonfire. Evening ,his boss called him to hand over his guard uniform. He's completely dressed up as a guard, completely covered in black uniform . His black leather belt gives him a heroic feeling. He holds up the walkie talkie in his hand. His boss snatches it back from him.

Boss: Don't touch anything not being authorized to you.

John: But boss, that's how I'll be able to communicate with other guards,

Boss: You don't have to communicate with any other guards! Your duty is in front of the junior's barrack.No leave . Quick!!!

John: (walking swifty and turning back) What about a bonfire, isn't it?

John's boss comes near him , orders him to bend and hits him hard on his buttalocks.

Boss: You've not come to the picnic. Remember it's a Military camp! Bonfire happens once a month,you're lucky to experience it. Now run ,you bloody clod !(furious loud voice).

John gets intimidated and runs quickly towards the Junior's barrack. As he stands there, it's all foggy and chilling cold. He tries to stay strong and stands stiff, but after three hours, his eyelids are heavy and he wants to sleep. He is fascinated by sleeping in his cozy hostel bed with a blanket. All he thinks is that, the day before yesterday, he was all there! It's three thirty pm in the morning ,his boss comes to check him and finds him sitting on the ground and drooling. His boss hits him hard with his boot and then with a stick eight times and then makes him do a hundred squirrel jumps, due to which his body is heated up. He's tired and thirsty but of course not sleepy anymore, due to his boss's punishment. He doesn't want to get hit by his boss more than this. In all that consternation, there's just one hope of returning back to his University's room, where that one bed is seraphic to him. He did his duty as a guard till five thirty in the morning, when he realized that it's time for soldiers to go for a ten km run, he went into his barrack as he wanted to get ready to leave towards his University. As he was changing his dress, his senior came inside, asked him to change to a physical training dress as he had to go for a run along with others. When he tried to say 'Sir, this is the time for me to leave for my university' ,the reply was that he isn't supposed to ask any questions. John was absolutely miserable and tired, unaware that he has to go through this much strain and his punishment has been increased. He vowed to himself that he'll never propose to a girl in his life as now he can see that the consequences of it are grave. As he wore white T-shirt and white jogging pants.

As he reached the race, there were around a hundred men in jogging uniform. His boss came there to make an announcement.

Boss: As you see John was sleeping in his duty time, so not only has to run ten kilometers today but has to come first, or else he'll leave this place only next week.

John: What ! I can't ...I just can't. Yesterday I ran just three km. Running ten kilometers ,I'm dead.

John lies down on the ground as he faints. As he opens his eyes ,he finds himself surrounded by other soldiers, a few of them lift him up and push him up in the air, he soon realizes that he's tossed in the air. He's tossed four times and they all shout "John's life is boring,he wanna have fun, let's fulfill his life with a birthday bump". In the fifth one, they don't hold him, so he gets thrashed on the ground. His boss comes to him.

Boss: John, it was all a prank, before I could reveal that there's no run for you and you're going back to your University, you fainted. Haha(cackles).

Others laugh at him.

Boss: Now let me give you the price of your hard work.

Boss gives him a certificate and an envelope.

That envelope had some cash in it,as John opened it, it's just two units . In his certificate it's mentioned 'John has been a hardworking student to finish his short term course in Military regiment. He finished all tasks successfully. His score is 3.4/10 '

John: What the heck! Just two units of cash! Isn't that too less for all the hard work that I did?

Boss: Keep it man! Two units is your traveling allowance. The certificate is for your hard work.

John: But I got 3.4 out of 10. Why so stingy in giving scores?

Boss: Only 3 is your score. 0.4 is extra added as a grace mark. Now vacate the barrack space!

John: Thank you. It was a pleasure to experience all this!

Boss: You worked hard man(gives shoulder hug to John).

John packs up his bags and leaves the place. He isn't given any transportation while returning back, so he decides to take a bus towards Himbertown University.

Within one hour John packs up his belongings, changes dress to casual Shirt and gray pants with a Beanie and leaves the Military camp, by taking a lift for free in a garbage truck ,sitting next to the driver . As he reaches Johnson's market which is some one fourth way away from the University, he gets down near a pastry shop. It's decorated beautifully by bright pink and white flowers with bakery items displayed in a fancy way. He reads the board "Get melt by cakes- Taste that's exploding minds since 1953 ". He finds this bizarre and uproarious. As he enters the shop ,he finds a rogue person sitting at the counter with a big belly and giving a grave look at him . As he gets in with his big bag of luggage, he's stopped by that man from doing so and is asked to keep his bags outside in a locker. He enters the shop after keeping his bag in a locker, as he sits on one of the tables, unexpectedly there comes an exquisite lady in a light pink dress with a rose scarf . She takes his order of cheesecake and a cup of coffee. As he looks around the shop, seven to eight waitresses are working in a similar costume, they all look adorable. He thinks in his mind 'Dude, after so much struggle you have come to the right place....It's like a dream or an angel's land. Beauties all over'. John doubts that the man with pot belly is the odd one out, probably he's the manager or the owner. As he was looking at his two units of currency note, one waitress arrived to serve him with his order in a tray, John get's enlivened after seeing that it's Stella, Pamela's cousin. She's just looking adorable like others in pink frock,rose scarves, but has this blue ribbon with jasmine flowers printed on it which is tying her hair. There is a curl that she's putting back again and again as it is coming in front of her face . The curl is touching her nose and lips .She smiles at John,

Stella: John,I am pleased to see you here.

John: Stella, do you work here?You look beautiful.

Stella: Yes John .Thank you.

As John looks into her eyes, they're sparkling like sun rays hitting the sea. As Stella serves the coffee to John, they both look at each other's eyes and smile. There's a slight sadness in her eyes due to which her smile looks tiresome.

Stella: How come you are here today? You should've been in the University right?(raising her left eyebrow in sarcasm).

John: It's a long story.

Stella: But I can tell my father about you bunking here.

John: Yes Stella, go ahead and tell your dad Bidar Nelon about my misdoings. I am present in this world to get ordered by others. That's my identity(vexed). You too show it.

Stella: Hey no no(fixing her curl and putting it behind her right ear). I was just joking. I won't say anything to anyone.

John: Why are you working here as a waitress? I thought this year you would be joining Himbertown University!

Stella: I'm a pastry chef here, other girls you see are our employees. Me, Joana and Katy started this pastry shop just a month before. I don't want to go to University as I ain't passionate about it.

John: Really, so that guy sitting near reception is the owner.

Stella: No, he's our cashier.

John: Why did you choose such a cocky cashier?

Stella: Are you referring to Billy .He looks cocky but he has a disconsolate story! All he's living is for his one son.He's actually a kind hearted man.

John: Hmmm .Okay . Well the name of your shop sounds.....(still) hysterical! Haaaahaha.

Stella looks around as other girls are looking at both of them. She gets slightly self conscious.

Stella: Let's go out, there's a garden nearby !

John walks out in a rush, leaving his luggage bag outside the shop's locker. She whispers something in ear of her partner Joana, due to which Joana smiles and she too comes out of her shop with her silverish gray color purse that she's holding with her right hand which is half folded towards her back . John and Stella go to the nearby park. They sit on a bench. They start looking around. For two minutes there's an awkward silence. After seeing Stella quiet, John finds an urge to open up . John starts speaking about himself.

John:There's a girl whom I have loved since my school days.

Stella: I know ,she told me everything about what happened between you and her.

John: Do you know about her?

Stella:Yes, it's my cousin Pamela.

John: I'm just broken from inside.

Stella: Life has many options, people come . But all these experiences help us grow!

John: And our pastry chef Stella has a surprising philosophical side too.

Stella chuckles , she bends downwards to lift her bag up and hands over the wrapped items to John.

John: What's this(opening the wrapper). Yum. Strawberry pastries and chocolate cake!(Keeping food items in between both of them on the bench)

They make eye contact with each other and smile.

Stella:Yeah, you actually did not eat anything inside the bakery that's why I took your ordered items that you left on your booked table .So I got them wrapped for you.

John: Oh yes(shy laugh). That chocolate cake, I didn't order(shrugging his shoulders)!

Stella: Well it's a new bakery item in our shop, you can take that as a free item to try! But if you don't want to,I can give it to our cashier Billy.

John: No way. I'm gonna have everything you see!If you have anything better ,do get it now. I'm all in to try different items as your bakery food looks just scrumptious.

Stella: Ofcourse, but only the chocolate pastry is free ,for other stuff that you ordered, you need to pay.

John: Here you go(handing a note of two units of currency).

Stella:(chuckling) No way, it's too less money you're giving. Only coffee and strawberry pastry can be bought from this! What about other items that you'll order sir?

She stands up and puts her hands on her waist.

Stella(smiling): Who will pay for other items?

John: Since we're good acquaintances, I don't expect you to ask me to pay! Do you?

Stella laughs for sometime and then her smile fades her .Again the same sadness is observed by John in her eyes.

John: I was just joking Stella! I won't put your bakery in loss.

Stella: I know you won't. Don't worry about paying, just think that ,it's a treat from my side.

As John was about to take the first bite of his chocolate cake, he waited for five seconds and kept the pastry back on the bench as Stella still looked .

John:How has life treated you till now?

Stella: Not so good! There was a guy whom I was dating, but he ghosted me after two weeks of dating.

John: When did all this happen to you?

Stella: Two days before.

John: That guy is just an asshole. Forget about him, as you said "Life has many options, people come and leave. But all these experiences help us grow!".

After a gap of two seconds ,Stella smiles at John and they both start to beam at each other.

They visit the nearby shops of crockery and porsche artifacts, and John gets to know the amount of Renting a crockery shop. He talks to the businessmen whose shops are established for many years here about their experiences of ups and downs in business and how they handled it! He expresses his wish of establishing his own business to Stella, she seems to be very supportive towards that.

John had to return back to the University before six. Stella informs him that in his family his father is out for two days due to University work and his mom is at her grandmother's place ,she'll return only tomorrow. They both go to her house. John freshes himself and Stella cleans the room and removes her books from the bed and keeps them in another room. The doorbell rings, she goes near the door, receives the package overjoyfully and comes back to her bedroom. She turns off the lights and lightens up two lavender candles just two meters away from bed. As John comes out of shower, she is waiting for him, sitting in a gorgeous red night gown in the afternoon with only red lipstick and no makeup. There's a lavender fragrance all over the room. John sits next to her. He looks at her face. She looks at him for a second and starts looking slightly down with shyness. Her cheeks are pink, she's blushing with a faint smile which shows a little nervousness on her face. There's a slight cleavage,John's eyes are going there ,although he's trying to establish eye contact with her.

Stella: This gown, it's not mine.I borrowed it from Joana. She came when you were taking shower. Do you like my lipstick(pointing her index finger towards her lips).?

John: Yes, I do. You look stunning in this dress and those red lips are intoxicatingly beautiful!

Stella smiles and looks down again. She looks pressured while trying to stop smiling as she's unable to. She again looks at John ,but this time she looks confused!

Stella: Have you done this before?

John: I've been in a relationship twice before. So yes. I have done sex many times.

Stella: I was in girls school, I never got a chance to be close to any guy!I'm nervous.It's the first time I'm that close to any man.

John: Stella, each experience is unique. If you're not ready for it then we can leave things here itself!

Stella: I want this,especially with you!

He comes closer to her , she can feel him breathing heavily and he starts kissing her on her lips, she moves backward .

John: What happened? Why did you move back?
Stella: I'm too nervous!
John: Are you not ready?
Stella: I think I am. Let's try it again!(she breathes heavily).
John: Just relax(deep voice). Many people do it, it's going to be smooth, as we aren't experimenting to go to the Moon!

John kisses her on her lips again, this time this lasted a little longer as Stella holds the bedsheet of her bed tight. He starts to remove her gown. She's wearing a cream colored bra with a blue panty. Second, he thinks "what a guiltless girl, blue with cream,raw and simple, he finds it lovely ". He uncovers her bra and touches her everywhere. He kisses on her neck, cheeks, on the cleavage and holds her breasts .She starts breathing heavily. He kisses her navel and starts licking her on her back, shoulders and other parts of body. Stella's body feels tremendous heat. Then he kisses passionately on her thighs. Her breathing becomes very fast. She's holding his hair and he's about to give her the love that she always craved for.

She tells him in a soft voice that she's liked him since the first time they met. He smiles at her and kisses back again on her lips. With that awkwardness ,she hugs him, strokes his hair, touches his masculine shoulders . He interlocks his fingers with her and they become one after that. After two hours of quality time with each other, John takes a bus to his hostel. Stella is feeling sad after his departure. She wonders when will be the next time when both of them will see each other.Although John loved her passionately but now she's longing for his love the next time. She's lying on her bed and recalling the precious moments shared with him .

John reaches his University. As he enters the hostel room, he doesn't find anybody! He hears the footsteps of someone coming.

As Mumkin enters his hostel room, he gets freaked out by John.

Mumkin: John buddy! Where were you?

Mumkin hugs him but detaches himself immediately and slightly pushes Mumkin back. Mumkin is dumbstruck with John's bizarre behavior.

John: You never tried to search for me.

Mumkin punches John lightly in his stomach and says "you have no idea how we got freaked out after you were missing, we searched for you in the whole University. Thanks to Ren's uncle Bison, who told him everything that you're in the Military camp! How are you brother, what experiences have you made from there?".

John: I worked really hard there ,took up the job of gardener and guard . Got this certificate in return! (showing his Military certificate of appreciation).

Mumkin: Woah man! Congratulations, keep it safe! It has a lot of value! You look very tired, it's probably due to the hard work you did there!

John: That's there. But there's something else also to it!

Mumkin: Really, what's that(excited)? Did you get any position in the military?

John: Who'd like to be Military huh? Life is so difficult there.

Mumkin: Then what's the good news brother?

John: Guess what, this entire afternoon, I was with Stella Bidar. Yeah, we made love bro.

Mumkin : I'm so happy for you (giving a tight hug).

John: She's just the kind of girl whom I always dreamt of!Sweet ,guiltless and adorable.....

Mumkin: Do you have any plans with her in future?

John: I am not sure. Just now we started dating so.....(silence).

Mumkin: Probably she's the one for you.

John: What about Laila? Do you have any plans or are you two just having fun?

Mumkin: Just fun...No brother. We two are deeply committed towards each other. In Fact I plan to spend the rest of my life with her.

John: Great, if things go right then surely I will be uncle John in future.

Mumkin: Uncle John....(chuckles) ...John,you're acting naughty today, Probably apart from the gardener and guard role, the military trained you for comedy too.

John: Maybe. A military man is an all rounder.

They both laugh together and talk to each other for some more time and then they move to the refreshment room to play carrom.

The next day both of them go to the University, they are getting ready to attend the classes. Everyone is affectionate to John after having him back to campus. People are friendly, punching his shoulders amicably and giving him high five. Mumkin and John, both are sitting together. Pamela enters the class and hugs John ,shouting his name, but then she awkwardly moves one step back from him.

Pamela: John, we were worried about you!

John: I know, you two really care about me.

Pamela: I'm sorry John, I'm actually dating Ren. I could never come to know that you like me.

John: Pamela, no nonsense please! Why are you sorry? If I like you ,but you don't feel the same, then you can always say no. And how will you come to know that I like you, as I never told or confessed my love towards you! Also forget about whatever I said about Ren to you that he's self obsessed or loves only Janny, ignores you. Now as he proposed to you,shows that he wants you and will keep you happy in life! In Fact I was wrong in judging him. I'm delighted to see this new person in your life !

Pamela: Thanks John, you're the best! You talk like a saint. I don't know when and how you've grown this maturity. I don't want to lose a friend like you(hugging John) .

Mumkin: Ofcourse, he sounds more like that of a philosopher . Probably this is all coming from Stella!

Pamela:Oh now I get it! It's Stella's magic on you. She's the one who talks all philosophy.

The trio laugh together.

John was called at that time by Warden Atricka Bloom near Prof Olivia's office.

Prof Olivia: Mr. John Greza, come inside. It's been found that you did a fine job in the Military camp as your punishment! Congratulations. We might consider you for a good position in school!

John: Prof Olivia, I'm fine here. It was tiresome. I don't want to be the school's gardener or guard. Or as Mumkin pointed out, the school's comedian.

Prof Olivia: Not the position in your mind. Don't you think Pamela and Ren are too close, I've heard that you loved Pamela!

John is dumbstuck as Prof Olivia is asking this.

Prof Olivia: John, don't be too private, sit down. Have this(passing a cup of coffee).

John is a little skeptical about Prof Olivia's behavior.

Prof Olivia: You didn't answer my question!

John: Yes ,I loved Pamela ,but ultimately it's her choice of choosing the person of herself.

Prof Olivia: You're adulting huh! Everyone knows ,since the time they joined the committee ,Mumkin and Pamela have been kind of separated from you. Your trio friend circle is broken. Ren took over your place in Pamela's heart.

John: No(standing up), no one can take my place in Pamela's heart. Who the heck is Ren?A boy who brags because of his uncle ,who's a trustee of University.

Prof Olivia: I too don't like his uncle! That's why I thought of removing Ren from the committee. Would you like to take his place? By this Pamela can come closer to you!Deal?

John: Yes, deal!

Prof Olivia: You know why John is there in the committee? Because his uncle Bison gave him full knowledge about it, that's why he passed all the tests. You don't know yet that Ren told the same to Pamela as he liked her and Pamela told the same to Mumkin. That's why three of them made it to selections. Unfortunately, Pamela also wanted you to know about all the secretive answers to be part of the committee but you were already out of testing.

John: Really!

Prof Olivia: So I have one condition. If you know something about the committee, Ren will be replaced by you . He entered the committee through knowing about the extra information from his uncle. Although it was cheating, it was his smart move to steal and use the information for his own good. Because he had a lot of secret information about the secret committee that's why he proved to be resourceful. Now it's your turn to show your smartness by revealing almost every information about the secret committee. Come on John, it's your test to get your darling Pamela.

John: Yes I know something about it that the committee is established for secret work.

Prof Olivia: This is very general information that everyone knows in the University. Even one simple but unique piece of information from your side can fulfill your wish to replace Ren.

John:The committee is establishing an action plan!

Prof Olivia(attentive): What action plan?

John: The plan is to talk to aliens I guess, that's why it's so secretive. I saw in a movie that such committees are formed to contact the aliens.

Prof Olivia: Are you joking or trying to behave like a fool!

John: I seriously don't know anything about it. But please keep me in!

Prof Olivia: Keep you in. What about Stella?

John: How do you know her?

Prof Olivia: Your boss from the Military camp was so much impressed by your work that he spied upon you till the time you reached University.

John is dumbstruck.

Prof Olivia: In life choices need to be based on values. If these are your values, then you might get your love by breaking the trust of others.

John: No Prof, I love both Pamela and Stella. They're cousins and resemble each other so much.

Prof Olviia makes John leave her office immediately and makes a phone call stating "John Greza, isn't the culprit".

The next day all four students of the secret committee, all students of first year psychology and second year business management are asked to get accumulated on the basis of the committees assigned by the University. John and Benny are in the committee of serving differently abled people, Laila is with another girl named Kristine in the committee of education. And finally Mumkin, Pamela ,Ren and Bessy are in a different committee to conserve water as mentioned to them prior by Prof Olivia. All students are provided with respective guides. The guide for Mumkin's group is Prof Olivia. John thanks God for not being in Pamela's group. After hearing Prof Olivia's advice on values that morning, he made his decision to be with Stella. Now he is getting more inclined towards Prof Olivia morally and emotionally as she is her guide of service to differently abled people. Prof Olivia takes them to Gandhi Hall, where she gives them the instructions.

Prof Olivia: Four of you,pack your all belongings, be back here at ten twenty! Run. Ren ,your family has already made arrangements!

Ren:Do you mean my uncle Silver Bison has made all the arrangements?

Prof Olivia doesn't give any reply to him.

As they run towards their hostel rooms, they realize that it's a time to leave the University now, their group is for the training of the Committee. They trio return back to Gandhi hall . Pamela is five minutes late as she goes back to bring her cat. Prof Olivia ,tells her to pick four extra bags ,two each from Mumkin and Bessy. As Mumkin comes towards her to help her out in lifting the bags, Prof Olivia stops him from doing so and warns him that consequences would be substandard if he displays the same behavior again during the Committee training time as it's hindering Pamela's punishment and behavior management process. Pamela is a rule breaker and she needs to learn through the punishments! She drags the bags with a lot of whack and finally comes near the luggage truck twenty five minutes late with five plus three bags . She's out of breath and sweating badly.

They all keep their luggage in a Military truck which is huge! Pamela is very worn out to even climb the stairs of the truck .She takes out her water bottle .As she looks around expecting Ren pitting her, she finds him looking at the clouds. As they were waiting for the Military bus for their commutation, Prof Olivia arrived there!

Prof Olivia: What are you all waiting for? Get in fast.

Ren: It's a truck Professor, not even a bus where we can sit! There aren't any seats!

Prof Olivia: Get in princess!

As the truck is filled with their luggage in the starting, so they sit on the back side on the truck's floor. It's a menacing cold. As the truck starts moving they get a feeling that they're cattles going to the butcher! Among all Ren looks unstirred by unkind weather. Pamela is just half dead ,Mumkin and Bessy are trying to stay strong .They see ,there's a single peach colored quill near the luggage on the other side of the truck. Mumkin gets an idea.

Mumkin: Let's play a small game to warm up! One by one I'll pose a few puzzles ,for every correct solution, you'll take a step towards the opposite side, where our luggage is being kept!

Ren: Why to move towards the luggage?

Mumkin: Look at that quill which is peach in color. The one who reaches first will get the quill.

So the first puzzle is "I am not sun, not moon but a bow.My shape is acceptable both upside down " .

They all guess together except Pamela who's irritated due to two things- the chilling cold and coldness of Ren towards her. Ren comes with the answer that it's a hemisphere. Mumkin tells Ren to take one step forwards and Pamela and Bessy need to bend to take the shape of a bow!

As Bessy and Pamela do ,their bodies feel warmer with movement. Ren gets exhilarated by taking a step forward. Mumkin asks the second puzzle "People think that god controls everything but in reality that's me! No one knows who made me, but my eternality is not defined!" .Ren replies quickly-The Universe, Bessy guesses-it's life and Pamela replies- time. God created time, that controls everything but no one knows whether it's eternal or not!

Mumkin: Take one step forward Pamela. Ren and Bessy make a clock!

Ren: Wait, why do we make ourselves a clock and what kind of stupid question you're asking!

Mumkin: Just stand like a tree with one foot up and hands in rotating direction.

Bessy stands but Ren doesn't as he's agitated .Pamela asks Ren to calm down and take the game as game only! But this time Mumkin gives Ren a chance to ask the puzzle.

Ren: I'm seen only in movies,dreams or in reflections of saints. Everyone talks about me but reality my entire existence exists in none!

Bessy: Ghosts?

Ren(chuckles): Some ghosts exist in all of us! Isn't it?

Bessy(embarrassed):I see, I don't know the answer!

Pamela: I know the answer, it's love!

Ren: Kind of ambiguous answer.

Pamela: As ambiguous as your question is! (Pamela was actually referring to the careless demeanor of Ren towards her. During the proposal he behaved as if he loved her ,but his love is just like the puzzle- only seen in movies and dreams but in reality it isn't existing at all towards her).

Mumkin: I know the puzzle, the answer is "character", which is seen in heroes of movies, reflections of saints but in reality it exists in very small quantities in all of us! No man on earth can be called as hundred percent full of character! But I don't know how character and dream are connected together.

Ren: Take one step forward man!

Mumkin says yes with thumbs up in excitement and he takes one step forward.

Ren asks Pamela and Bessy to bend down. Pamela asks the next puzzle!

Pamela: I like painting, I like making money but I can choose the former only.

Bessy answers that an entrepreneur can be a person who likes to make money but choses painting as their hobby. Pamela says that she guessed it wrong. Ren answers that a woman's lover makes women's nude paintings to make money. Pamela rebukes Ren by saying "a woman's nude painting isn't always painted by a woman's lover !in fact a woman's nude painting is an art which sometimes may or may not make money". Mumkin answers that it's a woman's story. He regards it a sad part of our society. Pamela says that " it's a gender stereotype, where women aren't able to take roles in money making or business but art work is regarded to belong to women. Mumkin is somewhat correct". Pamela gives permission to Mumkin to take one step forward. She asks Bessy and Ren to lie down, which turns out to be the worst nightmare for both of them as the truck's surface is damn frigid. The game continues, all give their weird self made onspot puzzles in rotation and ultimately,it's Mumkin who reaches to the blanket. However their bodies are already warm enough to not to feel that cold. Mumkin decides to share the blanket among four for the rest of the way. Pamela and Bessy are delighted to do so whereas Ren believes that it's Mumkin who's supposed to be there in a blanket as he earned it after winning the puzzle game so he doesn't accept Mumkin's proposal to even step inside the blanket . After a few minutes of enjoying the luxury of a blanket, the truck stops and a smartly dressed Military personnel opens the exit shutter of the truck. Ren stands up to go out .

Military man: Wait mister, were you the one making so many jumping noises inside the truck?

Ren: Not only me, eventually it's all of us.

Military Man:You chaps had enough fun! Now come out, chop chop.

As the four of them come out of the truck, the Military Man asks them to call him sergeant Davis. He calls out the names of the foursome and assigns the roll numbers according to their groups alpha, charlie, Sierra and November. Sergeant Davis takes them to a place he calls the Hub. At this place ,it's all huge walls surrounding the four sides with the sky open. The sky is looking beautiful with hazel blue color and it's providing comfort in the chilling cold! The smell of fresh whitewash on walls is weirdly appetizing to Pamela as she's lacks calcium. She sometimes craves for clay, rock and mud after when it rains. Within a few minutes some new people joined the foursome. They find that there are some twenty more students just like them but of different Universities. There comes a similar face to welcome them, it is Colonel Hielmaster. There's another soldier standing next to him who looks like a junior Colonel. He orders to make two seperate lines, one for girls and other for boys! This time he doesn't make eye contact with any of the students from Himbertown University. He orders everyone to get acquainted with the places. A soldier takes them to all places including the parade ground, ammunition rooms, mess, barracks and local prayer room! He introduces them to their trainers and prominent teachers of various subjects including gun handling, shooting, drill and mess etiquettes. He informs them about the timings of waking up and sleeping starting the day at 3:30AM in morning and ending at 11:00PM at night which gave the foursome disquiet! Then the next knowledge about being a night guard in rotation with zero sleep ,kind of made them rethink for a second if they are at the right place. This might cause them so much of sleep deprivation and exhastion that even sleeping like kumbkarna for six months won't do their recovery. Kumbhkarna is a characther in Ramayana, younger brother of Ravana who's envy of lord rama because he kindnapped lord Rama's wife Seeta.

As they return back to Hub, Colonel Hielmaster addresses them again.

Hielmaster: I'm sure smart chaps like you have understood this place's structure and ambience!Before you leave, I want to introduce you to your sub seniors of the camp. Ren,Mumkin, Pamela and Bessy, step forward and face the opposite of your juniors(referring to the other twenty students)!

The foursome follow the order! Mumkin can hear his heartbeat...lub dub lub dub....His body is feeling very warm as the blood is rushing fast! There's a warm feeling dealing with the promise to make his father proud! Pamela still isn't believing that she's also been given the position of subsenior on the first day of her training. She's both happy and nervous. Ofcouse when Captain Lidiya Cheriyan said that she lacks bravery,for sometime she lost confidence on herself. But with this new position of subsenior of one of the company in Military training camp ,she feels very powerful again. Whereas Bessy has an optimistic mindset with a calm demeanor and Ren doesn't care about the happenings in his surroundings as he feels entitled to this new position. All he's interested in is the adventure that he's yet to see in Military missions.

Hielmaster: The foursome are from Himbertown University! Alma mater of Captain Lidiya Cheriyan! They are your sub seniors, who will directly report to their senior Sergeant Davis. You four can wait here whereas others can disperse for lunch.

Hielmaster came near the foursome with Sergeant Davis standing to his immediate left side.

He shakes hands with each one of them and expresses his best wishes before leaving from there. Sergeant Davis orders them their first task, that is to clean the lawn of Colonel Hielmaster. As the foursome start walking ,Sergeant asks them to double up and follow him. On the way they encountered eucalyptus trees whose base was covered with red and white paints. There are fully furnished big wooden houses with parking lawns that are painted white from outside and have railings all around. Each house has a small garden in it. He informed them that these are the houses of senior officers. His speed was just equivalent to a thunderstorm, reaching the destination within a few seconds. Pamela was still three hundred meters away from them, whereas the other three were catching their breath until they looked into the huge lawn of Colonel Hielmaster which has a swimming pool, a fish pond, a horse house ,a dog house and a garden full of blooming flowers with dandelion and crabgrass weed. His house was double the size of the previous houses as Sergeant informed that Colonel Hielmaster is the senior most officer here. Pamela reaches near them.

Sergeant Davis: You should loose those extra pounds then only you can sustain here(referring to Pamela).

Pamela: Sure sergeant.

Sergeant Davis: Colonel told me that you don't understand rules much.

Pamela: Do you mean Colonel Hielmaster?

Sergeant Davis chuckles.

Sergeant Davis: Yes, then about whom I would be referring too. He's the only person at the rank of Colonel with you four since day one of your slections. You idiot girl.

Pamela feels humiliated.

Sergeant Davis: Are you crying girl. This humiliation is a part and parcel of Military life. You need to be always ready for it.

He looks at Pamela and then others.

Sergeant Davis: It's not only for her but also for each of you too. Be ready to get humiliated. Even Colonel Hielmaster had to go through this humiliation during the time of his training.

Pamela was looking at the lavish residence of Colonel Hielmaster.

Sergeant Davis : Girl, where your eyes are wandering?

Pamela asks him whether Colonel Hielmasters family is also living here with him as his residence is huge, the sergeant tell her the tragic story where his three years old daughter and wife were kidnapped and murdered by Watson's men in revenge of one of the successful mission that destroyed Watson's illegal workplace. So the Colonel lives alone!. They are staggered as the Colonel Hielmaster always acted funny to everyone except Pamela .She thinks that he's a rude person as he gave Pamela a nick name of leech on sunflower. But still he has such an intense history that has shocked all four of them!

The foursome start removing the weed from the lawn, indeed a tiresome work. When it came to cleaning up the stable, the horse peeped out, it's a black colored horse with the shiniest hair. The dearest of the Colonel, named him Dhurandhar, which means an expert as the horse was bought from one of the fetes in Himachal Pradesh. As Mumkin opens the door of the stable, Dhurandhar remains indolent, unaffected by their presence. As he holds the bridle of Dhurander, Dhurandhar takes a high jump and starts galloping all over the lawn destroying all flowers creating clutter. Finally he falls over the pond and starts snorting, as the Sergeant comes back there, he holds his bridle, however they find that Dhurandhar isn't able to walk any more as his front leg knee is bleeding. Sergeant tells the foursome that Col Hielmaster won't like this ,but since they are young chaps he won't take any action against them. He tells them to clean the ponds and dog's house before leaving from there with Dhurandhar for his leg's treatment! This time they divide the work. Mumkin and Bessy decide to clean the dog's house whereas Pamela and Ren decide to clean the pond. As Mumkin reaches towards the dog house, Bessy stops him immediately as she wants to do the job of taking the dog out of his den. She takes a breath and takes one step forward, leans downwards and opens the small yellow colored door of the wooden den, but discovers that there's no dog in there! Both Bessy and Mumkin get relief as the work will be easier now. On the other hand, Pamela and Ren take two skimmers to remove any pond sludge and dirt debris. Ren also takes out the different types of fishes in the pond that include goldfish, sunfish , algae eater and shubunkin to show others. Pamela also starts to do the same and they both start throwing sludge on each other . Both were having fun. This time in Pamela's skimmer there comes a shiny fish.

Pamela: Wow, Colonel Hielmaster has eeil too in his pond! Full pisciculture Colonel(taking out the fish from the pond)

Ren(deep voice): That's not an eeil, it's a snake Pamela, beware it can be poisonous.

As Pemela looks at the fish ,there's slithering movement, she shouts loudly out of fear and throws back the skimmer in the pool and the snake falls inside it. She runs towards the cottage where she collides with someone. It's Colonel Hielmaster with his American Bulldog, which starts jumping towards her ferociously with non stop barking.

She turns back and runs towards Mumkin and hugs him tight, crying hard.

Col Hielmaster calms his dog by saying "Stop barking Binny, few guests have come(pointing towards the foursome). So behave yourself". He comes near them.

Col Hielmaster: Looks like you four have done a good job except injuring my horse and scaring my snake! Well it's dusk, so clean yourself up and move towards the mess dinner.

As they move, Pamela realizes that Ren is moving way ahead of her and is just ignorant towards her. She realizes that it's because she hugged Mumkin. She doubles up near him to talk.

Pamela: Ren, I'm really sorry, it all happened so fast that I didn't realize that I hugged Mumkin. I was scared.

Ren: Don't say sorry! Ensure that it doesn't repeat by any chance. You are my girlfriend not Mumkin.

She promises him so, however there's an inner voice saying to her something that "Pamela, no whatever happened wasn't your fault. It was an all natural response. So why are you apologetic to Ren?He needs to grow up to understand you" The foursome reach the Mess following a soldier who was their guide. They get to eat the world's most unappetizing taste like food which has tender salted chicken, burnt garlic rice with protein shake. It's already ten forty five nights where they are taken to separate barracks according to their company where they meet the other students whom they met upon their arrival in the hub. They're provided the matrices to sleep on so called bed which is actually a cemented elevation, some three feet up from the floor and slightly slanted at an angle of fifteen degrees due to which the sleep after full day look like ghost chanting mantras of reminding that no more dreams as it's Military training. In the Mumkin's barrack, it's found that all of them were doing the same task of cleaning the lawns on their first day, that makes him wonder why the foursome were made the seniors of the training if the task is the same for all, i.e.cleaning of lawns?

The next morning, walking up at four in the morning and going to pick the trash from the huge campus of the Military. It was all dark,foggy and chilling. Street lights were playing a heroic role in showing the way! Mumkin was addressing his group and sharing the responsibility of work to members of the team Alpha, he heard a loud outcry from team Sierra whose incharge was Bessy. As Mumkin, Pamela and Ren address their team mates to remain at their places and pick up the trash from parade ground, football stadium, and the area in front of the recreational theater. The trio ran towards the cavalry unit where Bessy's team was about to clean. As they reach, they see a crowd of Sierra team members that has been covering somebody who is weeping. As the trio enter the crowd by snaking inside ,sidelining four to five people, they see a fictitious lady in uniform lying down, with her head facing the ground and blood is dropping from her nose. Due to the shadow of military cap, her face isn't fully visible .At another corner it's Bessy whose hands have been tied with handcuffs by another soldier. She's weeping. The nurse arrives, sits next to the lady soldier, puts cotton on her nose and then a bandage. Within a few seconds she stands up straight with both hands backward and starts looking at everyone with a grave look, as she removes her cap, it's Captain Lydia whose nose is red now with a few drops of blood at the shoulder of her uniform.

Captain Lydia Cheriyan:Everyone back to your work now. Ren, Mumkin and Pamela stay back! Team Sierra pick the trash here within fifteen minutes(snuffles for a second)

She starts walking and the trio start following her .The soldier also follows her, dragging handcuffed Bessy along with him. Bessy is constantly apologizing to her, giving the reason that it was all dark and due to it she attacked to defend herself assuming it's a goon. She didn't realize that it was Prof Olivia aka Captain Lydia. Captain Lydia takes them to a small triangular room which has orange lights in it and chairs are arranged in organized two cross three ways. She orders Mumkin, Pamela and Ren to occupy seats on the extreme left whereas she herself takes a chair, she puts her legs crossways on a chair facing opposite to Bessy on the extreme right! Bessy looks timorous. She starts repeating her request for apology along with weeping.

Captain Lydia Cheriyan: Stop crying! You're handcuffed not because you attacked me .But because you breached the law. An important law of this committee. Before you question our judgements, better introspect yourself.

Bessy: (weeping) I don't know anything. I haven't done anything wrong!

Captain Lydia Cheriyan::Better think before speaking. Larry,your boyfriend, didn't you tell everything about the committee's plan?

Bessy(shocked): Now I recall! I did tell him everything, but he's a trustworthy man. He won't reveal anything to anyone until my death.

Captain Lydia Cheriyan:: Shut up you nincompoop! He not only knows everything but he's passed the whole information about the committee to Watson and his men failing our plan completely.

Bessy: I just can't believe that Larry did this!

Captain Lydia Cheriyan:: You are more of a culprit than him as you revealed the secret information ,thus breaching the Military's code of conduct! Your boyfriend is in our custody. Soon you'll join him too until the mission is complete.

The soldier takes Bessy out of the room saying to her that "Despite being chosen, not everyone can be a part of the Military".

Mumkin, Ren and Pamela are just dumbstuck after the revelation. They aren't sure about their future plans.

Captain Lydia Cheriyan:: We have new members with us. Benny Sebastian and John Greze came inside. (John enters the room). Plan will be modified. Pamela and John ,you're the senior most of Sierra now,thus taking the place of Bessy and Benny you'll take the place of November aka nurturers. Since the plan is revealed to Watson, now it's all up to you four to modify it further and give Watson an unexpected surprise that'll result in ultimate collapse of his power. Understood(loud and bold)!

All say yes ma'am. She stops them from saying anything.

Pamela:Thank you Captain Cheriyan for giving me this role.I promise ,I won't let you down.

Captain Lydia Cheriyan: It's by the senior team not by me!(grave look at Pamela). Your psychology testing during the committee selection says that you lack bravery (sighs). However, you're best suited in supportive roles. That's why John will be your counterpart as your vacant courage factor is balanced through him, making both of you a good team in support of ammunition. Also from the past few days we see an improvement in you, be it following the armed forces routine or keeping the committee secret safe . John be attentive in proving help to team Sierra whenever Pamela gets incapacitated.

John nods his head soberly.

Captain Lydia Cheriyan: Always remember, the battle cry "royalty with loyalty" ..

All say together "royalty with loyalty"

Captain Lydia Cheriyan: The training for you all will be for two months, the next month Tonio village's youth will join you too. Plan is changed completely. Soon when the training is over, the first week now will be destroying the malefactors, and the second week in establishing peace .Third and fourth week in reconstructing the Surae village. Prominently three weeks of training will happen in Tonio village itself as Watson isn't expecting this! Remember , Tonio is a highly resourceless village with a scarcity of basic facilities ,be ready. Don't forget to instill love and faith in the hearts of naive villages with your courage and good deeds.

Captain Cheriya lifts her right hand up and says"royalty with loyalty".The foursome repeat after her loudly and valorously. Just at that time they hear the sound of every soldier saying together "royalty with loyalty".The voice of the slogan reverberates in the entire military camp. There comes another soldier with the same board on which the map is stuck. Captain Cheriyan explains the plan again to John and Benny. She asks Pamela to focus as she's now the pivotal part of the Sierra team.

Captain Cheriyan:I am repeating the plan. Keep your senses open as I am adding new information too. Diewa is an important Military base with an armory. Surae is 160 km away from Diewa with the facility of Military Hospital, troops , small armory unit and a small air force base. Marvo village ,210 km away from Surae is where Malefactors are trained by Watson .People of Marvo Village are oppressed by these malefactors. Piklin is the city where Watson is presently residing which is 60 km away from village Surae. In the village Tonio which is 290 km away from Piklin is the place where the mission will start. This village has trained youth by Himbertown Military to fight the injustice happening in Marvo village by malefactors of Watson. The task of the selected committee members is to overthrow Watson's oppression in Marvo Village and hamper Watson's master plan by nobbing him from city Piklin. There are two roads that connect Diewa and Surae, one unsettled road connects Diewa to Piklin, three roads connect three cities to Marvo and Tonio.

Seniors of Charlie, Alpha and ex seniors of Sierra and November gave suggestions last time that since Marvo is in complete control of Watson's malefactors, there is tight security at the bridge for people to enter from Tonio to Marvo. Look here(pointing towards the bridge connecting Marvo and Tonio) . They thought of making an underground tunnel from Piklin to Marvo. Not from Surae or Dieve as Watson might be aware about the Military base and Military facilities at two cities, he would be expecting any action to happen from these cities. So as to give the enemy a bleeding nose under its roof and since Piklin is 60km away from Diewa,ammunition support can be easily provided, their plan got further accentuated by making an underground tunnel from Piklin to Marvo. The second step of the plan was to send troops from Piklin to Marvo after capturing the bridge connecting Tonio to Marvo ,thus sending the troops two ways viz. Piklin and Tonio. They considered the youth of Tonio village as a paramount resource.

Mumkin, Pamela and Ren are astonished as Captain Lidiya wasn't there when Mumkin, Ren ,Bessy and Pamela had the discussion last time about the plan .However she's completely aware of their ideas that they had discussed at that time. Even more aware than Pamela is as she has completely forgotten about the ideas that were discussed among each other.

Captain Cheriyan: Unfortunately, Watson is aware of the Tunnel's plan. All thanks to Bessy's imperceptive love towards Larry and her lack of self control. Now the plan is not to create an underground tunnel, instead create tunnels in the mind of Watson. For security purposes, a plan will be told to you just sometime before its execution to prevent a past nemesis! Sergeant Krodie, take them to their respective places.

Sergeant Krodie is a 6.5 feet tall handsome man in his mid thirties with a big mustache. He enters the room, says "royalty with loyalty" to captain Cheriyan with a salute to display respect to Captain Heriyan whois senior to him .She repeats the slogan and salutes back to him. He gives a quick glance at all five of them and then takes them to an old hut which was made up of mud. The area had dilapidated small walls with bricks lying around.

Sergeant Krodie: You five need to go to the nearby market to buy a few things before you head towards Tonio Village. Remember, be nice with civilians, use public transport, buy items from Extra Busy shops that have only military items available.

He hands over a few notes with a list of items to John and Pamela.

Sergeant Krodie: You can proceed now!

As all five of them proceed, he stops them by saying "Stop all of you ".

Sergeant Kroodie: First, money is given to two ,only they will proceed. Second, say the battle field slogan before and after seeing any senior. Third, be in an attention position when order is given!

He teaches them the attention and stands at ease by giving them a demo. Complete focus, straight legs, erect head and neck with arms at your side is the attention position.

Sergeant Krodie: Stand at ease is position with your eyes and head directly turned to your senior.

John: In my school's assembly we had both these positions. I always thought standing at ease is the time to chill.

Sergeant Krodie orders John to bend . He then orders foursome also to bend like John and hits them all hard on his bums with a stick lying near the dilapidated wall.

Sergeant Krodie: Even after getting punished in Military training camp, you're still cracked from the brain. Remember (loud and grave voice) it's not a place to chill, you all have a mission to complete. If any one of you makes a mistake, damages will be paid together in a team. At ease of position,you can move ,however you need to remain standing with your mouth shut on your right foot in place. Troops disperse in a certain way. The first step is taking two steps left, then one step forward and then they turn towards the right side . Last step is standing on the toes for two seconds!

Mumkin dispersed successfully, whereas Pamela is all perplexed. Sergeant orders them to bend again and hits each one of them thrice on their bums. He then demonstrates proper dispersal, making them repeat it five times, before letting Pamela and Mumkin go to the market. He also ordered both to take an outpass which has a deadline time!

Mumkin and Pamela run near the gate where the guard makes their exit entry with time written as 19:00 hours. That is their return time! As they move out, it's all jungle area where there's no bus stop . They need to go to the address :13/2 Abis Garden, Vincent Street .They both glaze at the chit ,but the address is new for both of them. The guard shouts at them,telling them that the nearest bus stop is one mile away towards their north. Since Mumkin is aware of the directions, he takes perplexed Pamela with him towards the north side ,they briskly walk one kilometer and find a bus stop. Three buses pass by but none take them to destined Vincent street until the forth bus where the driver stops and tells them that they need to change the bus at BWoni Park. They sit in that empty bus, the conductor looks friendly and he charges a minimal amount from both . He informs them to get down when BWoni Park arrives and also gives the information of the buses to get in to reach Vincent street.

They briskly walk towards the nearest bus stop, the first bus stop has boldly written "Vincent street". They both swiftly get into the bus,however there's a lot of rush, not even space to breathe. The conductor charges the fare from them. Pamela stands next to the seat of an old woman who starts to screech at her after waking up from her nap grumbling that she's standing too close to her. Pamela takes a step away from her .

Mumkin also takes a step back to provide more space to Pamela as he is now holding the bus hangers from both sides like being in swing. Pamela notices a one year old baby concealing his face into his mother's lap just next to the left side seat where she's standing. She starts to play with her, however the baby looks exhausted as she isn't trying to sleep in the thong and people are slightly hitting the baby inadvertently . She tells Mumkin how bad she's feeling after seeing the baby and her mother's condition. The baby's mother also looks a few months pregnant . Mumkin raises his voice requesting others to give some space to the mother and the baby.

Mumkin: Please move slightly away from the baby and the mother as the baby isn't able to sleep.

People don't listen to him at all as they seem inconsiderate .He calls the conductor and the bus driver ,due to which the three of them move people slightly away from the child and the mother. This allowed the baby to sleep, due to which the mother was also in a better comfortable state! The mother of the baby smiles at Mumkin to give him a gesture of thanks, he takes off his cap as a token of respect with a blameless smile.

After twenty minutes of puff and blow ,they finally get down at Vincent street, which is crowded near the fountain as there's a mime artist performing. They see all shops of colorful costumes and decorations and interior design material. Mumkin asks an interior design material seller about the address of the place where the listed items can be bought and in return he tells him to take the immediate left ,then take a round turn where they'll find the shop. Mumkin hurriedly walks towards the immediate left, he looks at his watch to tell the time to Pamela. Not hearing any response puts him into suspicion, so he quickly turns back and his suspicion was right, Pamela wasn't there. So he runs towards the mime artist crowd as that's the most probable place to find a three years old by heart in a nineteen years old teenager. As he reaches there ,he starts searching for her in the crowd asking people if they've seen a chubby girl of around five feet five inch, with brown hair wearing navy blue petticoat with yellow apparel. Seven to eight people say no, until one old man calls Mumkin near him and inform that he saw a girl similar to his description along with three to four danger looking men. He smells that something isn't right ,so go near two persons in police uniform standing in front of a restaurant.

Mumkin: Sir my name is Mumkin Chamburt. I am a student of Himbertown University. I came here with my classmate Pamela ,but she's missing in the crowd. One old man said that she was seen by him with four hooligans.

Sergeant Kamy and constable Maideem start searching for Pamela along with Mumkin, they also inform that at this place murder and kidnapping is at it's upsurge. They tell Mumkin to be careful as they enter an alley where goons were playing carrom and cards and drunkards were swinging. They knock at a door where a crooked woman wearing mexi in her mid fifteen comes out. They give a description of Pamela, she looks gall now . She leaves the door open and goes back inside her home. The policeman reaffirms Mumkin that Pamela will be fine. The woman comes back holding the wrist of a teenage girl looking similar to Pamela with respect to height, hair and dress color. But that isn't Pamela. Mumkin is disappointed as it's already getting late and he's worried in what conditions Pamela would be. Sergeant Kamy tells him that this place is a brothel where everyday young girls are kidnapped and put. As they move out of the array, they see a girl facing back kind of looking similar to Pamela ,she has cotton candy in her hand. She's sitting in seats outside the cotton candy shop. Mumkin goes near her, she smiles at him and he is amazed to see how Pamela can be that much cool, not realizing that he got so much worried about her.

Mumkin: Pamela, are you nuts? Where were you?

Pamela: Wait, why do you look so annoyed? I was just searching for the shop and then two guys asked me out if I wanted to hang out with them. I refused ,but they bought chocolate and cotton candy for me.Look(raising her hand with cotton candy). I was just waiting for you here as I was exhausted.

Mumkin : I'll request Sergeant Krodie to never make us a team again.

Mumkin's eyes turned red and watery. Pamela gets saddened and she keeps her cotton candy on a seat adjacent to her.

Sergeant Kamy: Listen young lady, this is no park. This area is rising in criminal cases, you've come here for the first time. You wasted a lot of our time and put your friend into trouble too. Do you know we can charge you for this?

Pamela starts crying.

Mumkin apologizes for both Pamela and his side from the Policemen. As the policeman leaves from there, he offers Pamela his handkerchief and asks her to stop crying. They both go to the shop.

They purchase the required items given on the list- combat uniforms, black leather belts, drill shoes and physical training shoes and ten other items. All five in pairs. With six heavy carry bags ,they rush towards the bus stop and get into the crowded bus, they change to another bus at BWoni park and reach the Military training area fifteen minutes late. After reaching they distribute the items to others. Happy all five members are to see themselves shining in olive green combats bought by Mumkin and Pamela. Their new nameplates also added to their jubilation. However, just after dinner, it was time to wash the utensils ,punishment given to three people in the military for coming late .Those were Pamela, John and Benny. It was a time to learn ultra cleanliness to clean the men's toilet of barracks for Mumkin and Ren. Pamela along with John and Benny start to wash utensils that take them a lot of time as ten cauldrons, on which the food of the whole military was cooked were there to be washed too. Mumkin and Ren start cleaning the toilets in the alpha team barracks. Ren curiously asks Mumkin of why he and Pamela were late.

Mumkin replies back giving the reason for the bus change and the market was far.

Ren:I thought you and Pamela were having an affair, she was cheating on me with you that's why you both were late.

Mumkin: Ren don't you dare to talk absurd about us. You know I thought Pamela was kidnapped and took help of Police there in Vincent street. It wasn't easy to spot her again ,near the cotton candy parlor.

Ren:I knew it. I had a bet about it with Benny that Pamela will create some turmoil .You know what, she has not only got a lover but also a twin.

Mumkin gasps towards what Ren said.

Mumkin: What do you mean man?

Ren re-explains saying Pamela and John are so similar in creating a state of turmoil .Mumkin ignores what Ren says and continues his toilet cleaning work with his scrubbing brush hard,which is extremely fetid. Ren also starts moving the scrubbing brush leisurely . Mumkin is vexed from inside after seeing that Ren is not only taking Pamela for granted but he also has potential to harm her innocence as he might break her heart in future. Ren is utterly insensitive and disrespectful towards both John and Pamela. Mumkin, for a second doubts his own loyalties towards John and Pamela .He realizes that keeping quiet won't fetch anything but accentuate Ren's meanness towards his friends. He decides to confront him.

Mumkin: Ren, just be more quick, this lethargy won't help. We need to clean up every toilet and wake up tomorrow at 4AM. It's just one hour before midnight.

Ren: Didn't expect that you'd talk like this.

Ren starts to clean up the washrooms swiftly now.

Mumkin: It has to be neat and clean Ren. Also I got to wear my heart on my sleeves and say something to you,(gasps) Don't be mean to Pamela or John. Pamela loves you and John isn't into Pamela anymore .And truly speaking ,it's disgusting that you, being boyfriend of Pamela, are trying to pair up her with John. Where are your loyalties(stern look)?

Ren: Three more toilets to clean the alpha barrack. And you, just don't take Pamela's side .

Mumkin: Ren, I'm worried if you love her or despise her.Whatever she does , you're always vexed by her.

Ren: My issue with her is her being so kind to everyone. She never asks for anything ,the way Janny used to. Her simplicity makes me envious of her. Sometimes ,I even wonder if she requires me in her life or not. How do I be her provider? I think the only way to do so is to make her believe that she's less than others,so that she'll look upon me for help to make her emotional and fulfill her emotional needs..

Mumkin: You know that she's a guiltless person! I don't wish for a change in her . Now she's a bubbly individual and you want her to be sad just to entertain your manhood! That's not very nice to do with a girl.

Ren: Look, this is the paramount which a woman has to offer, their intimacy is the most alluring. Pamela displays mostly happiness . I want to see other emotions and expressions on her face when she's in my arms filled with sadness that she has from this whole world.

Mumkin: Don't you dare to do that with her. Let her be on her own terms. I know sometimes she behaves like a child, however that's what she is. And believe me, how much you try , a leopard cannot change its spots.

Ren doesn't speak anything but he starts his cleaning work again. Both of them complete the whole task by 12:30 AM and go to sleep for three hours . The other team completed the work by midnight . The next day a huge alarm sounded with Slogan song "royalty with loyalty,Dis, qu'est-ce que c'est. A song in french language.

,La victoire ne vient que du travail acharné,alors, lève-toi, fais-le et gagne, translated as "royalty with loyalty, what is it, victory only comes through hard work, so get up, work hard and win

". Announcement is made using a microphone that the one who doesn't get ready for physical training in the next ten minutes will be sleeping at their own risk. The four seniors with their junior trainees of Alpha, Charlie and Sierra company looked outside the glass windows, it's all dark like coca cola and fog is flying all over like they show in movies. Everyone observes that all the soldiers are ready with a full sleeve black shirt and camouflage pants with brown leather PT shoes. Mumkin, John, Pamela and Ren get ready immediately along with Juniors of Alpha, Sierra and Charlie in the barrack Juniors of Alpha, Sierra and Charlie companies .The common washrooms are full in all three companies ,however the four seniors make two persons of same gender to share one bathroom and divided two rooms of each gender for changing night dress to physical training dress. All were coming out in pairs out of bathrooms wrapped in their towels. They first wore their innerwears inside the towel and tossed it away, showed their curves before wearing their PT uniforms. Within twenty minutes when every junior changed, the seniors of three teams changed too and they all ran towards the training ground. Pamela changed in the girls room and the three boys in the boys room. Whereas Benny, the senior of November company is with his thirteen junior trainee boys and seven junior trainee girls . As Benny is still sleeping, he's informed by one of the November girls to wake up after listening to the announcement. However he excuses himself saying that he got only two hours due to last night's imposition ,and he's feeling sick. After seeing their Senior Benny sleeping, the juniors also go to sleep. Just after two minutes , ten masked men get inside the November Company barrack and start covering the faces of all trainees with paints of blue, gray , red and green color. Within a short span of time, all November junior trainees along with their Senior Benny are having colored faces looking like peacocks.

One masked man ,in his high pitched voice, orders them to wear a Physical Training uniform and double up to ground. He starts counting in reverse order from ten. All get ready, except Benny who's still searching for his Physical training shoes. The masked men make all twenty junior trainees stand in front of their November barrack . They order Benny to stand in front of his junior and run barefoot ensuring that he's always ahead of them! As they shout: Three, two ,one ,Runnn. Benny and his juniors start running towards the physical training ground. Benny's feet now are badly abraded with bleeding.

As the November company reaches near the fitness ground, they have to jump down the staircase which is four feet each to reach the ground. First their senior Benny jumps down and then other members of his team follow him. He finds that Alpha, Sierra and Charlie companies are already standing in discipline one after the other with their seniors Mumkin , John, Pamela and Ren. Three members of the November team fall down while climbing down the stairs. They are given immediate first aid. Sergeant Krodie asks Benny and his junior trainees to stand facing the Alpha, Sierra and Charlie team. Benny is again standing in front of his November company. Sergeant Krodie stands next to Benny.

Sergeant Krodie: Can you recognize them all? From their physical training dress , it's letter N, which means November Company. However they aren't November trainees anymore. They're Ninny(a fool) November or nincompoops November troops ! Look at their hideousness. Their colored faces. Look at the legs of this ninny Senior(pointing towards Benny). What a incapacitated leader. Indeed unfortunate juniors to be under him. (whispering in ear of Benny)Now it's all up to you Senior Sabastian to win again the trust of your young juniors as your sleep has put them into trouble. You've made the november team a flock of peacocks who haven't come for a mission but are ready to do a rain dance.

All juniors of Alpha, Charlie and Sierra start to laugh after seeing November company's condition . Mumkin immediately orders his Alpha company juniors to keep their mouths shut, followed by John of Sierra company.

Sergeant Krodie: Now all of you will go for a run of five km in eighteen minutes. Those coming late will be imposed with more strenuous exercises.

As they run a few kilometers Benny sits down in front of Mumkin .Mumkin stops running and looks at Benny's state, with all his legs bleeding profusely ,pebbles and dirt assorted with blood. He sits next to him,tells him to stay motivated, everyone is proud of his dedication, it's just a little more way. He stands up and gives his hand to Benny to provide support, pulls him up on his feet and then takes him three and a half kilometers in a brisk walk fashion, until Benny falls down and faints. Mumkin looks around but there's no one as everyone has surpassed them in running,he finds that there's a wood house three hundred meters away. He runs towards it, amidst a forest filled with bushes, acacia, bougainvillea thorns .As he reaches near the tree house, left his leg is bleeding, he bends to take out stem of blackberry plant and hears some sound, as he takes a step forwards, there's a sudden thrust and now he's in upside down state ten feet above the ground inside a net. It's like a web, he struggles and shouts for help but there's no one around. He feels immense pain on his head as if someone has hit him hard. As he opens his eyes, he sees himself on the ground with two monster looking men, who start yelling at him giving a description of how the hell will look like as they are taking him there. There comes another man twenty times his size, who's sitting on a huge animal. The animal gives the breed of ox and yak. Its face is highly aggressive . The man makes Mumkin sit on his yak. Mumkin and the huge man are looking like that of a squirrel and an elephant sitting together on a moving mountain. He takes him amidst the clouds. Mumkin is seeing the other side of the world for the first time. There's a pinkish sparkling light breeze blowing all around. They enter a floating ground whose roof is held by four pillars. It's all made of plasma . Mumkin is scared to step down on it . The man gets down from his animal and pulls Mumkin down ,where he doesn't feel any burn and he finds himself very light weighted. The man displays a huge screen on which he sees his mother, Pamela ,John and others crying and the holy person doing his last rites saying "Oh lord, may the soul of late Mumkin Chamburt rest in peace forever under your pitiful espionage". Mumkin's body is put in a coffin and buried in front of the screen. He's in shock. He finds his father standing in front of him and smiling, spreading arms to hug him. Mumkin reaches near him and sees his father for the first time after his death. His father says the word welcome to him, telling all soldiers who died fighting a war for peace and their people are given heaven. Mumkin hears a voice, with a completely white light that his eyes aren't able to take anymore, he finds his father and the huge man kneeling down in front of that light. The voice says: "His soul has to offer more karmas, take him back, this is not the right time for him". The huge man sits on his animal again and makes Mumkin also sit on it. And the next second he opens his eyes surrounded by Sergeant Krodie, Pamela, John and other soldiers. There's a doctor sitting next to him, where he has something black in color in his hands.

Doctor: Look, every trainee needs to know this, these purple black berries if eaten more than seven can cause death. This boy is lucky to not die. Be careful next time chap(slapping Mumkin tightly on his arm)

The doctor stands up and starts to walk away. Pamela and John come near Mumkin, give him a tight hug.

Pamela: Mumkin, why did you eat these berries in excess, you know for a second we thought ,we'll lose you! (crying).

John's eyes are watery too.

Sergeant Krodie: What an auspicious day, the two seniors are Alpha and November companies are hospitalized due to their recklessness. I think we'll make an army of nincompoops!Jinx!

He leaves from there ..

As Mumkin tries to wake up, he finds his body very exhausted ,he's breathing heavily. He asks Pamela about Benny.

Pamela: Benny is very thankful to you as you brought help for him very quickly.

Mumkin: Do you mean ,someone saw me inside the tree house and came out to help Benny?

Pamela: There's no one in the tree house, they told us that you ran with very high speed and informed Sergeant Krodie about Benny . However, after receiving this information from you , as the Sergeant was hospitalizing him, you went somewhere in the jungle and were found unconscious as you ate excessive poisonous berries.

Mumkin realizes that his reality has been tweaked to make this world and the other world look the same as he feels that whatever happened to him in the other world isn't a dream or hallucination!

Just in the afternoon they go for shooting training, five bullets each are given to them in kote. Mumkin, John, Pamela and Ren were given rifles. They're given a demonstration of holding a rifle ,lying facing ground,left leg at forty five degrees from body making straight line along with right leg and keeping rifle on right side of shoulder . Instruction is given that when the gun recoils, push the right shoulder also backward to balance .The foursome are asked to demonstrate the same in front of their juniors of Alpha, Charlie, Sierra and November companies. Pamela makes a mistake while doing so. The shooting instructor orders Mumkin to come forward in front of juniors of all four companies. Then he asks everyone to watch carefully the steps done by him. The foursome seniors are now asked to slap ground with both hands as a part of the warming up process with counting. As Pamela does it lightly,she's asked to apply more force. Her hands are abraded. They're taken to the firing ground, where they have to use five bullets to hit a target fifty meters away from them. It's a lot sunny. The second instruction comes is to meet the target with a rifle keeping one eye closed for accuracy. For John all five bullets are washed out, Ren meets first and last bullet with the target whereas the other three he misses out. Mumkin meets four bullets to target and misses one. Whereas to the surprise of everyone, Pamela shoots all five bullets to the target with pinpoint accuracy. Colonel Banzazi, is highly impressed with newly discovered talent and he provides her with three extra bullets as a prize which she shoots again with pinpoint accuracy. Colonel Banzazi, makes a statement "We've got a leader who will head the whole mission to destroy Watson. That's our new shooter, Miss Brown". Pamela is just half dead after acknowledging her talent. She can't believe that she's so good at shooting. Being a head of the whole mission is just increasing butterflies in her heart and stomach both. It's recognition with self doubt which is through the evidence of her psychological testing mentioned to her by prof Olivia in the past where she stated that she lacks courage and probably confidence too. While leaving towards the barracks, she's self absorbed in such thoughts while Ren comes near her.

Ren: You know , Mumkin shooted three, for me it was four bullets with pinpoint accuracy, John was a complete non stopper with all five bullets gone for a flop. I heard the trainer saying that the missing bullets depicted missed the enemy target. What a loser, I've no idea why Captain Cheriyan brought him here.

Pamela: Really, you won't ask about my performance? I too did well Ren.

Ren: Who's interested in others? Everyone here is looking for fulfilling self motives. I'm sure that it's a washout for you! As usual you might have disappointed both your trainer and your team of November company.

Pamela : I'm in Sierra now and all five bullets of mine hit the target!(giving a sober look).

Ren kind of ignores Pamela completely and starts talking to his junior trainee of Charlie company. Mumkin and John come near her.

John: What a performance Pamela, for me it was a complete washout,

Mumkin: But you did a good show Pamela. Do you remember what Colonel Banzazi was saying(enliven)?

Pamela: Just don't talk about it! It doesn't matter how much ever I try.....He's just always unhappy with me.

Pamela pushes John back and leaves from there.

John: Woah,(moving backward with a jerk and balancing himself) hold on, imprudent ego? Why is her behavior so indignant ?

Mumkin: John, her behavior might be despicable but the reason is not her ego but the ignorance and bit by bit suppression by Ren leading her to self loathing. And now you see, she isn't even happy for being good at shooting.

John looks staggered.

John: Yes,I see her unsatisfied all the time.

Mumkin: Her relationship isn't healthy at all.

Both of them leave from there near the Trainee Mess to have their lunch.They find Pamela eating food all alone. Ren is sitting with junior boys and girls of his Charlie company. As Mumkin and John stand in line to take their lunch, they make eye contact with Pamela ,however she starts to ignore them. As they move towards her , she is putting her head down and keeps having her soup with a frowning face. As she looks around and finds both of them sitting three dining tables away from her. She grabs her lunch and goes near them .She asks John to move aside and sits next to him.

Pamela: I'm sorry John for pushing you and ignoring you both.

John: Naah girl! Just don't talk about what happened in the past. Would you like a honey bun?

Pamela: How did you get it? It wasn't there when I took lunch!

John: Yes, only three were left when I visited here before, I took all. Come on guys, help yourself!(giving two honeybun each to Mumkin and Pamela).

All three of them were raising a toast with their buns ,before a guard came and warned them to eat food quietly or else they won't see the food for the next three days as part of their punishment.

CHAPTER EIGHT

Not riding but jumping over the horse!

One week went in learning the basic techniques of march past. The next week was the day of selections of the trainee troops into various categories in the Military. It was a type of temporary promotion, to gain a new experience in Military for skill improvement. With zero idea everyone was standing in their formations with five seniors of four companies including Benny. He recovered on the third day of his injury and now he joined again for physical training. From his bedridden condition as an example such that no one broke the physical training law including him. All juniors were of total two hundred in number, but made to stand mixing all companies in a line of thirteen people each excluding the five leaders who were made to stand behind their juniors. All are given the instruction that as Sergeant Krodie will whistle, at that time the front line will run, raise themselves up and jump the horse. Due to being standing at the end, the fivesome aren't able to see anything however they hear their front row junior students murmuring. Juniors Karen, Arek and Shawn are ten years old school kids belonging to Alpha, November and Charlie companies. Arek and Shawn have Australian features whereas Karen has asian features. Shawn is standing in between Arek (left side) and Karen(right side).

Karen: What's this horse, and what's the point in making us jump over it.

Arek: Probably they want us to be flexible.

Karen: Flexible for what? To do ballet dancing or gymnasium?

Shawn: In the military, we do things, not what we think to do the things. So be prepared than becoming fussbudgets!(he gently slaps the necks of Karen and Arek with both his hands).

The fivesome laugh seeing the conversation of three of them. Mumkin says "That's true, in the Military you need to be jack of all trades but master of none" . They see Sergeant Krodie just standing behind them.

Sergeant Krodie: Although, all five jinx or so called " company" seniors, this is your only time to show that you deserve to be chosen at your position, or else a junior(pointing towards all 195 juniors of four companies), will take your position! Imagine a ten year old leading this mission and you being under him/her. What's the success rate of it ? Mumkin ,imagine that you are not being part of the mission even knowing the fact that Watson killed your father!

Mumkin looks exasperated.

Mumkin: This mission can't happen without me, Sergeant!

Sergeant Kroodie slightly holds Mumkin's neck, his hands are cold.

Sergeant Krodie: Then prove it!(giving a slight jerk to his neck). Anyone want to say something(staring at John)? Who has zero idea what's going on(starring Pamela) or wants to take a rest as the activity looks irrelevant (starring Benny)?

All five say together "No Sergeant".

As the fivesome can't see what's happening in front of them, they hear a lot of chaos and cry of their juniors. Pamela and Benny are getting chills discussing what might be happening with them, they're imagining if the horses might be kicking them with their legs or if they are getting hit while climbing the horses! As just two more lines are there in front of them, they see thirteen wrestling poles, four feets high with a flat square shaped seat on top, which are called as "horse" or "khemba" in local language, not the real horse,but a non living T shaped obstacle. Each trainee needs to run forward, reach near the pole, lift their bodies up making legs at 180 degree position, till the upper edge of the square seat of the pole and then jump to the other side. Most of the trainees aren't able to pass through them and hitting themselves hard with a blue bruise of thunder speed!That's why the fivesome heard the loud outcry.

As there's just one more line in front of them before their turn comes, Mumkin advices them the strategy to run with full strength, take a jump a step before reaching the khemba,together holding the seat with arm strength, lift one's body up with maximum strength and then pushing one's legs apart opposite to each other, making 180 degree angle. Ultimately jumping off the other side. He called it making an upside down 'T' posture on a khemba/pole which is already a T. In their front row almost all the trainees collapsed. Now it's their turn to jump on the horse. Mumkin is the fastest among all and his strategy with self conviction is superb to cross this hurdle. John too runs keeping in mind the strategy of Mumkin ,jumps to hold the square seat of the pole, he pulls himself up and jumps off successfully, just getting the sensation that the toe of his left leg is twisted a bit. Pamela runs fast with her full endeavor however is unable to pull herself up above the stand due to low muscular strength of her arms. She continuously tries to lift herself, second, third and fourth time, but all she's left with is teeth gritting , heavily breathing and lastly falling on ground with no strength. And Ren, as he jumps off the square seat, his thigh legs hit the seat, leaving himself bruised in pain . Benny is left with abraded again but this time his buttlocks. Now, Pamela is lying on the ground looking exhausted and sweaty, Ren and Benny are sitting with torment and discomfort. Sergeant Kroodie comes near them from behind.

Sergeant Kroodie: (His index finger of left hand is facing up with his fist is closed) One, this is just a starting.(He opens his middle finger and index finger)Two, tomorrow ,at the same time the same jump training will be done.Now stand up before you go to serve lunch as a promotion of being unsuccessful seniors, you three dumasses(referring to Pamela ,Ren and Benny).

The trio stand up to move. This time Ren and Benny are clinching to the shoulders of Pamela to get support to walk. Both of them are groaning in pain.In the midway towards trainee mess, Mumkin and John were waiting for the trio to come. Ren holds John's shoulder and Benny does the same to Mumkin. Both Ren and Benny are whimpering in pain.

Ren: Never knew that you would also succeed in the spooky jump.

John: I'm a fitness freak Ren,it was just a child's play for me.

Ren:(laughing in a shrieked tone) No, not at all a child's play. Since they call that T shaped pole with a seat a "horse".So you on top of it are like a donkey on a horse!

All four of them, including John, start staring at Ren for his dark humor.

John:Not a funny thing to say man.

Pamela also looks disappointed at Ren.

Pamela: Ren, why do you want to say such a thing to others?

Ren: Now what happened to my girlfriend? Do you have a soft corner for John?

Pamela: Just leave it Ren.

Ren: Why leave it? You should laugh at my funny jokes.

Benny:In fact what's more funny is now serving lunch to the whole regiment,standing with broken legs and buttlocks.

Ren:Yes, we have to. But before that I got to do important work.

He goes near Pamela and gives her a kiss on her forehead. The trio walks ahead from there and now it's just Pamela and Ren.

Pamela:It wasn't nice, the way you called John a donkey.

Ren:Oh, come on Pamela, it was just a joke. John and you, both of you are quite alike when it comes to reacting to jokes. Listen, (getting very close to her) I am unable to sleep these days due to loneliness at night in my bed.

Pamela(speaking abruptly):If that's true then why don't you join me during lunch time?

Ren:I'm always surrounded by juniors of Charlie company who don't leave me for a second. You tell me, how can I come to you during that time?

Pamela gets sentimental, He further comes closer to her such that his chest is kind of touching her shoulders and body.

Ren(directly looking into her eyes):This sunday is outing, shall we go for a movie?

Pamela gets euphoric after hearing, as it's the first time Ren has asked her to go out .Before she only saw Ren taking Janny out.

Ren:What you're thinking so deeply darling?

Pamela:Ofcourse, it's a big yes Ren, just can't wait for Sunday to come.

Ren hugs and kisses her on her lips. She's in a slight shock.

Ren:Now, we shall go to serve lunch as part of punishment.

Both leave towards the combined mess where both trainees and other soldiers were sitting. There were five counters .Pamela stood at counter one where all trainees with soldiers would collect utensils then move to counter two where Ren and Benny were standing to serve multiple dishes like chicken curry, rice, fennel seed bread and apple pie etc. Third and fourth counters were occupied by Mumkin and John ,for the hospitality and service of senior officers who had a separate cabin to eat food. The fifth counter was for collecting and washing utensils which was occupied by none as there was an automatic utensil washing machine. As every soldier and trainee took utensils from Pamela ,Ren and Benny started to distribute food. After half an hour, Ren looks very exhausted, so Pamela replaces him and he starts resting on a chair kept behind the dish washing machine so that no one would see him. Mumkin goes to serve inside the room. He is asked by Lieutenant Adwer to wear his cap in order to salute the senior officers inside. Lieutenant Adwer ordered him to set up a table where he had to cover the table with velvet cloth red in color, keeping dishes in extra porsche crockery printed with light pink color flowers. There were three extra dishes including belgium chocolate cake, red wine and alcohol. Mumkin wears his navy blue training cap with white gloves .As he prepares himself to walk with his rolling table to cater, he's stopped by Lieutenant Adver . He picks up all four wine glasses and makes Mumkin to reclean them again with a rag. He then quickly keeps one more glass and then gives Mumkin a set of instructions. He knocks on the officer's dining room with his mini rolling table on which wine and glasses are kept. He gets permission and keeps the rolling table aside for a minute. Gives a salute to five members sitting inside.He's asked to pour alcohol by a senior official in all five glasses .Mumkin hears the conversation of four members with someone present there. Sergeant Kroodie was also present at that time. All five, including Lieutenant Adwer, were having wine and talking . After overhearing the information, Mumkin runs towards his barrack from the Officer's cabin without having his lunch. All other four seniors of Charlie, Sierra and November companies have gone back to their respected barracks. Before the Military formation theory class by Lieutenant Adwer, Mumkin shares the same thing with all other four seniors. They decide to share the information with their junior trainees too. As they got inside the huge hall where the class was to be conducted,seniors shared the information to all junior trainees through addressing their company groups . As Lieutenant Adwer entered the room he saw utter chaos in the room, all trainees were taking a lot of time to sit at their places .Sergeant Kroodie quickly made an announcement for the five seniors to take charge. As Mumkin, Benny ,Pamela and John sat down at their places in disappointment, Ren was standing. His eyes looked provoked and disinterested. The junior trainees of Charlie's team were still moving and chatting. After seeing anarchy, Sergeant Kroodie warned Ren of punishment to him with his juniors and ordered him to bring his company trainees in discipline.But Ren looked indifferent, he ignored the second command by Sergeant Kroodie. Mumkin and Pamela asked Ren to sit down as of now, however he was still looking vexed with his chest expanded ,eyes looking up. Sergeant Kroodie comes near him. As Ren looks into his eyes, he smacks Ren's left cheek so tightly that Ren falls backwards. All become quiet and sit at their places as if nothing had happened. As the Lieutenant asked them questions related to the topic of section formation that was taught in the previous class,no one responded. Lieutenant Adwer finishes one hour of lecture and tells Sergeant Kroodie that "these nincompoops are good for nothing. They're just here to eat Military ration. Assholes". He orders Sergeant Kroodie to ensure that next time they're well prepared for class and he wants uttermost discipline from them. The very next day, nobody from all four companies was on time at the physical training ground. All looked completely sluggish and had no interest on their faces. Sergeant Kroodie decided not to punish the junior trainees as it was the responsibility of their seniors to bring them up on time, here seniors were only late. Due to that sloppy behavior from seniors he allowed the juniors to go and have breakfast and kept the seniors waiting on the physical training ground. As it was 10 AM , which was the parade time post breakfast, the seniors were directly sent to parade,empty stomach with no breakfast. They commanded their companies in the parade, however after the parade Kroodie made them rifle cleaning during the afternoon tea time break time, soon after that they had to learn a new drill known as commando march that required a huge energy expense as it required continuous walking with lifting legs till stomach . The seniors including Pamela had their stomach going inside with extreme hard work and no food. In evening duty they had to paint three walls of the recreation room,for that they cleaned up the table tennis, carrom board and organized books in the mini sports library from the room to the hall. As they finished room painting, it was already 8:30PM, which was half an hour post the dinner time. As they went to the dining hall, it was all leftover they found. They filled their tummies and with that utmost weariness and one time scrap food they wanted the bed, however their fate was calling them to wash cooking utensils. They had the comfort of sleep at 11PM. Sergeant Kroodie was confident that this punishment dosage is enough to remind them about where they are, what their duties are and how to fulfill them. However the next day too,almost the same lethargy was shown by seniors as well as junior trainees. Sergeant Kroodie repeats their punishment for the next consecutive days. However, on the third day, interference was made by Lieutenant Adwer, he takes all seniors to a room that is completely dark . It smells like rotten fish, a completely greasy place where there are jails down in which prisoners are captured.He shows them each prisoner cell where both old and young people are captured .He stops at a cell where two known persons are in deteriorated state. They are Bessy and her boyfriend Larry. They are in green suits, they look tired with dark circles as if they're suffering from some indisposition. When Adwer and fivesome look at them, they break eye contact and behave as if they don't know them at all in a disappointed face.

Lieutenant Adwer: Your friend Bessy and her so-called boyfriend are in this state due to their own fallacy thinking that turncoats are smarter than the Military which is working 24x7 for its people.

Ren:Why are you showing us them?

Lieutenant Adwer: It's a warning that you don't end up rotting like this in your entire life.

Ren:No. I never will. I'm out of this training. With one call my uncle would be here to pick me up.

Lieutenant Adwer: Your uncle Bison knows whatever is happening with you. Still he hasn't come up to provide you any sort of support because he wants you to be capable enough to make the mission succeed.

Ren: No, that can't be true. Uncle can't be that insensitive.

Lieutenant Adwer: Remember Ren, it was your decision to choose Military life as you wanted adventure over helping your uncle in business.

Ren keeps his mouth shut.

Lieutenant Adwer: Now before I put you all into this filthy dungeon ,continuous breaking of rules, where is this coming from?

Mumkin: When I entered into the officers cabin, I saw Tiger Watson sitting with sergeant Kroodie .They had this communication.

Mumkin describes the communication as follows:

Sergeant Kroodie:It's been a long time Tiger, that you came to Military camp.There's good news for you!

Tiger Watson: Military camp is just a reflection of Watson's security guards training camp. Infact out trainees can perform a thousand times better .

Sergeant Kroodie: Definitely, time does reflect reality.

Tiger Watson looks irked now,

Tiger Watson: You talk about the good news as my time for you Sergeant is limited as I have to leave!

Sergeant Kroodie: We've captured Captain Lidiya Cheriyan!

Tiger Watson: Wolah(tightly shakes hand with Kroodie), I've been waiting to hang her head outside my training camp.

Sergeant Kroodie: Amen, no more wait for you. The Military was searching for the gritty woman to surrender to court, what a fugitive who spoiled the name of the Military and killed innocent people of your camp .She's been hiding in one of the south Asian countries. After fifteen years she has come back thinking all is forgotten and forgiven. Our smart Military members captured her.

Tiger Watson(exasperated): No she'll not surrender before the court. Before that I need to teach her a lesson for the destruction she created at my security guards training camp almost seventeen years ago. Will just tear her apart into two pieces. She no longer has to hide because I'm Thanatos for her.

Sergeant Kroodie: As you wish my lord. Amen. On 30 Nov, is the day of her court trial in Himbertown as the case is opened again on request of the Military to punish her. While returning from court, we'll hand her to you .The military will declare her fugitive again. You can kill her as time fugitives for the second time in Military are shot dead .

Tiger Watson:What an idea Kroodie, you did not forget your lessons, just like a loyal dog you are(grimming).

Sergeant Kroodie smirks back at Tiger Watson and passes a glass of alcohol to him.

Tiger Watson: As I entered, I saw many young men and women..... What in the world are so many young kids doing in the military?

Sergeant Kroodie: We hired them for the namesake of military training. They are bonded laborers.

Tiger Watson:Bonded laborers? Are Himbertown University students too here? My nephew's best friend Larry came to know that the Military is training them for some mission. They're part of some committee.

Sergeant Kroodie: Ofcourse, they came here after becoming part of a committee. Highly successful in their mission in becoming the kings of asses . We made them the seniors to execute full work. Just rubbing them extremely for utmost output. He's one among them(pointing towards the carved wooden screen in front through which Mumkin was seen).

TigerWatson(clapping):Haha..Thankfully my nephew didn't know about this committee as I wanted him to as an undercover and reporting directly to me of what the heck is going on in Himbertown University under Bison's nose .I found things peculiar, when Ren asked me about Lidiya Cheriyan at my partner Bison's house at a party. When the committee thing came up, my mind boggled further and my suspicion became fathomless. Now I wonder why Bison took extra money from me and still didn't put my nephew here. Bison cares for me and he knows that King's nephew can't work as an unpaid donkey like him(pointing towards Mumkin as Mumkin isseen holding a wine bottle in a bar rack , then mocking at him by making the same position)! ....

Mumkin adds further about this whole event to Lieutenant Adwer.

Mumkin: As I came back to the evening class of yours(referring to Lieutenant Adwer), I shared the same with four other seniors of Charlie, Sierra and November Company. I told them how we're been misguided to accomplish a mission which isn't even real. Everyone including the junior trainees were in a state of turmoil as no one wants to be bonded labor. All of us are here with the wrong notion of supporting our country thus indirectly saving people from malefactors. If that's not happening then we don't want to be part of Military training anymore.

Lieutenant Adwer(septical): So this is the reason for undisciplined behavior !

Mumkin: We've got to say something else too. Captain Lidiya Cheriyan, she's already under the arrest of the Military where she'll be handed over to Tiger Watson soon on the day of court trial. Whatever is happening here in this Military camp is wrong and a fake representation of patriotism. Thus all five of us along with junior trainees are rebelling from the past three days by not performing our duties(making sober eye contact with Lieutenant Adwer).

Lieutenant Adwer: You talk like a three year old child Mumkin.

Mumkin: Why do you think like that?

Lieutenant Adwer: You think that the military camp has traitors right?

Mumkin: Yes, as that's apparent.

Lieutenant Adwer: Hallelujah! Do you know the birthplace of Sergeant Kroodie and what his father did for a living?

Mumkin:What kind of irrelevant question is it?

Lieutenant Adwer: It's as relevant as love for country and Captain Lidiya Cheriyan is to you all. So think about it and then answer!

Mumkin and the other four of them look exasperated as they aren't knowing the answer and aren't interested in answering any of Lieutenant Adwer's questions.

Lieutenant Adwer: I tell you as you five look pea brained. Sergeant Kroodie is from Marvo Village, it's the most crucial part of our mission as this is the place where the mission ends. The plan has both destruction of malefactors and construction of lives of villagers again. Out of those villagers, there's one family whose name is extinct. That's

Kroodie's family. Twenty years back when Kroodie was equal to your age, he was taking training at Watson's camp to become a male factor. As his father, a poor farmer couldn't pay the taxes to Watson, he and along with Kroodie's two elder sisters were brutally murdered by Watson. Kroodie still continued the training at Watson's camp until he became amity of Watson. In that course of time too he developed himself as a reliable gunner for Tiger Watson's security, where Tiger trusted him a lot. Kroodie joined the Military of Himbertown as his undercover. But the reality is, Kroodie's laceration of losing his family is undried. He's been working in the Military for ten years with a revenge that matches our mission. All he's doing is to confound to Tiger Watson. Whatever you heard that day is part of the mission. Such turmoil should not arise especially when we work for organizations like the Military. !Learn to trust your guts and the Military.

The fivesome are dumbstruck and things are more clearer to them now.

Lieutenant Adwer: Ranks will be given to you all just after your training, always remember to keep your morality, loyalty and faith towards your country's welfare and its Military. So young chaps(referring to fivesome), "royalty with loyalty".

They repeat the Military slogan after him and go to their grounds to continue their training of shooting with guns , horse aka "kemba", parade and serving food at night. Juniors too completely followed them.

Pamela was waiting for the weekend to arrive as it was the day of outing. Ren had asked her out . Early in the morning she wakes up with excitement in her barrack, her juniors help her in making a french braid for her hair. For clothes, she gets confused as she isn't able to find any dress that can allure Ren. As her junior decided to wear a delightful gown for the outing, she requests to borrow that from her. The gown is red in color,Pamela wears it and starts resembling a sun goddess. Pamela looks at herself and puts a lavender perfume especially at her neck .She looks at her cleavage which is more apparent than her usual outfit have.She puts a drop of perfume there starts to blush as her junior girl trainees start to give her a nickname calling her would be Mrs. Pamela Ren Bison and what not. She starts day dreaming of having children with him and becoming the queen in his heart. He would love her and provide her with all the resources of the world. Especially his uncle's huge Porsche car collections, their bungalows, jewelry he gifted to Janny and what not. Not Pamela will be a part of all that.For a second she stops daydreaming and thinks, what if the breakup happens…..Her heart is filled with fear. She tells herself 'Pamela, don't think like a gold digger, give your most love to Ren '.

She goes out of her barrack and starts to wait for Ren near the Church's praying room. Whoever passes by from that place gives a look at Pamela, two to three soldiers also compliment her for being so gorgeous.After forty minutes there comes a man to cherish her more than she could cherish herself. It's John not Ren. John visits the church to pray every sunday.He's wearing casual blue jeans and white T shirt.

Pamela:John, by any chance have you seen Ren? We were supposed to go on a date.

John admires Pamela's fresh look through looking into her eyes. Her pinkish blue eyeliner is glittering, making her look more beautiful.

John: No I haven't seen him! A date with Ren huh?That's why you've dressed up like this.

Pamela:Dressed up like what?

John:Like it's a new year party or christmas party for you. You're dressed up fully red, like red tulip flowers. Wait better than that, you're dressed up like a santa.(pulling Pamela's nose).

Pamela:Shut up Ren. My date isn't here till now. I was expecting red roses from Ren, guess what,he's late on the first date at Military camp . Since I can't get inside the Men trainee barracks of any company, can you please check and let me know?

John:No ways, it's my prayer time. Soon father Wilson will be here. I'm not gonna do a sin of missing any of my prayers for you.

Pamela:Please John, please. I'm sure Ren might have forgotten our place of meeting,he might have been searching for me.

Pamela starts to push John towards the direction of Charlie 's company barrack of boys. Mumkin arrived there for his church prayers. Pamela requests him too to search for Ren and bring him towards her in case he doesn't remember the meeting place from where they'll proceed for outing. Mumkin convinces John to accompany him till

Charlie barrack. Both run and go there and return back after some time with bad news .

Mumkin: Pamela, he already left for an outing with two junior trainees of Charlie company.

Pamela looks disappointed. Mumkin and John offer Pamela to hang out with them once the church prayers are done. However she refuses them feeling disheartened, she runs towards her barrack,changes her dress to gray sweatshirt and track pants and wets all her tissues. That day, she stays inside her barrack and plays with newborn puppies of abandoned bitch .

Evening during dinner time Pamela sees Ren ,having his dinner with his junior trainees. As he looks at her she ignores him. As she leaves from there towards the Sierra barrack for girl trainees.Ren calls her from behind.

Ren:Pamela, why are you ignoring me like this? What happened(hugging Pamela)

Pamela does't accept the hug warmly and pushes him after two seconds of hug.

Pamela:Don't you remember our date,we're supposed to go for a movie!

Ren:I remember it, but you see I was in the ammunition executive duty for the whole day. Sergeant Kroodie gave me this position due to my special abilities.

Pamela:Stop lying. Mumkin and John check from your barrack juniors, they told you that you went for an outing with two other juniors of Charlie company.

Ren:Just don't you dare to believe those dumb boys, they're big liers. Specially John is envious of me as we both are dating. He definitely would've provoked Mumkin also to lie.

Pamela:I believe that they're not lying. That's you, you're lying (sobbing)

Ren: Pamela, just forget whatever happened, it's all your misperception. I promise to take you next week(removing her tears with his thumbs and kissing her forehead). Listen, I love you a lot and nobody should come between us.

Pamela leaves from there in a confused mind. She forgives Ren ,but still feels that Mumkin and John can't lie to her and something isn't right with Ren. She meets John on the way.

John: You're crying again because of him? Do you really think he's into you?

Pamela:What do you mean by that?

John: Do you think he loves you?

Pamela: No, I think I'm getting clingy. If he wants to go out without me, then I needn't question his loyalty towards me.

John: Haha. How naive you're. Look, he's not even informing you where and when he's going out. Still you fall for him constantly.

Pamela: Aren't you jealous that I and Ren are together?

John: Pardon! You're becoming a nutshell head like him! I'm done with your friendship.

Pamela: Pardon me Ren ,ooops sorry John. I just wanted to make sure what Ren was saying to me wasn't right.

John:Nope.Instead do what your intuition says is right. Also don't forget that I'm dating Stella, your cousin. Someone's manipulation can create a castle of misapprehensions in one's mind.

Pamela: What do you mean , castles and misapprehensions.Please be direct.

John:Good bye Pamela.

Pamela:Please clarify John!

John turns his back and leaves from there.Pamela is still befuddled.Now she's believing John more than Ren, that Ren is actually manipulating her. However she remembers the kisses and care that she got from him ,due to which her mind and heart are in a conflicted state. She decides to forgive him with another seed of trust for outing the next week. However she wants to take this as her final call with Ren as if this time things don't go as decided, she'll break up with Ren!

As she was leaving towards the parking lawn to water the plants, Mumkin arrived there from behind. He starts to sprinkle water on the lawn with a pipe and Pamela does it with a watering can. Fresh fragrance of jasmine and rose lightens up her mood. Mumkin exchanges the sprinkling pipe with her water can as she was finding it difficult to carry. She comes near him.

Pamela: Do you think John has changed ?

Mumkin: Yes of course, he has become more responsible and mature now. The way he's executing his duties is commendable. His way of asking questions is also better.

Pamela: Not like that.

Mumkin: Well, it's probably magic of your sister Stella that he's more calm than what he was before. I hope this is what you meant.

Pamela: No Mumkin. Do you think he's a little arrogant nowadays? He just walked out when I asked him if he's jealous of my relationship with Ren.

Mumkin: What kind of question did you ask him? We're friends Pamela. In Fact he cares for you as a friend, He's happy if you're happy and sad when you cry in sadness.

Pamela: These are not my words but the words of my boyfriend Ren.

Mumkin: If Ren believes this then he is wrong in his belief system. The only person who has changed the most till now is Ren. Initially he made you your girlfriend but he hasn't been so kind to you. He sometimes does tumultuous and self seeking talk turning deaf ear to you and to others. Pamela, it's high time for you to not let people influence you. You decide which person is kind to you and which isn't. Yes, you decide based on his behavior's consistency.

Pamela goes into deep thinking.

Mumkin: Relax Pamela. Don't think so much.

They water the plants, go to the library to read a few good books. Pamela chooses a romantic novel and Mumkin gets to see the books that he always wanted. He's super excited like an atom to see a by Anleku Bonzina on Weaponries technological development from the past hundred years. In the book, there's a mention of a gun that's been developed after six hundred years of experience, capable of sucking a bullet from a distance of one meter. Mumkin rethinks about it, reads more and realizes that the book is just a parody, there's no logic. He keeps the book back, does more searches and finds a book of FG Wimperm, that shows how the business of armaments is happening in the current state in different countries, how his country is doing, what weaponaries technologies are present and absent and the ongoing research going on, on those. After reading the book, ultimately Mumkin ponders with the present information of how the country will face a war like situation with present resources, what can fill the gap and how it can be possible? It was already evening with the sky turning pink and blue with sunset. The color of tree leaves shined into golden colors as the last few rays of sun were falling, before the sun went to bed.They walked back towards their barracks with a clean whitewashed roads and disciplined bushes as the bushes were equally placed from each other, were three inches tall and with same castleton green color.

Pamela: This whitewash smell,I find it apetizing!

Mumkin: Really Pamela?

Pamela: Yes, I don't know why.

Mumkin: Probably you lack calcium ....well I think you need to consult a doctor for a proper diagnosis.

Pamela: Yes may be.

Mumkin:So, what did you read?

Pamela: It was an idealized story where both men and women lived in the dark world which separated both of them through huge mirrors. They would never talk to each other. An 18 years old girl falls in love from this world and a twenty years old boy from another world falls in love with each other.

Mumkin: Spellbinding story. What happens at the end ?

Pamela: From the world of women ,they support her to love the guy, but in the world of guy they regard this as law breaching due to which they create loot and violence in women's world. The two worlds get into an adverse situation and they start fighting until, the two lovers fly into space to reunite after worlds also reunite and the meaning of love is created in this world that way.

Mumkin: Fiction is always fun to read for a few people. But it's certainly not for me.(amorous smile). We've arrived at Alpha barrack for boys and your barrack is around two hundred meters away, it's already dark.

Pamela: No worries, I'll go all by myself.

Mumkin: I know that you're scared of the dark. There isn't any street light facility available. So, let me accompany you, till halfway,until there are guards with flashlights.

Pamela thinks that Mumkin is a kindhearted man. She knows that Laila is his inamorata(lover). Suddenly she doubts if he's attracted to her. She starts imagining her life with him as he's a perfect gentleman who can be a really great husband. However, her best friend's lover can't be her inamorato. In all her waves of thoughts were like sine waves,reaching zenith and nadir promptly. Suddenly she gets petrified. No it's not some street dog barking at her. It's the flash light of the guard on their face that has made everything white but imperceptible. They hear a very loud ,dissonant sound "Password?".

Pamela gets edgy, but Mumkin replies back to the night guard "Son of egg has become father today ".

The night guard allows them to go further . Mumkin's sharp memory has been praised by Pamela.

Mumkin: Password is hysterical isn't it?

Pamela: Mercifully ,you remembered it. I had blown my gasket as I got panicky!

Mumkin: I could see that. I know the reason too!

Pamela: Seriously, what's that?

Mumkin: You were thinking if I like you but how's that possible as I'm into Laila, why am I always so kind to you and.....so on.

Pamela: How do you know all this? Are you a sage from another world?

Ren: Since I read the diary of Captain Lidiya Cheriya, I've understood the thought process of a woman's mind a bit.

Pamela: Nevertheless all women are different!

Mumkin: You just said a variety. Nevertheless your personality traits kind of match with young Lidiya Cheriyan's traits.

Pamela: No way, was she timid, emotional trouble and struggling with a relationship with her boyfriend, like the way I am ?

Mumkin: I don't know what you're saying. According to me she was empathetic, determined, purposive, diligent and the list goes on. You're also like her.

Pamela: Do you think I have all those qualities in me?

Mumkin:That's up to you what you want to be!

Pamela: A true sage......and a philosopher you are(friendly banter)

Mumkin chuckles.

Mumkin:Don't put me on cloud nine. But you remember the password as that's paramount.

Pamela: Sure. Do you remember how much we searched about who's Lidiya Cheriyan? Remember Amrisk's shop and Prof Hashtik , the wine addict who punished John, me and you! Oh Lord, I was just flabbergasted to know the truth that the conceited Professor Olivia is only Lidiya Cheriya.

Both chuckles on what Pamela said just now.

Mumkin: It's been a long time since we three left University, how everything would have been at the University and at home(remembering his girlfriend Laila and his mother) .

Pamela gives a handshake to Mumkin and assures him that everything would be great.

As they talk, the Barrack of Sierra for girls arrievs. As Mumkin starts to walk back towards his barrack, he says this to Pamela ``Your thinking is valid. I do care for you so much as you and John are my two boon companions from day one of University. I want to be there for both of you always. I admire your candor and kindness. I'm in love with Laila,want to marry her in the future. I respect your dreams and fantasies,nevertheless a good man will be a part of them one day in reality .A word of advice, see how much other people value you, so you value them in return. Don't let others get on you. Good night ".

As Mumkin leaves from there, Pamela's vision is translucent as her eyes are watery from the last sentence of Mumkin. She ponders upon her relationship with Ren. She thinks if Ren is really valuing her.

As the time passed, the whole weekend went following the same so called mundane routine, that impoverished them completely, plus a new task was on their shoulders, to welcome and accommodate the youth of Tonio village after the two weeks. The whole routine of the seniors was to monitor and work along with their juniors of four companies to clean living areas, Mess, cutting the grass, cleaning washroom barracks, washing curtains ,drying and

• 151 •

ironing them, few of them including John and Benny were sent to the Bakery to help chefs in baking goodies for the senior officers. Pamela was put in a Cultural programme to ensure juniors are preparing a welcome song to praise lord followed by a dance and a skit displaying camaraderie of Himbertown Military with people of Tonio village. Pamela was also assigned to do a speech at the starting and end of the Programme. The hassle was all this had to be done in the evening hours which was the time to take a rest. The same physical training routine from 4 AM morning to afternoon drill training sessions were followed by theory classes on map studies that were causing nervous prostration . Ren developed a very good rapport with Sergeant Kroodie, due to which he and his Charlie company weren't supposed to participate in any of these things. Instead the whole charlie company was put into a quick reaction team where they had to be prepared in case of any emergency, where they had a full day of firing practice , buying and experimentation of new weaponries. It's been six days that Pamela hasn't seen Ren at all!Going for a movie or a date with Ren is just like a pipe dream for her. Next day was sunday, till afternoon it was an off for all.

After the breakfast,she was lying on her bed to repose after the back breaking week. Her Junior enters, wearing a black satin off shoulder dress, with gold chain and long dazzling earning. Pamela looks at her, admires her style for a second.

Pamela: Hey you look pretty junior? Are you going for a date?

Junior Katie: Was about to but had to come back to pass this message to you.Sergeant Kroodie wants to meet you immediately in the ammunition room.

After hearing this, hurtles towards the ammunition room with a jittery feeling of the reason for which Sergeant Krrodie called her. Her face starts to smolder after realizing that she might meet Ren there.She not only has butterflies in her stomach but these butterflies are causing tornadoes. After reaching the Ammunition room Sergeant Kroodie gave her the responsibility of keeping ten hefty boxes of ammunition to the firing range along with three boys and two girls of Charlie company juniors. They decide to keep the boxes one by one ,where four will hold corners and two will hold the door latch. As they start to walk ,it feels a more ponderous weight in boxes. The firing range was hundred meters away, in between they kept the box three times on ground ,until they reached the firing range. They repeat the process.Pamela gets a sound of jaggery in her stomach. Still she continues with them and they all keep the ten boxes within one hour. She doesn't see Ren anywhere. As she starts walking back to her barrack. On the way she finds Ren sitting on a chair under the flag area writing something. With all jitteriness and desperation, she goes near him.

Pamela: Ren , what are you writing? Is it too important that you can't leave?

Ren: Just some logistic stuff of ammunition.

He looks at her for a second and continues writing.

Pamela: Ren, you had promised that you'll take me for a movie. It's been a week since we saw each other and you aren't surprised or happy about it either.

Ren: Was just kidding. I'm not writing about logistics. I'm planning a routine so that both of us can spend our day together and we return back on time. See I don't want us to get punished as last time you went outside with one of your bosom friends , Mumkin due to which we all faced the punishment.

Pamela(felicitous):You're flabbergasting me, I mean really! Were you planning for me? Let's go out quickly so that we can return back on time.

Pamela is holding a big smile on her face. She's happy with Ren's surprise plan for her.

Ren: Whoever it was! What are you waiting for, just get ready. Just look at yourself, you're wearing trousers with a shirt full of mud and dust. I won't take you out like this!

Pamela: Don't worry, I'll come back in five minutes. I'm dirty as I had to keep the heavy boxes from Ammunition room to the firing range.

Ren: It won't be five minutes I know, You'll take at least an hour to wash those mucky hair, get dressed and apply makeup. Do all this within twenty minutes. Or else.....

Pamela: Or else what darling?

Ren: Or else I will take someone else.

Pamela runs towards her barrack quickly, she opens her wardrobe, searches for most pleasing dresses but gets discontented as none of her dresses will attract Ren. On the bed of her junior Katie it was Katie's black shoulderless dress that Pamela decides to wear without taking Katie's permission. She takes a bath with half shampooed hair, applies uneven foundation making her skin look unsmooth and wears a black dress with black shoes and runs towards Ren to keep the promise of coming back within twenty minutes. She looks delightful due to her smile and natural glow as she's happy and thrilled from inside. She finds Ren waiting for her there.

Ren: You arrived! Let's go, already we're late.

Ren pays no attention to her and starts walking holding her hand towards the parking lot.

Ren: I got keys, so that both of us can go in Sergeant Kroodie's motorbike.

Pamela: Are you sure, is this safe?

Ren: Absolutely, infact sergeant Kroodie gave me his keys by himself. Stop thinking much, let's move.

Ren sits on the motorbike, Pamela sits behind him, as she tries to hold his waist or shoulders to feel secure, she immediately thinks if Ren may not like it. It might spoil his mood. After all, after so much of endeavor he's taking her out, so she needs to avoid any mistake at all costs. So she doesn't hold his waist. They go to a fancy movie theater named "Mainstream House". She looks at popcorns and chocolates, craves for them as her mouth is watering. There's a painter who offers Pamela and Ren to paint them as he is looking to paint a couple like them. Within fifteen minutes, he makes a nice looking sketch of both of them and gives them a carbon copy of it, which Pamela keeps to herself as a memory. Ren pays money to the painter. As they move around the theater, there are plenty of good movies displayed in the hallway. Particularly there are two unearthly movies, one based on the biography of a famous popstar Garry Lee and another on politics and drama. She gets very excited to see another movie based on a psychological thriller. Ren asks her to wait for a minute there as he'll be back after buying the tickets. She was about to remind him for popcorn and chocolates, however she has the intuition that he'll get them for her as she has mentioned to him many times about her favorite popcorn flavor and chocolate before coming here. In the past she has seen that whenever he went out with Janny, he always cared for her needs by buying her favorite ice creams and goodies. So she patiently waited for him to test if he considered her wishes. But he returned back empty handed. They go inside the theater room, she is ravenous, but tries to hide it from Ren with a fake smile on her face. As the movie starts, she realizes that it's a passionate movie of a couple, where the boy is completely going crazy after his breakup and he's trying his best to win the girl back. Pamela wasn't interested in such movies as she lacked the connection there. In an emotional scene in the movie, where the boy craves for his girlfriend and shows explosive behavior in public beats up people. He gets a delirium of his ex-girlfriend coming near him, getting intimate and kissing him passionately, that calms the boy down. Ren associates with this movie scene and he kisses Pamela on her lips with such passion, but due to hunger, she shows detachment. She tells him that she isn't comfortable as she isn't feeling it. Ren gets annoyed after hearing this, he starts to look back at the movie with utter disappointment from inside. He again tries to persuade Pamela, but holding her hand and gently trying to kiss her neck, seeing him trying really hard to get close to her, she allows him. She doesn't feel for it at that time. In Fact she realizes that she isn't ready now and needs more time to get as things are getting very fast for her. Somehow she convinces Ren to postpone the second kiss as she's not in the mood probably due to hunger. Everyone in the theater is making out and getting intimate. Ren runs towards the Cinema cafe, he gets two burgers, one caramel popcorns and a strawberry smoothie. He gets back. The duo had burgers and caramelized popcorn, Ren was just waiting for the interval to get over as now is the time that Pamela will also get intimate with him. He is all excited. With the first sip of smoothie, Pamela feels jaggery in her stomach, she feels nauseous. She asks Ren if it's a strawberry smoothie as she's allergic to it. Ren looks at her and within the next two seconds she vomits out whatever she had, everyone in the movie theater is disgusted by her. She asks for help from Ren however, she sees he isn't next to her anymore. Probably went out to seek help from a nurse. With another wave of nausea she faints waking up her eyes straight away in the hospital. Doctor Ashyl is the one who gave her treatment.

Dr. Ashyl: Are you feeling better now?

Pamela: Yes I do, how did I arrive here in the hospital? Where am I? I just don't feel anything.

Dr. Ashyl: Well, your friends brought you here.

Pamela: I was in the movie theater. You mean a friend Right? He's not my friend but my boyfriend .His name is Ren.

Dr Ashyl allows the duo to come inside. It was Mumkin and John.

Dr. Ashyl: I was referring to them(pointing towards Mumkin and John).

Pamela: How did you guys get to know about me? Where's Ren?

Mumkin:The theater in which you went, juniors Karen and Arek of Alpha and Nurture company, who are dating were also present there. . They called me up after seeing you fainted in the theater. We immediately arrived there with an ambulance and brought you here.

Pamela: Do you know, Ren was also there with me inside the theater. I thought he brought me here.

John: He hasn't brought you here. We saw him playing squash just an hour after you were admitted to the hospital.

Both Mumkin and John say it together to Pamela that Ren isn't even a caring guy, she needs to let him go as begging for someone's love isn't even love.

Pamela thanks Mumkin and John for the help and asks them to leave as she needs alone time. After half an hour there's a rose bouquet that Pamela receives from the nurse. A big surprise to her is that the bouquet is coming from Isabella Martin, the lady who lives with Captain Lidiya Cheriyan as her maid. The message says: "Dear Pamela, regrettably you're unwell. Wishing for expeditious recuperation ". Pamela, remembers the time when she ,Mumkin and John actually helped Isabella Martin, when she was being robbed eight months ago. She wonders why is Isabella Martin sending her this wellness bouquet?

After two days Pamela returns back to the Military camp, the first thing she does after reaching her barrack was to take out something nostalgic. She opens her cupboard and starts searching for a piece of art that Mumkin had found in her hand in the cinema hall just a while before she was getting hospitalized. The task was to burn the only proof of her relationship with Ren, it's the carbon copy of the sketch made by the painter when they visited the movie theater. She went inside the washroom and used a matchbox to put the sketch on fire. As the painting was turning into ashes,she shrieked from inside as if her heart was broken into thousands of pieces. All these pieces are cut by a weapon called the conviction of being loved by Ren. After twenty minutes of crying, her junior Katie unlocks her toilet door, hugs her to calm her down. She tells her that her dress that was kept on the bed that day was because she wore it for a date but Bonnie from Charlie company did not turn up. She thanked Pamela for wearing her dress without permission and vomiting on it as she wouldn't have to wear that dress again, albeit she bought it with supposition to impress Bonnie. But that never happened unfortunately! She threw the dress away in the scrap when the nurse gave it to her in the hospital after dressing Pamela in hospital attire .

Junior Katie: I don't think that all men are the same, swung pigs, but these charlie boys are. I despise them!

Pamela laughs in an innocuous way after hearing this. She, along with Katie, go to the Mess to eat dinner. Ren was standing with Sergeant Kroodie and guffawing on some joke. Pamela holds his shoulder. As he turns towards her, she hands over a letter to him with an aggrieved expression. As Ren opens it, it's some money and change , ashes of paperlike material with a note, "A relationship shouldn't make a person worthless. I'm done with you. Giving you back the amount of vehicle and food of that day". Ren immediately excuses himself from Sergeant Kroodie and comes near Pamela.

Ren: Pamela, I went out to search for help for you, it was me only who called the ambulance to get you admitted!

Pamela:I know the truth whether it was you, or my two close friends who admitted me .How much you'll fall for your own trap of lies?

Ren: Your friends always turn up at all places wherever you are present. There's no name of privacy in your friendship with them.

Pamea: Shut up Ren. At least they are always there wherever I need them.

Ren: Listen, a vomiting girl like you, who isn't ready to give any physical satisfaction but wants every facility from her boy friend. I know gold diggers like you! Listen, I'll find many girls and I'm dating four more girls apart from you. In Fact you're more unprepossessing than them!

Pamela: Good for you Ren.

She blows the ashes of the painting that covers Ren's face and eyes and he goes to wash them in irritation.

She's completely dejected from inside after hearing all that from Ren. This time, she doesn't trust him at all. Mumkin and John come near her. John puts his hand over her shoulder and tells her not to worry and Mumkin says to her that "You made an absolutely right decision". She starts to move away without saying anything and goes inside the library where she picks a book of face reading art. As she starts flipping through the pages, she realizes that it's all blurred and obscure. She's trying to figure out by forcing her concentration on the book with a trifling discernment. With watery eyes, she takes a notebook and a pen from the library to write down, "Trust nobody, protect your heart".

Mumkin tells John not to worry about Pamela as she'll be alright ,whereas from inside Mumkin thinks in his mind that there's something off with her today. Evening is the day of the volleyball match between girls teams of Charlie and Sierra company. There's a referee, named Sergeant Bennet who's about to conduct the game. Everyone has arrived near the volleyball court . Both teams have arrived, twelve from Charlie team and eleven from Sierra team. As referee Bennet asks for the missing member, they find Pamela who's playing at Libro position is missing from the team Sierra. Mumkin,John and Junior Katie run towards the barrack of Sierra to look for Pamela. Katie runs through the hallway, checks the washroom and under all fifteen beds but finds no one there. They find her everywhere but she's nowhere to be found. They return back to the volleyball court. The match starts after another volleyball girl player of Sierra company who wasn't efficient enough takes the place of libero Pamela. Soon as the match starts Pamela arrives there wearing the libero dress, she had chocolate on her mouth. Her face was tired, with eyes filled with dark circles and hair scattered. As she enters the court, referee Bennet stops her as the match has already started. In return she replies back to Sergeant Bennet furiously saying that she had low vitality ,due to which she went out to the shop to purchase chocolates to get ready for the match. Hearing this, Sergeant Bennet hits her hard on her head with a stick in front of everybody. Mumkin and John pity her. Pamela, sits in the fourth row of spectators. As she's sobbing people look at her. Mumkin and John feel more bad for her, they want to support her but can't do that due to disciplinary issues. In that vulnerable state she makes eye contact with Ren by mistake .He seems thick skinned, talking to the other three guys sitting next to him, giggling and enjoying the volleyball match. The match ends at six pm in the evening. Charlie's team loses from Alpha. As everyone in alpha was celebrating their triumph, Pamela constantly looked at the brownish shade of the volleyball court. Sergeant Bennet calls her, and Sergeant Kroodie also arrives there.

Sergeant Bennet: This senior of Sierra broke the rule.

Sergeant Kroodie: So her complaint will be sent to Captain Lidiya Cheriyan.

Pamela gets stressed further. But,there was something this time that made her not to get apprehensive. The first thought that came to her mind was, let whatever may come upon me . This feeling gave her immense courage to not to say a word in front of either Sergeant Benner or Sergeant Kroodie. They see a tranquil face of her and they ask her to leave from there. She goes back near the mess area to have dinner in darkness and alone, there's no one inside the mess and food is already over. She puts hands in her pockets and starts munching the chocolate. Every other emotion inside her is rescinding. As she walks towards the Sierra barrack in darkness, she's just not petrified, as if there's nothing beyond death which is the ultimate. This time dogs bark at her, she gets uneasy for a second however continues to walk before she reaches the first light post where guards throw the flashlight on her asking for password. This time she remembers it and speaks it immediately, "My grandpa's brother is not my uncle". Guards let her go, as she reaches the barrack, other juniors of Sierra company gather around her to ask questions out of curiosity of what Sergeant Bennet and Sergeant Kroodie told her and what will happen to her after this. She furiously reminds them that she's their senior most not a friend on whom they can interrogate like this and she goes to bed after this. They have never seen Pamela showing authority or getting furious at them, they all are just dumbstuck and upset. Pamela orders all of them to go to sleep or else the next day will be their nightmare as she can punish them for not following her orders!

 The next day Pamela is the first person to wake up, she rigorously wakes up the other girls, gets ready and gets others ready,reaching the ground at four fifteen am before any other company. Sergeant Kroodie arrives and is astonished to see that Sierra girls are already present there. After that Mumkin arrives with his alpha boys and girls, Ren arrives there with Charlie girls and boys and finally John and Benny arrive with Sierra Company boys and Nurture Company boys with girls. As the physical training session starts with a five kilometer run, Pamela runs as fast as lioness and arrives first at the finish line surpassing both Mumkin and Ren, who are the first one to arrive always. For the first time Sergeant Kroodie says to her "Excellent Miss Brown, Keep it up!" .She's still impassive. As everyone moves towards the electrolyte drink counter, Mumkin and John see Pamela drinking five glasses of electrolyte.

Mumkin: Man, we just saw you drinking five glasses of electrolyte.Why?

Pamela: Why are you picking on me? If you also want to drink, you can drink on your own.

Mumkin: No buddy! It's just we're concerned about you.

Pamela leaves from there in indignation.

Mumkin stops her from behind .

Mumkin: We actually wanted to congratulate you on your excellent performance in running.

Pamela turns back and replies to both Mumkin and John.

Pamela: No need to congratulate me! I know what your purpose is.

She turns her back again and starts walking.

John shouts back from behind, "What intentions Pamela? What do you think of us, are wediscipable?"

Pamela gets piqued and swiftly runs from there crying.

Mumkin: John,she isn't well.

John(angry): She looks all fine. Don't you see that she drank five glasses of electrolyte?

Mumkin: I am referring to her mental and emotional health.

John: That doesn't mean she'll behave like a schizoid person! She's just not talking to us properly, shying away, brandishing her paroxysm on us. It's her breakup, but we're mortified!

Mumkin: Let's be kind to her. She's going through an experience that can be excruciating sometimes.

John:I don't have that stoicism . I'm getting overwhelmed due to it! If she does it more, I will start despising her!

Mumkin: Brother, try not to take things too personally, you can have your own boundaries.

John: You're just salt of the earth! I sometimes wonder how you have so much fortitude?

Mumkin: I don't think that I have too much of fortitude,instead I believe that I have to always be present for my loved ones especially during times of distress.

John: Do you like her?

Mumkin: For me it's only one person who's most close to my heart and that is Laila! Pamela needs me a lot as a friend, so I want to remain chivalrous so that she doesn't stop trusting me and other men in life.I want her to start dating again whenever she feels better!

John nods his head to show his agreement towards Mumkin.

Afternoon was the time of shooting, Pamela has adept with a record of ninety eight percent of pinpoint target till now. Mumkin and Ren with five other juniors got all five bullets hit the targets whereas Benny and John got three bullets hit and two washouts. This time almost all juniors and seniors had improved in their shooting except Pamela and junior Katie who were washed out this time. Sergeant Kroodie is despondent with them especially with Pamela as she is the senior of Sierra who is just not performing well in shooting, breaking rules of outing without permission for a trivial reason like buying a chocolate to eat. He warns her that she will be sent back home and no University will accept her again if she doesn't perform well. Her weight is reducing and Sergeant is been complaint by the Mess master to the Sergeant that she is missing out the food also. The afternoon Sergeant makes her eat a colossal amount of food so that she doesn't lose her health. Promptly, within ten days she gains four kilograms, which doesn't stop as she continues to gain weight eventually. Her face is pustule with red and black pus filled pimples. The smile on her face has completely vanished and now the escalation in her weight is making her underperform in most of the activities related to physical training. Sergeant Kroodie and Sergeant Bennet bait on her to make her perform better, this makes her angry and unloved. She completely ceases to talk or communicate with anyone. She craves for Ren, however he doesn't even look at her as her body is becoming a stout. Mumkin and John are highly worried about her health. As the arrival of Marvo students gets delayed for four more days,Mumkin and John plan to give a surprise to Pamela on her birthday. They book the storehouse ,buy a cake with balloons and candles with the money they get on their daily allowance and traveling allowance. They keep the chocolate cake on the center of the table with candles mentioning "P". On the cake it's written "Happy Birthday to the Princess of Earth ". The golden and silver color balloons are filled with rose petals , smoke and toffees. Mumkin tells the plan to Sierra Junior Katie. Katie brings Pamela, by blindfolding her from Sierra girls barrack to the storehouse. As Katie removes the blindfold ,Pamela feels astonished to see everything glimmering, kind of pricking her eyes. She smiles after a long time and that smile fades away within a few seconds.

Mumkin: What happened Pamela?

John: Yes your smile, it's completely gone.

Pamela: I just wonder if I ever deserve all this?

Mumkin:Why are you saying something like this on the day of your birthday? You do deserve everything.

John: And do you remember in University how greatly you celebrated the birthday of mine and Mumkin?

Mumkin: Absolutely Right John! Pamela, you have done so much for us, this is the least that we could do.

Pamela: I did all that because I think you two deserve love and happiness. But I don't because Ren wouldn't have left me then like this all heart broken!

Mumkin: Pamela, what you feel which is really beautiful, but Ren and you weren't supposed to be together. He doesn't deserve your love and he devalued you. Believe me, one day a great man will enter your life and you will forget about Ren completely.

John: Now you smile because with this serious face you look like piranha fish.

Pamela chuckles with Katie. Pamela hits John on his shoulder and in agony John says 'Aooo, it hurts Pamela'. Mumkin lights up the candles, she smiles after reading "Happy birthday princess of earth". She blows up the candles, cuts the cake. She takes square pieces of cake and offers it to Mumkin, John and Katie. All of them burst all the balloons, applied cakes on each other's face and had immense fun.

Mumkin: We have a surprise for you Pamela, come along with us and kindly stop laughing as your birthday was a secret act(smirking at Pamela).

Pamela laughs out a loud prompt. John says "shhhh " to her by putting his finger on his lips.

They go out in the dark and walk outside the main gate. It's cold. The guard looks at them with dubiety. He firstly asks them the password, which Mumkin tells confidently, his next question "what the heck are you doing at midnight 11PM and where are you all planning to go?"

Mumkin shows something to the guard after seeing it the guard gets happy. It is a finest packed glittering bottle of Lucas Bols vodka. The guard takes hold of it,lifts up to his eye level, grins like a Cheshire cat and starts drinking .He snarls on his first sip and stops any conversation with them.He places his right hand towards the direction outside the gate, thus allowing them to go outside near the bus stop. As they open the huge gate, trying to make a negligible sound. Pamela asks Mumkin and John again, however they ask her to keep quiet in an earnest way. It is all deserted and dark. They proceed towards the bus stop. On their way two trucks and one dumper passes by. Pamela sights a car that has an acquainted number and color. With euphoria in her heart she runs hell for leather. Mumkin, John and Katie, tell her to be careful while crossing the road. She cries in nostalgia and hugs the two people standing outside the car, one with brown hair and black jacket and the other with gray hair completely covered in shawl. They are Mr and Mrs Brown, her parents. Pamela's mother kisses her forehead and hugs her. They wish her a happy birthday. They brought a cake for her and a huge pink teddy bear that she was sleeping with before she left in the Military training. Her mother brought a bag full of goodies including homemade chocolate chip cookies, sticky toffees and potato chips etc. They cut the cake together. Enjoy the food.

As Pamela reconciles with her parents, Mumkin, John and Katie leave from the place back inside the Military through the same main gate. Pamela sits inside the car along with her parents.

Mr. Brown: Dear, it's been a long time. Mumkin told me everything about the way Ren treated you and the changes in you after the breakup.

Mrs. Brown: Never forget that we always love you . Take care of your health.

Pamela: Mom , dad, am I not beautiful? I mean my face is filled with pimples.

Mr. Brown: You look stunning even in your night pajamas. You look beautiful all the time! Look darling, you are our princess. These pimples make you look magnificent .You need to be proud as pimples are the sign of your infancy even though you're in teenagehood.How in this world such kind of doubt is coming to your mind ?

Pamela: It's Ren, I want to know the reason why he always ignored me and never cared for me even after knowing that I love him truly!'

Mrs. Brown: He will have his own reasons . It's time for you sweetheart to move on. Keep your chin up and always keep smiling. I can't see the dejection in your eyes. Be my little princess, come on smile and be happy!

Mrs. Brown: And before that you need to forget and forgive Ren. He was your past. My princess please stop brooding over it.

Mr. and Mrs. hug Pamela, all three of them rest inside the car till 2PM. After which Pamela says goodbye to her parents. Her father drops her near the gate in such a way that no one can see her, including guards. It is all caliginosity.

As Pamela tries to get inside the gate, she finds that it is locked from inside. The guard catches her and gets red handed as she was tampering with the lock to open the door. He holds his hands, as she looks at his face, it is a different person. She tells him the password but the guards warn her of chastising the law assuming that she is trying to run away from the Military training .The guard happens to be the security supervisor,the head of all three guards. He opens the lock of the gate,pulls Pamela inside the door and ties her both hands with a rope . She starts sobbing. There is black shiny car, after seeing that the guard salutes it. The guard goes near it and after a tête-à-tête he comes back and orders Pamela to sit inside the car. She resists and tells the guard that she doesn't want to sit as she is feeling scared(crying). However, the guard scornfully ordered her again. Pamela hesitantly sits inside the black car. Her biggest trepidation is inside that shining black car. She recalls what Sergeant Kroodie and Sergeant Bennet said to her. Now it's the time to tackle it! Colonel Hielmaster is driving the car and Captain Lidiya Cheriyan is sitting on the passenger seat. For a second she gazes at them the way the goat might have seen the lion.

Capt Lidiya: Turn on the lights Sir, so that she can get inside the car.

As Colonel Hielmaster turns on the lights of the car. Pamela gets inside . The entire way they do not speak anything whereas Pamela gets the reminiscence of the detention center, where Bessy and Larry are kept. They stop the car near the Sierra girls barrack. Pamela looks at Capt. Lidiya in a dubious manner.

Captain Lidiya: Did you not receive the bouquet and well being note from my maid Isabella in the hospital?

Pamela(haphazardly): Yes I did! I was skeptical of why the note was coming from her !

Capt. Lidiya: That's due to your scatterbrained habit! Do you think I will write my name "Captain Lidiya Cheriyan" to get caught by a nemesis ?

Pamela realizes that the note was actually from Capt Lidiya Cheriyan, not from her maid. Pamela nods her head in an apologetic way and thanks Captain Lidiya for the note.

Captain Lidiya: Kroodie and Bennet told me everything about you! The infraction of laws has been done by you. Your underperformance in shooting.

Pamela: Not by me, I lost my concentration.

Captain Lidiya: May I know the reason for your deflating concentration?

Pamela starts shivering, her legs are shaky.

Colonel Hielmaster: Relax girl(pointing to Pamela's shaking legs). Everyone faces breakups in life! For you it happened during the time of your training that made things worse as you aren't able to get the right support .

Capt. Lidiya: Is that the reason your parents came to meet you today,so that they can support you?

Pamela starts to sob as she's afraid after being caught, nodding her head agreeing to what Captain Lidiya asked.

Pamela: It was my birthday yesterday.

Captain Cheriyan: Don't you dare to think that we are not aware about the things happening here. We eye on your every move, .Now go back to sleep as 4:30 AM is training time. This is the last time you are forgiven for all the breaching of the law or else you will be at a place that you were reminiscing inside the car! Get lost(snapping at Pamela)!

Pamela goes inside the barrack and sleeps on her bed with teary eyes. As she wakes up, it's already 4:15 AM, half of the girls are ready. She promptly gets ready in five minutes wearing her physical training dress and leads the group of Sierra group towards the training ground.

Afternoon hour at two thirty , Mumkin visits the library during the study hour. He opens up the newspaper on which the front news is written as "The decade old fugitive from the MIlitary, court martialled Lidiya has been captured by Military intelligence,she will be taken to Taximtown after two days for her case trial.Certainly a good catch by Colonel Hielmaster".

Mumkin runs with the newspaper to show it to John and Pamela. All three of them go to Sergeant Kroodie who is administering the gun cleaning tasks. They wish him "royalty with loyalty" after which Mumkin hands over the newspaper to him.

Sergeant Kroodie reads the news and gazes at the trio for ten seconds.

Sergeant Kroodie: Chamburt, this is a mirage, completely untrue. As Captain Cheriyan is in fake capture of Colonel Hielmaster. Tiger Watson is also informed about the same information through the newspaper. I already called Tiger Watson regarding the same and now he would want Colonel Hielmaster to hand over Captain Cheriyan to him. However the plan is............

Mumkin: Please tell the plan to us Sergeant, we will contribute wherever required.

Sergeant Kroodie: I will not enunciate the plan .

Colonel Hielmaster entered the area with a gun. He takes the newspaper from Mumkin's hand, and starts reading out the front page of it.

Colonel Hielmaster: Cheers to the photo of mine on the front page for capturing Miss Cheriyan! I look handsome . Don't you think there's an artificial mole on my forehead(referring to the black print dot on the newspaper that's looking like a mole). Isn't that amazing that this artificial mission got me a lot of fame.Now the next step is to handover Miss Cheriyan to Watson , cause a military encounter on her as she tries to escape and declare her dead !

The trio with Kroodie look dumbstruck.

Colonel Hielmaster: Why are you looking at me like this? All this is counterfeit plans (referring to the trio and Sergeant Kroodie) so as to deceive Watson leaving an assumption in his mind that Cheriyan is killed. Keep it a secret trio group or else I am afraid to send you to the prison house of Bessy and her boyfriend.

He returns the newspaper to Mumkin, gives his gun to Sergeant Kroodie for cleaning and leaves from there in his car. Ren comes inside the gun cleaning space, he wishes Sergeant Kroodie "royalty with loyalty"and gives a quick glance at Mumkin, John and Pamela .He wishes hello to Mumkin and John and treats Pamela as if she doesn't exist in that world. Pamela also leaves quickly. Sergeant Kroodie takes the newspaper from Mumkin and shows the news to Ren as Ren is an ally to him now. They discuss first about the newspaper article ,then move their conversation to the various ammunition present with them at this time, which is the best of all and a bit about Colonel Hielmaster's passion for shooting and how he manages to fire a three digit number and practices for two hours everyday. Mumkin and John were still standing there looking at the faces of each other. Until Ren asks something from Sergeant Kroodie.

Ren: Sergeant Kroodie, is there any telephone facility available here? I need to call somebody.

Sergeant Kroodie: Of course, we have that facility ,but it is available only after your completion of three months of training here when you get enduring ranks of Military.

Mumkin and John, snigger looking at each other as Mumkin could call Pamela's parents through the only available telephone in the Military where Mumkin hoodwinked the guard incharge .Ren solicits Sergeant Kroodie that he has to make one call to ask the ammunition dealer if the material is ready or not. Sergeant Kroodie refuses him by saying that he himself will talk to the dealer. However Ren convinces Sergeant Kroodie that the Military will profit as his uncle Bison knows the dealer at a personal level, So he needs to allow Ren to talk. Mumkin and Ren leave from there. Ren and Sergeant have more conversations with each other up until Ren goes to the telephonic booth with a written permission from Sergeant Kroodie to make a phone call.

Two days go by, and on the third day , Captain Lidiya sits in the Military jeep that is completely painted green. She has handcuffs in her hands and she's proceeding for a court hearing. There are two male soldiers and one female soldier sitting in front of her and the other sitting next to her. Colonel Hielmaster visits the church to pray that everything needs to happen according to plan. There will be a fake encounter of Captain Lidiya by him and the other two soldiers as she tries to escape custody, hitting one soldier. The jeep will be overturned and ruptured by them to make everything look real. This encounter will declare her dead, thus Tiger Watson and his father will chase her away. The court proceedings will also close as the charges against the accused Lidiya will be abated after her death causing the case to close. Of Course retired Brigadier Blacksmith who is a dignified person of this country will say that her body was mutilated in the hustle so immediately it was taken to postmortem and cremated . The artificial evidence of her body's postpartum and cremation will be provided by the mortuary. With that he also prays that in all these atrocious planning and acts, Lidiya shouldn't get harmed at all .

Hielmaster sits on the passenger seat, the driver starts the jeep and they start to move.Captain Lidiya looks confident about the mission, however she's constantly moving her hands stuck in handcuffs, rubbing them with her pants.

Colonel Hielmaster: Lidiya, why are you disposing discomfort through your hands?

Capt Lidiya:These handcuffs are incising due to mini spikes in them.

Colonel Hielmaster: Remove them, you do not require those now, wear them when we click your pictures of fake encouncounter ,once we reach the site.

Their conversations keep happening until they reach the main site area, they see something that blows their senses. A jeep with the same number as theirs is overturned and ruptured. Captain Lidiya and Colonel Hielmaster get out of their jeep to reach the site. The three soldiers and driver also come along with their rifles in hand. There are two noises of bellowing. Captain Lidiya recognizes one of them and reaches near the Jeep, they take out the two men stuck inside after a lot of hassle. The person from the jeep turns out the man was wearing a hooded red robe and his driver. Both of their bodies are perforated with bullets through which blood is coming out. Captain Lidiya unveils the red hood to see his face. To her terror it is someone who's connected with her for years. It is Silver Bison. He's agonizing in pain and his driver just died after being taken out. Captain Lidiya goes near him, she sits down and Silver puts his head on her lap.Colonel Hielmaster gives the order to the driver to drive to the nearest hospital and get the medical team immediately .Silver is not in the state to be carried to the hospital.

Capt Lidiya(snivel): Silver, what happened to you? Who did all this?

Bison(precariously and agonizing):T,...Ti....Tiger Watson. Yesterday Ren called telling me about the brainless plan that you and the Military made. I knew that before you could create artificial death of your own, Tiger would kill you before, I know his deadly mind. My Olive's life was at stake(referring to her), so I wore this red robe with a hood, got the jeep with the same number and when Tiger arrived......he(snuffle)....he fired on us assuming that Olive you, you're behind this hood. Do you like my plan(wheezing and struggling to breathe)

Lidiya bends down to hug Bison.

Captain Lidiya(hugging and sniveling): Silver, you put your own life to save mine!

Bison: I love you Olivia, wish you could feel it too. From the day one, twenty years back when I saw you sitting inside the meditation room of University and reading a book with few of your curls covering your face, you looked beautiful.That impeccable smile was determined to steal my heart up until my death. I love you....I love you forever Ol...Oli...Olivia(breathe heavily).

Captain Lidiya looks into his eyes filled with tears, affliction and desire for her.

Bison: Stop staring like this or else my soul won't receive salvation, will cry forever for your love!

Captain Lidiya hugs him, his blood on right cheek and dress of her. Col Hielmaster comforts her, putting his hand on her shoulder. After a few seconds Bison's wheezing stops completely and his eyes remain open. He is dead. By then the driver comes back with an ambulance and. Hielmaster pulls away Lidiya from the dead body of Bison,so that the nurses from the ambulance could take Bison's body and his driver's body to the Mortuary for postmortem. Lidiya facing the ground which is filled with blood, she gets anamnesis of all the memories that she had with Silver Bison, how he always craved for her love, the mistrust and the judgment that she had on him that he is a cozener. He gave his life away for her, filled her with the feeling of rue and now she acknowledges the profundity of his love for the first time, after he is gone forever. All she has a stronger resolution to take vengeance from Tiger Watson and his father who murdered her enderament Mumkin's father Commander Major Chamburt ,her best friend Jonathan, her unrequited lover Silver Bison and many other innocuous people.

The very next evening is the funeral of Silver Bison and his driver .It is done covertly in the Military training camp ,so that Bison's business partner cum Military's adversary Tiger Watson does not get to know about it! Ren cries bitterly with the coffin of his uncle. Pamela feels downhearted for him, so does Mumkin and John as his Uncle was the only person for him. Bodies get cremated in the ancestral graveyard of Bison where the date written on their graves is two days advance, i.e. of 18 Dec whereas the actual death date is on 16 Dec. The next day there is news in the newspaper that Captain Lidiya Cheriyan is killed along with soldiers Barty Henry and Tulip Prince(fictitious names), where the strike was launched on them by unidentified assailants when she was taken for court trial in the Military jeep. The time mentioned in the newspaper is around 7:40PM, which was the time of attack on Silver Bison and his driver. On 18 Dec a news was launched declaring Silver Bison dead in a chopper crash over the sea and his body remained missing, the picture posted on newspaper is a forged one taken from a chopper crash in another country about three years ago. There's a second funeral of Bison done where Tiger Watson is also invited. Ren too goes in it. All the professors and students of University of Himbertown have assembled there including Principal Blacksmith. Tiger Watson too arrives there for the funeral of his business partner. Ren loses his temper inside himself after seeing Tiger Watson, however Principal Blacksmith calms him down whispering in his ears that there's always a right time for vengeance but this is not the one!

The same night there's a girl with long hair coming upto him back, she has big blue eyes and a mole on her neck and cheek. She resembles a famous celebrity Hiana Carter. She's full of fizz with dimples on both sides of her cheeks. Principal Blacksmith introduces her to Ren as his daughter Madeline. The principal talks to other people at the funeral. Madeline comes near Ren.

Madeline: Ren, I have heard a lot about you, dad keeps telling me the way you're the big cheese in the Military ammunition role.

Ren doesn't make an effort to talk back.

Madeline: What passion do you find in ammunition?

Ren:Our country has been doing pretty well in ammunition for the past fifty years.Since I am from a business management background at Himbertown University, I thought of why not take the supply chain of Defense to a different level.

Madeline: Interesting. How were you planning to do that?

Ren: Many things need to be changed, presently we are working on our supply chain management by enhancing transparency ,reducing financial losses, and improving on our unexplained inventory of ammunition. Also we're improving on our real time report so that it can be available all the time with complete accuracy that will help us out in taking critical decisions.

Madeline: Sounds good! What about Vendor's performance? Aren't you monitoring your vendor's performance or else spending on the wrong vendor can really make things go berserk.

Ren: That's a good point, we'll use it in the future purchasing of material.

Madeline: What about creating the Military's own manufacturing unit?

Ren: We will set that up too! For now it's an assignment of three months in which I have to take vengeance from our adversaries, the ones who killed my uncle.

Madeline: Do you believe in reincarnation or life after death?

Ren: I don't.

Madeline: Then you must believe in these concepts as your uncle's soul is vehemently seeking revenge. Go for it Ren.

Madeline leaves from there, she creates a profound impression on both his heart and mind, with her great looks and astute thinking.

CHAPTER NINE

Preparation to hunt him down

The very next day during the time of campfire of the unit, Ren is asked to go near the main gate to welcome the honorable guest. As the official car arrives with three diamond shaped flags in it, Retired Brigadier Blacksmith with the present Brigadier Arthur Vincent comes out of the car. From the back seat Brigadier Vincent's wife Mrs. Vincent comes out with Madeline. Ren looks delighted to see Madeline. Everyone is highly respectful of them, they all stand up upon themselves on their entry. They start with an orchestra, to perform a welcome song and start the campfire only after the permission from honorable guest Brigadier Blacksmith .Sergeant Kroodie asks Ren to escort Madeline to different places in the camp. Ren takes her for a visit to various areas of the camp like library, candidates Mess, Golf ground, recreation room where they play snooker and Madeline wins. Everything looks utter kempt as it has been unspotted and mopped before their arrival. The hallways are decorated with deep orange, white ,yellow and royal blue flags to display the unit's most reverent colors. Deep orange color depicts youth of soldiers, white represents astuteness, yellow represents fraternity and royal blue represents valor with loyalty. Finally Ren takes Madeline to the ammunition room as he assumes from the previous conversation between them that Madeline would want to see it .He displays the record book of ammunition about purchases that has been made till date. To impress her , he shows his written record of firing pic point target bullets. In that exhilaration, he takes her to the boys barrack and opens his cupboard to display his silver medal that he got in shooting last month .Madeline looks frigid. After a minute of silence, she asks Ren about the gold medalist for the same. Ren dithery takes the name of Pamela. Madeline says in response to Pamela's name "A girl is earning a gold medal especially in shooting, that is where revolution is happening in the Military, I would love to meet her".

Ren:Sure(dubiously). (Clearing throat)She was my girlfriend.

Madeline:Really! That's a very riveting piece of information. Take me to her.

Ren thinks that now Madeline no longer has interest in him. Instead she is uncanny right now. He goes near the campfire with Madeline. There Pamela was sitting with Sierra junior girls ,enjoying the dance and singing of juniors from other companies. Ren goes near Pamela.

Ren:(bending and whispering near Pamela's ear): Can I have a talk with you for a minute!

This sudden message from Pamela thrills her. She thinks Ren probably wants to apologize and he wants them to be back together. However this time she doesn't listen to any of the assumptions that her mind is making instead she decides to face it, so she goes near Ren,

Pamela(moist eyes):Did you call me Ren?What do you want to say?

Ren: Nothing! It's her(opening his right hand to direct towards Madeline).

Ren leaves from there. Pamela watches him moving away from her. She's not in mood to talk to anyone now, it's a feeling of heartbreak where despite of the fact that Ren doesn't want to be with her, she is forgiving him, leading her to denial of bad experiences with him and anger on trusting him .But she is desiring for him to be back in her life again. Just heart throbbing.

Madeline: I have heard from Ren about you winning various medals in shooting!

Pamela: Really ,did Ren say that(delighted and anxious)

Madeline: No do not take it like that, it was me who asked him about the gold medalist in shooting since Ren is a silver medalist. Happy to hear that girls are doing well.

Pamela:Thank you.

Madeline: What does your father do?

Pamela: Why suddenly this question?

Madeline: Well you must be knowing that my father is a retired Brigadier . He holds huge power. If you need any help, you can always ask for it.

Pamela: Thanks,but no thanks. I am learning here to be the best version of myself through toil.

Madeline: You're a quirky girl! Never mind, I will see you around.

Madeline goes near Ren. They cheer the glass of whisky together and start dancing.Pamela sees from far, clarity strikes her head. Getting Ren back by any chance is out of the question.

To get out of that state of mind she joins the circle of other forty people that included juniors of all five companies, trainers, staff members and her close friends Mumkin and John. They all run in a circle around the bonfire while singing the jingle bell songs for the arrival of christmas.

After a long time Pamela feels herself. Not with a lover, she is happy to live in the present moment. Mumkin and John pull her away from the group ,they offer her ice cream that they have stolen from from the Unit's canteen facility. As they try it, Pamela starts coughing due to the paprika powder sprinkled on the ice cream, Mumkin and John chuckles after their prank. She takes the ice cream in both of her hands to give a nice face massage to both of them. The trio chuckle ,John takes out another pack of ice cream but this time it is a mixed fruit flavor that is really delicious. Mumkin recommends that they need to go to bed on time as tomorrow afternoon the youth of Tonio village will arrive. The trio go to sleep so as to meet up with the next day's requirement. The day starts as usual from physical training ,breakfast, drill practice under the prickling heat of sun till noon followed by lunch. All this has breaks of ten minutes to change uniforms. Afternoon at 3PM, a green color bus arrives with the youth of Tonio village. Total fifty three in number with forty five men,who are six feet five inch to seven feet five inch tall, muscular bodies like wrestlers, back or dark brown hair, pinkish skin tone and stunning looks. However they all looked shabby as if they hadn't taken a bath for a long time. All these men aged from sixteen years to twenty five. There were six girls around the same age , lean, symmetrical faces and similar pinkish tones,gray brown eyes with prepossessing looks. There are two male and one female middle aged trainers of these youths. After a week's interaction these youth will be divided among the four companies irrespective of their gender. Sergeant Kroodie calls out all five seniors of the four companies. Ren looks at them scornfully. Sergeant Kroodie orders them to stand in front of the newly arrived youth. Sergeant introduces each senior of four companies to the youth to remind them that from now on the five seniors will be their seniors too. As Pamela notices them, many youths are making eye contact with her as they find her pretty even with extra few pounds of weight . One Tonio youth was constantly staring at her, she looked at him for a second. He smiles at her but she turns her face away.

The next day the five seniors along with Sergeant Kroodie take the youth to the khemba aka horse practice, however the Tonio boys, they're so damn pliant and swift that they complete their jumps as flat as pancakes. When it was the turn of Tonio girls,they showed a cut above performance. By running up to the horse, pulling their bodies up in an L shaped position, flipping 360 degrees round on the horse and then taking two to three summer salt flips with smooth landing on the ground. Everyone starts clapping after seeing their performance, sergeant Kroodie lifts his left hand up to order everyone to stop clapping. It is utter clear that the youth of Tonio village have sturdy bodies and tender hearts as even after being the best from the rest of the trainees in the Military ,they look exuberant and sane. Their trainers are proud of them. They are blending with these city junior trainees easily. However when it comes to food ,they become gourmand so there's always extra large food cooked in the Military. They are actually seeing so much food for the first time in their lives. Their village is filled with poverty in all areas including food.

With the same expectations, after a short break sergeant Kroodie takes the group for shooting. From the first round he finds that few of the members are bravura, means exceptionally good and few are just excrement and almost eighty other percent of youth aren't able to follow instructions, due to high illiteracy rate in the Tonio village as an outcome of blight influence of Watson on surrounding villages ,lack of teachers and constant physical, cognitive and economical grapple with Watson. When sergeant Kroodie re-explains instructions-hold the rifle by giving support of arms, take lying position ,then standing and ultimately sitting position for every five bullet, keep the alignment of target with front sight and rear sight of the rifle and finally he poses the question on the concept of gun recoil,but not even a single Tonio youth is aware of it. He explains the physics of recoil and give them few ways of reducing it like wearing protection, positioning the rifle with buttlock tight against shoulder's crook, keeping the left foot in case of a right handed person slightly in front and the other closed foot forty five degrees,12 inches behind and 24 inches away from your off foot. Leaning slightly forward. He himself made this sitting firing position. He gives another chance to them to fire five more bullets after his instructions. However again the results weren't sufficient. Dismayed by their performance,he again reiterates to hold the gun unyielding grip before leaving from the firing ground and making an announcement of the leadman who will teach Tonio youth. He makes Pamela, Mumkin and Ren as the leadman to teach them the instructions of shooting within three days.

Later that evening the cultural programme is conducted to gelatinize the Tonio village youth with previous trainees that are present in the Military camp. The first part is the welcome song, followed by a small skit to show the history of friendship cum partnership between the Tonio village and the Military of Himbertown, followed by the dance program that has folk songs of tonio village depicting the chauvinists of the village who twirled Watson's plan of attacking and capturing the village by influencing, motivating and accumulating village people's integration, attacking Watson's malefactors back and thus rescuing their village from getting attacked and captured.This is how Tonio village was saved from Watson. Out of the other villages, it is the most powerful village as it was rescued through the integrity of its people from Watson. The youth of Tonio get patriotic and few of them start crying after seeing the repercussions of the war. The end of songs give a message of crumbling away the Watson's rule in other villages forever and reestablishing cum recreating the lives of guiltless villagers whose lives are tarnished pathetically due to Watson. This generated empathy in villagers. In the end of part of the folk song, a proposal for a development model was kept to rebuild the education and resources of Tonio for ameliorated life. At the end of the programme ,Pamela was highly praised by Colonel Hielmaster on microphone for the smooth flow of activities that met the required target of hitting the heart of people and prompting their purpose to be here in the Military.

The night everyone had to sleep in the one hall before the separate barracks could be assigned the next. Mumkin and Pamela 's matrices were next to each other. There come two Tonio village youth, they ask if they can lay their matrices in between the duo. They introduce themselves as Ray and Sim. As they lay down, they start sharing their stories of Tonio village.

Ray: Our village's people are the first adversary of Watson. My father and Sim's father fought when Watson attacked our village for the first time. They were triumphant in withstanding and combating . However my father got martyred whereas Sim's father sustained injuries as bullets hit his legs due to which he became paraplegic.

Mumkin: Really touched to hear your story. My father was also murdered by Watson in an attack.

Sim: You both are from which place?

Mumkin: I am from Ranidetro village.

Ray and Sim: Ranidetro, the village of valorous persons.

Ray: What's your father's name?

Mumkin: It is commander Major Charles Chamburt.

Both Ray and Sim bow down towards Mumkin .Mumkin is surprised to see them doing that. They reveal the reason that Commander Major Chamburt played the marshal's role in evacuating Watson, it was also his first mission as he was a newly commissioned officer at that time. Their fathers tell his legend to them. In Fact in each house of Tonio ,he is invoked daily. There's a War memorial of Commander Major Chamburt in the center of Tonio village . His legend galvanized each youth of Tonio to fight against injustice happening in Marvo village. They regard Mumkin for being a son of this kind and braveheart soldier.

Both Ray and Sim are interested in developing friendship with Pamela. Infact many of Tonio's youth find her attractive. His chubbiness ,beautiful smile and curly hair are appealing to most of them.

Ray: And you Belle(referring to Pamela), you are from which place?

Pamela: I am from Himbertown.

Sim: Tell us more about yourself, like what your parents do and do you have a boyfriend?

Pamela:Why do you want to know? Do you wish to forward our marriage proposal to my parents?

Mumkin and Sim chuckles.

Ray: Goddess, just wanted to know about the creator of this angel! Do you have a charmer?

Pamela: No I do not have prince charming, in fact I don't need one as I am a queen in myself.

Upon hearing this Mumkin, Ray and Sim start to applaud Pamela for being such a frondeur in the community which has been patriarchal for centuries.

Sim: Do you know there's a lady in our village who's just similar to you?

Sim shares the various witchcraft stories of their village.

Sim: There was a woman named Mebil, who looked like you. She was considered as the queen of witches. She could predict the future with necromancy. She would cure any disease or emergency with her knowledge of wizardry. Snake bite, fevers, typhoid and child birthlike problems were just cured in minutes. Whole village would go to her for diagnosis and cure, they forgot about village doctors. Until one day Mebil........(silence)

Mumkin, Pamela and Ray curiously look at Sim.

Sim: Mebil gets proposed to by a warlock, she refuses him saying exactly what you said " I do not need a prince charming, in fact I don't need the one as I am a queen in myself. " Guess what, the warlock barters his proposal to Mebil's servant Eliza. The warlock and his newly wed wife Eliza had a positive ending. Poor Mebil dies at ninety four all single, unaccompanied and miserable. So Pamela the moral of the story is - If someone is proposing , take it up, who knows you might not have any other choice in future. And for now you have two good choices- Me and Ray, you can choose any of us.

Pamela chuckles and others chortle too.

Pamela: Not at all a miserable tale . I am glad that she lived up to ninety four years!

Sim covers his face with hands, he is smirking but his eyes are crinkled as Pamela isn't interested in him or Ray. Sim and Ray start telling Mumkin and Pamela about the peculiar things in their village, like a flying pot on which sorcery is done, the cursed banyan tree and the occult practice due to which there are evil souls wandering and twirling in the village. Many kids are possessed by ghosts due to which they pee on their beds, start hitting their loved ones, crawl upside down on the wall etc. Ray also starts to give his personal experiences based on the Village's ghosts.

Ray: I remember that it was the new moon's night when I was asked by my mother to get salt from the grocery store, which was around two miles away. I took my bicycle and started riding. It was all dark with huge banyan trees . No human voice, only owls communicating with each other as if making their mastermind mind to do something devilish allying with village ghosts. On my back journey as I bought the salt , my bicycle slipped and I fell down and the next second I saw the salt packet had opened and grains were just in air tornado.

Now Mumkin, Pamela and Sim are hearing things with more focus and they look anxious. They put their heads down.

Ray hears a voice from behind: Why did your mom need the salt at night?

Ray: I don't remember that, probably for cooking. I'm sorry, it was for removing ghosts as they are afraid of salt.

Ray get smacked by sergeant Kroodie who was just standing behind him, listening to Ray. Sim starts to laugh, so the other smacking was given to him. He orders them to sleep right away. Sergeant Kroodie elucidates that the sorcery stories and occult stories were just hoaxes, just for divertissement. He orders the foursome to sleep away right now. Even though stories were fake, the foursome were enjoying one another company. Even though they try sleeping inside their sleeping bags, they fall asleep only after an hour after they murmured among each other.

The next morning at 2 AM Mumkin and John go near the telephone facility room with a bag in which they wrapped something with a towel. As the guard starts to interrogate them, they take out the same analogous weapon again, one out of the two wine bottles with alcohol in it as a bribe to talk to their girlfriends. These bottles are stolen by them from the Military Mess. The guard permits them blithely as their weapon(wine) is an apple of eye to guard as it helps them to stay away at night duties. Guards here call it a megastar, heroine and idol etc . Guard gives them the time allotted is only one minute to each of them, so they need to hurry up. Mumkin calls Laila first in the Girls hostel of Himbertown University. As the Warden picks the phone , he introduces himself as the Librarian of Himbertown University and tells her that he immediately needs to talk to Laila as she needs to return the book early in the morning as library cleaning is going on at Himbertown University and the book that she has borrowed is paramount as it's been used by many scholars. As the Warden calls Laila, she comes half asleep and yawns. Initially she refuses to Warden as she claims to not have visited the library, however Mumkin aka fake librarian, insists the Warden to make him talk to her in order to remind and reprimand her. The warden hands over the phone to Laila.

Laila: I don't have any book ,as I do not visit the Library.

Mumkin: You need not to visit the library as the library is in your heart.(library analogous to love)

Laila: Mumkin(exhilarated). How are the books there?(books analogous to training)

Mumkin: All fine except the books are resilient . Everyday it's painful.'

Laila: Wish I could come there to help you in cleaning books.

Mumkin :Your writing is printed in my heart,after reading them I get motivation to read the books.

The guard is puzzled to see that the new generation talks about books in place of love these days. Mumkin and Laila talk for a minute, John hands over the second bottle of wine to the guard, due to which they get an extra two minutes to talk. John also talks to Stella, however, Mr. Nelon picks the phone, he asks John about Pamela and hands over the phone to Stella. Those six to seven minutes of talking to their girlfriends reviving both Mumkin and John of their rugged military training. They decide to bring Pamela also, so that she could talk to her parents. However as she has developed friendship with Sim and Ray, she appears cheerful in their both humorous but also silly jokes. That afternoon Ren visited Madeline. It appears that she's captivated by his intelligence and looks. For one hour they spend time in the garden discussing the subjects of philosophy, aliens, evolution and of course love making. Sergeant Kroodie is now a stronger ally of Ren as Ren is now dating the daughter of retired Brigadier. Pamela is definitely covetous of their new relationship with Ren and Madeline, however the new friendship that she developed with Sim and Ray is based on hilarity, trust and acceptance and is non toxic.

For the next one month Marvo youth are trained along with Military students. Mumkin and Ren are the finest seniors when it comes to their physique ,intelligence activities like assault demo, khemba performance and ammunition reading. John is the third and Benny is the fourth prime senior to them. Pamela is marvelous with her shooting skills. They all played a huge role in upskilling ,indoctrinating and disciplining the Tonio youth. Sim and Ray are the two seniors representing Tonio youth. Now it is time to leave for the main mission . Before that two days are given for them to meet their loving ones. After months of training all ex students are Himbertown University are going to go back to their homes.

On the first day Mumkin catches a train to his village Ranidetro. The village is extremely beautiful with lots of greenery all around. As he enters his village, the fresh air leaves him feeling cold. He now knows that his village and his father are paramount for many people. He gets a lift on the village head's son's motorcycle .The place is filled with huge farming and dairy sectors encircling the little village of Ranidetro with a population of around two thousand people. Mumkin recalls back his memories of his childhood of him climbing trees, eating berries and plucking flowers to create a bouquet that he would give his mother every time. He reminisces the flashback of that two bedroom hall house, in which one room was for cooking purposes and the other one was a bedroom cum storeroom where Mumkin's old books from nursery to senior school were stored. He remembered going out in the chilling cold sometimes to relieve himself and other times to take a bath as the bathroom and toilet were twenty steps away from the house. This was the house allotted to Mrs. Chamburt after her husband's martyrdoom. Thoughts after thoughts were making him nostalgic, until his house reached and he quickly went inside to meet his mother and the only member of his family. She was sitting on a chair knitting a cream colored sweater, as usual her hands are shivering ,her spectacles are at her nose and she is closely monitoring her loop stitching. He goes from behind, hugs her ,leaving her astonished completely. She pampers him and immediately goes to the kitchen to bring the hot chocolate milk with cinnamon buns. The mother and the son enjoy the time and for the rest of the day. Mumkin helps his mother with laundry and dishes. She tries to shower as much love as she could on her son. There is a transgender elderly coulple who lives in Mumkin's neighbourhood . They come to meet and bless Mumkin. Evening he visits each and every household of his village to meet them and seek out to give any assistance if needed.At night he had this conversation with his mother-

Mrs. Chamburt: Mumkin, how's committee work going?

Mumkin: Mom, it's a mission, something similar to what dad did!

Mrs. Chamburt hugs Mumkin and reveals her fear of losing him. In return Mumkin makes a commitment to his mother that once the committee work is over,he'll be back home and he'll take her to the place where his mother met his father for the first time and to the second place where both of them got married.

The next day Mumkin goes to meet Laila at Amrisk's shop. Amrisk has hired two students of Himbertown University who are working part time in his shop. As usual Amrisk is ready with a cup of coffee with his long conversations. Mumkin and Laila sit along with him and he keeps on talking about the dead and burials. About how he managed this shop with his father, the financial crises, name changing and the hefty trust of the military on the shop etc..etc..!Laila is a good listener however, she's exhausted from listening to him uninterruptedly. Once Amrisk moves near the cashier counter to handle a customer who's into bargaining. Laila and Mumkin hide away from Amrisk and run towards the second storey of the shop. They talk for four hours hiding behind the last book shelf. As they return back to the ground floor, they spot Amrisk standing outside as he's about to close the shop! They come in front of him and plead not to lock them with their sweet apologies. Amrisk smiles and tells them ,in fact he's sorry for loquacious talk and not letting the couple spend precious time with each other disregarding the fact that they're meeting after a long time only for one day before Mumkin leaves back to Military training. Amrisk opens up the back door,and hands over the keys to Laila, so that after spending the time together she can return the keys to him tomorrow. The couple thanked him. They spent two more hours together ,holding hands and sitting quietly ,just feeling their presence. Laila shares her personal history that how in her childhood her mother was an adultress and she cheated on another man, leaving her father and her and younger brother in despondency due to which she was abstained from mother's love. As she shares her vulnerability with Mumkin, he gives her a snug hug.

Pamela doesn't want to see her parents as it will be difficult for her to leave them behind to go for the mission. She, on the other hand, goes with Ray and Sim in Tonio village . They all sit together in a horse tonga, they see gigantic farms of grape vines. Ray stops the horse tonga, gets down and plucks a bunch of black grapes that look like sparkling black pearls and taste fresh and sweet . Upon entering the villlage, many people gaze at pamela as she's modern girl with her spick and span looks .She's in a village with poverty and people are looking scruffy. She's like a star in the audience. Ray and Sim introduce her to others in the village, make her meet their families and on the first day she spends her day near the river bank, catching fishes with Sim and Ray. She is wearing a red color cap with a truffled long skirt and white top. The water looks fresh with a great deal of fish caught.Afternoon she joins the hand of three village cooks.She chopped onions, garlic ,mushrooms and broccoli. Sim and Ray rinse the fishes, remove scale and intestines of fishes. The cooks set up the firewood cookstoves to cook the conventional dish named kahjupzi, Tonio's version of fish curry . The first day was spent in amusement. Pamela is elated after tasting the tropic flavors used in the kahjupzi. Next day she went near a paramount location of the village. It is a ten cross ten feet room where the Military transmission happens.There's a checkpost forty feet above the ground on which three soldiers are sitting ,completely in combat uniform with their fully loaded assault rifles in right hand and binoculars on left hand . She climbs up the checkpost. One soldier hands over his binoculars to show Piklin is the city where Watson is presently residing . He also shows the road that connects Piklin City to Tonio and then Tonio to Surae village. The soldier informs them that the mission might start from either Tonio or Surae as per orders. He shows the direction towards Marvo village where Watson and malefactors are wrecking everything. From there the trio move to the nearby church where they find a church father who blesses them with holy water .The church's chapel is fully embellished alluringly. Father informs them that it is for a wedding the next day. Pamela looks excitable. She entreats the church father if she could also become an indispensable part of the marriage. Ray, Sim and court father looked muddled, she reexplained saying that she wishes to be married ,just now. For a second, Sim and Ray are shocked and they start to chuckle.

Ray: I just can't stop laughing. Are you serious? Why such a swerve? I'm surprised. I mean the burning question is to whom do you want to be married?

Sim: Yes, is it someone you're seeing in Tonio?

Pamela: We'll be going on a mission tomorrow. I believe that it is the right time to enjoy this time in a brimful manner. Regarding my groom, any one of you can opt for it! Why not you Sim?

Sim is astonished as he doesn't know what to say. They think that it's a kind of shaggy dog story.

Ray: We'll why Sim? Why not me?

Pamela: You too can join Ray. So I will have two husbands.

Father : Child(referring to Pamela) you cannot marry two men at the same time.

Pamela: Father, I want to be married today, it's been my childhood dream. Probably in the future, I might not even be alive tomorrow.

Father: I understand your emotions. Infact, you can be married under the will of god. Sim and Ray will be your groom's best man. You can wear the wedding gown and accessories in the nearby house.

Sim and Ray arrange flowers for Pamela. The nearby house had a kind middle aged woman with no kids. She dresses her up and does the farding job. Pamela looks lovely,Sim and Ray have their jaws starkly open upon seeing her in the white wedding dress .She's decorated with white roses and gold jewelry. Sim hands flowers to her. Both Sim and Ray walk along with her . Upon reaching near the prayer place, father reads out the sermon which starts with a message "love is kind, love is creation and …….".Father blesses Pamela,Ray and Sim lay their hands and bow their heads to support Pamela and her invisible husband in case of any trouble. She exchanges vows to herself about being supportive to her invisible husband in case of any adversary.For the unity ceremony she hugs herself and kisses flowers..Father pronounces the wedding . They call the village cooks and Pamela gives the list of items to be cooked including a few traditional dishes of the village and sweets that are of five tyles. Evening they offer the feast in the village for her wedding. The village band plays folk music using fiddle, accordion, squeezebox and melodeon. Group of girls dress up Pamela in white and red traditional costume with a crown made of gold and silver. They bring sticks, handkerchiefs and colorful ribbons .Making her sit at the center in a chair and they start performing dance on the folk music. It is the traditional custom of Tonio village that they celebrate marriage by making the couple sit at the center of stage and considering them king and queen for that particular day.Pamela thinks that finally she is also wed. She feels she is exonerated into a fierce, intrepid and astute person as now all she needs to focus is on her expedition, her personal life is already absolute. Ray shows the traditional sword of their village that has been used for the last ten centuries in his village, the sword chops off the head of the enemy like a corn removed from its plant. At night when the first night for Pamela arrives ,she is given a small room decorated with flowers and filled with chocolates, cookies and dry fruits etc. Her bed is filled with rose and Jasmine flowers. As the girl who walks along with her inside her room chuckles after looking at her. She smiles at herself in the mirror with shyness. She closes the door and puts on a light pink blanket on herself. She feels the high sexual urge so she finally masterbates rubbing her clitoris and sleeps with peace.

On the other hand Ren spends the two days while going for a cruise with Madeline funded by her father as both of them have manifested love for each other. Ren has given a word of honor to her that once their mission is complete, he'll marry her and they will have at least ten babies together as they believe that for them a cricket team would be enough to keep their endearment vigorous.

John Grez meets Stella in her bakery.They became one the second time in that tempo. During the same evening he took a bus towards his parent's house in Himbertown. He rangs the bell and it's his dad who opens the door. He's a man with a big gut and golden spectacles with chains. As John hugs his father upon seeing him at the door.

John:Dad, I missed you and mom.

His father takes a step back,pushes him away and looks at him with suspicion.

Mr. Grez: What have you come here to get now?

John: Daddy, I'm sorry that I couldn't meet your expectations of joining the business school of Himbertown. But I got thousands of meaningful experiences to tell. One of them is the committee selection process.

Mr. Grez: I know your poppycock conversations! You've come here for two things-one to make a monkey out of your mom by scrounging my money and second is to eat food for free here. For how many days are you planning to do this misdemeanor.

John: I am not here either for scrounging your money or for free food. In Fact I thought of paying for my food and lodging in the house for one day and two nights, but now I think, I should rather spend the same amount of money on food from pantries and sleep in the park. Can I get one blanket from my bedroom so that I can leave?

Mr. Grez: Pay for it! Also think about returning the thousands of dollars that we've spent in your education.

John: I thought staying away from you for a few months will change your heart, fill it up with longing to see me, but you haven't changed a bit. Same money mindset who wants to slurp me away. And for now, get a shovel. I will pay from my boot polish allowance.

Mr. Grez: Whatever, at your age, one needs to prepare to be a manager, lawyer and accountant etc. They have the most dazzling girlfriends. But what are you doing? Nothing, you joined that stupid psychology cheap course. Remember, like this you'll die of hunger.

Mr. Grez goes inside to get a blanket. John still stands there with an empty bottle in his hand. He's hesitating to ask for water. Mrs. Grez,who's John's stepmother has a little degree of presbycusis,she comes out to check if someone is at the door. However she's pleased to see John, she gives in hugs and kisses on both sides of his cheeks. Meanwhile John's father comes out with a blanket, he separates John from his step mother. Finally John decides to hide away all the information about the committee. As he plans to sleep in the park, his stepmother quarrels with his father and convinces him to let John stay in the house for at least one day. She showers her love on him and his father maligns him for not being a good son, not getting a white collar job and calling him an insufficient young man! And throws him out of the house at night 1PM. John despises his father for this act. He takes his bag and goes to the nearby park as he opens his bag, he finds a cozy blanket inside thinking that his stepmother might have kept it inside. But in reality it was his father who kept the blanket. John's stepmother is like a chameleon who's internally envious of John, as he's the heir of the ancestral property of the Grez family as the decision was taken by John's grandfather before dying. Her three children own only three fourth of the property that is owned by their father Mr. Grez. The owner of rest one fourth is again John Grez. She doesn't want to leave a chance to harm John Grez and his father is aware of it. Thus his father has been behaving evil with him since his childhood in order to keep him away from the house and his step mother.

The next day John visits his University, where he keeps his identity concealed with help of Sylin, who's carbon copy of John in looks. Stylin takes balky leave by staying back in the hostel ,whereas John goes in to attend the Management classes in place of him. The only stumbling block was the tanning and body thinning of John due to Military training. So he wears a black colored hoodie of Stylin, which he normally wears and he keeps his face hidden non stop. Management classes where he attends classes about strategic management, human resource management and risk management etc were awesome according to him. He decides that once the Military mission gets over, he'll continue his ambition of starting his own business. While going back to the hostel ,he's thunderstuck to see Bessy and Larry together walking down the stairs from the front building towards the campus cafeteria !John hastens towards them, hiding away his face with a hoodie .They enter the cafeteria where each round table has four seats. As they occupy a table sitting next to each other ,John just sits at a table just behind them to listen to their conversation. However, apart from their University research product and deciding upon the order from the menu and appreciating the taste of filtered coffee ,he doesn't find anything.Finally John decides to confront them. He walks towards their table and occupies one of the seats facing front of them.

John: You guys may not know me, I am Stylin from the management course. When did you all join the University as from the past three months I didn't see you both. Also ,please don't mistake me for asking such a question. It's my younger brother who wants to join the University as he doesn't like the present course in another college.

Bessy: You don't have to introduce yourself to John like this! Also stop lying that you're Stylin and you have a younger brother.

John: Are you guys able to recognize me? How?

Larry: Although you are tanned and have a scrawny appearance. However we remember the despicable visit that you guys did with Lieutenant Adwer just a few months before!

John: How did you guys reach here in University again?

Bessy: After months of being in prison, we were given another opportunity to live a normal life. Larry realized that he was brainwashed by Tiger Watson's men. So Colonel Hielmaster sent us for rehabilitation and counseling .Let bygones be bygones . Finally gave us a chance to complete our courses at Himbertown University and live a normal life.

John spends some time with them and then leaves towards his hostel.

Benny goes to his grandparents house. They love him strongly as he is the only apple of their eyes . Ever since Benny's parents have divorced, he's dependent on his grandparents' endearment. His father has been visiting him infrequently for the last ten years.

It is the time for all five seniors of the Military training camp to show their comradeship in spite of the fact that all of them come from broken ,fragmented and deficient homes. It's the same as establishing a warrior from tragedy.

On the third day morning all five seniors with Sim and Ray meet in front of the Military training camp. The juniors and Tonio youth will arrive tomorrow. Sergeant takes them to Cafeteria where they have their breakfast. Due to sleeping in the park, John has fever and loose motions, so he is sent to the clinic where he is diagnosed with dengue. Because of his bad health the mission was further postponed to commence after a week. The next day all the juniors and youth of Tonio join back. Next week's training is abyss. The four seniors excluding John are taken to a forest ,left in the middle of it where they learn basic survival skills with zero food but only one liter of water with each person and no weaponry support. Their task is to come out of the jungle before six in the evening. Mumkin and Ren use their map reading skills to spot directions and the starting point.It is all boiling hot, their water bottles are already empty. Mumkin also figures out the water point on the map where they refill their bottles.Upon reaching the place, they find a dried pond where they can find fishes swimming only in their fantasy. There's muddy water that they fill up. They find plum and mango trees with a few ripped fruits on them. Pamela ,the toxophilite of the group, plucks out the fruits by throwing stones . They satiate themselves and take a rest for half an hour before continuing their journeys. They reach the starting point of the jungle before fifteen minutes. As an award of task completion they get to eat an appetizing meal upon which they hoover.

The next day of training was climbing a modest hill with jotting stones and rough terrain . With that drill, firing, navigation, close quarter combat techniques, martial arts, stress management techniques, meditation ,archery and swimming training continues where John also joins them on the fourth day after his dengue recovery. That day another task of cleaning the stinking tail of horses was given, that proved to be the backbreaking work. The intensity of all tasks increases thousands of times as now they involve their juniors and Tonio youth in it, creating ruckus as now it's over two hundred people working together to achieve all the tasks. However they all complete all the tasks successfully.

The next day is the day of their departure towards the main mission which will be explained to them before they leave the camp. They'll depart with their trainee juniors to various locations as per assigned by their companies. At night two am, Mumkin, Pamela, John, Benny ,Ren ,Ray and Sim meet up in the cooking area basement to celebrate their final day of being together as they don't know who will be placed where due to plan change!They make a painting together of five seniors with Ray and Sim standing at both extreme sides and all the juniors standing behind . In the middle of the painting is Sergeant Kroodie,their trainer waving a flag, manifesting their victory. They drink a glass of beer hooraying each other anticipating their victory!

On the other hand, in the mind of Tiger Watson ,the murder of Captain Lidiya Ceriyan by his hoodlums is a highly guarded affair. He did not swell after reportage in the newspaper about the death of his business partner Bison. Bison was a crackerjack in business and ingenious in various deals, enriching man to Watson when it came to Business partnership. So terminating him wasn't Watson's preference. But after his death ,it's uncomplicated to assassinate poor Ren who was the heir of Bison and usurp every single thing that belonged to Bison. For him it is a zenith cadence where he has the best of both worlds. As Tiger and his father are in zenith enjoying their seventh heaven, Lidiya with Colonel Hielmaster are preparing their entombment.Captain Lidiya has amended the whole plan.

The next day all are bedecked in their combat uniforms. Colonel Hielmaster arrives in his black Porsche car. The first thing he does is to make everyone do a hundred pushups saying "Dear seniors and trainees,probably this is the last punishment of this Military training committee, however it can be the last punishment of your life too!Be positive. It's the last punishment of your life from my side. Next time you will be able to punish your juniors and I might be transferred to a different place.We meet until my retirement. Come on! Go for a century ,with each soar give a roar 'royalty with loyalty' ".With a gusto each senior and trainee crowned each pushup blaring up the battle cry. Now it is the time to divide seniors of Himbertown University into various tasks and split up Marvo youth and juniors of the military along with them.

Everyone was doing hundred pushups.On the 99th push up,the second Mumkin gasps to breathe, Sergeant Kroodie comes near him with a big shining appetizing chocolate ball and he puts it inside Mumkin's mouth. On seeing that few more people obviously open their mouths to taste the luscious , Sergeant Kroodie repeats the same act with them ,filling their mouths with chocolate balls. Their faces turn red in flustering as the chocolate ball is actually a mud ball with a twist of sand and pebbles stones. Colonel Hielmaster says "A treat for those who asked for it. Bastards, a second of rest will sieve your chest with bullets. Circumspection !". Sergeant Kroodie hands over the list of names to him where he reads it out : "Congratulations to all five seniors . Their tentative ranks , company names, place of duty and task allotment is declared, so come up forward and wear prestigious badges unveiling your names with ranks:

Cadet Under Officer Mumkin and Cadet under officer Ren, C for Charlie Company, role is combat, Cadet Junior Under Officer Pamela, A for Alpha Company ,role is combat and weaponry supply, Counseling and rehabilitation. Cadet Sergeant John, S for Sierra Company, role is ration supply ,administration and weaponry supply in case of emergency. Cadet Corporal Benny,N for Nurture Company ,role is combat and rehabilitation concomitantly during the time of mission. Cadet Lance Corporal Ray ,Alpha Company, role is nurture ,administration and weaponry supply.

During the mission follow the order of seniors on the report of hierarchy. In case of discrepancy slash rebuff, the heretic will face immediate damnation. Cadet Under Officer Mumkin ,Cadet Under Officer Ren, Cadet Junior under officer Pamela, Cadet Sergeant John and Cadet Lance Corporal Ray will go to Diewa first, which is a Military base with an armory to inspect and stockpile weaponries. Same afternoon, the second destination is to go to Surae , 160 km away from Diewa to take a team of healthcare , combat , ration and ammunition supply troops. All four teams are trained and edified under Captain Lidiya Cheriyan .Cadet Under Officer Mumkin will visit the Air force base prior to avail for dropping off soldiers including newly recruited (referring to junior trainees) near the entrance point of Marvo village which has exorbitant security by Watson, henceforth river bridge plan rebuked. An undercover named 'Bull's Eye' will pave the way to Marvo and provide Cadet Senior Under Officer Mumkin with a map of Marvo village,elucidating it meticulously in task .Divide team, only few enter Marvo to read the state of affairs and others stay back till indication by the ones who already entered. Upon entering of first few folks the village,they keep identity hidden.Task is to destroy again the ten bases of Malefactors present on the map that are training centers of Watson .Paramount heed to be given to safeguard life of each villager .All three cadet officers- Mumkin, Pamela and Ren execute the above two tasks.Cadet Senior Under Officer Ren, collect concurrent evidence of abuse on villagers of Marvo by Watson. Cadet Sergeant John, administers the ration ,weaponry and healthcare supply in case of emergency. He is the ascendant in an emergency. The second ascendant cum succour to him is Cadet Lance Corporal Ray. Predominant person, Cadet Corporal Benny will be in combat role and concurrently will administer the regular supply of ration and ammunition and rehabilitation with Cadet Sim i.e.once the mission is achieved -opening closed schools, taking care of the farming sector and skill development cum job creation of villagers.Benny and Tonio village will forter their support in the rehabilitation of Marvo villagers. Pamela, mainly superintendent for counseling and mental rehabilitation. Coeval mission,paramount : Captain Lidiya and Mumkin slithering to Piklin within three days of first mission to do coeval mission viz to ambush Watson. By today afternoon ,a convoy will move to Tonio. My reiteration and your enshine that all alterations from previous plan, i.e. this time no use of roads or bridge of river to reach Marvo as restricted ways will be used ,apprised military archangels anterior to start of mission."

Col Hielmaster further divides the Tonio youth and the junior trainees under 20-24 under each senior. In five military airless trucks the convoy moved to Diewa city directly. They stopped near a huge building in the midst of the houses and market, there isn't any clue if it is Military base in reality or not as usually they are in a segregated location. There are twenty stories of the building and the five seniors need to climb the eighteenth floor to meet the seniors present there. The juniors are climbing steps ,following the seniors. However in between a person of Corporal rank stops them, asking the juniors to step back ,go downstairs and run fifty rounds of the building to warm up till the time seniors arrive back.The reason was juniors can't enter the building as one of the MIlitary rules. Upon reaching the eighteenth storey, the five seniors are gasping for air. There comes out Colonel Pasha, who orders them to visit the ammunition cartridge space which is in a colossal room in the backyard of the building! The room was filled with rifles, grenades and two cannons. All juniors are asked to pick their rifles, remember the numbers and visit the firing range series wise in groups of ten to inspect its accuracy. Cadet Lance corporal ensures that order of Cadet under officer Mumkin is followed. They clean the rifles and get ready to cock it in the air to ensure there isn't any bullet from prior shooting practice. Pamela goes near a junior cadet and slaps him tightly on his head with the way he's holding because his rifle's nozzle was pointing towards him during the cleaning process. She orders all of them to keep the rifles on the ground and hold their hands at their back, bend such that their heads rub the ground. This painful discipline is keeping the junior trainees in tank position. After two minutes as the junior trainees come back to their standing position, they feel dizzy as the blood rushes to their heads. She orders them to hold the rifle while standing perpendicular to the targets in the nearby firing range, keeping their legs and shoulders wide apart. For others it was a dry fire, but for the same junior trainee, a bullet popped out of his barrel and it hit the target straight away. He gets panic stricken for a second. Cadet junior under officer Mumkin arrives there and recapitulates that a rifle is just like a spouse, one has to keep it close .However the barrel of it should always face the enemy!

Mumkin prepares a list of weaponaries to stockpile after consulting his complement Ren. He ordered Cadet Corporal Ren to list down the cadets with their rifle number. With that he takes bombs, grenades, missiles, warheads and bullets etc and requests Colonel Pasha to make an arrangement of cannon in case needed in emegency hereafter and Corporal Ren will be intermediary for bestowing of the same. After the lunch they loaded the ammunition in a heavy armored vehicle in between the other vehicles where Mumkin and John were escorting it, in other regular trucks with logistics of cadets handled by Ren ,Pamela, Benny, Ray and Sim . They ensure the mobility of the convoy to avert any attack. They keep lethal weapons handy especially in high risk areas. Mumkin took prior measures of regrouping the quick reaction team with formidable confronting and blowing away the muggers or assailanters .He and the other ten were in ceaseless connection with the intelligence on walkie talkie and remote sensors, in advance he gathered and presented the information to those ten people. The Air Force was also doing air surveillance on helicopters. With no harm, in the afternoon they reached the entrance of Surae. A dilapidated place which was once ruled by Watson. They, at full tilt, set up their tent houses. There isn't a single winged bird, quietude. Mumkin divides the tasks among the rank holders with a deadline of 5PM. Each senior will have two juniors assigned for veritable tasks except for Pamela . On Military bullets with his black shining goggles on ,he takes his trajectory towards the paramount task.

Pamela visits the hospital to take the team of doctors and nurses to handle the emergency! She rides a bicycle to discover a tumbledown place which has the hospital sign. She gets inside ,where a guard wearing combat gear stops her. She introduces herself as the Military cadet at the rank of Cadet Junior Under officer. He doesn't trust her as her combat uniform is of black color .She then displays the insignia on her shoulders of Himbertown Military, due to which he allows her. She finds nobody in the hospital, the guard informs her that the team has already left to meet the concerned person and she'll waste her time in searching for them here as it's been two hours. Pamela gets suspicious about him after hearing the whispering sound coming from somewhere inside. Upon inquiring the guard refuses to reveal anything, so she gets inside the building again. As she climbs the stairs, the whispering is increasing . Now it's clear that there's something off with the medical team as none of them are present here. The voice is clamorous now as if a group is talking about committing the felony .She is getting inclined towards self defense instinct as she reaches the third floor.The guard has also furiously followed her. It's a long hall with shining chunks of fragmented glass. She takes out her gun and asks the guard to keep quiet , she moves towards the room and upon getting inside she finds no one. The guard is dumbstruck too. There's still a voice coming from the room. Bewildered, she climbs the loft to uncover a walkie talkie that is on. The guard starts to chortle. She finds it funny too that it was the walkie talkie from which so much of sound was coming. She tells the guard to stop laughing, keeps the walkie talkie in her pocket and rides back the bicycle to the tent area to locate the healthcare team.

There too she finds no one, except her junior trainees with Sim as the caretaker of junior trainees. She inquires about others and the healthcare team if they arrived here! But Sim informs her that everyone is following the orders of Mumkin ,all have left for their tasks .Nobody has arrived here. Pamela decides to wait there. On the other hand, Ren visits the Combat unit which he doubted to be operating inside the ramshackled areas . He took two juniors on a Military truck along with the driver with him. He sat on the passenger seat with a mission to reconnoiter until they found a dead road with a precipitous valley upon seeing which soul would jump out of the body and recoil back like a slinky. Ren finds that in the map, it's written Surae Armory base but in reality the area is at such a height that it's fully covered with clouds. No one knows what is down.There is a dead road that stops near the area. He gets down the truck to peep,what lies after the dead road, it was even craggier. It was like the Military camp was decamped. As he looks below the clouds, it's all dark green, if you throw a stone down, you'll hear its sound hitting the ground on your deathbed, so steep and deep .He further investigates the map, involving his juniors to see if there's any mistake he made while reading, but their position was ultrafine after a vigilant run through. There came a man wearing a combat Uniform. After seeing him, Ren took a sign of relief as his Uniform's insignia were similar to that of Ren and his two juniors of Himbertown Military. Ren saluted him through his left hand saying "royalty with loyalty". His juniors stood on his left side with the same salute. The soldier too mirrored their actions. He took introduction of Ren and then introduced himself as Corporal kzajjar, who has done five years of service in Himbertown Armoury Unit. He further reveals to them the secret that the valley is just 500 meters height and it's creating an illusion as if it were ten kilometers away down from the this dead road. This place was selected a decade ago by military intellectuals. He asked the driver to bring the truck near the dead road and keep the engine on , along with Ren and juniors, he pushed the truck. Now on the dead road ,the front two tires of the truck are in the air and the behind ones are still on the dead road until he asks the driver to turn to low gear. With another thrust the truck is in the air and all four of them clinge through the protrusions of the truck and now everyone's heart is pumping ,with a potent jerk, the truck is moving downhill with speed of a roller coaster and within a span of five minutes they reach a impenetrable forest through which the Military truck got accessorized with barks ,stems and leaves of the trees. They reached the Military Armory Camp of Himbertown which is located in this dark jungle. That is the reason that when John peeped near the dead road, he noticed everything green. Upon reaching down, their eyes couldn't believe what they saw. Inside the jungle was an immense area with various sectors of wireless internet, agriculture, coal ,mining ,iron and steel. It looks like infinite land from all other three sides, like a huge maze! Ren asked Corporal kzajjar about the number of industries and area of military operating here, his answer was everyday is metamorphosis and innovation here, so he himself isn't aware about the number of Industries operating. Also he's just a diminutive corporal here, high ranking officers and professionals working here must be aware about the complete information .But the Military intelligence has built its base here only. Ren observes industrious soldiers with civilians with a strong likelihood of belonging to Diewa village. All working in conjunction. Even four to five workers with threadbare looks, working with hydraulic presses and carrying mine carts had their limbs amputated. Ren asked if it happened due to accidents due to working in mine, however Corporal Kxajjar informs him that it's due to their involvement in the war with Watson's malefactors .They are still working with their desire to serve more like jingoism towards their country. One man had lost his eye too. Corporal Kxajjar suffused that they were once soldiers who wore Uniforms and upon becoming disabled, the Military is paying them adequately so that they can take care of their family. Ren asked him if they can be given any other work as working in Mine needs more huskiness. His answer was that they have been allotted in preponderance departments here based on their possible course of action.

As Ren,Corporal Kxajjar and the two junior trainees, entered the Military Ammunition unit, it was similar to the ammunition of their Military camp, but tenfold of the size. They met the senior official. Not only did they get an extra ammunition of four tankers but also ten grenades and sixteen snipers . They were gifted with the twenty deferential ,hale and heath soldiers wearing steep dark combat with dark google . They came along with them after the passing of the order of Commanding officer of Military Armory Camp.He gets to interact with them. They had astounding fighting talent. They claim to be trained by Captain Lidiya Cheriyan and Colonel Hielmaster. While returning back, there's something peculiar in the map i.e. the AirForce center was almost clashing with the Military Ammunition Unit. He discerns that there is no way for Mumkin to enter this place as he recalls the entrance is sort of impossible to breach. They all reach the Diewa training center with all ammunition and accomplished soldiers.

Mumkin rides to the Air Force Base of Diewa. He finds a huge gate with the name "Diewa Air Force training and Combat Center ".The guard wearing the blue uniform doesn't inquire about anything but let's Mumkin inside where there is number 8 squadron situated .He meets the Squadron Leader Danial Joshua ,a handsome air force officer wearing the blue flight suits with his black goggles on.He's flight instructor who trains young pilots . He takes Mumkin for a quick round around the base while informing him that there are twenty aircrafts with one twenty hundred airmen and twenty six officers. Out of those aircrafts, there are four for transport ,six for training and the rest are bomber, fighter and reconnaisance. He displays his three helicopters which will be able to accommodate thirty crew members. Mumkin discusses the time ,place, region and secrecy involved in dropping the soldiers. They go to a guest room where he asks Mumkin ``The entrance to this place is an uphill task.Even overachievers and champions fail to enter here after the dead end road until Diewa Military sends helpmeet to them, but to my surprise you were on time . How did you manage to arrive?". Mumkin replies "Even I got tumultuous after seeing the road, however I read in one of the Military Journal from the exclusive library of the Military training center that sometimes a dead end isn't actually what's visible ,through that idea I made my way". He appreciates Mumkin's brilliance.

After some time ,a team of five doctors, ten nurses, four ambulances with medical facilities like first aid, mini lab for testing, medicines and blood banks etc arrieve near the Diewa training center. The doctors are wearing white coats and nurses are wearing white nursing frocks. One of the doctors enters the barracks of seniors where Pamela and Sim are sitting,having coffee. He inquires " who is Cadet junior under officer Pamela". Pamela quickly stands up to reply.

Pamela: I am Pamela, I visited the Diewa Military hospital, but found everyone missing except for the guard. Where were all of you? Do you know the meaning of punctuality ?

Doctor David: Is this you've learnt in your training hitherto? Is this the way to salute seniors?

Doctor David takes off his white coat and underneath is the Military Uniform with rank of Captain and name on the nameplate as " Rabbi David" . Pamela immediately apologizes to him, Sim also stands up and they both salute to him. He looked conceited and replied to Pamela "No one asked you to come to receive me and my team . We went to the Medical Lab for our vaccination and to prepare for the vaccination of the trainee cadets starting with you both(referring to Pamela and Sim)". He makes them set a table, takes out his medical box with cotton and vaccination shots to prevent diseases like blood infections, measles ,rubella and tetanus etc. Starting with Pamela, he injects vaccination shot on her arm followed by Sim whose spooked of injection since his childhood. It hurts ten times more for him than Pamela. Both of them make arrangements for the trainee cadets to get vaccinated. As their vaccination is almost half done in an hour, Pamela gets a mild fever. Dr, David upon inquiry gives her medicines to build immunity as these are her menstruating days.

On the other hand, John and Benny with two other junior trainee cadets go near the Military ration store in a luggage cart , they find a small ration store with two soldiers sitting inside. John gives them the list of items to be procured to one of the soldiers. In return the soldier calls two more soldiers from inside and fills the luggage cart with two hundred packets each of bread, wheat flour, oil, canned fish ,pineapple, rice , milk powder and coffee etc in tonnes. The luggage cart is overloaded, its movement is encumbered. The soldier gives them around eighty packets of peanut butter toffees with an abundance of energy drinks, but there isn't any place to keep anything. Benny sits next to the driver and John with juniors sit inside the luggage cart over the rice packets and reach the Diewa training center like a bobble head doll.

Upon reaching they get themselves vaccinated by healthcare staff after keeping the ration to the store room. By five pm all the four tasks related to the Diewa training center are done! The trainee soldiers under the leadership of Pamela and Sim, cooked pasta,chicken pie with watermelon juice , egg sandwiches and coffee. The food was insipid in taste due to overdose of salt and other indispensable flavors, everyone ate it except the healthcare workers with a doctor as the disparager calling them "atrocious cooks". They just had watermelon juice and peanut butter with bread. This time the sleeping time was 6:30PM to 9PM. This time each cadet was given a separate space to sleep made by all five seniors .They tied thick ropes all across the sleeping hall,thus creating three hundred square shaped chambers of eight feet each. This was done so that all trainee cadets can sleep at a distance in a reticent manner from each other! This physical rest is paramount for the far reaching future. Mumkin ,Ren and John ensure that everyone sleeps by taking an uninterrupted superintendent of their sleep. They go to sleep after half an hour.

CHAPTER TEN

Do or die!

At 9:30PM all of them are woken up by a siren's sound, they start wearing the battlefield uniform(camouflage) with their unloaded rifles in their hands with an ammo belt each. The quick reaction team headed by Mumkin and Ren are ready with their fifty soldiers consisting of twenty soldiers from Military Armory Camp, ten Tonio youth and ten Military soldiers who are teenagers and ten trainee cadets. All these have breathtaking dogfaces. John stays back with Ray for ration ,weaponry supply in emergency and administers the four tankers, five grenades and ten sniper rifles in reserve to use promptly in case of emergency. Pamela , Benny and Sim got ready for combat roles with five juniors each under them. The rest of the human resource stayed back with John and Ray so that they could be readily available for the mission wherever needed in future. They shout loudly ""royalty with loyalty" and start running towards the Military truck, three in number that accomodated all seventy of them and in that stark dark where the chilling breeze was thrusting them, the intensity got ten times with blades rotating about a vertical axis creating bombastic sound! For the first time Mumkin and Pamela, along with a preponderance of trainee cadets sat in a helicopter. The pilots were ready with their black helmets, gloves and black flight suit with Diewa Air Force wings. Two air crew members in each helicopter are wearing combat camouflage patterns. The two helicopters accommodate them. Few cadets were sweating due to the spanking cold breeze, like folks from Alaska are going to track down an inexplicable planet to repulse aliens and save the vernaculars. No one has ever seen Watson and his malefactors. The division of teams is done based on Charlie, Alpha,Sierra and Nurture company.Charlie is headed by Mumkin and Ren. Alpha headed by Pamela ,John is heading Sierra as part of administration and ration supply with Benny heading Nurture with a combat role . These are all tentative roles!

All seventy people reach near the entrance of Marvo in twenty minutes. Upon hearing the sound fifteen kilometers away, the security of Watson present there is alert and it points towards the helicopters. But a man wearing white fur coat and binoculars in hand with the insignia of Watson's malefactor informs them that the helicopter sound is a sign of the arrival of Tiger Watson. He orders the guards to be alert on duty and the illumination of headlight falls on his shoulder with insignia depicting a huge lion and a puppy's head under it .He sits in his Mercedes car at the back seat. He orders the driver to drive towards the helicopter landing area of Marvo. On the way, the driver alternates the route away from the helipad and starts driving in an unheeding way hastily. He points his gun at the driver, the driver removes his cap ,he gets topsy turvy until the car stops. As he gets out, there are some seventy people standing with the majority young population. There arrives another conundrum, a person wearing a completely brown color coat with hoodie on. He's looking robust. The driver removes his white cap again and few of them start grinning like a cheshire cat. He's Colonel Hielmaster in diver's Uniform. Colonel introduces the man to the team as Vicor, who is undercover of Himbertown Military, presently working with Watson mimically. Then he introduces Bull's eye who hands over the map to Mumkin. The Colonel says that bull's eye is the paramount person who will lead the mission. Bull's eye removes his coat , it's Captain Lidiya Cheriyan, who's more sinewy body now. She folds the coat and keeps it on her arm, while addressing them.

Captain Lidiya Cheriyan: This is the first step of the mission. Victor is the chief security officer of Watson. Watson's pseudo devotee. Or a fake devotee of Watson, Three of you will enter Marvo right away. Once the orders from me are given ,the other sixty four will be skulking through a map in an underground tunnel that will eventually lead to Marvo village's lavatory which is non operational. Three going now, will hide the identity ,if in case someone asks, reveal as incarcerated youth held by Watson from Tonio village to work as bonded laborers . Adjust your looks accordingly belonging to the vernaculars of Marvo. Mumkin is to review with Malefactors of Watson with Victor's help,Ren to review with market and business and Pamela to review females and other healthcare workers .Ray will stay back here with the rest. Third day assemble in Marvo slaughterhouse to uproot the ungodly in conjunction." Royalty with loyalty".

Others repeat the same after her. Colonel Hielmaster with Ray go near the underground tunnel which has crude hidden five cross five feet capsules almost fifty in number . Ten are filled with ration and ammunition and three toilets with a deep underground pool for bathing and drinking water.

On the other hand Captain Lidiya wears her coat with a hoodie on. All black glasses of Mercedes are closed .Mumkin,Ren and Pamela sit with Victor, where Lidiya drives them towards Marvo, as they reach back the entrance , the trio bend down in the car, Victor pulls down his window half to order the guards to be vigilant until he escorts Junior Watson to his cottage(closing window immediately). The soldiers salute towards the seat next to Victor assuming Tiger's presence in the car. It's all shiny golden way with pillars on both sides as if made from gold, illuminating diamond gold sparkling light for almost five minutes until they reach a gate named Welcome to Sir Watson's Cottage. The cottage is twenty thousand square meters with forty car parkings, five swimming pools, nine gardens,ballroom, theater and ninety rooms etc with around two hundred workers in total. Any person can be struck in that captivity .Mumkin asks Victor about the mission tied with the cottage. Fascinatingly Captain Lidiya asks Mumkin not to ask now, instead descry ,not the aesthetic but the particulars. They get inside the parking lot of the car that has a dark and narrow hallway leading to the godown filled with grain sacks and a few inches tall unpaid guests scuttling left and right shrouding back somewhere near sacks. There's a soft chappling sound of lizards as they get down. Captain Lidiya calls Mumkin as AV, Ren as Havi and Pamela Kam Bi as their new names for the mission. They are supposed to react naturally assuming that these are their original names. She explains Pamela about her role as healthcare workers trying to help the prostitutes that are bonded by Watson, Ren is the incharge of bondsman in the marketplace. Victor is the first person of contact. Victor distributes the shabby trench coats to them which are their costumes and calls the trisome as the youngest Undercovers of Himbertown Military. He shows them the way towards a public toilet that hasn't been cleaned ,half cemented with sizable wall damps. Smells like rotten fishes or eggs, Victor takes Pamela and Ren along with him . Mumkin stays back with Captain Lidiya, for five seconds they both are muted.

Capt Lidiya:You will work as Janitor boy and laundry maid. Task is to scrutinize the arrival and departure of Watson and his son, particulars of other illicit activities done by them, weaponries possessed, absolute figure of total malefactors and infirmities to apprehend them.The intelligence gathered will be shared at this godown(throwing purple pants and gray shirt with a dust cloth towards Mumkin). Remember that it is a temporary job ,put only acting efforts not the real one.

Mumkin chuckles.

Captain Lidiya gawps and gives a faint smile saying "your smile reminds me of someone", Mumkin replies "I know my father's, my mom says the same".

Her face turns earnest.

Captain Lidiya Cheriyan: Keep the camera inside the trunk coat safe!

As Mumkin puts his hand inside the pocket, there's a bulky button camera inside. As they get ready, Mumkin is given the first task to go to clean the library and find evidence. Victor takes Pamela and Ren in his car . He drops her near the Healthcare center. Women are sitting outside the clinic ,four on chairs ,two standing and others on ground in a hassled state. It's her first time encountering women pitous way, their clothes are torn, few are bleeding , bruises are all over their bodies as if it was their tussle with a saltwater crocodile. Just injured. Her heart splinters to see a man bringing a ten year old bawling with stains on her frock and lacerations on her body. Her one eye is closed with white discharge from it,just excruciating to see it. Upon victor enquiry from one of the healthcare workers, it's Watson's man who has molested and assaulted her as if bitten by ferocious dogs. Victor in melancholy looks at Pamela and whispers to her that this is her work, to stop malefactors, rescue and rehabilitate women of Marvo . The man who came with the girl to the hospital was her father. Pamela too is in desolation now. Victor takes Pamela inside of clinic where he introduced her to the Doctor Emma as Kam Bi sent by Watson to monitor women in healthcare and prostitute house and do the survey on count, marital status and child status etc as Watson's men want the A-1 quality in data. Dr. Emman looks at him in repugnance. He leaves from there. Ren, who's waiting in the car, sees countless boys of his age in an excruciating state on the road. Victor informs him that it's Watson who makes young boys work till dire and then hurls them here. Few come to only healthcare of Marvo in a hankering that out of two hundred standing in their front, they will also be catered for medical service some day. Few die here on the road and few survive but their bodies are just on their last legs. The medical facility given here to the patients is like someone getting a lottery ticket. Most luckiest ones get it. Only one hospital, one doctor and three nurses are present here. They're just not able to save lives despite their best efforts as the facilities of healthcare are breadcrumbing by Watson to its people.

He takes Ren to the Market . Just like Pamela, he told Watson's men, sitting in the various shops for revenue collection, that Havi(Ren) is here to monitor every shop and do the survey. He is sent by Tiger Watson. Ren kept his button cameras in his pockets and Victor kept them inside the car . He further explains Ren secretively the way to use it. Victor goes to the Chief Security officer at Watson's Cottage. He informs him that Tiger Watson brought three laborers from Tonio village named as A V, Havi and Kam bi (Mumkin, Ren and Pamela). But he tells him that due to their good educational qualification from Tonio, they've been given roles . He further adds that there are some eight more workers to join . He displays the fake record book for the same. He displays five extra fake names which don't exist.

Chief Security Officer(flipping through the record book): Everyday there are plenty of butterflies and cockroaches come here, you don't have to show each one of them. (immediately closes the record book as he hears from guard the sound that Watson's car is arriving).

He runs to welcome Watson. Victor runs towards the recreational room to announce "Sir Watson is arriving, all servants in service" Mumkin was mopping the floors and Lidiya was ironing clothes, they leave the work there itself and run towards the window of tenth floor that has a balcony and a transparent glass through which they can peep in. They see a guy , six feet tall with long hair and a huge beard all silver in color. He's surrounded by at least ten bodyguards. As Mumkin tries to take a photo of Watson by taking out the camera, the manager comes across, throws his camera on floor and smashes it into tiny pieces by pressing his foot on it. Lidiya watches far from behind in exasperation at the Manager, He tells Mumkin "You, kiddo stop playing with your third or fourth hand broken ass camera and start working, if you're seen again like this, you'll be thrown out from here!". Mumkin in dispondenly starts mopping the floor, Lidiya takes a step back and takes lift to the ground floor. She takes the pillow covers in hand from one of the bedrooms and goes near the reception area where she finds the guy from Watson's car going inside the conference room along with his security and a few other people, all of whom are men. As Lidiya gets near the conference room, she gets stopped by the receptionist at gunpoint, he inquires from Lidiya of what she's doing and who she is. In return Victor arrives to defend Lidiya by betting that She's a deaf and dumb mother of a child named AV, two out of eight people brought by Tiger Watson to work at Watson's cottage. All she's searching for is Watson's room to fix new pillow covers. The receptionist refuses to tell by saying there's already a maid working for it.

Victor to receptionist :She is the mother of the partially deaf and but fully dumb shouldn't come as a hurdle while making the maid do the work. In Fact she can be helping her. Now she's in the laundry but try to use her everywhere .Make Sir Watson's room maid as her mentor at work and attach her in parties work too as I firmly believe that these differently abled are just awesome at industrious labor!

The receptionist brings the bell and from there a young lady aged in mid thirties comes. Her eyes are wet and swollen, face is fully red with slight vexing on her face. The receptionist orders the maid to tell the various roles played here and ensure that she becomes her image by the end of two days.

The receptionist takes Lidiya with her in the laundry, Watson's room made looks downcasted .Both collect golden color bedsheets and pillow covers and they move towards the third floor where at one extreme corner, there's a hall, inside which there is a room and another room inside it,there lies bedroom of Watson, with theme color of blue and orange ,the room would be six thousand square feet with as rare as hen's teeth items. A gold vase with violet flowers, mannequins carved on stone wearing skirts of diamonds, the roof has ursa major constellation with

Pictures of young watson kissing his guns after murdering people. His sofa is made up of rhino's and lion's skin. There's a 3-D mirror with which you can see yourself 360 degrees. The maid starts changing the pillow cover and whimpers simultaneously. She starts mumbling "I am doing work here just to save myself! I am being a mianslay here, that's why they haven't assaulted me till now, not even a single female worker could pull through here,all are either incapacitated till death or sent in blight state to brothels, you partially deaf woman should've eaten poison in Tonio rather than been brought upto Marvo. They didn't spare my ten years old niece, who assaulted her pitilessly yesterday(weeps)(referring to the assaulted girl that Pamela saw in the hospital). Just do your work in an idealist way or else your body will be seen hanging in one of the diamond chandeliers! Don't think about escaping, you'll not only be caught but the death that you'll get heebie-jeebies to imagine what happens hereafter. But you take no worries, I'll teach you things to perfection so that no one can point a finger at you. You'll get luscious food to eat here twice a day,here eat this apple as you look unfed."

She picks apples from Sir Watson's bedroom's refrigerator. Lidiya munches on the apple and observes the maid scrupulously, realizing that she can be way too knowledgeable about Watson and helpful when it comes to breaking any rule just like pilfering Joe Blake's apple.

She speaks further :My name is Eliza, since you're tongue tied so you can't tell your name, so I'll call you maid Ava.(Whispering loudly in ear of Lidiya)

"Do you know Ava, this Watson and his son, mmmm..his son's name is Leopard .....no no... Tiger ...Tiger Watson ,they are the biggest satyrs in this world. Every Sunday they have parties with dances of young girls from brothels followed by squalid acts". Lidiya gets irritated with the loud shuting in her ear, but she finds it climacteric information. Lidiya chokes the apple and starts wheezing, Eliza runs towards the water purifier ,some two hundred meters away muttering "Poor Ava, I shouldn't have intimidated her, but that's not my mistake.I am doing favor on her by telling her the reality . To let her know that this place is the abyss".

Meanwhile, Lidiya takes out her camera and promptly takes pictures. As Eliza comes with a glass of water, Lidiya drinks it placidly.

Mumkin goes near the 4th floor's library to clean the floor. He starts cleaning and alternatively looks at the librarian. The librarian was half asleep sitting with thumb in his mouth. Mumkin drops a few books while cleaning. The librarian comes and slaps him on his neck "you idiot, how dare you to touch even a single library book. Who will clear the mess that you created?". "I will clean it sir, I am literate, I have passed all my primary grades"replies AV(Mumkin). The librarian chuckles and makes jokes about him. Assuming AV is uneducated, he takes out a book to check Mumkin's reading. Mumkin reads it with intentional blunders"The ...h ...ho..hog Hog's.... Histuriyi". But in his mind he read as "The Hog's History". The librarian chuckles,hits Mumkin again and forces Mumkin to read the front page about the synopsis"The hog born in 1915, served in Himbertown Military for twelve years killed our homie. This book is about how rakehell was assassinated. People called this grunter Commander Major Chamburt. ". Mumkin is shocked to read his father's name in the book. The librarian hits him ,gets close to Mumkin's face and says in a chuckling way "More spanking, better reading!, now keep all books in order as just now you graduated in english. A single mistake will ruin your life" . Mumkin reads the 359 page of a book mentioned about his father, where he gets aggrieved because cuss words are used for his dad. More astounding things are mentioned about his mother,the way his parents met, his own birth and his relationship with Lidiya Cheriyan. The book ends with a note "Probing to liquidate hog and slut's son,drink his fresh blood.". The book is from 1940, when Mumkin would be 5 years old . He searches for other books there, all related to Himbertown University , Watson's business , and his capture in various cities and towns. He surprisingly finds another book based on Lidiya Cheriyan calling her a harlot(slut). Mumkin gets shocked for a second to read revelations -first Lidiya was pregnant when Mumkin's father died and second a prophesy that Lidiya is alive, it was her lover Bison who was murdered. Mumkin's legs are shaking to see the last page, it's written "To be continued till her slaughter". The book was written eighteen years ago and still information has been added in it about Lidiya! The first question that's clicking in his mind is who's the writer of these books and how do they know each and every event about Mumkin's father and Lidiya? He keeps on searching for other books but most are about Watson's achievement in being the Business Tycoon of Himbertown. But in one book he finds the name of the writer, Junior Akiba. The books that Mumkin discovered were completely against his dad and Captain

Lidiya.

It's late at night. Mumkin keeps all books in order , asks the librarian if he knows about the writer of this book, the librarian replies- "You illiterate of Tonio village, just now I taught you reading and you got wings to do literature review on arcane knowledge!".

To this Mumkin replies "Sir, you are a stunning pedagogue that is illiterate like me, starting reading like a scholar. You're a fountain of knowledge. A petty creature like me got enlightened under you today(bowing down with his hands joined together) " says Mumkin.

Mumkin holds his bucket and mop sticks and starts to walk away, the librarian stops him and says "You've recognized me well. You're not a nitwit, don't tell anyone(keeping his spectacles on nose), these books are written by someone very close to Sir Watson. He often visits him here and wears the Uniform of Himbertown military''.

Mumkin returns back to the Godown, he finds Lidiya and Victor working on photos.Since the exposure on camera was a subminiature 16 MM film, they were busy in developing the film .Mumkin goes near Lidiya and informs her about the shocking revelations i.e. the book written about her and Mumkin's father ,all using cuss words. In the former they're probing for Mumkin to assassinate him,but he saw his name nowhere.The writer isn't aware of Mumkin's name. Second thing he asks Lidiya is "Captain, were you expecting during the death of my father?" . Lidiya replies "That's hoax, the reason your mother is safe in Ranidetro with you is because we created a misjudgement in mind of enemy by spreading fake rumors in newspaper - ' fugitive Lidiya, wife of Commander Major Chamburt who sustained injuries in bomb blast is expecting'. This was done, so that people will give sympathy as I was considered a criminal at that time. Slowely more hoax were spreaded- 'Lidiya is not fugitive,it's conspiracy, someone else did deplorable act of killing innocent people(referring to planting bomb at building ,resulting in killing Watson's malefactors)'". Through this way we could remove the aggrieved public who got tranquil against Lidiya as there were both bittersweet news about Captain Lidiya Cheriyan at that time". Mumkin informs about the second prophesy in one of the book i.e Lidiya is alive, it was Bison who was murdered and the enemy is blood thirsty. Captain Lidiya says " The sanguinary writer of these bloody books! Who is it ?" .

Mumkin replies " In one book it's written as Junior Akiba. The librarian mentioned that it's a man very close to Watson and pivotally ,he wears the uniform of Himbertown Military."

Victor : The only person closer to Tiger Watson is Sergeant Kroodie. He acts closest to Tiger Watson ,emulating to help him in finding Lidiya. Who knows he became a turncoat ,vicious man ,swindling own country(speaking in a bellicose way)?

Lidiya :Don't make assumptions Victor, remember his history. His heart is still burning with what Watson did to his family.

Concurrently she gets the photos ready . They do a comprehensive review ,but find no corroboration of involvement of Kroodie. As Victor keeps one photo back to its place, Mumkin holds his hand and takes the photo back. His eyes catch three fourth figures of a tall man wearing a three piece suit with a shirt and a tie,standing behind Watson as he's feeding a piece of cake to his son Tiger on his birthday.

Mumkin: "Captain,this man(pointing at the man in photo),is so well dressed and clean shaved,do you think he has any military connection as normally military people live with suc discipline."

Lidiya looks at the photo ,but she gets fondled for a second, she says "My eyes can't fool me. He's AJ Handon, my trainer during the Military training. Now it clicks the pen name, bloody Junior Akiba for AJ. What a bloody trickster ".

Mumkin: "But how does he know about the fake death of your Captain?"

Captain Lidiya :He still works for the Military and is a junior of Lt. General of Himbertown, presently working at the rank of Colonel in the headquarters, it's time for the traitor to stop his Renegade. Victor, you inform Col Hielmaster that it's the time to kill this venomous serpent named AJ Handon out of its hole".

Victor follows her orders .Lidiya remembers all the punishment given by him during her training which was taken positively but today she feels repulsive on seeing him as a traitor for own country! .

Pamela goes in the prostitute house and gets goose pimples, women in pitful state . They are malnourished and few with kids are grappling to give them necessities of food and clothing. If anything goes wrong, if any prostitute doesn't want to work that day, she's maltreated with belt. The cicatrix on their bodies are trenchant of persecution.Anyone can get distressed after seeing them in this pathetic state. She takes photos of them and starts writing an anecdote in her diary of whatever she's seeing. She goes near a woman in worse condition, wearing a torn blanket with no clothes inside, she has feverishness in which she's babbling. Pamela goes further close to her and she's taking someone's name "Peter, peter....please come back baby". Pamela sits near her and there comes a young woman. Pamela asks the young woman for how long has she been here ? The woman replies that it's her second year, she's forteen. Pamela is startled by the girl's looks as she seems to be at least 30 years old. The girl introduces herself as Annie, she glazes over Pamela's notebook . Pamela asks the lady back how this woman's body is bruised everywhere?

Pamela introduces herself as Kam Bi, sent by Watson for survey in healthcare and brothel.She shakes her hand with the girl with a sympathetic and warm smile. The girl's hands, shoulder and face have deep cuts.Pamela asks the girl if she knows total count of people here with ages, upon which the girl replies that she isn't not a library catalog to answer this, but as per her understanding there are more than fifty girls living in a four bedroom quarter in brothel sharing one common toilet. Pamela writes the information, the girls reveal more information about herself and her younger sister were playing in the farm, the two men came and nabbed them. The next time they opened their eyes in a brothel around rapacious men who changed their lives. Pamela asks her about her sister in return for where her sister is right now? She replies that her sister is more charming than her ,so she's specifically kept to cater to a few suprintendent in Marvo. The girl says' ' initially it's tough here but we get used to it as we meet other girls here. Sometimes when another person's ache is killing then our own problems are forgotten easily. She asks Pamela if Pamela is here to take their interview also.

She further adds " Look at this sick woman, her name is Hilda .Her four year old son Peter has been taken away to work in a coal mine or other labor work and she's non stop crying from the past ten days, has been grasped and beaten by Watson's men. That's why everyone here is out of pain seeing the bigger pain of other.Pamela writes all these points."

Pamela inquires further "Do you know the coal mine here?".

Annie :No idea, we aren't allowed to step outside or else our limbs will be chopped off. I have to get ready, today it's time to dance at the house party of Sir Watson. Let me remind other girls.

Annie shouts names of girls to be ready . Pamela tells Annie that she also wishes to be a part of the party to which Annie laughs off and says " it's not a cultural program Tonio village but an exhibition of females , they choose girls, you better not come. If you're their eye candy then men present there will nibble you away,if not still they'll nibble you for being not good enough for them".

Pamela insists and finally all girls are dressed in sparkling red frocks with black stockings. She makes the sick lady wear a loose nighty and take her also with the girls in a lorry. As the driver refuses to take them she tells him that she's a princess aka the most favorite girl of Tiger Watson and she'll complain against him if he refuses to do what she says. The driver agrees with that intimidation. In the Market's way, Pamela asks the driver to stop the lorry . Ren comes to take Hilda with him halfwitting the driver that Tiger asked to do so. When Ren sees Pamela, she looks gorgeous. He isn't able to take his eyes from her. She feels admired for a second but she takes her eyes away from him and says "cadet senior under officer Ren, please hospitalize her. Junior Pamela seeks permission to leave".

"Permission granted(earnest)" says Ren. She gets inside the lorry and sits soberly.

Upon reaching there Lidiya was already present in the room as a waiter. Watson , Tiger Watson and many other men were sitting there in their third piece suits like a business meeting.A hell lot of free alcohol with dark colorful light setting. The songs play, girls start moving their waists except Pamela who's struggling to match steps in embarrassment. One by one men stand up and come to take girls away with them to various rooms. A guy comes near Pamela, holds her waist tight and starts taking her away, she goes along with him in a room on the fifth floor. It's the first time Pamela has entered here, huge space with cream and white theme on walls,sofas and vase with white lilies in it , the man takes her to the bedroom, where he opens her back chain, she knocks him down on his mouth by punching on it,he promptly stands up in aggression, grabs her waist tightly, pushes her down on floor, slapping her twice. She tells him to not to guzzle instead take it slow just like tasting a glass of wine (whispering in his ear and slightly biting it). All she wanted was to seduce him ,get information and lock him inside and run away.

But her strategy fails, he gets tremendously forceful on her that she is at the extent of giving in physically pecking her lips hard. She closes her eyes and sees herself in Military Uniform saluting her flag saying "royalty with loyalty". She pushes him with vigor, he falls on the ground, with watery eyes, red face and red scars of forcefulness that are giving her the throbbing pain. She hits him constantly four to five punches on his nose where her energy get's low tenth punch. His nose is bleeding profusely,he's howling in pain. She takes her high heel sandals and hits him hard ,with a loud outcry he grabs her leg to stand up, she hits his head, her teeth are clenching . She hastily runs towards the door ,unlocks and then goes to the front door, unlocks that too. As she looks behind, the demon is running towards her with a hockey stick in his hand, with one meter of distance. She promptly closes the main door, luckily locking him. She gets inside the lift to reach the party area, everything is just the same, the process of choosing girls is still going on.Dark room with colorful light is camouflaging her. She feels gagged , until someone holds her hand down the stairs, it's Captain Lidiya. They both reach the godown area, Lidiya rushes to bring sterile and cotton to clean Pamela's wounds. Pamela hugs the captain tightly and cries her eyes out. Lidiya looks cold-blooded, she keeps cleaning Pamela's wounds .

Lidiya :Pamela, tell me who you are and why are you here?

Pamela: Pardon captain Lidiya, why such a question when I am in this state?

Captain Lidiya repeats the question, upon which Pamela answers "I am Pamela...I'm here to..", Lidiya interrupts, "You are not Pamela , you are Cadet Junior Under Officer Pamela, you are here to put an end to Watson's rule and unshackle women's life. To liberate them. You are here to free everyone not to get fettered and become a victim. Who asked you to dress up and present yourself like this? Did you watch too many movies or read various so-called psychological thrillers with romance in them? One more menace like this, you'll be dismissed from the mission. Got it?(Lidiya is holding Pamela's shoulders tight and is speaking very close to her with immediate eye contact)".

Pamela takes an hour to recover herself, Victor along with Mumkin leave her near the healthcare. Mumkin feels miserable seeing the state of women. Victor drives his way towards the Mining factory of Marvo . Victor introduces Mumkin as a one day worker at mining as there wasn't any work for him at Sir Watson's residence. The head of mining sends Mumkin with a cart inside the mining cave. Mumkin goes inside , fills his cart with coal and starts to call out to his boss in the mining cave that someone has been called by the head of mining outside and he is Peter. Seven to eight men of different body structures with gangster looks come ahead with their names as Peter. Mumkin says that it's a small boy named Peter, but there isn't anybody named Peter exists ,infant boys below ten years of age aren't taken in mining as their bodies are incapable. Mumkin feels saddened as he isn't able to find Peter anywhere. But one of the men named Peter comes near him and reveals that there's a four years old boy named Peter who developed friendship with him but soon was taken away somewhere, but he isn't aware about the place. Mumkin peep near the dark office of his mining boss . He pushes his mining cart towards the right side of the boss's office due to which the coal falls down producing a crashing sound. He quickly hides himself behind the wall, as the boss comes to scrutinize Mumkin, gets inside his office and hides himself in a carton box. After an hour and half the boss moves out. Mumkin takes the register away on which the information about workers is written with addresses. He looks at the data from four days back and finds the name of Peter with address of 13/3,Woovin Residence lane 6, Marvo. After noting down the address ,he turns back and his boss is just standing behind him. Mumkin tries to explain that it's his first day at this job so he was searching for hand gloves as his hands are just getting peeled off. The boss pushes him back and throws him outside calling a loafer and orders him that he has to work constantly till one am . The same man with Peter name, helps Mumkin in escaping where he sits inside the coal cart with coal on his top. Upon breaking free from there, Mumkin reaches the address with the help of Victor in his car . Mumkin has coal all over his body. The address is a small bungalow , but looks aristocratic. To his surprise, the head of the mining company enters it with his car and there are two security personnels. Mumkin tries to transpass by climbing through the wall, but there's broken glass on top of the wall due to which he's hurt and his hand is bleeding. He ties it with a handkerchief and looks through the glass window and sees the head of mining hugging a woman, probably his wife. In the next window he sees nothing but in the third window, he sees a small boy probably four years old. But the minute the servant calls him by the name of Peter, Mumkin realizes that he's the son of Hielda. He climbs till the window and gets inside Peter's room when nobody is there. As Peter gets inside, he introduces himself as the Umbrella man from his story book and he's here to play a game with him .He needs to keep quiet until they reach the end of the game. It's stark dark outside, Mumkin holds the child and gets down the house, but to his horror he finds the head of the mining company waiting with his wife. He gunpoints at Mumkin calling him a burglar and they identify him through the blood that is all from the glass on wall through garden to their son's Peter's room. He takes Peter away from Mumkin. Mumkin calls the allegations as false ,and says that he's here to reunite Peter with his mother who's on her death bed without him. The lady stops him in doing so and says that Peter is her only hope as he's recently adopted by her and her husband. Mumkin calls it an illegal adoption as the mother of the child is still alive , but the mining head shoots towards Mumkin but due to darkness, he misses it. Mumkin throws a stone from the ground that hits his hand, runs towards him and pushes to overpower. He catches the gun and points it towards them, holds the boy in his lap and escapes in Victor's car .Upon reaching the healthcare center Hielda is disconsolate, with her eyes swollen and she being numb. Pamela tells the Doctor that Hielda is to be taken away for corneal donation, the doctor stops her from doing so causing it an unscrupulous act, but Pamela informs that the donee is Sir Watson's comrade. Doctor allows her in dismay .Pamela takes Hielda in gurney and makes her sit inside the car along with her son Peter .Upon seeing her son back, Hielda's face blooms as if someone has showered a withered plant with blessed water. Hielda hugs him and wipes her tears of joy. Pamela goes back to the healthcare center. Victor starts to drive with Mumkin who is sitting next to him , Hielda and her son Peter ,where both are sitting in the back seats. He tells both Mumkin that they did a great job and he will drive Hielda and her son to Tonio village with a route of least security. Mumkin feels an extreme sense of contentment.

As he returns back to the godown with Victor , he doesn't find Captain Lidiya there. They start working on the photographic film collected from Pamela. It was Captain Lidiya who had kept previously collected evidence. She leaves a note on the study table of Victor ,informing that she is going to finish the task of revealing about traitor AJ Handon to Principal Blacksmith and update him concurrently about the mission . The next day Mumkin sits in Victor's car in a concealed way to head towards the market. They meet Ren working as a clerk at an aristocratic shop of sofas and chandeliers. He observes a huge class disparity. Workers were in a selfsame state, working at lowest wages facing highest ill treatment. These workers are mostly the breadwinners for their families. Mumkin clicks the photos of the worker's pathetic state as evidence. Two days pass by and the plan looks subdued. Lidiya doesn't arrive back either and there is no information about her. The security everywhere is unassailable if they have seen Lidiya somewhere. Even Victor isn't able to know where Lidiya can be. Collection of evidence is not that easy now without her and the ones collected are just missing from the place as if they have been stolen . Mumkin hides himself in the car trunk and Victor drives him away to the tunnel. They walk for eight kilometers till they meet Colonel Hielmaster who informs him that Captain Lidiya hasn't met any one of the senior officials till now in both formal and informal setup hitherto. Infact AJ Handon's reality,i.e. he is a traitor!, they are hearing it for the first time from Mumkin's mouth. This truth is shocking to Colonel Hielmaster too. He is concerned about where Lidiya would be. With missing evidence and no information about Lidiya causes wariness in Mumkin's mind too.

Lidiya wakes up from her dream world . She finds her both hands tied apart,she struggles to breathe, it's all dark. She's wearing some loose dark color one piece which doesn't belong to her. As she closes her eyes to remember what actually had happened. She recalls getting hit in the head while she was heading towards Watson's house after collecting a few more pieces of evidence from his room. She is tired ,thirsty and hungry to think anything more.

There comes a man who stands in front of her. She looks at him with her tired eyes, seeking for help from him to release her tied hands. But eventually he hits her with a belt on each of her legs coercioning her to speak up about the planning against Watson . Then he holds her hair, pulls them saying "Lidiya! tell your plan or else we'll tumble you into pieces making you a living mummy".

Her mouth seems padlocked. Her heart is throbbing out of fear and her body is completely red due to high flow of blood. He further smacks her badly thrice until she blanks out, bleeding pitiyingly from mouth. In her mind she's in a stage where pain is at its extreme and the heart is anticipating what's next torment would be. Luckily the man leaves from there at that time.

At night they repeat the same savage act with her. She's out of existence with that unbearable pain, unwillingly she wants to beg for her own death. Dirty clothes covered in blood and bleeding mouth ,she remembers her dearest old mother who prays for her safety in church everyday. Lidiya is praying to the lord to release her from this situation . In her closed eyes ,she wants her mother's lap to comfort her . AJ Hondon enters the prison gate,he thumps her too. She is now like a lifeless doll. He sits on her legs and another man smacks her fingers and toe nails repeating the same question that was asked in the morning tormenting. "Lidiya, reveals the plan of the military of Himbertown against Sir Watson" .Her legs and fingers are numb,heated up where the heart beat is experienced intensely. Her mouth is stuck, until a man broughts scythe to him. He's Tiger Watson. He says "Lidiya, my lost beauty, I never knew that you are alive otherwise I wouldn't have fantasized your head hanging from my office. But don't worry ,it's not your head, full body in a copped state decorating the Christmas theme of my office(grinning)".

WIth his brutally violent words ,he takes the scythe and lifts it above his head and then hits it that there's squawk that can quaver people with trepidation. All that is seen is the blood around her. No wonder ,it's been few days since she's locked here, but now her story is at termination with goals unachieved as she never opened her mouth to reveal anything about the military's plan to terminate Watson's rule.

Is she dead? No she's not. She looks lifeless. Tiger Watson and AJ Handon leave from there. As she opens her eyes, the prison guards around her are laughing and smoking . She looks at the bars of prison that seem infinite . It will lead her to the next life as in this life it's her death that will occur inside these bars. For the first time in her life, she's hopeless about her situation . She closes her eyes. With heavy breathing ,she moves her left leg apart to relax. She discovers a piece of folded chit with a one feet long stick next to her three chopped fingers that was attached to the scythe. Drained with blood,she opens it. The chit looks like a ten years old well preserved flat paper with both sides filled . She reads it in a quiet voice ,hiding away from prison guards.

Looking back in time ,your name just got me stuck,

As calm your face looked, your actions was about to create a young punk,

As I escorted your bygone principal to college, he looked perturbed,

No I am not disturbed he said, it's Miss Cheriyan's Work,

A rebellious kid of martyred Military officer is wearing a dog's tether,

Showing that analogy that University's uniform can't do students fetter,

He said more, but the girl is bescuited,

With full scholarship she's recruited,

Marvelous in all subjects, she's always thrilled,

Tell me Chamburt,how to discipline her, so I answered that she needs a Military drill,

I proposed to Principal, let her be part of Military explorations,

Her intelligence will have many applications,

The moment your potential was amuck,

The research project at University and recruitment by blacksmith brought you to your real work,

The luck lied there as I noticed you everytime ,that fresh face got me stuck,

Those innocent eyes, that sparkling smile ,one girl in military men but that braveheart attitude, how can one not resist,

Saving you from devil instructor and being your protector in training camps , taking you to makeshift relivings and coring you through my tall jeans, all looked funny Lidiya ,yes still it persists,

Remembering the days of us sitting in front of convoy, soldiers singing with tamburing from behind,

Comical: to maintain regulations, with dummy fake long face you made them quiet, seeing children in our soldiers, from inside you had a huge smile ,

Big heart with sharp edged brain are your way,

Kind girl, flamboyant bird and love doll of clay,

That it is our eternal love that's never ending,

Our's is undefined bonding, your jealousy is not erroneous,

Seeing my wife with me made you feel less joyous,

Wooks that fake smile isn't undeceived,

Your eyes question me Lidiya, why I gave you wounds that you will never heal,

Here writing everything on my couch as today is probably my last day on earth,

They have found me as master in their slaughtering long back, they will never let you give birth,

If we had our child ,they will not let it be alive,

That's why I married another woman whom I call as my wife as they can't trail that Ranidetro is her hive which they could do for you due to your city life,

This was to bemuse the enemy, still I do really love my wife,

All I want you is to appreciate the beauty of our uncontaminated love and your delightful life,

As few love don't have the end of line.

If I am not there tomorrow,

Live happily your life ,

You are a queen Lydia ,

The kingdom of my heart will always have you as its best price………

The poem was dated just a day before the death of commander major Chemburt. Lydia looked at her remaining thumb and little finger of right hand tied with a cloth which she tore from her skirt. She sees Commander Major Chamburt sitting next to her in his white Uniform, with all the light of stars falling at him. All he says to her is "You're the strongest, most beautiful and you must fight", kissing her injured hand ,wiping her tears and disappearing. Lydia cries openly in grief and happiness that finally she knows that her Commander Major Chamburt loved her truly, but due to circumstances he couldn't marry her. She flips the page with a map on it and a small plan. She gets firm again. She decides to go for the plan on the chit sent by some unknown person. She is now completely trusting this unknown person assuming that they are her well wisher . She starts digging the ground continuously with her left hand. The prisoner guards look at her, calling her a mad person and laugh at her. She continues until making a hole of one feet and closes her left hand intact and peeps through it multiple times and smiling . With that she tries to save her right hand which has lost three fingers as it was attacked by Tiger Watson by a scythe. The guards get suspicious. She tells them she discovered a valuable thing that's sparkling a lot, very hard and it can make her rich again. As the tow of guards decide to inform Watson assuming about her finding diamonds, she corrupts them telling that the diamonds will be sold in eight digits. She can share with them in return for giving her food to eat. The two guards agree upon it and they ask for the diamond from her beforehand. She shows a diamond ring from left hand, covered in mud which she always kept inside her hair rubber band in the past to use in extremity. They hold her hand to snatch it , she shakes her hand off,due to which the ring falls down behind the prison bars , making it impossible to reach it. She recapitulates "The ring is all yours master,I am starving ,just give me some food please!". One of them brings a sandwich and both of them are dribbling over the diamond ring! She snatches the sandwhich from them and starts eating , and one of the guards aggressively slaps her for not keeping the promise. She says: "Listen, I will give you this ring, but there might be few more inside this area, this land is sort of impenetrable." They look at each other in a gluttonous way. She says "Sir, if both of you enter the prison, it'll be dubious.Small mouth big talk, if any of you stand at the main door and help me in digging the ground, it will be very helpful in searching for more diamond rings ,your majesty." They again look at each other and one goes near the main door with a gun in his hand and the other runs to get a small hoe from an attached junk room,unlocks the lock and opens up the prison locker and starts digging the land from hoe along with Lidiya. After ten minutes of drudgery he says "I don't think there's anything here!", to which Lidiya replies, "Dig deeper sir, so that your partner can also get three more rings just the way you have kept the first three in your pockets. Majesty there needs to be equality ,this a tied up Military officer saying to you." The other guard comes near them to check on the jewels discovered. As they get into a quarrel , Lidiya asks the other guard to check the pockets of his partner. As he goes for it, her eyes deviate from his partner's pocket to the other hand. As he shifts his gun to next hand, she promptly snatches it, jumps two steps backwards and locks the two guards at gunpoint and runs towards the junk room .She tone with her map ,where she starts removing old tyres, broken tables with huge spider webs, dog's bones etc until she finds a mini door ,she glide by it until she falls straight through a long and dark pipe, wrenching her leg, loosing the grip of gun and falling on something soft. Wollah, she's outside the house.

Two masked people hold her to throw her at the back seat of the car ,take the gun with them and they open up the throttle .She wears the seat belt and they take her far in a jungle .Stopping the car, Mumkin and Colonel Hielmaster bring to light their faces by removing their masks. Medical team with three nurses arrive there with Doctor Emma who is a healthcare worker of Marvo. They tell her that it's three ferocious dogs that attacked this robust lady when she came walking here. Emma incredulously provides first aid to Lidiya, telling her that the nearby area is a red zone, high level menacing from where screeches of maltreatment of human beings is heard. She concurrently sterilizes her right hand wounds in three amputated fingers, apply moist gauze wrap and necessary injections. After the medical team leaves , Mumkin and Hielmaster display their ruth on Lidiya,but she says,many people lose and have lost their lives in this area,she's a lucky one to not to be slaughtered here. She further inquiries that how did they save her? Hielmaster replies that they foraged everywhere confidentially but it was futile. But Principal Blacksmith has apprehended the personal driver of AJ Hundon who is well informed about missions. The driver mentioned this place ,where prisoners work as bonded laborers starting from chopping grass to work like drugs, animals and tree smuggling. Everything happens through this forest. The small house where Lidiya was kept is known as the torture house. Torture happens when the labourers become inoperative. It is the end stage of the labour. He drew a map that had private ways to exit. The chit attached to the scythe was sent through our right hand with the presupposition that grass work would be assigned to you initially because it's more soul destroying than other tasks. Regrettably we never knew that it's used to scathing your fingers as you're directly put in the torture house! Lidiya says"It's destiny, destiny of this Village, in all likelihood, Hundon's driver gave incomplete information .Since Watson and malefactors know that I absconded ,now they're more alert about our plans. At Least proofs are safe with you in the form of a video.`` They inform her that the video proof ,along with other ones are discovered and seized by Watson. But Lidiya tells them that all proofs are lying safe with Pamela as she handled them clandestinely ahead of time.The video has comprehensive illicit activities , number of weaponries possessed, downright list of malefactors etc. Their vulnerabilities to attack and capture them. As Lidiya starts to move with Hielmaster, Mumkin stands behind. He says "The letter I discovered in the piled up documents of my father, when I recently visited my mother. I kept it inside my pocket as I didn't know what to do with it``.Mumkin was talking about the chit on which the poetry written by Mumkin's father motivated her to escape. Lidiya turns towards him ,remains hushed till she starts to walk again with Hielmaster .

Lidiya gets bed rest ,Hielmaster replaces her for the mission after a week's time.She is in one of the resting chambers of the tunnel. The very next day he brings thirty more soldiers with their identities hidden and maps them with Mumkin, Ren and Pamela. Concurrently John supplied the weaponries. Sir Watson's Mansion's hidden basement is made the base of the mission, forty more soldiers including the twenty deferential soldiers wearing steep dark combat ,a special trained team of captain Lidiya also join the mission .They are under Colonel Hielmaster. Mumkin talks through the list of malefactors and suspicious people from the list of evidence collected.

On the other hand Victor shares with Colonel Hielmaster the delightful news of an excursion plan for Watson and its malefactors to a nearby lake ,followed by their cricket match after two days . Duties are assigned concurrently to do the right steps during excursion and cricket match ,probably this is the time to kill the enemy under its own nose .Everyone is ready for the action.

Victor is given the task of security to take care of V.I.P. cars pertaining to Watson, AJ Hondon and his daughter Natasha.On the way to the market ,near hospital, Victor encounters despondent male workers agonizing the pain of destitution under the despotism of Watson. Few are already dead bodies lying in garbage, underfed children, women working as prostitutes and bulk went missing. No school opened and one hospital, giving the null service to it's people due to the lack of staff members. Complete dystopia. His blood is boiling seeing the pathetic condition of his people in the village.

Since this is saturday,again there's a party in the evening where girls are selected by lodgers for pleasure. Pamela gets dressed up again with one more idea. She has put together to sway with other girls in a seductive way. This time also the man who was forceful on her the last time is present. His eyes are scarlet in color and he's gawking at Pamela in a group while dancing like a cat drools over the fish in a pond! He's just ruffled and aggressive to attack her once he gets to choose a girl. In his mind ,he wants to attack and abuse her. Pamela is conscious of him . But she considers the collection of evidence and success of the task more important than her own safety.

Drinks are offered to all guests. During the time of selection of girls he jumps towards Pamela and holds her tight saying "Today, you'll see how bitter revenge is taken. I won't let you breathe, you'll be under my arms inside the room ". Upon reaching the first floor in the lift, he sees another Pamela coming from left and right until he gets troubled with vertigo before going bananas kissing the floor ,getting treated by the god of sleep!

Correspondingly other men too sleep and now start the humongous task of conveying these forty seven sleeping, not so beauties in terms of humanity to the prisoner cells in a truck set out by Victor . They are sleeping due to drugs inside their drinks. Ren arrives with ten soldiers . All women prostitutes also help in concluding this task of conveying these forty seven men inside the truck.Ren sits next to Pamela in the front seat. The strike starts to move, the soldiers with Pamela and Ren have guns fully loaded to be prepared in case of any trouble. Ren looks at Pamela's face,her lipstick is merged leaving her in sweat and pink tint on her lips. He says "Macaca". She glances for a second and turns her face towards her right ,watching out of the window.

Ren :Macaca is the scientific name for monkeys, I read in a journal.

Pamela :Do you read? I thought you only like to play, play with people's mind! Sort of manipulating them.

Ren: Come one , this was just to make you laugh . Your merged lipstik makes you look like a monkey.

Pamela:These favors of making me laugh aren't required,we're here for a mission,not on a comedy show.

Ren :Till now you haven't forgotten how cocky you want to be with me! This will be the last mission in which I wish to be with you as I will put forth a special request to Colonel Hielmaster to not to map us together again.

Pamela remains silent. As they reach the entrance of Marvo village, everyone's hearts start thumping , it has a brimming security. Suddenly ,the malefactors point their firearms towards the truck seeking for a security check. Ren comes out of the truck's door saying that Sir Tiger Watson has asked me to take luggage to the other side of Marvo. The malefactor asked him to show his identification card. He displays a card from his pocket ,the malefactor checks it and after approval, Ren gets inside the truck and closes the door of it. The malefactor knocks at the door. Ren says to the driver, "probably they want to check the truck". He tells the women to put tarpaulin on unconscious forty seven men in order to hide themselves underneath. He takes a few seconds and holds the door handle to open the truck's door . Pamela is all vigilant to monitor their conversation. After opening the door, the malefactor gets heavy on Ren, putting the gun on his jawline saying "How the hell do you know what lies on the other side of Marvo when you aren't authorized to cross the border?". He points the rifle towards Ren's head. Pamela takes her rifle out and shoots the malefactor. The two other malefactors start heavy firing. Pamela pulls Ren back through holding his hand inside the truck ,standing in the front fire . She tells Ren and the soldiers to support fire, the other soldiers shoot at malefactors from the window. They hit the two other malefactors until the fourth one knocks her down ,Ren immediately shoots him with five bullets too. Pamela is all bloodsoaked, with her half eyes open she's taking her last few breaths . All malefactors are dead. But Pamela is whispering something in the ears of Ren. He looks around ,discovering two girls, one soldier is also hit by a bullet. He tells the driver to hurry up towards the Diewa hospital, out of injured only one girl could get the treatment and others lost their lives. Pamela is no more. That's why they say "Respect the love when it knocks at your door or else you'll lose it forever".This was a lesson for Ren. It's all warm around Ren,he's seeing blue light around him in guilt for not behaving kindly with Pamela. His cheeks are just red and he's sweating and breathing heavily to see the dead bodies near him in the hospital . Doctors and the nurses are all looking at him . He hears the sweet voice of a girl, "Sir, do I have to write their names?"Ren murmurs "Do it .Write the names of both dead and injured!". Again voice "But sir, they're just unconscious,after one hour only they'll get back to their consciousness".......The voice gets louder "From their identity card ,we're able to do so"....The voice changes "They'll tell about their ancestors once they get back to conscious, write their names. Chop chop". Ren gets shaken up swiftly by somebody "Wake up Shehzaade before I disintegrate you from the mission,denounce your crownship". Ren opens his eyes,looks around and finds himself in the Diewa hopital that's more advanced than he saw in his dream,next to him is Captain Lidiya Cheriyan and a trainee nurse. The nurse was of his age ,with a sweet voice and big spectacles. Captain Lidiya is scowling at him. He inquires about Pamela saying "royalty with loyalty Captain. How is she? My junior Pamela?I mean Cadet junior under Officer Pamela ".

Captain Lidiya Cheriyan: Royalty with loyalty. Out of your mind are you?

Captain Lidiya leaves from there. Ren sees Pamela standing next to the operating theater room. She's wearing casual clothes ,a red shirt and white pants ,talking to the doctor. She looks invigorating . Ren comes near her.

Pamela:Hi Cadet Senior Under officer Ren. Good evening to you sir. Hope you dozed well.

Ren: Saw a bad dream, you got killed in the tussle with malefactors as you came in front to protect me.

Pamela:Well in that case,I would rather send you in front(smiling) .Why would I ever want to protect my senior who has been unkind to me.

Ren: Come on Pamela, don't bring the past. I am happy that you are alive.

Pamela: Why are you happy? You only wished that this should be our last mission and look you got me terminated in dream.Haha.

Ren: I was never in love with you ,but I don't hate you either. I will never wish for your termination. After this mission ,we're like two peas in a pod,yes colleague wise! But your bravery can make me change my mind, I am afraid to fall for you again .

Pamela:When was the first time when you fell for me? In Fact you never fell for me.You were just bridging the gap of your ex girlfriend Janny ,when she left you. I was just a substitute for you, never a desire.

Ren :When I saw you for the first time, I got intrigued by you! Lost it afterwards, I am intrigued again.

Her face is sober as if nothing affects her.

Pamela: I fell in love with you when you proposed to me. I forgave you so many times. But you....You never respected my love as you weren't mature enough to do so.

Ren wakes up from his real dream as he was dreaming in a dream. He is sitting on a chair and the funeral of martyred soldiers has been held including Pamela in Himbertown. Everyone is dressed in black, her parents are downcasted to lose their only daughter. They are accompanied by her uncle Nelon. Out of her two best friends only John is present there.Mumkin is still in the mission. Everyone is dejected. The family of the deceased soldier has also arrived. The Military arrives with their services headed by Captain Lidiya . They had garlands, flowers and medals of bravery in action .For Pamela a special medal " Lioness of Himbertown" was decided by the Military for a brave act of close monitoring and taking the front position to protect her senior colleague Ren, getting into prompt action for success of mission by risking her own life.

People around her parents start murmuring and pitting them saying "they've lost their only daughter and what bad luck". Lidiya stands near Pamela's mother where she annonces to everyone " Pamela wanted to leave the Military in starting but she was the bravest of the brave to sustain hardship. She altered the record by becoming the bravest of the brave "Lioness of Himbertown". Long live Lioness of Himbertown, the braveheart . Rest in peace the sacrificial goddess, Rest in peace. "Everyone repeated after Captain Lidiya including Pamela's parents with tearful eyes ``Rest in peace Sacrificial goddess, long live lioness of Himbertown' '. After the funeral Captain Lidiya hands over the special medal of bravery to Pamela's parents. Her mother expresses the wish that they should've taken Pamela out from the Military when she was at her lowest and feeling weak i.e. when they met her on her birthday, after the bad breakup with Ren . Her father however resists and calls Pamela ,his brave daughter who fought bravely to save lives.

Ren comes near them to give condolences and further tells them that he was a rank senior to her and he worked with her closely in the mission too. He says "She was a lionhearted girl who made the whole Himbertown Military proud and saved various lives.Without her,it was nearly impossible to complete the mission".Ren meets Captain Lidiya and gives full report to her and also about Pamela's closet in healthcare center where the evidences are kept.

John cried massively after seeing paying respect to Pamela through a garland on her coffin. He just can't believe that his best friend is no more, probably the trauma of losing her will take years for him to heal. Mumkin isn't even aware of it as no information is conveyed to his group.

Pamela's Tonio friends , Ray and Sim, are also present at the funeral. They are just remisinscating about her marriage to herself and crying.

Mumkin talks through the list of malefactors and suspicious people along with Victor. He assigns duty to people in order to assign the fake security to V.I.P. pertaining to Watson, his son Tiger, AJ Hondon and his daughter Natasha. Captain Lidiya reaches the location where late Pamela and Ren had created a way to enter Marvo after expulsion of malefactors. Captain Lidiya also has a convoy of trainee soldiers with John ,Ren, Benny , Ray and Sim. Sergeant

Kroodie also joined them. This is probably the last part of the mission.

This side all are enjoying the excursion of fun parks and the cricket match that is started by the umpire in the match. It is actually Colonel Hielmaster in the guise of the umpire. There are two teams,one is headed by Tiger Watson and the other by the finest cricket players of Watson. There are various malefactors in that area . There is a minor population of Watson who are unimpeachable. They are present on ground , as helpers ,spectators in the match and as bus drivers etc. At the top position of the stadium it's Watson with AJ Hondon and his daughter to view the match. Mumkin is in the guise of a field boy who keeps in check of the cricket ball and spraying medicines to remove mosquitos. He is carrying a backpack . He starts spreading it at various places. One of the spectators enquired about what he's doing. In return Mumkin says "I am spraying the drug that is used for sedation! ". The person stands up furiously and holds his collar, Mumkin replies in return " Haha. I .....I was joking sir, this is just sanitizing and removing mosquitos. " . The spectator leaves his collar and starts clapping as Tiger Watson hits a six. The umpire shows six.

There are a few more soldiers who start sanitizing the place by spraying the mosquito spray. The second time Tiger hits a four, the umpire shows a four. Third time when Tiger hits six, five is shown by the umpire due to which Tiger's and his team got infuriated with the umpire. Public has no reaction as all the spectators are in deep sleep! The umpire blames Tiger for cheating and provokes the other team which has majority of Himbertown Military soldiers guised as the finest cricket players of Watson ``. The two teams start hand to hand fighting with each other, Tiger is hit dead on his head by his opposite team member and he's lying in the pool of blood just like few other members from his team. Watson watches his son dying from far as he tries to make a move, he finds his body numb completely. AJ Hondon and his daughter Natasha too are just trying to help him move, but soon he realizes that his body has been paralysed completely. Their four bodyguards come to help him but instead they rotate his chair one eighty degrees . AJ Hondon gasps after seeing Lydia dressed as one of the body guards. Mumkin, Hielmaser and Sergeant Kroodie are the other three bodyguards. She sees Watson for the first time, a heavily old man on his deathbed, but with an evil mind. She keeps the trigger of the gun on AJ Hondon and says "You will get the price for keeping traitorhood". She puts her mask on followed by the other three bodyguards and she opens the door due to which the gas enters the room and three of them viz Watson, AJ Handon and his daughter Natasha faint. The rest are handled by all the soldiers gathered by John,Renm Benny , Ray and Sim with other soldiers. All members of Watson including his malefactors are loaded in the trucks . They open their eyes in a prison which is completely different from their aristocratic lifestyle. Lidiya presents all the necessary evidence in the Himbertown court along with Hielamster, Kroodie and Victor due to which AJ Watson and Handon were regarded as guilty of dictatorship in Marvo village. Both are given a life sentence in jail. AJ Hondon is also court martialed .

Marvo is rehabilitated by the team. The restoration team containing Benny , John and Ray is already .Mumkin arrives there too,His eyes are looking for one more person i.e. Pamela as she was mainly assigned the duty of nurturing people.He meets John who reveals in Mumkin's ears about the martyrdom of Pamela in the mission, due to which Mumkin feels that he has lost half of the person in him. There's a sudden pain in his heart like thunder to accept that his dearest best friend Pamela is gone forever. All he remembers is her innocent memories and bubbly nature that made him always feel to protect her from any evil. He feels although the mission is successful he has failed!

They all are invited to the Military cum government function. The mayor of Himbertown is on the stage.Lidiya Cheriyan is given her stars and her respect back officially by the government ,promoting her to the rank of colonel. Her piping ceremony is done where her mother puts her rank. Her sister Isabella and her maids Lucas and Isabella are extremely happy to see that. Colonel Hielmaster is promoted to the rank of Brigadier. Mumkin and Ren are given the official ranks of captain , followed by John and Benny are given promotion to the rank of Lieutenant in the Military. Hielmaster is promoted to Brigadier. Mumkin is smiling at Laila and his mother from the crowd ,who are just elated... Lidiya or we say Colonel Lidiya comes near Captain Mumkin and says "There's another mission captain".

Mumkin :Ready for it always, this time combat with better and improved weapons.

She smiles at him with pride. Mumkin started the military entrepreneurship with a separate research wing of innovative self protective guarding materials for soldiers that supported the soldiers in almost all the missions successfully. The branch of Military run by him became a business tycoon later selling the products of Himbertown Military to other countries. concurrently contributing all wealth in restoration and education of people of villages like Marvo, Tonio and of course Mumkin's own village Ranidetro. He's married to Laila. John married Stella.

Lidiya found a person to whom she can connect to, it's Brigadier Hielmaster. Ren is married to Blacksmith's daughter Madeline. They've a beautiful daughter whom they name as Pamela. For him she's a gift of god .He can't come over the guilt of not acknowledging Pamela's kindness. He always tells his daughter "There was an angel who flew to the sky to become a star due to which he got the gift of this life" Today is the tenth death anniversary of Cadet Junior under officer Pamela. Ren and his wife reach there with flowers. A car arrives where Mumkin ,Laila and their daughter get down. They've named her Pamela too. John arrived there with his family and Pamela's parents . They salute her and remember her for bravery!

Lidiya publishes a new book named "Destiny made of Ranidetro- from Nadir to Zenith" based on experience in the mission . Her latest book is "The turbulent champion: Braveheart Lioness of Himbertown". You decide to whom it's dedicated!

Sometimes Mumkin feels that if Pamela were alive, she would have become the younger version of his senior Colonel Lidiya as for him both are loyal to their countries, brave and kind women.

As the trio wcrc walking towards the reception ,John offered to make Mumkin make him as his partner in business with a partnership of 30 percent first then changing it to 20 percent and tell how his middle class working father always put him down. His father always tells him not to dream too big as one day John will end up wasting all his hard earned money from the bank job. His father is a clerk in an old bank run by the government in Himbertown and his step mother is a housewife. Mumkin too shares that his father's martyrdoom has made his mother to upbring him with a lot of difficulties seeing his mother getting major emotional breakdowns.

They reach reception where Pamela grabs her brand new books of psychology and makes the two guys load them back till the classroom.

During recess time Mumkin, Pamela and John were sitting together waiting for Uncle Nelon.

Mr.Bidar Nelon has been working from fifteen years in this college, he is a good observant and knows almost everyone in the school. Be it a student or faculty.Or probably his job demands that. He is also the maternal uncle of Pamela. He's bald in the center of his head,a short heighted man who has a dimple on one side of his cheek and a long pointed nose. His big belly tells a story that his job requires him to sit on a chair in order to keep records of students and teachers precisely. He's one of the most trusted people of college and has received Best employer of the College award incessantly for five years. He's dedicated to college and believes to be a well wisher of students. Probably due to his graciousness, many students approach when their hall tickets for exams are blocked due to attendance shortage. He adds up the genuine certificates of sports or health so as to unblock their hall tickets due to which almost a hundred students could write their exams in the past. He's like an alarm clock who reminds students of their crises time and sometimes act 'sankat mochan ' for them,

Pamela: Uncle(runs and hug him)

Nelon: Pamela, dear child. I'm so happy to see you and your friends. Very pleased to meet you John(punching on John's arm playfully) Do visit Stella and her mother with friends for dinner this weekend.

Pamela: Uncle, I hope you remember that outstanding acting done by John and Stella to make you fool,so that John could get in there!

Nelon: You were involved too Pamela. I actually wanted to beat the hell out of him but soon I realized that it's the plan of all three of them,not only his fault as Stella was also involved. Forget about it Pam, stop pulling his legs. Poor John, I have forgiven him but now Pamela wants to dance on his head!

Pamela(coughing): Yeah uncle, I'll stop this fun, after all he's your future son in law.

John:You're a serious bully Pamela, you'll have to pay for it one day(earnest).

Pamela: John, I am just joking(holding his hand with both of her hands and slightly falling towards him in a childish way). Leave it John. Uncle how is aunty and Stella?

Nelon:They're doing fine. Your aunt enjoys her cooking and Stella wants to study something in Business.`

Pamela: In what area does Stella want to do business?

Nelon: I am not too sure ,but I think it's business in food!

Pamela: Well said uncle, she wants to do business in food and John wants a business in vessels and crockery stuff. Our future couple can run a restaurant well!(giggling).

After a slight slap to John on his shoulder,Pamela starts running towards the corridor.

Uncle Nelon laughs after seeing this, annoyed John runs behind Pamela but she shows her teeth making a monkey face that annoys him further. John attempts to follow her but she hides herself in the girls washroom.

Mumkin keeps looking for both of them to come back to the corridor crowded with students.

Nelon: God knows,when she'll grow up,still a naughty kid even after joining college.

Bell rings..

Nelon: Let me go to see them both, you hurry up to meet the principal and other members of the University. There is a meeting right now.

Mumkin: Only with me?

Nelon: No, not only you. It's all the students of the College.

He stands up in front of the entrance of the corridor and claps thrice to announce "All new students head up to attend the meeting in the Xavier hall."

New student: where's Xavier hall?

Nelon:It's that way, just behind the recycling building and there is Xavier hall in the block four ,third floor. Make sure you reach them on time or else gates will be closed and seats will be full. Even if you manage to get inside after being late, then learn to sit on the ground as you won't get any seat to sit. You won't want the first day of your college to look like that! Do you?

John comes and stands next to Mumkin. Pamela arrives and stands behind him. As John aggressively tries to hold her hand, she haphazardly says "save me Mumkin,protect me from this orangutan!". Mumkin asks both of them to stop as they need to go for a meeting . All three along with other students headed towards the hall. There's a huge paper recycling unit . There's fresh air blowing from the three banyan trees inside the unit ,like just in the middle. The recycling unit has thatch over it. Pamela peeps inside it and says "Is this a recycling unit? It looks like a junkyard to me. I mean look at all these machines! Isn't these machines should produce something marvelous out of waste, but I think they make good waste.".

John: For a second will you shut your mouth Pamela, can't you see it's a paper recycling unit! This is not a junkyard, these are machines that recycle paper and look to your right, can you see little cardboard houses? These are made after recycling paper. Once you color them ,they'll look more resplendent.

Pamela: Okay ,Mr. Erudite! That's the trifling thing to discuss, aren't you aware that we're getting late now?

John: Wait Pamela, I'll murder you and dig your grave in this paper recycling unit! Wasn't it you who started questioning the purpose of this junkyard, ahh(vexed) ,I mean recycling unit. You'll drive me nuts.

Pamela starts walking swiftly and turns back and says "Do all the planning of murdering me later, now's the time to reach the Xavier hall". She starts running, Mumkin and John follow her. John "I don't know why rags me down".

Mumkin :She's kind of playful,try not to take her seriously.

John: Haha. You took my words away. I've been doing that for a long time. Sometimes she acts weird.

Mumkin: You mean like a hypocrite?

John: Yeah!

Mumkin: She's just trying to put a trick on you.

John: That's a childish thing to do. Despite knowing what irritates me,she does it! One day,I'll make her taste her own medicine!

Mumkin: Haha,try let it go .Let's go!

As they reach the Xavier hall, it's all crowded with too many people. The trio chose the last row for them to sit, whereas the guard showed a baton, asking them to occupy the first few rows.As they look around, the other security guards are shifting other last seaters in the first few rows. Pamela chooses to sit in the sixth row where the access of security guards is minimal. John and Mumkin sit next to her.

There was a student who held the baton of a security guard "Tujhe pata hai mera baap kon hai?(you don't know who my dad is?)"

Guard: Tujhe vaadil kon ahet? (Who's your father?)Kon he re tera baap, bol na sale, kisne paida kiya tujh jaise sapole ko?(Tell me, who created snakelete like you?)

Students: How dare you talk to me like that?Huh? Vardi utarva dunga tera(I will get you dismissed from your job)

Guard: Tula majha uniform kadhayla of Miles?Tumi te kaise karte? Le tumi murkha(Miles to take off my uniform! How you'll do it, take this idiot).

The guard starts hitting the student with his baton ,the student howls in pain and other students occupy the seats within a few seconds.

A teacher arrives there and says "thambva raja(stop king)" to the security guard. "Follow what our guards say, or else they'll turn your life upside down! no matter whether you're the son of a billionaire (to the student)or a widowed mother(looking at Mumkin). Sarva tvareta base (all settle quickly)"

Mumkin gasps for a second.

Pamela:Asabhya sṭapha membara niẏe ki asabhya kaleja(What a savage college with savage staff member).

John:Shut up or else you'll get one savage from him.

Pamela:Mala koṇihi maru sakata nahi!(No one can hit me!)

John:Are,baghuya, surakṣa rakṣakala sema gosṭa sanga(oho, let's see, say the same thing to the security guard)

Mumkin: I don't understand what you both are saying, but you both seem to be augmenting again.

The security guard hits Mumkin at his back with his baton and says "Bola na chup reh(don't speak, shut up)". Pamela and John become quiet after that. They laughed quietly, keeping their hands on their mouths.

The principal enters and everyone stands up. He looks like a 65 years old man dressed in a plain gray shirt and black pants. He had a piece of paper in his hand which he handed over to Kimsu, the guard of the College.It was the welcome speech of the principal that he wrote thrice,not because he was a dolt or dullard. It's because he was a perfectionist and prescient who would never tolerate even a single mistake either from his side or from others. The trio are asked by Kimsu to get up,he tells Pamela to come in front and hands over a bouquet of tulips to her that is to be presented to principal Blacksmith. Mumkin and John sit back at their seats. There are more than five hundred other students in the hall. Principal Henry Blacksmith reaches up on stage, he checks the microphone first "Check 1,2,3....3,2,1..... 2,1,3.... 2,3,1.... 3,1,2 ......check .....you give the last combination....who knows? Many of you might be saying 'Oh no....I don't know anything.....Because I hate math....haha, how many of you do not like math?'

Many students raise their hands to express their dislike whereas Pamela raises both of her hands to give confession that she hates it double. Mumkin has been a huge fan of this subject. According to him math is used for managing money, handling finances, understanding cooking, sports etc.Especially the business and finance part of it he regularly reads magazines, newspapers and journals of it.

Principal Blacksmith: Good morning everyone!

Students reply to him murmuring.

Principal Blacksmith: What, didn't eat breakfast? Be loud , come again!

Students reply again to them in comparatively high pitch now!

Principal Blacksmith: The question that was posed is from math. Math is like a goldmine, the one who knows it is as smart as a whip!Person with math knowledge will be able to solve any problem in life like a pro. All my dear students who have joined this year, first of all I would like to congratulate you. This is one of the top colleges of the world. It's the dream of many students to join here, build their lives and finally leave the college making a big impact in the field of research, technology and innovation . We have produced successful people from all fields. Our alumni as scientists, musicians, engineers, doctors and businessmen etc are all flourishing in their fields. Our motto 'Faith and hard work' has made many students go from rags to riches .This year has been an auspicious year for us as we have a total 550 newcomers . Every Year 400 was the limit. As requested by our very able teacher Professor Olivia, the management has increased 150 more seats. You have been here after tough competition. Hope you will respect your decision to join this College. Ensure that you make good use of this time. A degree is a treasure for you to survive in this world. Also ensure that you keep the people happy who hold a great standard of trust in you by completing your degree. Make use of all resources and we wish to see you as great psychotherapists ,scientists, artists, doctors and managers etc. in future. I wish you all great luck. Hope you achieve all your dreams and make your parents and loved ones proud. All the very best...Also there's one new committee to be made . Please ensure that you all take part in it. It's open to all students however my special expectations are from the first years to take part in it . This is a request from an old man aged 76 years with 20 years of experience in college teaching.``

All are shocked to know about his age as he looks quite twenty years younger than that. He has served a few years in corporates after his retirement from the Military. He was also involved in the wars for almost thirty years where he got commissioned at the age of 19 .

John whispers in ears of a boy sitting next to him "To khupa goda manusa ahe ase(he seems to be a very sweet man)"

The boy quietly says "hoya(yes)" .Both are hit by the guard at their backs saying "Bola na chup kar dono, mooh bandh rakho, dande khao tum(I told you both to shut up ! Take my beatings)"

Principal blacksmith "thambava(stop), eat your blood pressure medicines,students haven't joined to be beaten by you(to the guard). And students, keep quiet! Especially when I talk".

The guard takes four steps behind them and says "theek ahe sara(okay sir)".

Miss Olivia went to the stage, she called Pamela and asked her to go back after handling the bouquet which she gave to the Principal blacksmith. He happily received it but Olivia seems to be indiffeRent. As Principal Blacksmith gets down to occupy the first few seats .

Olivia: Prof Caleb William teaches developmental psychology , Prof. Rustin Henry.... statistical psychology, prof Rasko George.... behavioral psychology, Prof Alexander Keats..... research, prof Angola Kinman...... counseling and prof Rehman..... administration and teaching clinical psychology. Prof. Jaquiline Gomes teaches Sociological Theories, Prof Gretsha Jones ..... religion and Society and Prof Xiang Zin .... political sociology. and......(continues names of teachers and corresponding subjects in psychology for next few minutes).

Then she takes names of ninety eight teachers of other departments like mathematics, hotel management, Medical research etc.

Olivia: You are supposed to know the names of your faculty. No student will take leave without notification. If taken, with genuine reason ,take signature of pre and post leave permission from faculties. Once entered college, bunking any class the entire day is actionable. The set of non negotiable rules are: roaming in campus with no purpose is punishable, no plagiarism in academics and playing with practical instruments during practical sessions is prohibited, follow the formal dress code ,misbehavior on the side of students is considered as a serious offense,students need to keep an eye on notice board,especially on the circulars regarding examinations, placements and scholarships, ninety five percent of attendance needed to write term examinations,home assignment and tests are to be completed on time either graded or ungraded, parking of vehicles need to be made on parking stand , follow class schedules class, no taking leave after class, proper behavior to be displayed in classroom,hoteliers are expected to follow rules ,maintaining decorum of class(for next 8 minutes students are warned about the basic rules that need to be followed).

Pamela whispers in Mumkin's ear "What a boring teacher with a boring lecture".Then she turns towards John and says "nirupoyagi college(useless college), my fees are fully wasted here". In return John replies "oh hoshiyar bai,guard ke dande khane ka bahut shawk hai kya?(oh smart girl ,are you passionate of getting hit by guard)"

Mumkin signals Pamela to keep quiet by keeping his finger on his lips doing "shhhhhh".

Pamela: I've arrived here to learn, not to waste my time! What's wrong with everybody here?

The guard comes near her to warn 'Shanta mulagi(shut up girl)'.

Pamela:(To the guard) Ok uncle.

She whispers in Mumkin's ear "My father still has the marriage option open for me. He says if something pressures me ,be it in College studies or a future job, his doors will always welcome me. The restaurateur guy is also a sweet person. Actually I am the only child,the most pampered one!"

John: (whispering): I am also only child, but most tortured one!If I ever go back to my dad's house ,he'll treat me like a peice of shit!

Panela: My dad beats his chest with pride,when he introduces me to others. Mumkin, what about you?

Mumkin: I don't have one.

Prof Olivia finished her so-called speech that had just information about the college rules and faculty information. Professor Rehman on stage.

Prof Rehman: What's up babies. Yes babies you all are,when it comes to learning. A wise man once said ,if you think you lack knowledge ,you actually build it after acknowledgement as you avoid ignorance. So be a knowledge seeker. I am professor Rehman, you can call me Reyh. I am from the department of counseling. My job is to keep you students happy and teach you guys exciting ways everyday,especially when to deal with so-called firecrackers that explode in their life. Me and my colleagues,we are always there in your entire College journey .You are most welcome to stay in touch even after college. You can always visit the mindspace activities beside the auditorium .Welcome students to this lovely phase of your life called college.

The caravan of speech lasted for the next four hours.The trio started to sleep as they found it way too boring. The fall asleep sitting posture. With the sudden sound of a bell, they wake up seeing everybody has gotten up and people are starting to leave. They follow the que. That day Pamela and John went to their respective hostels but Mumkin was asked to sleep in an open area of the college's hostel corridor as he hadn't paid any hostel fee that was not part of scholarship. He makes his fat bag as his pillow ,as he covers himself with a bedsheet like a baby, he doesn't find this citation difficult. There has been a time in his life where he had to actually sleep on an empty stomach with mosquitoes especially on the hospital floor as his mother's health wasn't that good. She had to go through a cervical biopsy. Her mother's health improved after that,however Mumkin was just seven years old at that time .Today he didn't think the same way as he thought when he was young, this time he didn't question himself why he had to sleep in the open as he knows that money is the issue! This time the sleeping is more comfortable ,probably he is in deep sleep. He hears a heavenly voice 'Wake up sir, you got to come with me!' .There's bright light all around. He tries to open his eyes, rubbing them slightly to discover the College guard Kimsu standing with his torsch flashing on his face. The guard closes his torch and reiterates 'Take your bags sir, you need to come with me'. Mumkin is still breathing fast ,no wonder why and where the guard wants to take him.

Mumkin: What happened? Can you put the torch off?
Kimsu: Oh sorry(turning off the torch light). You can sleep with me.
Mumkin: With you?
Kimsu: Yes, just for today! From tomorrow you can go back to your hostel room.
Mumkin: Room? But I can't avail hostel facilities for now!
Kimsu: No sir, a room has been allotted to you in the hostel.
Mumkin: Who allotted the room?
Kimsu: I don't know.
Mumkin: How come, I still don't get it, do you know that I come under hostel fee offenders?
Kimsu: I don't know all that. I am just following the orders.
Mumkin: Who gave you the orders Mr. Kimsu?
Kimsu: My senior, the security supervisor of College. For now come with me.

Mumkin and Kimsu go to the guard dormitory. There were few guards,still in their blue uniform chit chatting at one o'clock at night. Three guards were sitting on a round table and drinking whisky,talking about all their experiences-their villages, wifes, childRen, cows ,properties and murders etc.

There's a huge man in his black and white night suit, he tells Mumkin to sleep in any one of the bedrooms and his hostel fee has already been paid by someone for him.Kimsu reveals that that huge man is the college's security supervisor. Mumkin sleeps in a relaxed way with this question in his head i.e. 'Who paid his hostel fee?'